EMPIRE OF BLOOD

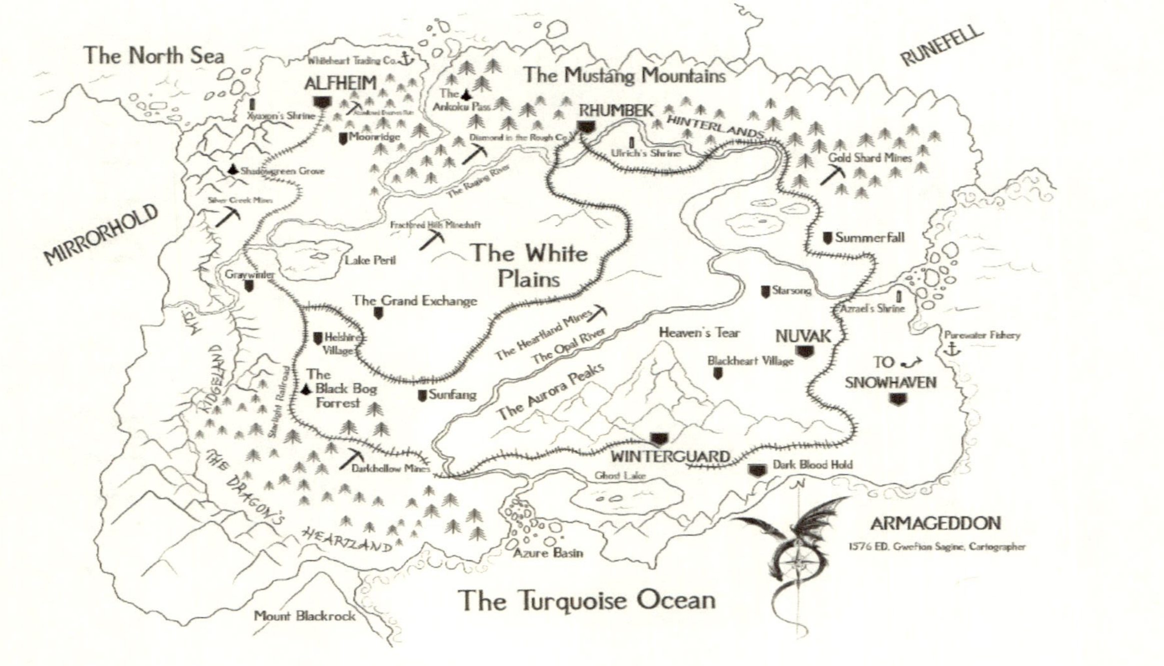

The North Sea
RUNEFELL
MIRRORHOLD
The Mustang Mountains
Whiteheart Trading Co.
ALFHEIM
Xyaxon's Shrine
Moonridge
The Ankoku Pass
RHUMBEK
HINTERLANDS
Diamond in the Rough Co.
Ulrich's Shrine
Gold Shard Mines
Shadowgreen Grove
The Raging River
Silver Creek Mines
Summerfall
Fractured Hills Mineshaft
Lake Peril
The White Plains
Graywinter
The Grand Exchange
Starsong
Azrael's Shrine
The Heartland Mines
Heaven's Tear
NUVAK
Purewater Fishery
Helshire Village
The Opal River
Blackheart Village
TO SNOWHAVEN
The Black Bog Forrest
Sunfang
The Aurora Peaks
WINTERGUARD
Ghost Lake
Dark Blood Hold
Darkhollow Mines
KIDGELAND
Starlight Railroad
MTS.
THE DRAGON'S HEARTLAND
Azure Basin
ARMAGEDDON
1576 ED. Gwefian Sagine, Cartographer
Mount Blackrock
The Turquoise Ocean
N

EMPIRE OF BLOOD

Book 2 in the Armageddon Trilogy

C.D. MULLER

Lunar Wolf Press

To Richard,
You were as cold as winter.

To the reader,
Sometimes, no matter how hard you try, some stories aren't
meant to have a happy ending.

CONTENTS

CHAPTER 1: DRAGONFIRE AND STEEL

Seventeen-year-old Selena Liongod and Rahim Branwen were intensely locked in a life or death struggle. The two glared at each other through the blazing sun, ignoring Dragonstone Estate's trickling water fountain beside them, occasionally splashing on their cheeks; she feared Rahim would make his move that may end it all.

He squinted at the sun and closed his eyes. "This will be your end."

A sneer played upon Selena's lips as she did her best to anticipate what her opponent would do next. "We will see about that."

Rahim breathed deeply, and his eyes fluttered open. He raised a hand and, with great care, picked up his piece on the chessboard sitting neatly on the ground between them. The two had been locked in a timeless battle over strategy; it was the third round, with Selena winning every game. However, Rahim was not giving up; it would be different this time.

Through his smug grin, he slowly set his bishop down on the square that would take Selena's king. "Check."

Selena stretched, feeling more relaxed. She reached for her queen, ticking off all the ways she could win in the best way possible. As she was about to make her move, Rahim pointed above her head. "Look over there."

Selena huffed, as she had come to suspect and expect he would try to manipulate their game. "Why?"

"Just because—look over there."

"Rahim, if I do, you're either going to switch the pieces, or you're going to flip the board over and blame either Thor or Silver when they're not even here."

"No, I won't. I promise, now look over there." Rahim stretched his arm further, shaking his finger. Giving up, Selena sighed and ruefully looked in the direction he mentioned. Rahim then grabbed the chessboard set and tossed it over, scattering the pieces and ruining their game.

Selena groaned and dropped her queen when Rahim pretended to act shocked and surprised. "Oh no, look at what Thor did: he must have knocked it over with his tail. Oh, well." Rahim casually stood up and dusted off his wrinkled light amber shirt and black trousers.

"Thor isn't even here," Selena repeated, although it was her fault for letting Rahim distract her.

He looked up at the sky, thinking of another excuse. "Hmm. Well, it must have been an earthquake—a huge one."

"You don't take losing very well."

"Not true; I let you win the first two games."

She nudged his shoulder. "Admit it."

"You're supposed to let me win. It was my sixteenth birthday, remember?" Rahim made a disgusted face, and the two picked up their mess. His birthday was about two months after the Battle of Alfheim—and two months following Selena's birthdate—on the sixteenth of Arelion, but it was now the eighteenth; Rahim groaned when Selena reminded him that it had already passed.

Selena said, "I also seem to recall that Silver threw you a party as he did for me. Cakes are expensive and are served only to royalty." Silver was a famous scholar known as Genesis Altessa, a sixteen-thousand-year-old shapeshifting demigod who served the imperial family and was a captain in Her Imperial Majesty's Air Force. Upon their initial meeting, he helped Selena and her friends arrive safely in Alfheim.

"But as the Divine Crown Princess, I'm sure you can pull some strings." The two laughed at Selena's recently discovered identity. The strange mark etched into her left palm was the imperial family insignia, which wasn't well known outside Alfheim, marking her Silver's first and only success to resurrect the dead without necromancy.

Selena was originally the stillborn child of Her Imperial Majesty, Empress Aryl Aurora, but was revived through Silver's project: the Well of Souls. Considered dragon-born, the only way for this design to work was for her to be re-born from a Divinity Dragon: a species that could wield many abilities others could not. As elemental masters, Divinity Dragons were created by the Divines to maintain peace and banish evil from their realm; even the old guardians from the Mythic Flight feared and respected their power.

However, a few slight errors resulted from Silver's formulas, such as the mark on her hand and her race change from elf to human—as her parents were elves. The only resemblance she shared with her mother was her copper-kissed skin tone that accentuated the hue of her emerald eyes gleaming against her chocolate-brown hair. Regardless, the Well of Souls was a massive breakthrough in magic.

Her partner and twin flame, Thor, was such a Divinity Dragon, as he and Selena shared the same Divine mother. Trying to distinguish one was folly, for it was nearly impossible to identify one unless they had fully realized their power; otherwise, they could easily be mistaken for another breed. Thor, for instance, was suspected of being a cross between the Fire Ridgebacks and the Blackland Steelwings, only recently confirmed by Silver's team of scholars to have been blessed by the Divines.

Although only one Divinity Dragon could exist at any time, Silver somehow found a way around Xyaxon's rule—the Divine over life and creation—and Selena received the same blessing as her half-brother. Though she was human, the Divinity Dragon's blood ran through her veins, thus granting her their powers, but she had no control.

The Day of Eternal Darkness—an eclipse that would empower their feared nemesis known only as the Lich and his accumulated army to god-like strength—lingered over the horizon on the winter solstice. The twenty-second of Moonstar was about four months away, and Selena wasn't close to figuring out how to control her dragon powers.

Yet, since the Battle of Alfheim, Selena and Thor had been hard at work training relentlessly with Colonel Theron Cyres and his Onyxian Steelbelly partner, Onyxria. She was a heavy-weight fire-breather with more than forty years of combat experience; she worked more directly with Thor to perfect his fire abilities. Meanwhile, Silver helped him practice his other elemental powers in Dragonspire; even now, Selena could hear the loud noises and feel the earth shake from Thor's might.

Selena hissed through her teeth as she peered over her shoulder, ensuring their conversation remained clandestine. "Even though we're at Silver's manor, please refrain from calling me that, as the Council still isn't aware of who I am."

Rahim groaned. "I don't think those foul old gits would hear; Dragonstone is safe."

Selena cringed as she knew how ruthless their leader, Vidar Helios, could be. The Council remained oblivious to her guise; women were forbidden to be dragon riders, so she hid under the alias of Andric Liongod, disguised as a boy, to protect her bond with Thor. Although the Council sent two riders—brothers and Flying Officers Gromm and Beck Steelmane on the Empress' order—to rescue her from the Lich's clutches near the new year, Vidar knew *of* her but not Thor; he neither recognized Selena's name nor where she came from. The pair safely hid within Her Imperial Majesty's Air Force for the past several months without detection, completed basic training by mid-Xol, and the two became war heroes in the Battle of Alfheim.

Though General Araneus and his partner, Aracania, relied on their unique powers, Selena remained hidden for other reasons: her existence defied the natural order, as her parents and Silver dabbled in illegal magic to resurrect her. As Silver finished the Well of Souls, although sparing the Empress, the Council arrested her father, Phantom Dust—the Shadow Emperor—and sentenced him to death. Yet, he escaped Mortemholdt and had been in hiding for over two hundred years. Dust only recently made his return to help Selena forge her sword, Dragonheart, and participate in her seventeenth birthday party.

Selena and Rahim felt the ground shake again, and the two saw an earth wall erupt around Dragonspire beyond Silver's property. "I told you there must have been an earthquake." Rahim sneered, and Selena elbowed his arm.

She folded up the game board. "What are your plans for the evening?"

Rahim shrugged. "I dunno. I'm thinking of meeting with Niamh and maybe Maria." His face flushed when he mentioned Niamh's name. Selena knew he liked her, but Rahim refused to admit his affections. They had the pleasure of forming a new acquaintance with Niamh Wood shortly after arriving in Alfheim. At the time, Myrrdin, or the Lich in disguise, was the one who introduced her.

On the other hand, Maria was someone Rahim wanted to avoid. He believed her to be a vampire, although Selena knew she wasn't. In all actuality, Maria was the great-granddaughter of Varathka Gundisalvus, the brilliant and insane war general from the One Hundred Years' War who led the Empire to victory over the Lich. Gundisalvus was also a terrific writer whose works Selena enjoyed, along with Silver's. Although Maria lived in the Sky District, Niamh often invited her to Dragonstone Estate in the Garden District.

Silver granted Niamh and Rahim room and board as long as they agreed to stay away from his forbidden alchemy tower, where he held many of his medicinal experiments. Before former Captain Ashur Bel vanished after his suspension for abuse and maltreatment of the recruits—Selena in particular—his manor, Norrington Hall, was open to Niamh and Rahim. However, the Council assumed control over Ashur's assets and estate when he disappeared, leaving it in the hands of the Oracle triplets: Nona, Cassandra, and Morta.

Yet, it was already late afternoon, and Selena had finished with Colonel Cyres for the day, granting her this small window to spend however she saw fit. Rahim feared Niamh and Maria were probably busy, as the two hadn't returned to the manor, and he sighed.

Instead of letting the tense atmosphere steep, Selena bluntly asked, "Have you told Niamh how you felt yet?"

Rahim shook his head. "No, but I know I should. It's just...." His voice trailed off, and his face burned crimson.

There was a pucker in Selena's brow. "Did something happen?"

"Er, it's been a little awkward since Niamh found out you were a lady. She grew fond of you, remember? Honestly, that still stings." Rahim looked down at his feet to hide his embarrassment.

Selena understood how he felt. Niamh admitted her affections and went as far as to kiss her. It wasn't until the eve of battle that Selena told her and Maria the truth; as Selena expected, it was quite a shock for Niamh. "Forgive me." Selena's voice was quiet, but Rahim held up his hand.

"No, it's fine—really. I have no reason to be mad at you. I wish Niamh would give me a chance." Rahim avoided making eye contact, hanging his head in defeat and shame.

"Be a little more confident and assertive in wanting to take her out and do a fun activity. How about dancing or playing a game?" Selena smiled. "Give it some time, and I bet you all the gold I have that Niamh will come around."

"Okay, I'll try," Rahim smiled back, his voice ringing like the tolls of a bell. When Selena declared she should return to the barracks, the two waved farewell, and Rahim dashed through the manor's double doors.

Selena smiled, and she felt Thor's tendrils of thought nudge and prod her mind. His voice was like the steady ocean wave: relaxing and soothing. **Did you beat him again?**

The two shared a telepathic link, allowing direct and intimate communication between only a dragon and their handler, no matter how far apart they were. *Yes, but he knew I was about to win again, so he knocked over the game and blamed it on you.*

Of course, he did. Although, my training hasn't exactly been quiet.

Did you and Silver finish?

Instead of answering her directly, Selena peered up when she heard the soft flail of wings rapidly descending upon her. She moved out of the way in time for Thor to land on his haunches beside the trickling water fountain, displaying his fifteen-ton magnificence. Though he was still a young dragon of seven months, Thor's growth knew no bounds; his size already outmatched many of the Force's heavy-weight dragons, save for the older fighters like Onyxria.

Though he presented a formidable appearance donning the bone mask, Selena couldn't help but admire that Thor also exhibited a regal aura, given his crown-shaped horns, while two larger spikes curled from his jaw like gigantic goat tusks. His blood-red diamond scales gleamed with the rubies set within his golden chain, awarded by Aracania for saving Selena from the Marcupo Ashur Bel released.

Unfolding his five-spined wings like a lady's fan and edges dabbled in purple, red, and yellow ovals, Thor's smoldering membranes caught the fleeting sun's rays like stained glass windows from the Fire Temple, magnifying his blazing, golden chest scales. Though Silver and Selena had just augmented his harness, Selena feared they would have to resize again to accommodate Thor's new growth spurt from the last two months.

Thor wrapped his long, thick, gem-encrusted tail around the water fountain's base as he gently landed on his front paws, the ground yielding to his majesty and grandeur.

We just finished, my dear one, Thor said, **Silver has shown me how to hold my breaths and use more than one element in a single attack.**

That's wonderful. You'll make a mighty Divinity Dragon yet.

Satisfied, Thor snorted, smoke wafting from his nostrils; he extended his paw for her to climb on, and after ensuring Selena was safe within his clawed cage, he flapped his colossal wings and swept himself off the ground in one leap. Selena watched as his tail slithered like a snake, and the two soared heavenward.

The grand ivory city of Alfheim drifted below their feet, swirling with activity as the locals prepared for the evening; even Rune Citadel, home to the imperial family, drooped in weariness upon its mountain pedestal. Although their flight was short from Dragonstone to the barracks, Selena enjoyed their brief moment of respite; Thor purred and hummed in ecstasy.

As Thor landed near the entrance hall and Selena dismounted, he added, **I want us to fly together later this evening if you're able.**

There should be no reason why I can't. I would love to.

The training courtyard buzzed with a new group of dragon riders Aracania had finished working with; the clutch of eggs the Council had set aside for fresh soldiers before the Battle of Alfheim hatched shortly after. Their assigned riders were nearing the completion of the second phase of their training, and the hatchlings were like ravenous weeds: always hungry and forever growing.

Though venomous dragons were rare—save for Aracania and Jade—the Force finally welcomed a Typhoon Wraithclaw youngling, the first wind dragon in years. However, the news regarding its handler wasn't uplifting as it hatched to Volt White, a cadet who harassed Selena before. Though he kept his distance since Silver intervened, the two occasionally shared hostile expressions whenever passing through the common areas.

As she returned the game to the recreation room, Selena had the displeasure of seeing Volt prattle about his new dragon to his gang, but they stopped when she passed by, watching her like a hawk eyeing its prey. All brawn with a head as empty as a flower pot, Selena wondered how a dragon chose him as its handler and shuddered. Yet, they remained civil, even when Selena left as quickly as she came, possibly not to invoke Silver's wrath again.

She marched to the dining hall for supper, overhearing news of Silver's recent promotion, skipping several ranks to reach Admiral, one class directly below General Araneus. Since his advancement, a new captain took over training recruits: Captain Faelar Allendreth. A young elf man whose complexion was as pale as a porcelain vase, yet with blue hair as dark as midnight's curtain, General Araneus had been training the new captain to take over Ashur's old position. His dragon, a heavy-weight male Malachite Diamondwing with earth powers whose rough, jade scales were the envy of other dragons, was dubbed Venerius. He and Thor had the pleasure of forming a new acquaintance before the general announced the new captain earlier that morning.

Since Silver's promotion last week, she had hardly seen him recently; until today, General Araneus kept Silver busy carrying out various tasks and orders. Selena had yet to congratulate him, purposefully wandering past his office near the dining room, but she grew disappointed it had remained empty.

Instead, Selena ruefully ambled towards the post office, which was a falcon sanctuary. The intelligent birds were bred and trained to read and deliver messages quickly across the Empire. Selena had meant to write a letter to Chaliss to re-establish contact. She lived in Nuvak since the Lich's followers, the Obsidian Order, destroyed Helshire Village; Selena had started hundreds of letters but never sent them.

Selena sighed and left the falcon tower, strolling around the fortress, fists stuffed into her pockets until an idea came to her. *My dear, since your bullion horde is still locked in a safe, I want to surprise you with a new gift tomorrow. It's now my weekend off, and I wish to go shopping.*

The thought of gold tore Thor's attention away from his evening meal. **Oh? May I ask what it is?**

It's a surprise, my dear. I know the Council paid us a hefty sum after the battle, but I have yet to see what they deposited into my account.

I look forward to whatever it is you have planned.

You don't mind me going into town tomorrow?
Not at all, but you will return soon to me, yes?
Certainly.

Keeping her promise to Thor, Selena skipped breakfast the following day and took a carriage ride into Alfheim towards the Imperial Bank. Never dealing with bankers before, upon confirming her identity with the front tellers, she was instantly conducted to a private office and greeted warmly by Mr. Copperbrow, a dwarf financier. He happily informed her that the prize money from the battle came to "twenty thousand gold," striking Selena speechless.

Yes, they paid us your weight in gold, Selena teased, and Thor replied with chirps and purrs. Mr. Copperbrow offered her a glass of brandy to share in her success before taking away a handful of banknotes and gold, leaving more than half of her earned wealth locked away in a fund for future endowments.

In the distance, she heard the train's whistle before it departed Alfheim. Since the battle, the train hadn't made its run nearly as often as the business had returned to normal, and the call for war supplies ended.

Selena smiled and happily made her way to the Market District, checking out shops specifically selling equipment and accessories for dragons. Various merchants lined the streets: jewelry and antique stalls, stores selling weapon and armor goods, all showcasing an array of their finest wares. Bell chimes twinkled through Selena's ears as the people strolled in and out, entranced by the merchandise. Civilians flocked to them like a moth to a lamp; the sweet sound of the crinkling coin was like music.

She strolled into a shop, 'Dragonfire and Steel,' a blacksmith and jeweler warehouse ran by dwarves; rows upon rows were chocked full of a vast display of valuable goods. Mannequins lined the front dressed in armor and uniforms the soldiers wore, a forge and a giant smelter sitting in the very back within a private atrium. Aside from jewelry, armor, and weapons, the dwarves sold various ingots and gems, priced close to what the Council paid her; Thor was pleased to hear that he sat upon a mountain of wealth locked safely away in Silver's house vault.

The shopkeeper clad in a blacksmith apron approached her, wiping the sweat off his brow with a handkerchief. "Welcome to me store," he greeted, "just call me Gronbol. See anythin' ya like?" Answering her inquiry, Gronbol beckoned her to follow him to the jewelry displays. Selena's eyes shimmered over the exquisitely jeweled neckpieces, talon-sheaths, and decorated chains for horns and tail; with every piece, Selena imagined Thor's happiness at receiving his new gift.

Once Gronbol gave her the grand tour, Selena finally settled upon a pair of twenty-two karat gold bracelets, set with perfectly cut white diamonds: completely colorless with flawless clarity and excellent polish. The pieces were designed with an adjustable clasp that could be extended as Thor grew. Although the price was enough to make her slightly quiver, Selena still hastily signed the cheque and waited while one of Gronbol's assistants ran to certify the amount with the Bank. Once cleared, Selena immediately bore away the well-wrapped pieces with slight difficulty from their massive weight.

Upon returning to the courtyard, Thor's bliss in his new bracelets was so great as to rescue Selena's carelessness in spending nearly half her earnings. Once she clasped the bracelets over his thick wrists, the golden pieces looked dazzling against his red scales, and his pupils widened and sparkled tremendously upon closer examination of the diamond's clarity.

They are exquisitely beautiful, and I love them so much, my dear one. And I love diamonds, probably more than rubies.

It's worth seeing you look so handsome, my dear.

Oh, Selena, I'm so happy. Not even Aracania has anything nearly so lovely. He wrapped his colossal arms around her, chittering in deep satisfaction.

Selena smiled upon her preening dragon, silently gloating over his new trinkets, but their moment of solace was wholly interrupted when an orange blur dashed across the messy courtyard. It was Loki, Her Imperial Majesty's messenger shapeshifting fox.

He must have recently returned from Nuvak, Selena thought as he rushed towards the pair with a roll of parchment tied around his neck.

"Good day, Liongod. I'm glad to see you're doing well." He bowed, tail happily wagging like a dog's.

"It's a pleasure, Loki. How is *Matu?*"

"Quite well, but she misses you and Rahim dearly."

Selena gave Loki a half-crooked smile; after exchanging pleasantries, Loki mentioned he carried a summons from Vidar Helios himself. Heart racing, Selena eagerly snatched the parcel; as she unfolded and read it, she flipped the message around to see if there was more. Her eyes scanned it once again to her disbelief.

"He wants to meet me at noon, but he doesn't say why." She tried convincing herself that this request couldn't be it; there had to be more. No matter how many times she looked it over, the message stayed the same.

Loki licked his chops and scratched his ear. "Her Imperial Majesty stated she will be waiting for you at the Fire Temple as she agreed to escort you to Vidar's office." He and Selena looked up when the Pyre chimed ten in the morning. "I would leave at once: Vidar is not a patient man."

After Loki dismissed himself and vanished through the diminishing crowd, Thor nudged her backside, pulling her from her fixated gaze. **My dear, what's wrong?**

I dunno. I pray to get this meeting done and over.

He plucked her from the ground; Thor launched skyward, and Selena busied with making herself look more presentable. Her fingers fumbled as she patted down her hair and re-adjusted her military uniform for the Council. Selena dismally stuffed the summoned parcel into her trouser pockets as the pair drifted over the gleaming ivory city. She snorted, preparing herself to meet with the pompous half-elf who made her want to retch; yet, he and Her Imperial Majesty were her commanders-in-chief, and she must follow orders.

*****

CHAPTER 2: A DRAGON'S SECRET

Vidar Helios paced about his office on the top floor of the Council headquarters, overlooking Alfheim's glory. He nicely arranged his mahogany desk with books and pieces of parchment with messages from the members of the Council, including one scheduled crucial meeting with a specific dragon rider. Near the scribbled parchment was a report regarding the egg health of the Mythic Flight clutch. Admiral Altessa's scholars had thoroughly examined the hatchlings and made the alarming discovery that, judging from the hardening of their shells, they were close to hatching: anywhere from several weeks to four months. Yet, he was more concerned about the leather-bound journal hand-delivered to him from former Captain Ashur Bel on top of the pile, detailing startling news needing his immediate attention.

Disgruntled and impatient, he sauntered towards his large window. The sunlight caught in his shoulder-length snow-white hair while he watched the citizens below like a hawk, his usually tan complexion drained of all color, save for his burning crimson cheeks ready to explode like an angry tea kettle. His piercing ice-blue eyes darted from one person to the next, unflinching when he heard a voice coming behind him. "Grandfather."

Vidar spun on his heels to see General Araneus and said in a sharp tone: "Ah, what impeccable timing, as always."

It had been a while since the two spoke. Resembling more of an elf than his grandfather, his mother of pure blood and father with a watered-down bloodline, Araneus Morleth was considered the youngest war general in history at age twenty-four. He wasn't as fair in complexion as most elves, but the alikeness was evident upon his narrow face; his maroon hair christened with silver streaks couldn't hide his pointed ears, nor his deep purple eyes.

His companion, Aracania, was a rare species with venomous abilities, called the Aracania Venomtooth—hence the name. Her daintier and slender frame compared to dragons like Thor and Onyxria made her more agile and acrobatic while airborne and was still strong enough to carry the weight of about fifteen fully grown men. The only other known dragon breed with similar powers were the strikingly white Imperial Pearlscales. Jade, the only Pearlscale in Armageddon, had voluntarily taken a leave of absence after the battle since his handler, Ashur Bel, vanished.

General Araneus' voice nearly matched Vidar's growing temper. "Aracania and I had to pause training with Captain Allendreth and Venerius when we heard you set up a meeting without our knowledge. We demand to know what's going on."

Vidar sneered and scoffed. "No need to be so angry, my dear boy. I will explain everything soon, but I have a favor to ask you." General Araneus' shoulders slumped forward slightly, but he did his best to remain upright. Vidar turned to look back out his window, scooping the scenery. "Before I do, however, you must understand why I would make this ludicrous request."

Araneus squinted at him and snarled through his teeth. "What are you playing at?" When Vidar didn't answer, Araneus asked, "Which soldier did you summon?"

Vidar's reply sent a cold shiver down Araneus' spine. "Do I need to answer that? No matter—I am expecting Liongod."

The general took a quick step forward. "Why?"

"I'm afraid that my orders will overrule yours in this instance: I want Liongod arrested and put in prison immediately."

This abrupt announcement and order made Araneus' knees buckle, but he quickly recovered his bearings. "Have you lost your mind? I will do no such thing. What has Liongod done to warrant an arrest?"

There was a sharp gleam in Vidar's eye as he spun on the balls of his heels, piercing certain darkness trailing the edges of his pudgy face. "We received disturbing reports of his new, unstable power. Not only that," Vidar reached for the leather journal and waved it in front of the general's face, "but we have proof that Liongod isn't who he claims to be, thanks to Captain Ashur Bel."

General Araneus fumed. "As you're well aware, I have a warrant for the former captain's arrest, and you're telling me you allowed him to waltz in here—"

"Believe me, what he brought to my attention cleared him of all charges."

"Nothing in this world would ever clear that man for what he's done." Araneus' fists shook at his side as it took every ounce of energy to keep from lashing out at his grandfather for his insurrection. "How dare you question my authority and decide this behind my back?" When Vidar still wouldn't answer, the general headed towards the door. "When Liongod arrives, I will dismiss him immediately."

Vidar's lips curled into a sneer. "She," he corrected, leaving the general at a loss. "You mean, 'she.'"

"I'm not following you."

His grandfather held up the journal again. "Read it."

He glared at Vidar for another moment before finally snatching the journal. Araneus opened the first page through clenched teeth, but his expression changed as he shuffled through the entries. Vidar scoffed when Araneus' eyes widened, and his mouth trembled. After he finished, General Araneus tossed it on Vidar's desk and looked away after grabbing his chin, falling deep in thought. As Vidar had expected, the general's face burned with rage, but all Araneus could say was, "Where did Ashur find this?"

Vidar squinted at him, confused and bewildered. "I was expecting more of a reaction from you, my boy, upon discovering this dragon's secret. Aren't you disgusted that one of your soldiers is a young woman disguised as a gentleman? Not only that, but she is the result of illegal magic."

Araneus returned his grandfather's gaze and held his head high. "It doesn't matter if she's an Orc; she is the Crown Princess. All I care about is that a dragon chose her, and they decided to serve Her Imperial Majesty."

"She is the abomination of illegal magic," Vidar repeated; he grabbed the journal and waved it in front of Araneus' face. "I had an odd feeling about this 'Andric Liongod' fellow when she and that dragon of hers showed up unannounced. Remember Flying Officers Gromm and Beck Steelmane and their mission?"

"No need to remind me—"

Vidar ignored him. "We wasted our time, money, and resources in rescuing and harboring the dead child of the Empress."

"Watch your tongue. Liongod is the Crown Princess—how dare you speak ill of the imperial family?"

"Oh, may the Divines strike me down, then." Araneus cringed when Vidar began mocking their oath. "We have laws and rules for a reason, and this child has broken enough to be sent to the gallows a hundred times over."

"Who are you to pass judgment over the imperial family, not to mention a Divinity Dragon? For Divine's sake, Grandfather, think about this for a moment—"

Yet, Vidar continued spewing his nonsense that made Araneus want to vomit. He grabbed his chin and began pacing about his office, ignoring his grandson's disapproving glances. "The Emperor is still alive and hiding somewhere within the Empire. I knew it, and we will find him and condemn him for his crimes. Then, I will prepare a trial for the Empress and Admiral Altessa. Yes, Selena Liongod will be tried for her crimes, and I will send them all to the gallows."

"I will not hear anymore of this," General Araneus sternly interrupted, "and I will see to it that she and Thor remain in our ranks. We can use their abilities; they helped us win the Battle of Alfheim. They're heroes."

"She's a woman and a disgrace—Liongod will never be worth anything."

Araneus snarled as he had enough of Vidar's sexist remarks. "Oh, I beg to differ. I see that she and Thor are enough to frighten you and the Council." It was time for Vidar to growl. "I will fight for Liongod during the trial. If we kill her now, what will happen to Thor? He and Selena are Divinity Dragons; we couldn't be luckier than having them in our ranks. If you sentence them, the entire Force will turn against the Council."

"Not if they find out who and what Liongod is." As if to play on his grandson's words from earlier, Vidar's smirk vanished, and his face suddenly turned pale. "You will have to convince the rest of the members of the Council, as we all feel unsafe and fear her Divine powers."

"You say she's not worth anything, yet you hide in the corner, shaking in your boots. Think this through, I beg of you. Selena Liongod outranks all of my other soldiers in skill alone. How many have stood against the Lich and his army?"

Vidar's expression changed, and an eerie smile played upon his lips. "If you fight for them, do you think you can win?"

The general took a step back, appalled by his grandfather's sudden change in demeanor; he wasn't sure if this was a trick, but he said, "I will prepare my stance to keep her in. I will see that she will have the full support of Her Imperial Majesty's Air Force."

"We will see, but unfortunately, I cannot say much more. It's not something I can openly discuss with you, my dear boy. We have our plans." Vidar turned his back to him. The general couldn't bring himself to move; it was as if Vidar purposefully pushed him into the corner, testing his intuition. He wasn't sure whether to trust his grandfather. The two stood in uncomfortable silence before Vidar said again: "I believe you have someone to arrest."

*****

Upon seeing Her Imperial Majesty waiting for the pair upon the Fire Temple's steps, Thor finally made his slow and graceful descent, still carefully carrying Selena in his protective clawed hold. The sun perfectly captured the beauty of his exquisite gold and diamonds, glimmering with his deep ruby chain he polished to a flawless shine.

Instead of donning her usual dark blue cloak, the Empress stood out in the open, her imperial magnificence on full display. Her long hair and thin, silver-tinted eyebrows burned like a beautiful white flame, magnifying her blue eyes gleaming against her narrow sun-kissed face and golden crown set with dazzling sapphires. Though Alfheim's denizens were a perfect rainbow of skin color, hers and Selena's hues were an identical match, no mistaking their relationship.

The Empress smiled upon seeing Thor's new trinkets, and regardless of all formalities, she bowed as Selena stepped forth from Thor's paws. Overcoming her surprise, since Her Imperial Majesty lowered herself, Selena immediately dropped to her knees to keep up the respectful appearance. Since an imperial ruler bowed, Selena needed to bend lower.

Ignoring the confused public behind them, the Empress said, "It's wonderful to see you again, Liongod."

"Thank you for granting us an audience, Your Imperial Majesty." Yet, her mother's eyes glossed over at the overly formal exchange as if she desperately wanted to beg Selena that this ruse was no longer necessary. "I pray we haven't kept you waiting long."

"Not at all, my dear child. You've arrived plenty early, but Vidar is not a patient man. He's anxiously waiting to meet you, Liongod."

Selena couldn't find the strength to step forward when the Empress spun around. Thor lowered his head and nudged her along with his snout, but she blurted out, "I'm sorry for what I said before, at the funeral. I didn't mean to lose my temper."

Her mother paused, but she didn't meet Selena's apologetic gaze. "I'm afraid I don't know what you mean." Her answer was cold.

"I don't understand—"

"There is no reason to talk about this." The Empress' voice turned to ice-shards that pierced Selena's chest.

Thor snarled through clamped fangs and swept his tail around the water fountain beside the temple. **My dear, you need to back off.**

I was trying to apologize, but she won't accept it—

Thor's roar made the ivory city pause dead in its tracks. **Enough! I understand, but right now is not a good time and place.**

But—

We're out in the open where everyone can hear you, and I will not allow the Council to take you away from me.

"Vidar is waiting." The Empress acted as if the previous conversation had never happened and strolled inside, head held high with her eyes closed.

Thor's throat echoed from the deep grumbles as if he were about to roar in Selena's stead but nodded; he sat down, tail whipping in circles. **I will wait here until your meeting is over.**

Selena tore her shimmering gaze from her indifferent mother and leaned against Thor's foreclaw. *I'm sorry. I promise to be more careful.*

My dear one. Thor snaked his head around and sniffed her short hair. His slippery red forked tongue danced through his clamped serrated fangs and licked her cheek before Selena followed the Empress inside the temple.

The stone-cold sanctuary wasn't nearly as inviting as when she first stepped foot inside, yet their presence made the candles flicker on the shrine to Xyaxon, the Fire Lion, upon trekking inside; even the paintings displaying the Divines' perfect tableaux looked dreary. It gave Selena an uneasy feeling to return, and the hair on the back of her neck stood on end.

Before Selena could muster another word to her mother, the Empress abruptly halted and peered over her shoulder. "Please know that I was never angry with you, my dear child—it's not safe here."

Just as the Empress strutted forward, the wall behind Xyaxon's statue crumbled away, revealing a hidden passage with a massive marble staircase. General Araneus trudged down the stone steps with two guards following behind.

"Sir, it's great to see you." Selena immediately saluted but froze when she noticed that he didn't return the gesture. Head hung in defeat, Araneus even refused to meet her gaze. Instead of formalities, he snapped his fingers, and his guards immediately drew their weapons.

Selena flinched and stepped back, confused; the desperation to run erupted from the thundering ticking of her heart as his voice echoed: "Andric Liongod, you're under arrest."

Before Selena could demand the reason for her warrant, the Empress stepped forward and held out her arms, shielding her. "What is the meaning of this?"

General Araneus avoided eye contact as his guards rushed past Her Imperial Majesty and forced Selena to her knees, binding her hands behind her back; the cold metal cuffs made her skin prickle.

Selena couldn't think about losing Thor. Her friends: Silver, Kain, her father, everyone told her they would be safe. *This nightmare couldn't be happening—*

"Selena Liongod," the general stated with her real name this time, "you are being charged with joining Her Imperial Majesty's Air Force under fraudulent enlistment and endangering the Empire."

How could I have been so careless to let my guard down? No, the Divines wouldn't do this to them, to her. She couldn't walk to the gallows or watch them kill Thor. She couldn't—

The Empress stepped forward but was pushed back by the guards. "General Araneus, I order you and your men to stand down this instant."

"My orders are not my own, Your Imperial Majesty."

"Then whose are they, Vidar's?"

Araneus held his tongue and turned his back on her. Selena struggled, but the guards shoved her face into the marble. She relayed what was going on to Thor, and his roars made the earth tremble. Araneus and his guards looked up in time to see flames trickling from the closed temple doors; dragging the bound Selena with them, they rushed out of the way, and the stone doors burst open from Thor's deadly inferno blast, his flames reaching the hallway end, singing the walls and carpet.

His fire died away, and one of Thor's claws thrashed wildly from the threshold. General Araneus immediately pushed through the dissipating smoke, drew a dagger hidden in his belt, and pressed the blade to Selena's throat. "Thor, stand down, or I will kill your handler now."

Thor stopped and slowly pulled back his claw. He lowered his massive head to the ground through thundering roars and peered through the entrance with his colossal, smoldering eye, burning like a volcano's fury.

Selena hissed through her teeth, but she reassured, *My dear one, now is not the time. Please, do as he says.*

Thor only backed away when he confirmed Selena remained unharmed. **If they kill you, I will destroy everyone and everything in this damn city.**

Thor carefully backed away from the temple, and on the general's command, numerous heavily armed guards surrounded and pointed their rifles at him. Snarling through the wafting embers licking his clamped maw, Thor neither moved nor budged when the guards bound him to the ground in heavily weighted chains.

Satisfied that Thor was finally cooperating, the general put his weapon away with his back to Selena, even as his sentries forced her to her feet. "Your dragon will be detained until further notice." He pointed at the escorting guards, still refusing to meet the Empress' pleading gaze.

"Take her to the crystal chamber until we're ready. The Council will prepare for your trial, Liongod."

*****

CHAPTER 3: THE AYNU

Despite the late summer months, the landscape donned a snow coat deep within the Hinterlands. The sun drifted below the skyline, leaving an oil-spilt canvas with the dusk's beautiful colors. Shadows danced across the ground from the hovering clouds, and the heavens grew shrouded with silvers and blues; the unforgiving torrential blizzard didn't take long to sweep over the ancient emerald nightmare.

The feared and fabled Aynu pack knew the land. They lived inside the Hinterlands as wolves that could shapeshift into humans, always wearing wolf masks, granting them the power to survive Armageddon's harsh tundra forest. The pack never tolerated newcomers: they showed no mercy and killed all in their path.

Two wolves from the pack zipped through the sea of green and white, following an unusual yet delectable scent luring their attention. Within the meadow clearing ahead was a human with three large hunting hounds on leather leashes, looking for the perfect spot to set up camp after tracking a wounded elk that had eluded them for days. The muscular man donned heavy furs from previous kills, protecting him from the blizzard's embrace. His loyal dogs, laikas, were suitable for the hostile weather and were quite versatile hunting dogs: capable of hunting game of all different shapes and sizes. Typically, he wouldn't consider hunting in the northern part of the Hinterlands, but his last few trips proved profitable after selling to Alfheim's butchers.

The wolves growled, piercing yellow eyes fixated on their prey. Three more hid well within the trees behind the hunter's new campsite, silent and ruthless hunters ready to strike at a moment's notice. Yet, they bowed their heads as the She-Wolf, whose fur was white as the forest's snow fleece, stepped forward slightly, nose twitching from the human's scent. The alpha would have been entirely invisible if it weren't for the red-painted claw marks across her face.

The Aynu watched the human set up a post, tethering his dogs, his tiny tent, and a campfire in the meadow clearing before collapsing with his hounds; one laid its head in its owner's lap, whimpering for affection. The wolves tilted their heads, quizzically studying the strange interaction as the human stroked the dog with a free hand and fed the fire with the other.

As the man and his hunting hounds cuddled around the new fire, the She-Wolf lowered her head, her blazing yellow eyes glowing like a full moon. Without turning around, she gave her orders to her unit telepathically: *Wait until they sleep.* Like other wildlife, the Aynu communicated telepathically in their wolf forms after learning from the dragons many years ago when they allied with mortals. Yet, they retained verbal speech upon assuming their human guises.

Her pack gave low, impatient growls, eager to strike now, but the She-Wolf's intense stare kept them in position. She knew they were hungry, but it wasn't the right time; the alpha watched and waited until the perfect moment, as they had been following their prey all day.

The blizzard eased finally; as her unit of seven wolves circled the camp, concealed in the darkness and thick, verdant brush, one member's paws gently and purposefully brushed against the leaves. The hunting party sneered when one hound's ears picked up the sound and growled as its head whipped forward; the She-Wolf gave it an intense glare, but she remained hidden as the three dogs howled and barked.

Heeding the warning, the hunter grabbed his rifle beside him and loaded the chamber; the alpha ordered her unit to step back, and all was still and quiet once more. However, the three laikas growled through their fangs, hair bristling on their backs, eyes still fixed to where the wolf pack retreated. Yet, they whimpered when the hunter withdrew to his tent and fell asleep, leaving his hounds tied to the pole outside.

The following day when the human awoke, he found his campsite trashed, and one of his dogs was gone with blood trailing across the ground; his two surviving hounds huddled together in fear, away from the massive crimson pawprints tracking through the ancient grove. Judging by the size of their prints, the hunter understood that their predators were like dire wolves.

As the man snatched his hunting rifle, he heard his two dogs whine, and when he looked over, he saw the majestic and snow-white She-Wolf, like the harbinger of Death. She dwarfed his dogs; the man stumbled backwards, and his hands trembled as he fingered the trigger, but she spun around and dashed back into the trees before he could unleash a single shot.

The hunter spent the remainder of the day in fear, keeping his gun ready as he tried to find his way out of the forest, keeping his dogs close. However, the trees grew thicker and darker, as if the Hinterlands were trying to imprison them forever.

The sun dipped behind the trees; the blizzard clouds continued brewing overhead, and the storm would settle again soon. Hopeless and lost, the man set up camp far away from their previous site and tethered his whimpering dogs to the post before setting up a new tent. As soon as the man went inside his pavilion and unpacked food, he heard sudden rustling and his dogs whining and snarling.

A shrill howl echoed, and the man came out to find that a hunting party of seven wolves had returned for his dogs. Ear-shattering snarls thundered across the site as the wolves threw themselves at the hounds. As he snatched his rifle beside his sleeping bag, the She-Wolf appeared through the pell-mell mess like a ghost. Her yellow eyes blazed hotter than the sun as they fixated on him.

Yet, as the wolves killed his second dog upon snapping its neck, the man shot one of the alpha's members down, an omega. The She-Wolf and her remaining party didn't have time to grieve for their fallen comrade and retreated with another prize.

The wolves tracking them tormented the unfortunate hunter, and he didn't know what to do. With not enough food to make it through and only one hound left, the man knew they would die in the Hinterlands. Yet, the pair endured the evening, his last pup sleeping as if nothing had happened to its brothers.

Howls followed them throughout the following day, but the hunter caught no sight of the wolves. However, he knew they were tracking them, and a bullet to the head began to look friendly. It didn't take long for the wolves to make their grand appearance once nightfall settled, and his last dog barked and snarled.

Like a spirit, the She-Wolf appeared from the thick sward, tail wagging and whimpering as she approached the hound. Believing that she wanted to play, the dog conceded to her behavior, whining to go and be with her. The man immediately rushed to untie the leather leash, but his companion quickly dashed away as soon as it was free, pulling the strap from his hands.

Sneering, the She-Wolf bounced backwards, luring the playful hound deeper into the forest; the man watched in horror, unable to stop his final dog from falling into the alpha's trap. When the trees swallowed the two, there came a grisly yelp and eerie silence.

When the She-Wolf returned, blood staining her front claws and white muzzle, the hunter had his rifle ready and began firing a volley of shots. She dodged with lightning speed; the alpha disarmed and knocked the man down, pinning him with her large front paws, preventing him from grabbing his dropped gun.

While he struggled to push this dire wolf off, the surviving members of her hunting party swarmed the camp and ravaged what remained of the man's supplies. With one massive swipe of her large teeth, she clamped her jaws around the hunter's throat with a sickening crunch. Her prey trembled, and the man's blood poured out like a river. The wolves howled in victory as they retreated with their spoils.

They traveled home to where the Raging River met the North Sea at an enormous waterfall cast with an incandescent radiance from dawn's lancing sunlight. Lovely cliff dwellings carved into the mountain range gleaming like copper—called the Ankoku Pass—hid behind the waterfall. The terrain around its ruins was rugged, with steep-sided canyons cut into the amber mountainside. Their fortress was a rock castle built from the earth. The wolves were experts in using earth magic as they communed with nature; the Aynu had used their abilities to make their wonderland home hidden away from civilization.

Maru was the Alpha Male of the pack, a beautiful black-furred dire wolf with matching red-painted claw marks on his face; he and his mate resided in the bottom stone apartments while their family lived above. This arrangement allowed the alphas to protect their members.

He and his hunting party had just arrived as the morning sun crested over the Mustang Mountains and brought their spoils to the nearby cave stocked with food and other supplies taken from weary travelers. There was always an abundance of snow, and meats lasted for weeks when packed in ice. The Aynu loaded their food hollow to the brim with giant ice blocks from the North Sea, preserving their perishables. Already, lower members of the pack began prepping the meats for the curing process and wrapped them in oilskin when finished to save for later.

After giving his orders, Maru shapeshifted into his human form; though short-statured and adolescent in appearance, the Alpha Male and the She-Wolf were at least three hundred years old. His black hair matched the hue of his fur, and his different colored eyes shined from his wolf mask: his right ice-blue and the left a chocolate-brown. The pack was a diverse culture of humans and elves, but they especially hated dwarves: some of the elves from the Aynu were part of the rebellion. As the Aynu preferred their wolf forms, they usually didn't wear clothes and strutted about naked.

It wasn't long before he picked up his mate's scent; the She-Wolf, Kiba, emerged from the thickened trees, helping her unit carry the bounty of their hunt. They hiked down the hill towards the glassy sea, passing by the gathered wildlife surrounding the river. Deer, foxes, rabbits, and various bird species, all stepped back and bowed as Kiba's hunting party strode by; they recognized the Aynu as forest protectors.

The pack believed the Hinterlands were a gift from their goddess Artio; they guarded her blessing: a solid gold egg-shaped paragon possessing powers to help regrow the forest. It blazed from its stone pedestal within a shrine dedicated to the goddess of the wilderness. The Aynu worshiped Artio and prayed to her daily to keep the Hinterlands well and plentiful. The trees were fruitful when she was pleased, and the prey was abundant. When Artio was angry, she would curse the pack with natural disasters and famine; the Aynu offered her the blood sacrifice of traitors and trespassers to quell her wrath. Anyone not permitted by a pack member was hunted and killed on sight.

When they reached the pass, Kiba and her unit delivered their rich bounty; they resumed their mortal guises to assist the other pack members, but the Alpha Female broke away. Like the others, she retained her wolf mask covering her face from the mouth up: all white, like her long, flowing locks, save for the same red-painted marks over the eyes. Like Maru, she could have fooled the outside world regarding her age by appearance alone.

After she and Maru exchanged pleasantries, she delivered the news of their fallen omega, and the two agreed that the pack would mourn her death; every member was valued, no matter what role they played. Yet, their interaction was interrupted; many wolves scuttled and scurried from their dens as soon as they picked up Kiba's and Maru's scent. Small pups rushed by, chasing each other while their mothers wove furs together.

That night, the pack got together—about fifty members, the most prominent wolf pack ever recorded—before the rising full moon beside the river. In their wild guises, Maru and Kiba stood within the formed circle. The Alpha Male threw his head towards the sky and gave out a long howl, and the She-Wolf soon followed. As their mournful cries rang like the tolling of a bell, their pack joined the chorus, and together, the Aynu howled in harmony, their song making Niflheim weep.

*****

39

CHAPTER 4: THE HEARING

Selena sat in isolation in the crystal catacombs underneath the Fire Temple for several days since her arrest, yet all she could think about was Thor's horrible torment. The alluring mineral pools lost their luster as she crouched beside a stream of trickling water and cocooned herself within her embrace.

Although her efforts were futile in trying to speak with Thor, she feared he wore the Silent Vow, Ashur Bel's treacherous invention: an enchanted necklace severing all telepathic communication between a dragon and their rider. The former captain had used this once when the pair started basic, separating them until training was nearly over. It took weeks for Silver to convince the Council to remove it finally.

I'm so sorry, my dear.

She held her trembling head. It all seemed like a dream or that maybe someone was playing a cruel trick on her. She was tired, too tired, but she didn't dare sleep. How could a reasonable person sleep while their companion was in chains? If Thor were dead, Selena would join him.

She pushed the thought away as she stood up and paced. *How could the Council have found out about us?* Selena immediately thought of Azrael, her rival and bunker buddy, and cursed his name. *That treacherous bastard, how could he—?*

No, it couldn't have been him; Azrael knew better. After their skirmish months ago, he and his dragon, a Sunbeam Shieldtail named Doragon, had both declared a silent truce. Though Azrael didn't quite warm up to her, he had at least begun showing respect. *If he did report me to the Council, Silver and the others would have addressed this issue by now.*

She then clenched her teeth when suspecting former Captain Ashur Bel's involvement. However, she wasn't sure how that would be possible, as he hadn't been seen since his suspension; even Jade took a leave of absence, possibly to join his handler. Yet, Selena couldn't understand how Ashur found out about her ruse. Clearing her mind, she prayed in silence to the Divines for a way out or to save Thor.

She paused when the wall before her rumbled and swung open like a massive door. Selena scowled and cringed upon seeing Azrael strutting calmly inside, with fists jammed into his pockets; behind him followed Admiral Silver Altessa, frantically spewing nonsense about the Council's atrocities.

Save for Rahim's birthday party, it had been weeks since Selena last saw Silver; her eyes darted to his new badge pinned to his jacket, declaring his high rank. Silver towered above her and Azrael—only the Shadow Emperor's height outmatched his. Yet, he was the same. A pair of rounded spectacles perched on the bridge of his nose, like glass cases protecting his ice-blue eyes. His waist-length silver hair matched his regal white jacket and waistcoat, fastened by an azure chain with teal-tipped feathers, accentuated with gold and blue trimmings and white breeches. Even his hessian boots completed his ensemble, though they were uncommon to be any color other than black.

Contrarily, Azrael looked depressing through his messy jet-black hair and deep blue eyes. His crescent-shaped scar through his right eye appeared darker than usual. Yet, he scowled at the rampaging Silver and turned away to avoid Selena's heated gaze; she couldn't understand why he would be willing to join Silver to see her in the dungeons. She dug her nails into her palm to see Azrael again. Lately, he had been doing his best to avoid her company, not being in their shared bunker whenever she was around, and Selena took it offensively.

Silver ignored their hostile exchange. "I'm sorry I'm late. I came as soon as I was able, but General Araneus won't tell me a bloody thing."

"As his orders came directly from Vidar, I doubt Araneus would." Selena sighed and snarled. "Do either of you know what they're doing with Thor?"

Azrael answered in Silver's place. "From what we know, he's fine for now—Doragon last saw him detained at Dragonspire."

"Very good." She bit her inner cheek until she tasted blood and scowled. "Why did you come here? Silver, I'd expect, but you—"

"Because I agreed to help," Azrael sternly replied.

Selena never thought that Azrael would be the one to offer her assistance; she was sure he would have been ecstatic to see her rotting in the catacombs. "I cannot understand your character: first, you and Doragon spent a good deal of time hunting us down for the Obsidian Order, then the general asked you to be a coroner. Now, you made a complete change by showing me *any* form of compassion—"

"That's enough from you," he hastily interrupted and nodded at Silver. "You don't know when to stop— you're just as bad as he is."

Silver smirked, taking the comparison as a compliment. Selena, however, hid her burning cheeks, hoping not to show her embarrassment. Since the two confessed their affections and kissed at her birthday party, she couldn't help but long for his company; she wondered if it dampened the small relationship the two shared, but Silver acted as if they had never been apart.

"If you two are ready to play nice," Silver said, "I would like to remind Azrael of the plan."

He hissed at Silver's cooled words but eventually nodded. "Let's hope your former fellow *captain* doesn't ruin it again."

Selena banged her fist against the large, smooth crystal beside her. "So, it was Ashur who was behind this. I swear by the Divines, if I ever see that rat again—"

"Not to worry, my dear," Silver interrupted, a smile brightening his face, "your father, Kain, and I came up with a plan. Although, as for your suggestion, Azrael, I'm beginning to question your sanity."

"It will work. I guarantee it."

Selena huffed but nodded. "What do you have in mind?"

Silver fixed his glasses. "We have one chance to show the Council how much of an asset you and Thor are. From what I gathered, General Araneus is planning a proposition to control your new awakened dragon state."

She immediately understood what he meant. "You mean like a weapon."

"Precisely." Silver's smile vanished when he noticed her lack of enthusiasm. "That may not be what you want to hear, but right now, that's his best argument to keep you two." His ice-blue eyes pierced Azrael's unrelenting expression. "Though, I still don't believe that, to wholly convince the Council—"

"Dammit, this will help get our point across." Azrael met Selena's smoldering stare. "I know you hate me, but can you trust me?"

Selena snorted. "Do I have a choice?"

Azrael sneered. "No," he said coolly.

Shortly after Silver and Azrael left to join the trial, General Araneus and his two sentry escorts arrived at the crystal catacombs. "Your trial will be held upstairs in the Council's headquarters. You and Thor are prohibited from speaking: Thor will continue wearing the Silent Vow until the Council decides."

Selena avoided the general's piercing gaze and trudged with heavy steps; he and the guards led her up the massive marble staircase branching into different wings within the mountain metropolis. Yet, she couldn't help but wonder if the Council would have kept her in the catacombs upon successfully relocating her before fleeing Helshire; Selena shuddered as her heart caught in her throat.

They passed many wings leading to Rune Citadel's different levels until marching through the main keep. However, General Araneus hastened his steps, and Selena was urged forward before taking in the lovely splendor of the throne room, taking the exit leading to another set of stairs behind the gold-streaked marble columns and red silk curtains.

The next chamber was a surprisingly shining welcome; the warm sunlight captured by the titanic glass dome ceiling and walls illuminated the marble floor's melting colors of ivory and silver. A beautiful water fountain with crystal-clear water sliding smoothly from a lovely mermaid statue was displayed in the center. As Araneus and the guards urged her to stand before the spring, Selena glimpsed at Alfheim's loveliness from the windowed walls, its glorious architecture and landscape glistening in magnificent radiance.

She and her party strutted to the middle, and the floor quivered, shifting beneath their feet. The marble lifted into the air as a moving platform and elevated to the room above.

The stage brought them to a large courthouse. Vidar was in position as the judge, shuffling through paperwork. All twelve members of the Council sat behind him in the stands, shrouded in cloaks and shadow. Five others were seated on the benches to the side: the Empress, Colonel Cyres, Silver, Azrael, and an unknown man she had never seen before. He wore formal military attire similar to former Captain Bel's dress: a dark red jacket and waistcoat with black and gold trimmings and buckles, black breeches, and polished boots. She assumed him to be one of the soldiers.

Engraved into the wall behind the Council was a giant sigil of a dragon taking flight. In its talons was a long scroll bearing the words, 'Enno etem Drvanis,' which meant 'Year of the Dragon' in the Elven Language. Abbreviated as 'ED,' it measured how many years had passed since the war between dragons and mortals ended. An alliance solidified the two about two hundred years later when dragons bonded with the first humans; elves and dwarves joined a few years later.

My old captain couldn't even make it to my hearing. Such a coward—I swear by the Divines he will deal with me if I somehow make it out alive.

General Araneus ordered Selena to sit in the oversized metal chair facing the podium in the middle of the dark courtroom. She did so carefully while the two guards took their post to stand beside Vidar's stage. The many windows above the surrounding benches were closed save for one, catching the sunlight beaming upon her seat like Divine's judgment.

"This is a court-martial trial for the Crown Princess Selena Liongod, also known as Andric Liongod, on the twenty-third of Arelion," Vidar began.

She saw Azrael and Silver sitting beside each other; their heads hung low. Her Imperial Majesty was seated in the back, her face covered by a dark blue cowl. General Araneus took his position to Vidar's right, keeping his posture as he stared forward intensely, yet he ignored Selena's burning eyes.

"During the time of this trial, your dragon, Thor, will be detained until further notice, wearing the Silent Vow. With permission from the rest of the Council, I will be the one making the final decision on the outcome."

The twelve said simultaneously: "Yes, Your Honor."

"Very well then." Vidar then pointed his gavel to Selena. "Please state your full true name for the court to hear."

"Selena Liongod." Her words tasted vile, and she wanted to vomit.

"Very good. Now, will the accused please stand and raise their right hand?" Selena did. "Do you swear by the Divines that you will present nothing but the truth?"

"I do."

"Good. Sit back down. Now, shall we decide in your favor, this will allow you to remain as a Flying Officer in the Imperial Air Force and keep your dragon, Thor, and all charges should be dropped against you. If not, you and your dragon will be executed by sundown." Selena believed Silver had more reaction than she did; she peered up to see him adjust uncomfortably in his seat. Her mother, however, remained still.

Vidar continued: "The court has been asked to hear the two opposing arguments before deciding your fate. The first was submitted to me as a legal document from former Captain Ashur Bel, who unfortunately took ill and could not make it to the proceedings. He declared that a legal representative would take his place in the meantime." Vidar nodded to the unknown individual. "Please take the stand."

The formerly dressed man stood up and cleared his throat. "Thank you, Your Honor. My name is Derik Nuwolf, appointed advocate for former Captain Ashur Bel. His argument is this: Selena Liongod was an abomination created by illegal magic with a terrifying power that she could easily use against the Empire. From the reports following the defeat of the Lich, witnesses noted that Liongod had no control over her dragon state when she awakened her ability.

"Furthermore, she disobeyed the Council's orders for relocation, hid an unreported dragon rescued by Flying Officers Gromm and Beck Steelmane, and committed fraudulent enlistment by falsifying documents. All of her crimes, Your Honor, are the highest offenses against the Empire and should be prosecuted as treason. Her punishment is clear, and we ask for the death penalty." Derik bowed and took his seat.

Vidar nodded. "You may be seated."

"Thank you, Your Honor."

"Next, we will hear the defense from General Araneus Morleth himself." Vidar's eyes darted over to the general.

He and Colonel Cyres exchanged glances and nodded; Araneus made his stand: "Thank you, Your Honor. As the general of Her Imperial Majesty's Air Force, my defending argument is this: I want to acquit Crown Princess Selena Liongod of all charges, keep her as a soldier, and her dragon, Thor, and use their power to fight against the Lich in the upcoming war. She has proven her dedication and loyalty to our Empire. I respect a dragon's choice in their rider and handler, despite her being the first female among our ranks. She neither chose the origin of her birth nor creation, but she decided to fight for us and serve the Empire.

"We have two Divinity Dragons willing to assist us when they don't grovel to anyone lesser than the Divines, and they could be our only chance to defeat the Lich once and for all. You may as well have surrendered and given up by sentencing them to death. Without them, we have no future, save for counting down the days until the winter solstice."

The Council members behind Vidar began whispering when they were reminded of the Day of Eternal Darkness, which fell on the twenty-second of Moonstar of this year. Silver had shared news of the upcoming eclipse with the Council, General Araneus, and Her Imperial Majesty to prepare a battle strategy. Selena scowled when everyone seemed to have forgotten that their days were numbered if they didn't give her and Thor a chance.

However, Vidar was the only one who seemed unconcerned about the looming eclipse; he leaned forward and propped his chin up. "Thank you, General Araneus. Liongod, I have some questions to ask you. Do you still plan on continuing to fight for us, even with your new dragon state powers?"

"Yes, of course."

"How long have you known you had these powers?"

"I was just as surprised as you were, Your Honor —after the Lich conceded defeat."

Vidar shuffled his paperwork as if to search for a missing puzzle piece. "Hmm. Do you recognize this?" he pulled out the journal that Silver gave her two months ago. Her face turned pale, and she trembled; Vidar sneered when she couldn't answer. "Liongod, need I remind you that you are under oath? Answer the question."

Selena almost choked on her tongue. "Yes."

"How long have you had this in your possession?"

"Not very long, Your Honor."

Vidar's eyes narrowed down at her. "That's not what I'm asking. I need you to be specific. How long?"

Selena lowered her head. "Shortly before the battle, Your Honor."

"So, you've known this before you fought the Lich? You just said that you found out after he admitted defeat. Which is it?" Vidar demanded.

Selena snarled; if she had complete control over her dragon powers, she would have assumed her Divine state now and struck him down. "I stand by my original answer: there was nothing in that journal stating I had other abilities as I had no idea until after the Lich impaled me, *sir.*"

Her sudden uncivil hostilities made the appalled courtroom buzz, but Vidar gave her a nasty sneer. Ignoring her insults, he cracked the journal open. "Did it not, now?"

He flipped through pages as Selena went through her thoughts. Did she misread any information? Missed? No matter how many times she thought about it, she never recalled reading about having any powers. She had skimmed through the book several times over, but her heart stopped when Vidar cleared his throat and read: "I'm wondering if I made a miscalculation or an error elsewhere. With the obvious mistakes of being human— and not elf—and the mark on her hand, the child may inherit some unknown side effects from being a dragon-born. I don't know yet, but only time will tell." His eyes darted back to her. "Does this sound familiar?"

"If it did, I would have mentioned it, Your Honor."

"Forgive me if I don't trust you. As I seem to recall, you have an aptitude for lying."

Selena growled and stood up from her chair. The two guards near the podium stepped forward, but she made no intention of leaving the vicinity of her chair;

General Araneus ordered them to stand down when he noticed. "With all due respect, *sir*, as a Divinity Dragon, I swore an oath to the Divines and told you the truth. I yield to them, not you. I have nothing left to hide, and all I can give you is the truth. Then again, you seem to have issues recognizing it."

The courtroom held their breath as Vidar's eyes gleamed with murderous intent. However, he scoffed and tossed the journal back into his paperwork pile. "Hmph. Very well. I have no further questions for the accused. However, I have some questions for you, Admiral Silver Altessa." All eyes turned to Silver as he squinted at Vidar like attempting to solve an ancient riddle. "How can we be so sure that you didn't create her as a weapon to oppose the Empire? What exactly were your intentions?"

Silver's upper lip twitched when he was called out, and he jolted to his feet with a raised fist. "That is absurd. My duty is to the Empire."

"You still haven't answered my question. Why did you create Liongod through illegal magic?"

"How dare you? Your Honor, with all due respect, I never created her. I brought her back to life—that is a huge difference. I only did it to help out an old friend who lost his daughter, but I'm sure you couldn't imagine that pain." Silver's voice echoed with passion and emotion.

"I believe I've spotted another liar in our midst. Explain to me, Admiral, why she got these powers in the first place. It should have been a simple procedure for someone of your talents to bring her back to life, but instead, you created a potential monster that could destroy us." Vidar's lips curved into a sneer when he saw that Silver was ready to erupt like a violent volcano.

Silver attempted to answer, but Selena spoke out instead. "Admiral Altessa has nothing to do with this. Leave him out of it—this trial is about me. How could he have known that it would have given me the power of a

Divinity Dragon? How dare you call that a simple procedure? I haven't seen any of you foul old gits accomplish what he's done. He has made the greatest discovery in history, and you're turning it against him."

Vidar smashed his gavel. "Order in the court!"

Azrael grumbled through the noisy blitz and immediately jumped down from the stands, pushing his way past the general; the astonished Araneus commanded, "Azrael, stand down."

Ignoring his superior, Azrael reared up and punched Selena hard in the jaw, her head nearly knocked clean from her shoulders. He pulled out a fully loaded pistol and aimed it directly at her forehead. "Go on, do it. Do it, now!"

"This is an outrage. Azrael, I order you to stop!"

Still ignoring the general, Araneus and the guards took up arms, but Vidar ordered them to stand down. Silver slowly sat back down, eyes fixated on the scene like a snake ready to strike, while Colonel Cyres hopped from the stands to pull Azrael away. Yet, Araneus surprisingly held him back when he noticed Silver's reaction.

The Council members were appalled, but the Empress was the only one who remained emotionless throughout the ordeal. On the other hand, Vidar was amused; he propped his chin up with his clasped hands, watching the now suddenly exciting presentation.

Selena spat some blood before looking up into the barrel, and Azrael mocked her. "That will be the last thing you ever see. Do it now—kill me. Show me your powers." His hands trembled, but Selena noticed he kept his fingers away from the trigger.

Understanding his ruse, Selena growled, "What are you waiting for? Shoot me."

The two stared at each other, ignoring the steeping, tense atmosphere that took the entire courtroom by surprise, leaving everyone anticipating what would happen next. However, their stand-off was interrupted by Vidar's eerie laugh. "Very well; I think I've made my decision."

CHAPTER 5: THE MYTHIC FLIGHT

"After reviewing this spectacular performance, I have decided to acquit Crown Princess Selena Liongod of all charges. She will retain her position as a Flying Officer, where she will continue being Thor's handler, under the following two conditions: first, she will be directly under Azrael's watch. If he suspects Liongod is using her Divine powers against the Empire, he and Doragon have the right to strike her and Thor down immediately.

"Secondly, you are prohibited from using your old alias. We are now required to release your valid name, as we in the Council cannot condone hiding fraudulent enlistees."

Selena's face drained of all color upon this announcement, and her head immediately shot up, ignoring the blood dripping from her nostrils. "Your Honor, that shouldn't be allowed—"

The jaded Vidar scoffed, growing weary of her headstrong antics. "Under normal circumstances, you are correct, but we cannot pretend to ignore that a female officer exists; given your unique situation, we are left without a choice."

Selena looked at Silver and her mother; the admiral squinted at Vidar like he was an insect waiting to be dissected or squashed, but her mother remained detached emotionally upon hearing the verdict. "Do the other officers have to know anything other than my actual name?"

Vidar jeered and waved his hand as if to shoo away a pest. "That's up to our discretion," he vaguely said, to which Selena was unsatisfied, "we may or may not release more information."

"That, my good sir, is a complete violation of her privacy," Silver shouted across the courtroom before Cyres or Araneus could protest, "if Liongod so wishes to withhold personal information, she has every right to—"

Vidar banged his gavel. "Silence. Admiral, if you can't restrain yourself, I will hold you in contempt of court."

Silver nearly argued back, his wrath ready to explode until he caught Selena's pleading gaze; he sighed and hung his head in defeat.

Pleased by retaining order, Vidar smirked; Selena understood that this was the Council's way of further punishing and humiliating her. She knew Vidar would completely display her connection to the imperial family for the world to see, possibly turning the public and the Force against her.

Once the other Council members agreed, Vidar banged his gavel. "Case dismissed."

Once everyone was excused from the courtroom, General Araneus ordered Aracania to remove the Silent Vow from Thor at once. During their trek back down the marble staircase, he made amends for Selena's abrupt arrest, explaining he didn't know Vidar's orders until she and Thor were on their way to the Fire Temple.

Yet, Selena was aware. "Sir, there is no need. I understand you wouldn't have just arrested me on the spot like that."

"But you still deserve to know. Once I heard Vidar planned that meeting, I met with him straight away, only for him to overrule my orders. I will not allow that to happen again, and I will do what I can to ensure the Council doesn't turn you into an exotic show for the other officers."

"Sir, I appreciate it. I mainly don't wish others to overwhelm me because I'm the Crown Princess."

Colonel Cyres scoffed. "There is no reason for the others to see your imperial and Divine heritage. Rest assured, you will have the full support of Her Imperial Majesty's Air Force."

General Araneus, however, growled. "Vidar hasn't heard the last of Aracania or me."

Silver's piercing glare shattered the oppressive air. "Sir, it's no wonder you hadn't told me anything. I take it Captain Allendreth didn't know?"

"No, nor did I want him involved. It was bad enough to have my two commanding officers mixed up in this mess." Araneus bit his bottom lip, surprising Selena and the others by his distress. "With everything surrounding Liongod's trial, I hadn't had time to meet with the Council regarding the Mythic Flight clutch. As soon as we received your report, Admiral, time is now against us to find them proper handlers to be the new Dark Knights before they hatch."

"I sent my report to Vidar last week as soon as their shells hardened, and he's been wrapped up around this nonsense—er, no offense, Liongod." Selena dismissed Silver's remark but kept her eyes fixed on Azrael as he strolled by, his gun surprisingly holstered to his belt. She considered it a miracle that the guards didn't confiscate it after that dramatic display. He ignored her gaze and raced ahead to reach the exit, possibly avoiding her looming questions regarding his methods.

Silver didn't notice as he continued, "The younglings could hatch either weeks or months from now, but we must act fast. The sooner, the better, as we can rely on their abilities to help us win this war—we will greatly need their assistance during the eclipse."

"Admiral, I couldn't agree with you more. Two Divinity Dragons and the elemental guardians from the Mythic Flight would give us the upper hand we desperately need." General Araneus paused as they reached the bottom of the staircase. "I will march back to Vidar's office and demand an audience regarding the clutch. This matter needs to be settled today." He bowed and saluted, to which Cyres, Silver, and Selena responded likewise. "I will have news for you three by tomorrow. If Vidar doesn't give me a decision, I will take it directly to Her Imperial Majesty for her final word."

Cyres and Silver agreed, and Araneus bade the three farewell before proceeding to his task. Silver urged Selena to follow him outside the temple when the general left, leaving Colonel Cyres bewildered by the admiral's sudden guardian role.

When Silver noticed Cyres' strange looks, he said, "I'll ensure that Liongod and Thor are reunited, Colonel."

Squinting at him, Cyres eventually conceded. "Very well. Liongod, I will see you back to work tomorrow morning. Onyxria and Aracania will be expecting Thor." He bowed as soon as Onyxria arrived with ebony flair, swirling around the populace. Her chest scales were like silver armor plates shining against her void-like hide, her five-spined wraith-like wings leaving wisps of shadow from every beat. She hovered before plucking Cyres off the ground, and the two soared towards the covert.

When the colonel was out of earshot, Silver said softly, "I'm sorry that I haven't been as tentative as I ought, but I will ensure your safety, my dear."

"I pray you won't have to always come to my aid."

The two looked up as Thor's massive flurry of wings descended upon them; he cast an enormous shadow covering the afternoon sun, and his voice returned to her after days of tormented solitude.

He landed upon his hind legs first before gracefully dropping on all four; Silver grinned when Thor extended his protective arm around her, chattering in pure ecstasy.

If I ever see Vidar, I will rip him apart. He will not separate us again. Yet, his pupils turned to slits upon seeing the dried blood on her face. **What in Oblivion happened to you?**

While she explained, Selena looked past Thor's foreleg blocking the streets, hoping to find Azrael among the common rabble, but he was nowhere to be seen. Thor snorted when she finished her tale. **I daresay we owe Azrael much for what he did, although I don't want to see you hurt.**

Silver handed her a handkerchief when she attempted to wipe the blood away. "Well, I suppose by this time tomorrow, I suspect everyone and their mother will know who you are, no thanks to those nasty gits."

Selena sighed. "Then I ought to stop trying to dress like a gentleman. Perhaps I should allow my hair to grow back."

She laughed, but her cheeks burned crimson when Silver said, "Your hair will look lovely either way." Before she could find the courage to look up from her hands, Silver had disappeared into the crowd, leaving her and Thor bemused.

Selena was already up before the clock struck four in the morning; although she no longer needed to mask her identity or gender, she still tightly wrapped her chest. Yet, as Silver predicted, by the time she and Thor reported for duty to Colonel Theron Cyres and Onyxria, the officers looked at her with mixed emotions and expressions.

During breakfast, she noticed posters hanging from the walls with her drawn portrait below her actual name; her brothers in arms pointed and whispered at each other whenever she passed by. She cringed when hearing remarks like "the Council allowed a woman in here" and "she belongs in the kitchen."

"A lady isn't meant to join our ranks—"

"But she's the Crown Princess—"

"Bullocks. I've never heard of the Empress having a daughter."

"Why haven't they arrested her already if she's so dangerous?"

Having enough of the rumors, Selena marched to the cadet waving a printed pamphlet at a gossiping group. "The Council released this statement—whoa!" He whimpered and flinched when she snatched it, scowling; underneath bore the warning:

"Extreme caution must be exercised by anyone in close contact with Crown Princess Selena 'Andric' Liongod. Other than wielding the devastating abilities of a Divinity Dragon, she is connected to endangering the Empire and fraudulent enlistment. If approached, please avoid at all costs." She crumpled it away, ignoring the troubled soldiers stuttering through crimson cheeks.

"Be careful, or she'll destroy us," one officer from the group warned, "if she was strong enough to make the Lich yield, who knows what she can do to us?" Everyone within the dining hall suddenly backed away, but Selena had already stormed out, ready to strike at Vidar.

Can you believe that he stooped this low to defame my name?

Yes, I can, but you give him power by allowing this to bother you: that is what he wants.

After stumbling to the training courtyard, Colonel Cyres had ordered the removal of the terrible fliers, but the damage was already done. Everyone within the Force knew who she was and feared her Divine nature.

However, Selena was grateful when General Araneus kept his promise: by the time the Pyre struck eight that morning, he requested a private audience with her, pulling her from Colonel Cyres' instruction. Yet, as he led her to his office, her mood soured from hearing more nasty murmurs from the Council's leaflets, but they stopped when the general glared at them with fiery eyes. "If I hear one more word about the Council's slander, you will be severely punished. Dismissed."

Those within the vicinity who caught wind of his threat fled, and Selena was ushered into the general's office, where Admiral Altessa and Azrael waited.

Only two chairs were available, and Azrael took one; Selena ruefully sat in the other. General Araneus snarled when seeing the Council's flier on top of his desk. "This is a damn outrage. I don't care what Vidar says; I will ensure these posters are gone by tomorrow."

"Sir, I appreciate what you're trying to do, but now the secret is out—throwing these away won't make them forget." Selena sighed, and Silver placed a comforting hand on her shoulder. "Did Vidar at least give you any decent answer regarding the Mythic Flight clutch?"

"That may be our only piece of good news. In fact," Araneus pulled out a sealed roll hidden away within his jacket and handed it to her, "I have an assignment specifically for you: this dossier contains all you need to know. Pray, tell me what you think."

"An assignment? For me?"

Araneus grinned. "After what you've endured, you might consider this a holiday. Vidar finally gave me a straight answer regarding the dragon eggs, though I wished he could have involved me instead of arranging this behind my back.

"Through a signed agreement, the Mythic Flight eggs are now the property of Snowhaven, the Water Kingdom capital. After much consideration on Vidar's part, I have vouched to put my best Flying Officer on the line."

Flattered by his faith in her abilities, Selena ripped open the dossier, which repeated the general's explanation, detailing her responsibility to securely transport the precious cargo to Snowhaven. "Once there, you will meet with Justiciar William Holland, with whom Vidar has made all the arrangements. The only condition is that Azrael and Doragon must join you two, per the Council." She and Azrael traded gloomy glances; Selena hung her head in silent defeat, and he snorted before crossing his arms.

She quickly reiterated the details to Thor, who chirped and chattered. **I'm ready to leave at a moment's notice if this will give us a fighting chance, but why does Snowhaven want them?**

When she repeated the question for Araneus and Silver, they shared hers and Thor's confusion. "Vidar never did say, but Snowhaven paid a hefty sum—one million gold for all four," striking Selena and Silver dumb; Azrael remained indifferent.

"Then we must go at once if we're to deliver the eggs on time," Selena resolved.

"It could take you four damn near a month to reach the coast by dragonback," Silver said; when Selena asked, he gave his firm opinion that the eggs could hatch before Selena and her company made it to Snowhaven.

"The dragons have already been in the shell since the One Hundred Years' War, reaching the end of their brooding; why Snowhaven wants us to make the delivery instead of sending their crew to pick up the eggs, I don't understand."

"Nor do I," Araneus said, "but Liongod is right." He gestured to both her and Azrael. "The most I can give you is two, maybe three days to prepare. It will be a long journey, but if you succeed, we may damn well have a chance to fight back. May the Divines help us."

*****

CHAPTER 6: OATHBOUND

That evening after finalizing Selena's trip to Snowhaven with General Araneus, Silver invited Her Imperial Majesty to Dragonstone for a private discussion. At first reluctant to grant him an audience, she only agreed once Silver briefly mentioned the nature of their future conversation.

The Pyre struck two in the morning. The lamps lining the wide dirt path leading to Silver's manor flickered like a tinderbox kindling fire as Loki the fox ran past. Yet, he paused when he reached the footman and peered over his shoulder, waiting for the large, majestic white wolf to catch up. It was the Empress herself, granted abilities of the dire wolf. Fur as flawless as Thor's perfect bracelet diamonds, her sapphire eyes blazed from the strung lanterns guiding their lane.

Loki clicked his tongue against his teeth. "I have a terrible feeling—I can't understand why I agreed to come here."

The Empress' nose and ears twitched as the footman slowly approached with a quizzical brow, yet upon seeing Loki, he nodded and withdrew inside to call for Silver. She lifted her chin and spoke through telepathy: *At least agree to be civil.*

"I make no promises." When Her Imperial Majesty gave him an icy stare, Loki whimpered, parts of his orange fur bristling. "Perhaps I ought to wait out here until you two finish business."

Her paws grew heavy; the Empress paused and suddenly heaved over, vomiting a bloody, putrid mess. Loki froze when he saw her gory pile. "Your Majesty." Though rare, he had seen Her Imperial Majesty grow this ill on a handful of occasions, yet he cringed to see her beautiful snow-white coat dyed crimson. "Has Silver not yet found a cure?"

She wiped her mouth with her paw. *There is no cure, but please don't fret—I will live.*

"Then perhaps medical treatment—"

I said I would live. There is nothing that can help my torment.

When Selena was stillborn, Her Imperial Majesty had attempted to bring her back before the Well of Souls was completed through human transmutation. The process required an equal exchange, but the value of life was unmatched; yet, she desperately attempted the folly ritual, which backfired horribly, nearly killing her. Since then, the Empress could never again bear another child, and she was always gravely sick. Though Silver had tried, neither cure nor treatment could ease her pain. She remembered that dreadful day when she first held her daughter, how Selena's skin was grey and cold, her lips black and blue, her eyes lifeless.

"I see," was all Loki could say, and he sighed. "I delivered your message to His Imperial Majesty as you requested, but he gave me no reply. I expected he would have hastily agreed and joined our meeting, but—"

Vulduin has his reasons, the Empress interrupted, *perhaps he believed it too risky for all of us to meet here.* Yet, her stomach tightened; she had hoped to see her husband again after the long years of being apart. Vulduin Xyrrion hid under the guise of Phantom Dust after fleeing Mortemholdt. Although Silver and Kain knew of his ruse, the Empress was the only one who referred to him by his actual name.

Moments later, the footman returned with Silver, and the two welcomed their new company. Loki, however, hissed and backed away when Silver snarled at him.

"I will wait for you out here, Your Majesty," Loki growled and immediately dashed towards the lake, ignoring Silver's fixed ice-blue eyes.

Once Silver escorted Her Imperial Majesty to the drawing room, the Empress released her spell and had transformed into her regal elven form. Yet, she was reluctant to pull back her dark blue silk cowl.

"Would you care for some tea, or perhaps something stronger, Your Imperial Majesty?" Silver offered, but the Empress declined all refreshments.

When she carefully sat down on the couch and folded her hands over her lap, the three Oracle triplets arrived down the marble staircase and grinned. "Hello, Your Imperial Majesty." The first sister, Nona, whose hair loosely swept past her knees, donned her evening satin blue gown, extravagantly trimmed and decorated with lace and ribbons. Cassandra, the second, tied her hair with a red ribbon, matching the color of her embellished dress. Lastly, Morta, the third sibling, clad in green fashion, adorned her hair with a series of braids meeting in a single, thick ponytail. Their cold, pale faces matched their white hair set ablaze by the drawing room's flickering lamps.

The Oracles bowed once the Empress did; other than Selena, the Oracles reserved the right not to bend the knee to anyone. Silver had invited the triplets earlier to help discover the hidden motives surrounding Selena's and Thor's mission, as Norrington Hall belonged to the Council, deeming it unsafe.

Although Her Imperial Majesty refused refreshments, Silver still served evening tea with tiny glasses of punch on the side for the sisters, leaving extra in case the Empress changed her mind.

"Vulduin couldn't make it, could he?" Silver ruefully shook his head, and the Empress sighed. "I had hoped to see him again."

Silver offered, "If it helps, I will send him a message detailing our discussion." He turned away when the Empress agreed. "There is also a personal matter I wish to bring to his attention—and yours."

"What do you mean?"

Silver's cheeks flushed, but he shook his head. "It's nothing concerning, but I will wait until later. However, did General Araneus tell you of Selena's and Thor's new mission?"

The Empress' face turned paler than usual, and she nodded, her throat tightening. "He delivered me a full report and a copy of Selena's dossier, so I am well aware of their assignment," she sighed, her voice turning fragile, "I'm appalled by Vidar's sudden scrutiny and defamation —possibly as revenge against my headstrong child."

Silver smirked amidst stirring the lemon in his tea. "I find her quite admirable: she gives her opinion very decidedly for so young a lady." It took the Empress a moment, but she glanced sharply and grinned; the uncomfortable Silver shifted in his seat and cleared his throat. "I plan on hosting a ball here in their honor the evening before they set out—I've already sent out the proper invitations and put the news in the papers. Unfortunately, Vidar also wishes to attend, and it would have been rude of me not to extend the offer to him as a high-ranking official."

The Empress nodded and wholeheartedly agreed. "I'm sure Selena and Thor will appreciate the generous offer, but to tell you the truth, Admiral, I'm as lost and baffled as the general was with this arrangement. I'm not sure why Snowhaven was so interested in obtaining these eggs: they neither have dragons nor is there a covert within the capital."

"Perhaps they wish to change that."

"By tempting Vidar with a large sum for the most prized and powerful dragons? Something doesn't seem right." When Silver and the Empress turned to the Oracles, hoping they could share their visions; they immediately shook their heads, shattering their hopes.

"We tried, Admiral, but the future is uncertain right now," Nona said.

Cassandra wholly agreed. "Our visions are clouded by a darkened veil blinding us from the truth."

Morta finished with, "But what we know for sure is to exercise extreme caution: Snowhaven is a solid fortress of ice and snow far from the Council's reach."

"A city of secrets," Silver said quietly, and the triplets nodded.

"We will continue our work, but please give us some time, Your Imperial Majesty," the Oracles pleaded with the Empress in unison. "Indeed, the dragon eggs are close to hatching, but what you fear is the least concern."

The Empress shifted uncomfortably in her seat. "What do you mean?"

"All we could gather from our shrouded visions was this warning: be wary of those who wish to use the dragon eggs for malicious intent."

Silver's eyes widened, and his lips trembled when he caught their meaning. "Even in the shell, dragons are the ultimate source of magic. Remember when the Lich had Thor's egg? Only the Divines knew what he could accomplish from his alone. If someone had control of the Mythic Flight clutch, however, it would be like harnessing the power of a Divinity Dragon." He and the Oracles exchanged glances, and the four looked to the Empress for guidance and wisdom. "Your Imperial Majesty," Silver began, "what should we do?"

She leaned forward and closed her eyes. "If I step in and intervene, rather than simply dispatching another crew, I will face an inquiry from Vidar. If I allow Selena and Thor to continue, a possible danger awaits them. I don't know what to do."

Silver said, "Your Majesty, if I may. There could be a third option: we still send her and Thor but have them wait in Nuvak with Chaliss until the Shadow Emperor meets with His Majesty, King Boreas Tristan, and Justiciar William Holland. He can travel across the Empire as fast as a dragon; if he deems Snowhaven safe, Selena and Thor may continue their mission without disobeying Vidar's orders; we can ensure theirs and the eggs' safety."

The Empress shook her head. "His Majesty, King Camulus Urileth of the Air Kingdom, may not be so willing to oblige."

"Unless you gave the order."

"And risk having him report it to the Council? He made that threat when I relocated Chaliss and ordered him to take her in. He's extremely particular about who he allows in his city. I'm not sure which monarch is worse between him and His Majesty, King Dionysus Goldthane of Rhumbek."

Silver groaned but reinforced his suggestion of "if not Nuvak, then Starsong or perhaps Dark Blood Hold—yes, why not there? Lord Vincent Godfrey of the Shadow Templars would accept her and Thor, for they serve you, not the Council."

"Perhaps, but that would be out of the way, possibly adding another week or two to their already long journey. If this assignment goes as planned, we have to consider the safety and comfort of the eggs, securing and delivering them straightaway to the appointed Flying Officers waiting."

"At least have them wait in Starsong, Your Imperial Majesty," Silver pleaded, "until the Shadow Emperor is satisfied with Snowhaven's conditions."

The Empress sighed, and though she declined previous refreshments, she reached for the punch spiked with brandy. "I pray we're not sending Selena to her grave. Now, what was it that you wanted to tell Vulduin and me?"

*****

Doragon flew above the endless Hinterlands as his partner, Azrael, leaned up against his saddle seat with his arms crossed over his chest. As a Sunbeam Shieldtail, Doragon was a first-rate heavy-weight fire-breather whose size was comparable to Thor. However, the Divine dragon had already outgrown him by far in weight and size, and Doragon made it clear that he would not adjust his size anymore, though he easily could as a Spirit Beast.

Doragon's head was decorated with a crown of horns of all sizes, leaving his back bare. The moonlight caught his golden metallic scales, gleaming like a sharpened sword ready for battle. His silver-christened wing membranes enveloped the sky. His rider, Azrael, brushed aside the messy, jet-black hair covering his scar. As the two leisurely enjoyed their flight, Azrael hadn't belted himself into the harness; he kicked aside his straps and carabiners before leaning comfortably against the saddle's edge. Yet, he couldn't help but remain distracted, his thoughts racing over the trial and the mission granted by General Araneus. Surprisingly, both took a heavy toll on him and Silver.

Azrael was terrified when holding that pistol to Selena's head; he feared she would have assumed her dragon state and struck them all down, but he was pleasantly surprised when she remained in control. He couldn't seem to get her out of his mind for some odd reason.

When he noticed, Doragon snorted and poked through his swirling thoughts. **Why do you keep thinking about her?** He scowled when Azrael ignored him. **I pray you're listening to me. Please, don't tell me that you've suddenly grown fond of her. Selena loathes you, even after your saving grace.**

Azrael shook his head as he returned to reality and snapped at Doragon. *Enough of this nonsense. Selena wouldn't even be here if I had my choice— I probably shouldn't have helped her. I don't care for her.*

Then why did you help Silver with the Well of Souls? You and I both saw it wasn't her time yet.

I could have just let it go.

Rubbish. It would have been wrong not to intervene. We needed two Divinity Dragons if we were to fight back.

Azrael gritted his teeth and yelled at the sky. *Why can't anything go right?*

Doragon snarled but quickly paused his flight, and his head whipped around. His dragon growled before Azrael could ask what was wrong when his big, yellow pupil-slitted eyes caught shadows from a wolf hunting party scurrying across the ground.

What's wrong?

Doragon sniffed the air, and his tongue slithered between his teeth. **That same scent always lingers whenever I hunt: fresh blood.**

He followed the trail, diving into the opening within the ancient emerald sea, ignoring Azrael's pleas upon returning to Alfheim. Doragon shot through the Hinterlands with his wings tucked in, dodging all the guardian trees at incredible speed, making the air scream. Azrael's eyes watered as he grabbed the reins, suddenly regretting not belting himself into the harness.

As quickly as Doragon sped away, he stopped, flapping his wings forward and backwards simultaneously. His head swiveled around, his nostrils drawn to the delectable and alluring scent, and his slits nearly disappeared into his golden, smoldering eyes.

It's coming from over there.

When he deemed it safe to do so, Doragon gracefully landed in the clearing below, haunches first, and folded his wings, tucking them neatly away. Following his nose, he strode through the ancient grove with careful and heavy steps.

Azrael shivered; it was like walking along in a dark void and into the unknown. Yet, the aura was eerily familiar, and the hair prickled along his neck and arms when he suspected someone nearby had been brutally killed. However, Doragon remained focused on his pursuit, stomping through bushes and trees, the verdant lush yielding to his massive, golden presence; his sword-length curved ivory talons parted the shrubbery and limb.

When Doragon found what he sought, he abruptly paused; the scene made Azrael want to retch. Before the pair were two mutilated corpses, limbs scattered about with pools of blood and entrails. Pawprints and drag marks painted crimson circled the crime site before suddenly leading deeper into the forest.

Azrael hissed and gripped the edge of his saddle when Doragon, whose eyes returned to normal, somberly approached one of the unfortunate souls and bowed his head in respect. Their heads whipped up when high-pitched childish laughter and howls pierced the haunted sward, and the pair understood they interrupted the Aynu's hunting party.

We need to leave now. I believe we've scared the wolves off, but they'll return for their spoils.

Doragon unfurled his silver wings through snarls and growls and swept himself off the ground with one flap, flying as fast as possible as the howling grew close. When Azrael peered over his shoulder, his eyes widened when he saw a giant, majestic white wolf step forward; big yellow eyes fixated on them like they were the next hunt.

The flight to Alfheim remained in silence. Shadows crept along the ground, devouring the land, the trees whispering in the wind like they were sharing a secret. Yet, Azrael couldn't shake away the sound of their howls; he didn't scare easily, but the Aynu pack was enough to make him quiver in his hessian boots.

Instead of returning to the barracks, Doragon made a slight detour and soared towards Dragonstone Estate; he and Azrael were late in granting Silver a private audience to discuss their assignment. Yet, they saw Her Imperial Majesty strolling from the front door with Silver trailing behind, and Azrael faintly overheard the Empress serenely say, "…Selena would be delighted indeed. In both age and beauty, she would make anyone an excellent partner."

The Pyre struck three when they arrived. As Doragon made his elegant descent near the water fountain, Loki had already returned from scouting the lake with a frog dangling from his mouth. He yelped and dashed before the giant dragon landed on top of him, but Doragon gave him a series of chirps and clicks, offering a verbal apology for startling him in mid-meal. Loki scoffed but accepted it and devoured his catch.

Azrael climbed down his foreleg and approached the grinning and, in his opinion, foolish admiral. With every step Azrael took, a thin crust of ice covered the stone path, cold wisps wafting from his strut. Loki hissed and hid behind the waterfall when sensing Azrael's looming, deathly magic, but Azrael paid no mind to the quivering fox.

"I'm pleased to receive your blessing, Your Imperial Majesty." Silver bowed, having yet to take notice of Azrael's and Doragon's arrival. "However, I fear my greatest obstacle has yet to be faced: asking for the Shadow Emperor's approval."

"I'm certain Vulduin couldn't imagine a better suitor to ask for his daughter's hand." However, her smile disappeared when Azrael approached with an icy stare. "What a pleasant surprise."

Azrael crossed his arms, ignoring Silver's piercing eyes. "Always a pleasure."

"You're late, my good sir," Silver said sternly.

"Then perhaps you'll give me the quick rundown of what the meeting was about, save you stepping out of line—I don't need to know what you're planning." Doragon groaned and flickered his massive tail, but Azrael turned a deaf ear to his warning, **Back off**. "Do we have our stops planned accordingly? I'd hate to deal with the Aynu on our way to Snowhaven."

The Empress lifted her chin. "What do you mean?" Her face turned pale in the moonlight when Azrael regaled their findings, but she remained quiet, maintaining her composed demeanor. During his tale, he tried hiding his shivering; the idea of death typically didn't bother him, and he didn't want to admit his fear; their restless souls haunted him to his core.

The Empress hung her head in defeat and closed her eyes. "Admiral Altessa, would you please grant us a private audience?"

Silver snorted, but he bowed. "As you wish, Your Imperial Majesty." He and his footman withdrew to the manor, leaving them alone.

Azrael and the Empress stood for an eternity before the trickling azure water from Silver's marble fountain before Her Imperial Majesty finally said, "Please forgive me for my abrupt request, but if what you say is true, I cannot further risk my daughter's safety."

"Doragon and I have to watch her already. She and Thor are Divinity Dragons; I doubt the Aynu pack would pose a threat."

The Empress looked up at him with calm eyes, her sapphires as serene and deep as the ocean depths. Azrael understood her as always calm and collected, even when a situation forced her back to the wall; it was admirable. "Would you do it?" she quietly asked.

His eyes scanned over the dread in her delicate face, confused by her question. "I don't understand."

"Yes, you do. Would you do it?"

"I'm still not following you."

"You warned Vulduin and me of the possibility before—don't you remember? If what you've cautioned us was true, would you defy the laws of life and death? It would be an order."

Typically, his orders came from Phantom Dust, but seeing the Empress plead for his help made him uneasy. Even accompanying Selena and Thor meant that he couldn't change what may result from this mission; he and Doragon already came to terms with it.

He sighed and bit his bottom lip, afraid to meet her shimmering gaze. "This will disrupt the balance even more," was all he could muster.

"We all have a choice, even you, Azrael. I would even give up my time—"

Azrael snarled and interrupted, "You know that's not how it works. I can't just take away someone's remaining time only to give—"

"So you can see the remaining lifespans of everyone around you?" the Empress asked coldly.

Azrael bared his teeth and looked away. "Yes," he said quietly, "I can see everyone's lifespans."

"Can you see hers?"

"Err, everyone has one, but you know I can't disclose how much time you have left."

The Empress looked like she would shatter. "I never asked you how much time she had left. She is supposed to be immortal: the dragon's blood and magic were supposed to sustain her life because of the Well. But you indirectly said you could see hers—is this true?"

Azrael fumed with rage, insulted by Her Imperial Majesty. "Don't mock me. I've lived more lifetimes than all those who've existed in this world. That would go against everything that's been established since the beginning of time."

"I never intended to insult you, and I understand. But I need you to do what you must to keep my daughter safe."

Azrael crossed his arms and turned around. "I can't promise you anything."

Chattering, Doragon lowered his head and nudged his shoulder. **We ought to try.** Azrael scoffed at his dragon's words, but Doragon bared his fangs in a warning. **Tell her that we will.**

If we do, we'll be oathbound to Her Imperial Majesty.

Doragon roared and unfurled his wings, making Azrael flinch. **Without her and Thor, we have no chance of reclaiming Oblivion's throne. I'm willing to swear it, and you shall promise it, too.**

Azrael growled, but he nodded; they were bound to any deal or oath they made. "Doragon and I will try. That's the best we can do."

"Then swear it to me."

"We swear to you."

*****

CHAPTER 7: HIS DARK MAJESTY'S MERCY

Azrael had returned to the barracks around three-thirty, but Selena, unable to sleep, sat cross-legged on the floor with a deck of cards, building miniature houses to help pass the time. She only grunted when he said hello, focusing on stacking the cards, but he remained indifferent to her hostile greeting. She was utterly ignorant of his banter since he returned, and all he kept talking about was the Aynu.

Instead, she could only concentrate on the upcoming assignment and how she and Thor would have to settle with Azrael's claptrap. Since General Araneus announced the mission to Colonel Cyres and Onyxria, the two dismissed the pair for preparations, as they were set to leave in two days on the twenty-sixth of Arelion. Silver had notified them of his plans to host a ball at Dragonstone in their honor the evening before departure to see them off; however, Selena noted his anticipation in receiving her reservations for the affair, but she didn't think any of it.

Yet, Azrael seemed not bothered; he lay sprawled over his top bunk, one foot dangling freely over the edge. "You should have seen the grave state of those travelers—all chopped up like a butcher's work. Your mother won't stop worrying about your trip." He laughed, but when Selena didn't react, he added, "Quit being so quiet—you're beginning to spook me."

Selena scooted herself across the floor away from him. "Not talking."

Azrael sat up. "Do you still have mother issues you need to work through?"

Words fired like bullets. Selena jumped up and whipped her head around, her smoldering emerald eyes piercing through his deep blues. "Watch your tongue."

"I like seeing you angry," he paused when Selena wasn't amused, "have you tried talking to her? Since the trial, you've been very quiet—I thought you would be happy."

"I dunno how Thor and I will stand your unruly behavior." Her nostrils flared when Azrael only shrugged. "You knew former Captain Bel stole Silver's journal, didn't you? Why didn't you stop him?"

Azrael snarled. "What was I supposed to do?"

"You could have intervened."

"I swear you're mad as a hatter. I couldn't risk getting involved. Besides, your parents already knew, and Phantom Dust helped us plan the trial: it was just a matter of time before Ashur turned in the evidence, but we were ready."

Selena gritted her teeth and dug her nails into her palms, frustrated by his involvement. "For once in your life, leave me alone."

There was a furrow in Azrael's brow, but he shrugged. "I can't do that or risk the Council executing you."

"What's with your sudden change of heart? If you were indeed a traitor to the Lich this whole time, why did you try to kill my friends and me?"

Azrael answered bluntly, "To make my alliance more convincing—you wouldn't die. I remember Silver explaining mine and Doragon's secret alliance, as we want the Dark Master gone for more reasons than you can imagine." He paused and turned away from Selena's fiery gaze, hanging his head in defeat. "Your father also agreed to help us reclaim what's rightfully ours."

"And what's that?"

"That's personal."

She heard Thor's voice echo in her thoughts. **That won't help you get what you want from him.**

He's such a prick.

Come now—there's no need for insults. I would be grateful to him for saving your hide.

Infuriated and flustered, Selena threw her remaining deck into the card house. After what she endured from Azrael's torment, he stepped over the line of what she was willing to tolerate. Azrael climbed down and called for her attention, his voice sounding like a sword scraping against metal, making her cringe further. "How long will it take to realize that this is here?"

She turned around to see Azrael pointing to a single deep red rose sitting on her pillow. "How in the Divines' name…?" She ran over and brushed her fingertips against the fragile petals; she cupped the flower with great care. However, there was neither a note nor a hint to indicate who left it.

When she expressed her confusion, Azrael merely shrugged. "I dunno, your guess is as good as mine. Ugh— looking at it is disgusting." He turned away.

When her thoughts turned to Silver, her face burned crimson. "Do you suppose it's from the admiral?"

Azrael warned: "If it were, I would be careful—relationships between officers and their superiors are forbidden."

"I understand, but—" Although it was only her and Azrael, she looked around to ensure no one else saw her with the flower before tucking it away in her desk drawer.

Yet, Thor snickered. **I suspect it was Silver's doing.**

Do you believe that?

Yes, I wouldn't be surprised. I saw him rushing to the barracks earlier with purpose.

Azrael shrugged and looked up as if trying to find a way to change the subject. Selena guessed that any talk of romance or flowers were an awkward topic for him, but she was reminded of her irritation towards his suddenly friendly gestures.

She began: "Help me understand your character. You act as though you know our final hour like you're Death himself," Azrael fidgeted, but Selena paid no mind, "I gave you the benefit of the doubt before, but now, your new purpose has been to annoy me. I stood up for you when my father attacked you, but Thor tried persuading me otherwise. Even after you pushed me off the cliff, I couldn't stay angry with you, but for once, I want you to stop meddling in my affairs."

This news seemed to have struck a blow to Azrael; his face turned pale, but Selena disregarded his shock. However, it was his turn to flare with anger. "Don't be daft and dim-witted. You don't know what Doragon and I have gone through, and quite frankly, you don't deserve to know."

"Blast it, all I wanted was an apology, but you don't understand my troubled past either." Selena stomped to the door and threw it open, her face burning like Thor's flickering fire, but she stopped when Azrael asked her to stay.

"Please, I'm sorry—for everything. You're right, and that was too far. I pray you can forgive me."

His words rang genuinely; she froze with her hand over the doorknob. Her voice cracked when she finally said, "I want to forgive you, but it will take a lot for you to earn my mercy."

Azrael breathed deep, restraining himself from working into a frenzy. "Why? Their Imperial Majesties trust me enough to keep you safe. Honestly, you wouldn't be here if it weren't for my help. I'm not asking you to repay my kindness, but I would like to know why you still hate me."

Tears tracked her face, and her hands trembled. "I'll explain why. Do you know how much pain I went through after hearing you destroyed my village? Almost everyone died because of what you did, and I blame myself for it, even today. Maybe you can help me bring them back, or perhaps my original bunker buddy, Erik. He didn't deserve to die—I should have been there to save him."

Azrael stood with a dumbfounded expression but held his head in shame. "I-I'm sorry. If I could bring them all back, even Erik, I would, but...." he looked like he wanted to say more but held his tongue.

"Don't tell me that they deserved their fate."

"No, that's not what I was going to say. Ugh, you can be so infuriating sometimes. I'm trying to do the right thing here!"

"Now you want to do the right thing? How about this? Maybe you can track down those monsters who were with you that night and send them back to Oblivion for me."

"I would love to if I ever saw those tossers again," Azrael admitted, "the last I heard, some were hiding in the

Hinterlands near Aynu territory. Doragon and I have been working on rooting them out and eliminating them."

Selena snorted. "You two are foolish for trespassing into Aynu territory."

"Doragon and I can handle ourselves against a wolf pack. Perhaps you and Thor can join us: as Divinity Dragons, you two can sense demonic and undead presences. We can track them down." Selena abruptly turned around and stared at him, baffled and perplexed. "If we're to travel across the Empire together, perhaps we ought to set aside our differences," Azrael sighed, "and maybe you're right. It was my fault, and you deserve closure."

Selena squinted at him. She desperately wanted to leave right then and there, but she held herself back, suspecting a possible trap.

After listening, Thor said: **I would sleep on it. We can plan it out tomorrow.**

Do you think he's sincere?

I don't know, but why wouldn't he be?

"Thor and I will think about it," Selena announced; she closed the door and headed to bed, ignoring Azrael.

"Fine. I wouldn't expect you to leave now, but my offer still stands if you wish to join us." He sat down on the floor as Selena pulled the covers over her head and drifted to sleep.

Even when Selena awoke at the stroke of seven in the morning, Azrael hadn't stirred from his spot. His legs crossed and his head hung, he looked up sleepily, bags dragging under his eyes.

Selena turned away from him. "Why didn't you sleep?" That was all she could force out.

"Because I don't need to. Did you think about what I said?"

"I still need to talk to Thor." Her eyes darted back to where the rose rested in the drawer; her heart immediately raced, and her cheeks burned crimson.

Thor's voice interrupted and made her snap back to reality. **Deeply in love, are we? Stop thinking about that.**

I'm sorry.

Sure you are. Tell Azrael we will take him up on his offer, but it will just be us three—I don't want Doragon to be there if it is a trap.

Very well.

Selena repeated their conditions to Azrael. To her surprise, he didn't argue. "Fine by me. We'll prepare for tonight and head towards the pass."

After breakfast and coffee, while ignoring the snide and sexist comments made by the other soldiers, Thor met her within the training courtyard, offering to escort her to Alfheim's grand library. As he scooped her within his talons, the two watched Azrael meet with Doragon, and they soared away from the barracks towards the North Sea.

I would give him a chance, my dear one, Thor said, **I believe Azrael means well.**

I still don't know.

It will take some time.

Free of his harness, Thor liberally displayed his gold and jewels with his freshly cleaned and oiled scales. The large crowd dispersed when Thor gracefully landed before the grand library, and he released Selena from his clawed cage. Even as she marched up the massive marble steps, she needed to distract her wandering mind, though she was anxious about the planned trip and possibly running into Silver again. Selena had to remind herself to hold back instead of rushing to conclusions about his involvement regarding the red rose. However, he was the only one who would surprise her in that manner; her face burned when she understood the meaning behind the flower: beauty, romance, and love.

See if you can find more books on Divinity Dragons. Thor snorted, blowing a smoke ring, tousling her hair.

As she entered, her eyes scanned through the rows of ancient tomes decorating the august castle. Skeleton displays of various creatures—gryphons, dragons, Grootslangs, giants, trolls, all that she could imagine—embellished the atrium library, surrounded by skylight-covered spaces.

She sought out Apollo, a dragon librarian. As an older Viridian Longwing, Apollo was the only known dragon who could speak verbally and telepathically. He was small, matching Selena's height. His dull emerald leather-like hide revealed his age—Apollo recently celebrated his six-hundredth hatching day—and like Aster's physical features, two long, curved horns adorned Apollo's head. He adapted to walking on two legs instead of four, his wings always neatly folded and tucked to his sides, their tips brushing against the marble floors. Selena watched his long tail as it slithered past her like a giant, thin snake.

He was always ecstatic to see Selena in his library, as the two usually engaged in conversations regarding philosophy and religion. Apollo knew of her Divine draconic nature and considered her a fascinating phenomenon. As the two finished their debate, Apollo said: "You have indulged my weakness for speech yet again. Here. I saved these for you."

"Thank you. You're too kind." Selena smiled at him. "Thor was recently discovered as a rare breed, though I understand it's difficult to differentiate one."

Apollo nodded. "Indeed, yes. The only way to tell whether a dragon is one is tenuous at best. It requires extensive research and study to see if they can use other elemental magic or just one. I'm sure you know that only one can exist at any given time, though from what I hear from Admiral Altessa, I believe you and Thor are quite exquisite, defying the Divine order."

Selena smiled; Thor overheard her conversation and contributed, **Can you ask him something for me? How does that affect mating?**

Selena repeated his question, and Apollo chuckled. "They can still mate as normal, but unlike other breeds, Divinity Dragons can only produce a clutch of one egg at any given time. Once laid, they may choose to pass the blessing by offering a prayer to the Divines. Divinity Dragons are quite fascinating."

Thor hummed in delight, and Selena asked, *Are you satisfied?*

Yes.

Are you interested in finding a mate for yourself?

Don't be absurd. I was only curious.

Of course, you were.

Selena thanked Apollo by grabbing the two books he had set aside for her. The doors to the library suddenly opened; Selena didn't think any of it until Silver entered, leaving her astonished as she bowed. "Admiral Altessa."

Without a word, Silver gave her a firm, jerky nod. "Good day, Liongod."

There was an awkward pause until Selena offered, "Would you care to join me? I was getting some light reading done for the day."

Silver's lips trembled. He looked between her and Apollo and shook his head before pacing back and forth, leaving Selena confused about what he wanted. He stopped and nervously gestured to the building's general splendor. "I'm glad to see that you enjoy the library—it's about as old as Alfheim itself. Both Apollo and I did a great deal to it during early construction."

Selena smiled. "Yes, it is quite charming indeed."

Silver nodded and clasped his hands together, but he looked as though he wanted to say more. *I've never seen Silver act this way before.*

Apollo asked him, snaking his head over the counter, "Do you need anything, Admiral?"

Silver declined his offer; when the massive doors opened again, he jumped in his spot, and Rahim came inside with the Oracles carrying a hefty tome emblazoned with jewels. "Good day, Liongod." Silver bowed and left.

Both Rahim and the Oracles exchanged glances as Silver rushed past them while Selena stood there, bemused and intrigued. Raising a brow, Rahim asked, "What happened between you and Admiral Altessa?"

"I-I don't know," Selena admitted.

She spent the remainder of the day with Thor reading to him within his quarters; it didn't take long for her to attract an audience of other dragons within the covert—including Aster, Vulcan, and Doragon—to join them when they finished working with Aracania, Venerius, and Onyxria. The officer dragons listened with interest from their apartments and clicked their nails against the stones, applauding whenever Selena finished reading the glorious stories behind the powerful dragons from history.

General Araneus, Captain Allendreth, and Colonel Cyres attended briefly before withdrawing to the barracks, preparing anew for the morning; Silver, however, watched in admiration from the hall's entrance, smiling at the warm scene.

The lore behind the Divinity Dragons also attracted Mr. Kingsleigh, an older gentleman and Aster's handler, and the Steelmane brothers, Gromm and Beck. They watched as their companions collected together in a rainbow of scales glittering from the evening sun; even Azrael strolled across the dragon grounds and watched the display in amusement. Doragon chittered and chirped, urging him to join, but Azrael kept his distance.

As if jealous of the sudden attention Selena was receiving, Thor wrapped a protective arm and herded her close to his breast, pressing her into his gold and ruby chain. Selena laughed, but she enjoyed their shared respite; even if the soldiers wanted to be nasty behind her back, she was at least loved and adored by the dragons.

When evening settled in, Selena and Azrael returned to their bunker and packed for their short trip, leaving Thor to finish his meal of sheep and pigs.

Are you sure you're comfortable with him riding with us?

Of course. It's my idea, but I started wondering if this is wise.

Why?

It feels more like you want revenge than closure.

Now you're being daft. Revenge is what I want, and Azrael will help us.

She slung her prepared pack over her shoulder before grabbing Dragonheart, leaning against the wall; the rose-tinted ivory bone-cased scabbard glistened like her blood-thirsty blade. Courtesy of her father, a master blacksmith, her dragon bone and steel sword was the perfect weapon that struck fear in her enemies. Once belted to her waist, she and Azrael zipped through the four-towered fortress and met with Thor, hovering above the training courtyard, with his harness dangling from his talons.

As Thor helped them strap the saddle over his back, he arched his neck and snorted, plumes of smoke wafting from his nostrils. **I still don't believe this is what you want, my dear. Remember when I kept telling you**

to forgive yourself? You blamed yourself for Helshire—maybe you need to do the same for them.

No, they're demons and monsters who only understand evil and darkness. How could I ever forgive them?

After the two were situated and belted into the saddle, Thor launched himself skyward in one leap, his massive wings trailing through the evening sky like sails from a ship, and soared over the Hinterlands.

"Tell Thor to stay on the lookout," Azrael began, "after the Battle of Alfheim, these old gits somehow went undetected in the forest. They're few in number now, but we need to follow a stealth approach if we want to take them out without making a scene or attracting unwanted visitors."

The waning moon guided their path, leaving a silver tint lancing through the whispering leaves. Selena tightened her grip on Thor's reins as she scanned below, but Thor's steady wing beats had him sailing across the emerald dream.

Yet, Thor slowly succumbed to his worries. **What will happen if you turn into a dragon again? I hope your desire for revenge won't result in your powers destroying you.**

That won't happen to me, my dear. It's been a while since I've transformed—these monsters won't compare to Venexus.

Do you have to keep saying the Lich's name? It's like summoning him.

It doesn't matter. He will still try to kill us either way.

The three heard high-pitched laughter followed by the whistling of an unsettling melody from below. Closer to the mountains was a titanic green dragon thrice the size of Thor flying away in the distance, its wing flaps making the heavens quiver. Yet, the emerald behemoth continued south, following the guardian trees until it shrunk to a tiny jewel Selena could pluck from the sky.

They spent the next hour in uncomfortable silence. Azrael leaned over the edge, away from Selena's brewing rage, about to erupt like a violent volcano. She was ready to unleash the firestorm, prepared to incinerate those who've wronged her.

Suddenly, a quick, ear-shattering ring blasted through her thoughts; it was like Death's shrill, a calling to the grave. Thor roared as he heard it, too; as the two riders prepared for a fight, Thor dove into the forested abyss through one massive flap and tucked in his wings. The shriek nearly grew to an unbearable pitch, and Selena released the reins to cover her ears, but she couldn't block what stabbed her subconsciousness.

Thor zipped through the gripping trees, yielding to his might and power, his incredible velocity making them bend in respect. **My dear one, Azrael was right— you can sense them, too. Pray that the shadows will hide us as we make our descent.**

Selena and Azrael ducked, avoiding the whipping and bending branches threatening to cut them in half; Thor elegantly weaved in and out of the ancient grove until he found a large enough clearing to land. Thor allowed a downdraft waft over his wings, gliding upon the earth's hot breath, billowing dust from every flap he made.

Selena and Azrael dismounted as he descended, climbing down his forelegs with ready weapons. Yet, Thor withdrew into the shadows, his smoldering amber eyes and pearly fangs piercing the darkness.

I'll wait until the time is right, my dearest one. I fear the Order will scatter like roaches if they see me lurking nearby, as they should.

The shrill lessened, but Selena pointed to where the sound originated; Azrael nodded and summoned his blue Aether spirit pistols. Selena instinctively drew the energy around her through a determined and heated gaze, and her arms and hands were set ablaze with dragon fire, tickling her skin like winter's kiss.

Azrael followed her lead; the two ran across the ground in graceful strides. The moon hung low and lit their steps through the trees, the North Sea mirroring its blue-ore hue. Azrael paused and leaned against the tree, flinching and intimidated by Selena's furious blazing flames like the firestorm boiling from a dragon's throat. "Are you sure that you're ready for this?"

"I'm more than sure."

The two reached an eerie meadow: a small, empty campsite and a stone tower nearly falling apart from years of waste and decay. Guarding the campfire were three tents large enough to house thirty men—one housing a wooden table cluttered with blood-painted clippers and small bones—lined with animal furs and sacks full of food. A large metal pot sat over a roaring fire held by a metal rod strewn through cookware loops.

Azrael growled and winced. "Stay low."

She growled like a dragon, and she wanted to vomit. *Those monsters are going to get what's coming for them.*

She followed Azrael around the disgusting sight while reaching for her sword with lightning reflexes; even Dragonheart burned from its scabbard, waiting to unleash its blood-thirsty and inferno wrath.

Yet, before the two could adequately investigate the empty campsite, Thor's voice thundered across her thoughts: **Leave, now! You two are surrounded.**

Just as Thor finished, the deathly shrill from before shattered her mind like breaking glass; through smoke spires, a group of twenty robed zealots from the Lich's Obsidian Order emerged from the shadows. Selena snarled through gritted teeth to see their silver dragon-head-shaped masks decorated in a crown of horns; their dark blue robes trickled in steel buckles and trimmings, catching the moon's sinister glow.

She was about to unleash waves of dragon flames, but Azrael shook his head, as the Order hadn't exchanged hostile fire. One of them stepped forth with a sneer. "We knew you would come back one day, Azrael. We've been waiting for you. Our Dark Master has been longing to see you again." Snarling, Selena pulled out her sword, but Azrael held out his hand to stop her. She mouthed to him, "Why?" Yet, he didn't answer.

"Thank you for hand-delivering Liongod to us. Have you finally come to redeem yourself? I suppose we could forgive your traitorous acts—perhaps even His Dark Majesty will welcome you back with open arms."

She glared at the Order, then at Azrael to see him possibly contemplating this offer and joining them again. *I knew it. He lied to everyone.*

"Recite our blood oath," the cultist hissed, "we will seal our pact, and you will be welcome back once more. Seek His Dark Majesty's mercy, redeem yourself, and join our reign in the Kingdom of Oblivion."

Thor's growls grew. **What's happening?**

The Order is tempting Azrael to return.

I don't believe that. What is he doing?

Selena couldn't answer as she finally unsheathed Dragonheart, her blade whistling its deathly tune and glimmering from her blazing flames, but Azrael kept his back to her. Her heart throbbed in her throat as she anxiously waited for his answer. *How could we have been such fools to trust him?*

Finally, Azrael cleared his throat before Selena readied an attack. "Then I shall: my only oath is to see your Dark Master's demise."

The demonic group backed away, and the cultist who gave the offer to Azrael hissed and began reaching for his holstered weapons. "Your souls to Oblivion. You two can run, but you cannot hide—the Dark Master will find you."

I thought right: I'm coming for you now.

Before the Order could go so much as ready themselves, everyone cowered when Thor's loud and piercing roar blasted over the canopy, and the gale storm from his massive wings bent the treetops. His blood-red scales and golden underbelly gleamed with murderous intent as his silhouette loomed over the Obsidian Order.

Thor released another thunder as flames and smoke wafted from his maw. While the zealots organized against the Divine dragon, Azrael grabbed Selena's arm, unharmed by her fire, and the two dashed as far away as possible. She pulled away when she heard them shouting orders to bring Thor down, and she pleaded with Azrael to return and save him.

She paused, however, while watching Thor rear his head back like a snake ready to strike, and his chest began swelling. Just as the Order unleashed their melee volley—as magic was useless against a dragon—Thor opened his colossal maw, the inferno storm building within his throat. He exhaled an enormous torrent of flame, consuming the campsite and his enemies.

Selena and Azrael dropped and flattened themselves against the ground as his fire blasted in every direction as a shockwave, leveling the trees and brush within their vicinity. When Thor's flames extinguished, all that was left was an enormous crater of his size in its wake: the Obsidian Order and their campsite had been reduced to ash piles, but Selena and Azrael remained unharmed.

Satisfied, Thor landed haunches first on top of his rubble pile, wings wholly unfurled, waiting for his two riders to approach across the singed earth. Smoke plumed from his nostrils, and flickering embers licked from Thor's clamped maw as he extended his paw to the awe-struck Selena and Azrael.

As he ferried the two back to the training courtyard, Selena and Azrael couldn't meet each others' gazes; she extinguished her flames and sheathed Dragonheart, ashamed for doubting Azrael's alliance.

Thor landed as the moon dangled, a couple of hours before dawn, above the horizon and snaked his head down when the two dismounted. **I'm proud of your restraint, my dear. I pray that you've found closure and can finally put all this to rest.**

I don't want to keep blaming myself, but I promise you I will never forgive the Order or the Lich for what they've done.

Thor snorted, but he turned his muzzle towards Azrael, who stood dumb before their exchange; sweat beaded his forehead as he anticipated what Selena would do next.

To his surprise, she looked at him with soft eyes and embraced him. "I'm finally willing to forgive you. I'm sorry—I was wrong. Friends?"

He staggered backwards, but he gave her a small smile and returned the gesture. "Friends."

*****

CHAPTER 8: THE DRAGON'S DANCE

Azrael bade Selena farewell before she returned to their bunker as Doragon soared overhead. He and Thor exchanged civil pleasantries, and Thor excused himself, retiring to his quarters for the day. After ensuring his rider was well, Doragon and Azrael retreated to their stall and relaxed together in silence. Facing the Obsidian Order and his past was almost too much for Azrael to bear; he was exhausted.

Doragon wrapped his wings around him and nudged his arm in comfort. **You did the right thing.**

He leaned his head back and smiled at the heavens. *Yes, I suppose so.*

The rustling leaves near the forest edge disrupted his tranquil thoughts. Azrael saw a doe grazing when he whipped his head around; she ignored their gazes. Out of curiosity, Azrael left Doragon's protective wing and sauntered towards her with his hands stuffed in his pockets, not wishing to startle the gentle creature.

His eyes drifted over the doe's head, and his face drained of color. Azrael swiveled his head, but he couldn't find the looming threat. He was able to approach from behind without disturbing her, but the doe turned around.

To his surprise, she didn't flee; Azrael reached out to pet the animal, but she rejected his touch. The doe immediately sprinted, running deeper into the forest.

The ancient woodland called him into its pulsating heart. The deep, haunting ballad of its grisly song tinkled in his ears as Azrael stumbled through the over-arching vault of leaf and limb. The beauty of the setting moon's light had lanced through the lush, green turf. Black shadow adorned the groves—vaporous mists wrapped around the tall pine trees; the forest's damp breath overhung the hallowed ground. Yet, a grave silence lingered in the gloomy atmosphere.

Azrael followed, but the deer would dash away every time he drew close. Eventually, he paused, keeping his distance, and observed. Satisfied that he respected her privacy, she crouched down behind a hidden bush. When Azrael bent over and moved the leaves with extreme caution and care, he was shocked to see that the doe had a fawn with her; he guessed it must be a newborn.

The mother doe nudged her fawn, and the two pirouetted away from him in such grace and elegance, but she looked up at Azrael once more before leaving. Azrael moved away not to bother them, as he knew he couldn't stop their inevitable fate. However, he suddenly had a change of heart; his expression changed when the worst was soon to happen.

Just as the doe took her last step, a gunshot rang through the trees. She fell forward and landed in a pool of her blood, leaving the panicked fawn crying for its fallen mother. The baby hunkered beside the doe's corpse when Azrael rushed over, and he mourned this loss.

He snarled when the leaves and brush parted, and a hunter donned in furs and leather made his way through the foliage with a rifle in hand. "That's my kill. Get away from that now, or else."

As the man loaded another bullet, his face flaming red, Azrael gritted his teeth and summoned his spirit pistols. The hunter became intimidated when he saw his magic and ran back the way he came.

Releasing his Aether firearms, Azrael knelt beside the mother. She was already gone, but he wanted to help. He had to: she was a mother. *How could it have been her time?*

Azrael.

He ignored Doragon. *No, this isn't fair.*

Stop, and let her go.

I can do this.

However, Azrael knew it wasn't any use: he wasn't allowed to bring back the dead, no matter how unjust. He held up her head as he fought back his tears. Her body was limp and cold, and he saw it in her eyes. Azrael put her down and prayed in silence, and the fawn trembled beside her body, nuzzling its tiny head into her fur.

What should I do?

It's not going to be easy, but.... Doragon's voice trailed off.

What? Oh, no, absolutely not; I will do no such—

It won't survive without its mother, and it will die soon. At least, you can give it a gentle end.

He felt the sweat drench his skin and the throbbing of his heart. His fingers curled into a fist, digging his nails into his palm; Azrael eventually reached to pet the fawn. To his surprise, it didn't run away. While caressing the baby's face, he muttered a few words like a prayer to make it quick and painless, and the fawn finally stopped crying. It closed its eyes for the last time, and its body grew cold and grey.

He laid the fawn's head down and tearfully walked away. Azrael couldn't dare to look back, but soon he gave in to temptation. The forest glade haunted in the enhanced light of the glaring moon, and the wind whistled a ghastly melody.

*****

Azrael offered to show Selena more about Aether the following day before the anticipated ball since she had the aptitude. Doragon followed his example and extended the training to Thor; it didn't take long before the dragons' magic grew out of hand, accidentally summoning a spirit meteor shower that nearly destroyed their courtyard. If it weren't for Silver, the fort would have been annihilated.

"I would recommend practicing near the beach," Silver suggested, "I don't think General Araneus would appreciate losing the covert." Yet, he broke away from his tasks, observing and admiring their sparring match.

Thor and Doragon circled overhead until they found a location far enough away not to disturb their riders. While the dragons busied themselves with their magical ruckus and playful skirmishes, Selena couldn't help but blush when Silver leaned against a nearby boulder.

Thor sneered. **You missed him.**

She sighed in defeat. *Is it that obvious?*

Your awkwardness definitely stands out.

Azrael was amidst instruction and demonstration of summoning Aether strands, but Selena peered over her shoulder, growing nervous under Silver's watchful eye. When Azrael noticed her lack of interest, he called her name. "Pay attention; this is important."

Selena snapped herself back into reality and hunched her shoulders in shame. "Pray forgive me. I was distracted, but I won't let it happen again."

"You don't say. I'm trying to work with you."

"Okay, okay. I'm sorry."

Azrael cracked his knuckles and stomped forward, creating a rock-shaped dummy resembling the Obsidian Order cultist. "Now, with your power, I want you to roar like a mighty dragon and destroy that target."

She breathed in deep, drawing in the energy within her core, and expelled it through a roar that resonated among the trees and nearby rocks along the beach. A torrent of deadly dragon fire erupted from her mouth, beginning as a tiny flame that erupted into a blast as large as Thor's, decimating Azrael's stone dummy.

Thor and Doragon watched in amazement, their eyes twinkling by her dragon fire; Azrael nodded approvingly, and Silver applauded. When Azrael launched several earth disks into the air for target practice, Thor intervened: he soared past her head and exhaled his fire blasts, destroying the rock slabs before Selena had a chance.

Ignoring Azrael's fuming face, Thor tittered and landed behind them. **I'm sorry, my dear, but I couldn't resist.**

Azrael exclaimed, "We're working—get out of here."

Thor's lips twitched as he bared his fangs in annoyance, but Selena shook her head. "He's fine. Thor just wanted to be a part of the fun."

Ignoring Azrael's tantrum, she resumed her stance and focused on channeling the fire energy within her as Azrael prepared another volley; she unleashed another explosion from her mouth and fists, shattering each disk before they reached the ground.

Satisfied that she flawlessly executed her technique without further interference, Azrael gave a tiny grin. "Brilliant—I believe you can do anything; I wish I were as capable."

Selena smiled at his compliment. "What do you mean? You're proficient with Aether."

"Somewhat, but not as much as I would like. Understanding the differences between the elements is the best way to grow and become whole with Aether. It's spirit energy and the ultimate form of magic—even my spirit pistols are Aether in its purest form. There's much more to it, and quite frankly, I wish I was more accomplished."

Selena looked over at Silver, who eagerly watched their exchange as if they were part of his experiment. "Silver briefly taught me that there is energy all around us."

Azrael nodded. "There's positive and negative energy: light and dark Aether. Unless you're that Divine awful necromancer, nobody knows about dark Aether: it never existed until the Dark Master started using it. However, it's important to draw knowledge from the different elements to understand these energies. The greatest illusion is believing in separation; the four elements, for instance, aren't different at all but are one. Understanding them will help you grow powerful and whole."

Selena smiled. "We are all connected."

Azrael looked off to the side and grinned. "Exactly."

Silver strolled over with a huge smirk and straightened his glasses. "A fantastic lesson, I daresay."

Selena and Azrael bowed and saluted. "Admiral Altessa." She couldn't tear her eyes from her boots nor stop her cheeks from burning.

"I'm happy to see you two finally playing nicely." Azrael scowled from Silver's sarcasm, but the admiral ignored him. Rather, he was more interested in meeting Selena's attention. "Please forgive me for being absent from your instruction, but I will let you in on a little secret since you two discussed Aether. I started working with General Araneus in creating portals to traverse Armageddon safely."

Selena's head whipped up, and her eyes widened with wonder. She recalled Kain having summoned a portal himself during her battle with the Lich; to think of being able to use these gates as means of travel would prove incredible, unleashing a plethora of possibilities.

"That would simplify all future business with other capitals, not to mention traveling wherever you please within seconds and having the world at your disposal," she said eagerly.

Silver nodded but clarified that "the project is still in the beginning stages, so we're nowhere near finished. But think of all the good that will come of it once we can harness that kind of energy: we could travel from here to Snowhaven in seconds instead of months."

Selena smiled. "You never cease to amaze me, Admiral. Hopefully, we'll return to see your project finished."

Silver's eyes lit up. "Very good. Tonight, after the ball, Vidar will hand over the four Mythic Flight eggs to you and Thor. Please ensure that you two have your bags packed and ready before sunrise." He nodded to the two jeering dragons, and Selena's face deepened in embarrassment when she realized Thor and Doragon were teasing her. "I recommend for them to eat and rest plenty before the trip. With their size, they should be able to do without food and water for a few days at a time, but I want to ensure their comfort."

"Of course, Admiral. Although, sometimes Thor can be stubborn and push himself past the limit."

Azrael snorted, but he agreed that Doragon could be the same way; however, the snickering Thor was still more concerned about mocking Selena's demeanor. **It's too apparent, and I can see it in your face. What do you humans call it—blushing? Your face is turning red.**

Please, stop—not now.

I think you love him.

She bowed, turning a deaf ear to Thor. "Thank you."

Their exchange was interrupted by a screeching courier black falcon racing in their direction with a parcel tied to its talons. It slowed its speedy descent when its black, round eyes landed on Selena; as she extended her arm, the messenger bird perched on her bicep and allowed her to untie the roll. It had the Empress' seal stamped on the front; after the falcon confirmed she received the note, it released her arm through the flutter of its wings and dashed back to Rune Citadel.

Silver scoffed when he saw that Her Imperial Majesty withheld sending Loki to deliver the parcel. "I swore to be civil with that shapeshifting fox."

Selena laughed and tucked the secret message away into her trouser pockets, but the two stood in a brief moment of silence, blushing deeply. It was about as awkward as their exchange at the library.

Azrael squinted at her, and Selena bowed before walking away. "Pardon me, Admiral."

"May I see you back to the barracks?" Silver asked.

"Oh, no, thank you, as I'm fine with walking by myself. Good-bye, Admiral."

She strutted off, leaving both him and Azrael behind, calling herself stupid for how she acted under her breath. Yet, Thor left the snickering Doragon and soared overhead, hovering beside her, but Selena ignored him. **What was that all about?**

Please, not right now.

I know you better than that: I was teasing you earlier, but I'm beginning to believe you're in love with him.

Don't be absurd.

Admit it. That was the first time I've ever seen you act that way around him. He landed and whipped his head around as if their meeting were clandestine. **I thought relations with your superiors were forbidden.**

A knot tightened in her stomach as she felt worse. *They are. I feel bad enough about it already.*

Hmm. It's not deterring him.

Selena saw Azrael heading in her direction, and she sat down on a large rock near the courtyard, wholly undone. "I pray nothing is going on between you and the admiral," he said.

She immediately blushed again and looked away. "Don't be ridiculous—nothing is going on." When he didn't look satisfied with her answer, she added, "Silver and I kissed after the battle. Are you happy now?"

"You know I'm never happy. Do you realize you're risking everything because of Silver? You and Thor will be court-martialed for sure." When she couldn't reply, Azrael clicked his tongue against his teeth. "Why him out of everyone else? Isn't he a little too old for you?"

Selena shot him an angry eye. "Don't lecture me about what I can and cannot do. If you have a problem with it, talk to him."

Azrael backed away and held his hands up in defense. "It's not my place, but I know you've worked too hard to get here, and I don't believe you want to throw it all away because of this."

"It won't happen."

That afternoon, Selena and the other Flying Officers were ordered to be in uniform and formation with their weapons before noon. She and her unit paraded through Alfheim for two hours, hoisting their official firearms over their right shoulder. Erecting Dragonheart over her shoulder, Selena marched in front with the others who had one-handed swords. Soldiers with ranged weapons were positioned in the back.

General Araneus and his commanding officers led the march, displaying their badges of honor in order of highest rank to lowest: Admiral Altessa, Commodore Rhys Harlequin, Colonel Cyres, and Captain Allendreth. They rallied behind the general, with four rows of soldiers following in perfect and rhythmic sync. Flying above in three different v-shaped formations were Her Imperial Majesty's dragons, directed by Aracania; Thor was to her right, and Doragon covered her left flank.

Selena felt awkward when the townspeople gathered around the corners of the streets to gawk and watch. It became more so when the young ladies pushed through to be in the front, giggling when they saw a soldier they thought handsome. Selena did her best to ignore it when women tried calling her attention.

"Officers as far as the eye can see."

"Did you see that white-haired dreamboat? Isn't he an admiral?"

"I heard he's worth twenty thousand a year."

"Twenty thousand? The Divine's forbid—"

"I wonder if he's single."

One maiden tossed a handkerchief at Selena; she met eye contact with whom it belonged, and the two blushed. The soldiers marching beside her snickered and teased that, as a lady herself, she still attracted the other females; Selena wanted to ignore and forget, but it proved difficult.

After General Araneus dismissed them, Selena trekked through the dispersing crowd until she found Rahim, Niamh, and Maria near the Fire Temple. Earlier, she sent a letter asking to meet by the steps after the parade; the three smiled and waved her over. Selena attempted to enjoy this bittersweet moment, as this would be the last time she would see her friends for a long while.

Niamh had already bought more ribbons and lace for the ball, matching the color of her teal blue eyes and accentuating her dark brown shoulder-length hair and freckles dotting her nose and arms. Maria, however, had already donned her pink evening gown with white lace; she surprisingly wore a red hooded cloak, her long black hair curling freely over her shoulders.

Rahim, however, insisted upon coming to reunite with his mother in Nuvak. Although Selena was hesitant, she at least agreed to see if General Araneus would allow it. "It will be like I'm not even there," he said, "and I won't delay your trip nor cause any trouble. Besides, from what I hear, you and Azrael are now on good terms, yes? Someone needs to ensure peace continues between you two."

Selena nodded. "If the Divines shine upon us, we should return by the end of Stardusk."

Maria and Niamh exchanged glances, and Maria said sadly, "Two months is still quite a long journey, and I wish I could be here waiting for your return."

Selena was shocked. "What do you mean?"

"I will be leaving Alfheim tonight before the ball." Maria quickly addressed their confusion and concerns, explaining her mother had passed away a fortnight ago after battling a deadly illness. "My mother didn't wish to bother the admiral for a cure, despite my protests; I've already made the proper funerary arrangements with the House of the Dead caretakers."

Selena pleaded, "Do you need anything? Please, we want to help."

"There is no need. Her Imperial Majesty already arranged escorts for me; I'll be heading for Winterguard before the sun sets."

Selena's gut tightened in a knot. She was grateful that her mother was incredibly generous in helping her friend, but she wished that the Empress would put in as much effort to see her daughter. "That was most gracious of her."

Rahim's brow wrinkled in confusion. "Winterguard is on the other side of the Empire. Do you have more family there?"

Maria nodded. "Yes, I do, and I'm glad everything has been arranged. It makes things easier."

Selena thought that Maria and her mother were Gundisalvus' only living descendants unless there were others not related by blood. Even still, she believed her story to be a lie. Maria probably had her reasons, and Selena felt it would be rude of her to pry further. "Are you sure that you can't stay for the party?"

Maria shook her head. "I don't like social situations—I prefer staying away from large crowds." She laughed but sighed. "I do need to finish packing. Safe travels, and goodbye." Before returning to the Sky District, she gave the three one final hug.

After watching Maria disappear down the cobblestone road, Selena said, "I pray you two can make it. After all, it will be in Dragonstone."

Niamh blushed and turned away. Rahim's face matched Niamh's deep crimson hue, and he stumbled to find the right way to ask her to join him in the affair. It wasn't until Selena gave him silent cues, urging him to keep trying before missing his chance.

Rahim cleared his throat. "Err, well, um…. W-would you like to come to, uh, dinner with me?" He couldn't take his question back now if Niamh were to reject him.

To his delight, her eyes flickered and lit up. She kept looking between Selena and Rahim before she grinned and nodded. "Yes, I will." She curtsied and bowed.

Rahim sighed in relief and gave her a half-crooked grin. "V-very good; I'll see you then."

Without warning, Niamh leaned in and kissed him on the cheek. Even as she walked away, Rahim kept touching where she kissed him.

Selena nudged him and laughed. "I told you."

The afternoon passed, and evening came. The moon hung oppressively low to the ground that night, with heavy clouds blotching the sky. Lanterns were strung along Silver's lampposts with festive-looking decor. Carriages and dragons lined his estate and clustered together near the marble water fountain embellished with jeweled lamps. The first guests to arrive were the Council, followed by the decorated officers from the Air Force.

Cooks walked inside and out, carrying platters of food for the grand feast within Silver's magnificently massive dining hall: whole-roasted deer with sprigs of rosemary and basil lining the platter. The chefs served grilled salmon and trout with lemons and limes; next were honey-glazed hams and game hens stuffed with breading inside, shimmering like gems. Mounds of rice and potatoes drenched in butter and spices lay before the guests in the buffet room. The cooks displayed countless cheeses and loaves of bread in baskets near the other varieties of salads and side dishes; the guests flocked to the banquet once the mouth-watering treasures were set.

Silver had a feeding pen put together near trees beyond the lake with a line of chefs preparing a row of whole roasted pigs, cows, and sheep on enormous spits, the delectable string of jewels luring Her Imperial Majesty's dragons. However, from Silver's request, the dragons agreed to wait until the festivities began, though they couldn't help but drool.

Azrael and Doragon had already left for the celebratory feast and ball, but Selena groaned when she couldn't think of what she should wear. Before, she only had a regal suit for formal military fashion. However, upon returning to her bunker, she saw a noble dinner dress folded neatly upon her bed with a note written in her mother's hand.

"Now, there should be no debate on how you wish to dress—a lovely lady ought to choose."

She smiled and decided to finally unroll the note she had received from the messenger falcon earlier. Yet, she read a series of spelling errors:

"To my ddear Selena,

Please excuse my lack of communication. Our last conversetion was extremely umpleasant and tore right through me, but you deserved an answer. Pray know that I've been watchin you.

Words cannot discribe the pain I feel every time we are togethe, and I cannot eVen talk to or address you as my daughter iin public. It dwas even risky to have this delivered to you.

Stey safe—you father and I love you. Pray don't foget that."

"This doesn't make any sense; she knows how to write." Selena groaned but paused when she re-read the note again. She scanned over the errors in detail, and with her head buzzing, she immediately grabbed her fountain pen and inkwell to write out the mistakes underneath the message. "First one is 'd'. 'Conversetion' is supposed to have an 'a' in it, and this has an 'n.' This is missing a 'g,'… 'e,' 'r.' They're not mistakes," she continued to search for the remaining errors, "v, i, d, a, r." When Selena finished, she read the cryptic message: "Danger Vidar."

Her throat squeezed when she called for Thor, and he was nearly as confused as she was. *What does it mean?*

Perhaps your mother is warning us that Vidar may be up to something. We need to be cautious. When she didn't reply, Thor changed the subject. **I will meet you down in the courtyard when you finish getting ready, my dear one. Pray that the party hasn't begun without you.**

She had already bathed in the steam baths once the officers had left; she unfolded the extravagantly trimmed short-sleeved pearly-white gown decorated in pink lace. Selena was surprised by the low cut bearing her bosom upon donning the unfamiliar attire, as she was accustomed to wearing gentlemen's dress. She saw the pile of pink ribbons and a pair of white gloves underneath where the dress was, and she blushed, unsure of how to properly decorate her gown.

What is going to happen at your special event? Thor asked.

It's just a big dinner party with dancing, promoting etiquette and civility.

That sounds very boring, but pray let me know how it goes. I'm looking forward to snatching those pigs and cows for myself.

Unsure of what to do for shoes, Selena muttered, "Oh, to Oblivion with it," and decided to slip on her polished hessian boots. She could give a damn if the others took issue with her ensemble; after all, this ball and feast were in her honor, and she may very well dress however she saw fit.

While attempting to figure out how to tie her ribbons and laces together, she glimpsed her reflection in the full-body mirror. Though human, Selena exhibited similar elven beauty as her mother: a spitting image minus the pointed ears. She had stopped trimming her hair since the trial, and already it had grown to her jawline. She hadn't any makeup, but Selena didn't need any to accentuate her natural loveliness. Contrarily, her thin yet muscular build bore a resemblance to her brothers in arms from months of bitter work and training without taking away her feminine beauty.

She bit her bottom lip as she failed to figure out how to tie her laces and ribbons together. *You wouldn't happen to know how to lace a dress appropriately, do you?*

Why would I know something like that?

"Blast it all." She draped the ribbons over her shoulders for the time being, and her eyes darted to her dresser drawer that hid the rose. She wondered at clipping the stem and sewing the flower to her neckline. Her face burned crimson at possibly sparking a reaction from

Silver; she wouldn't know how to proceed with their relationship if it had.

Hesitant at first, Selena pulled out the deep red rose and a pair of scissors she kept to trim her hair. After cutting it down, she grabbed a piece of her ribbon and sliced it into strips. Satisfied, she tied the rosebud to her neckline, but before she could examine her handiwork, there was a light knock on her door.

Confused, she went to open it, only to be surprised to see Silver. He had traded in his usual white attire for a black frock coat decorated with golden trimmings and buttons, a gilded chain pinned from his right shoulder and tucked into his left pocket; a gold pocket watch fastened to his coat. His jacket and waistcoat matched his black breeches and gleaming boots.

Upon seeing her in a dinner dress for the first time, Silver reddened and turned away. "I-I'm happy you found the gift your mother had delivered. I came to see if you were ready as the party had already begun."

It was Selena's turn to blush. "I'm nearly finished dressing."

Silver found the courage to meet her gaze; his eyes flickered, and he smiled. "You look lovely, and what a beautiful rose, I might add."

He noticed. "Thank you." She bit her cheek and gingerly grabbed the ribbons still draped over her shoulder. "I hope it's not too much to ask, and since my mother can't right now, do you know how to lace a dinner dress correctly? I've never worn one before."

Silver looked down at his feet and laughed. "As a gentleman, I don't believe it would be appropriate of me —"

"As a lady, I permit you to help me dress."

He gave her a tiny smile. "If you insist, my dear." He guided her to the mirror and helped her adequately decorate her already extravagant gown. However, when Silver went to tie the back, he quietly cautioned that "you're not wearing a corset."

"I detest corsets."

"Aren't you afraid of the others noticing you're not properly dressed?"

"Who decided that corsets were proper? Should I also wear a fish on my head if that was expected?"

Silver laughed. "Of course not, my dear. You may wear whatever you like." He finished, and Selena was satisfied.

"Thank you, Admiral."

"Please, no need to address me so formally." He cleared his throat when Selena went to slip on her white gloves. "If I may be so bold, will you go with me to the ball?"

His abrupt request left her dumb; her face flushed. "I-I would be honored, but wouldn't that be strange for the others to see you dancing with a Flying Officer?"

"I don't care. The others can piss off." He held up his arm for her to take. "If you're ready, my dear."

Together, her arms laced through his, they strolled to the courtyard where Thor patiently waited, donned in his diamond bracelets and polished ruby necklace. He carried the couple through a gentle flight to the busy estate where hundreds gathered outside the dazzling affair, already drunk with the festive spirit.

Thor dropped them off near the busy water fountain, and he snickered to see their almost romantic display as they stepped off his paws. **Oh, I see. This party**

seems like it will be much more than just civility and etiquette—you can't fool me.

Please, don't—

Thor stuck his tongue out before launching himself heavenward, flying towards the communion of dragons ready to attack the jeweled delicacy that would be their feast. **You will hear it from me long after tonight.**

How about you find yourself a lady dragon friend so I can tease you?

Ha, ha, you're too funny.

Selena stared up at the glowing moon as she and Silver followed the line of guests. "It's a lovely night."

"Yes, very lovely indeed," but Silver wasn't looking up at the sky, "I pray you find this ball more than adequate to show our appreciation for your dedication and hard work."

"Of course, I will—after all, you put this together, and you've already done more than enough to help me." She was unsure why her feelings were strong enough to make her feel this weak: Silver was a sixteen-thousand-year-old shapeshifting demigod, after all. Yet, she blushed every time she caught him smiling at her.

Like her, all the women were clad in white evening gowns decorated with soft shades of lace and ribbon; the men were either donned in red and black officer uniforms or black and white curved-back coats and waistcoats with matching neckcloths. Silver's various rooms were occupied with different activities—cards, buffet, and punch—but the largest and finest ground-level apartment within his manor had been converted to a ballroom lit by an exquisitely jeweled chandelier, a swirl of elegant dance.

Selena caught herself admiring the splendor of the ball. "It's lovely and breathtaking, Admiral."

"I'm pleased to hear you say so."

She searched over the sea of red and black coats; General Araneus, followed by Colonel Cyres and Captain Allendreth, made haste to greet Vidar and a select few from the Council near buffet. She caught a glimpse of Commodore Harlequin between the common rabble, a young human gentleman of twenty-seven. Among them was Azrael, but he was quiet while sipping his brandy; he gave her a jerky nod when the two made eye contact. Selena couldn't help but admire the general's slick maroon silver-streaked hair and clean-shaven face. His neat and orderly attire bore similar to Silver's with golden trimmings and buckles, but his decorated awards and stripes exhibited his high rank.

When Araneus saw her and Silver enter together, his face flushed as he approached and bowed. "Liongod, it's damn good to see you, though," he cleared his throat, "You'll have to forgive me—I'm not used to seeing you out of uniform."

Selena curtsied and bowed. "Sir, likewise, and I suppose it doesn't hurt to wear an evening dress at least once." She laughed, but her superiors nervously grinned as the other officers gawked and doted on her. Nearly half of the soldiers whispered the slanders publicly announced by the Council, while the others admired her loveliness from afar. To her surprise, Volt and his gang of misfits were among the adoring crowd; when she caught his staring, Volt blushed and quickly turned away, muttering, "I can't believe a lady bested me."

Selena glared at Volt menacingly and gave him the "I'm watching you" hand gesture, and the whimpering Volt backed off. Silver, however, snickered in amusement.

Vidar peered over the general's shoulder with smoldering eyes, but Selena met his gaze with equal intensity. Araneus, however, was indifferent to their silent yet hostile exchange. "When the ball is over, you and Azrael will report to Vidar and me at the Fire Temple, where we will have the dragon eggs ready."

Selena smiled at him. "Sir, Thor and I thank you. We appreciate all you've done on our behalf."

"Of course, though, I wish I could have done more, Your Highness. You two have certainly left an impression on Aracania, and she has pledged herself to you and Thor. We will fight for you until the end if we must, not only as a member of the imperial family but also because you two are heroes. You and Thor saved Alfheim and have the full support of Her Imperial Majesty's Air Force."

The general excused himself and left with the colonel and captain following his steps. Selena took her small opportunity to look around, but she couldn't see her mother anywhere near. When she asked, Silver mentioned he saw her slip into the ballroom. The two made their way past the sea of dancers, and true to Silver's word, the Empress overlooked the affair from the very end of the room.

She smiled when Silver and Selena walked in together; the two approached Her Imperial Majesty and bowed. "I'm very pleased that you're here, my child."

Selena swallowed hard but nodded. "So am I, Your Imperial Majesty." She leaned in slightly and whispered, "Thor and I will heed your warning."

The Empress didn't respond, but her cumbersome expression was enough. When Silver asked what she meant, Selena pulled him away past the dancers and briefly explained the note she had received from the courier falcon. "I understand, and it's true," he said sadly, "Vidar Helios has seemed odd lately. Best be wary."

Selena watched as dancers lined up in the center of the hall in two lines of about seven couples, their partners facing each other. Men lined up on one side and women on the other, preparing to start the reel folk dance; the couples advanced towards each other at a four-step count, and they retired four steps back into place. They resumed forward, joining hands, and made a complete turn before returning into position.

The music was loud and vibrant as the musicians played their classical tunes for the party. Selena grew even more nervous as she watched the dance continue with the partners passing each other from right shoulder to right shoulder while crossing arms, then repeating by the left. She smiled when she saw Rahim and Niamh among the line of couples, but they didn't notice her arrival; oblivious, they were enjoying each other's company.

Silver cleared his throat and asked, "I apologize if this seems straightforward, but may I have the next dance?"

Selena swallowed hard and nodded. "You may."

When the floor opened to new dancers and the music began again, Selena and Silver joined the couples as they formed the two lines again. When she stood on the women's side, the ladies gawked and giggled at her, whispering about how she was improperly dressed. Others watched and doted on Silver with interest and lustful eyes. Selena felt a slight sting of jealousy, but Silver paid no attention to his adoring crowd. Instead, he kept looking at her.

It was as though he read her mind. "Don't worry about them. It's just you and me right now." Selena's face flushed, and she smiled.

The live music echoed across the ballroom, and everyone in both lines bowed to their partners. Selena watched as Silver and a few others from his line stepped up; the dragon began her dance, following the ladies from her row, swirling around each other.

Silver remarked, "I know I said it before, but you look lovely—even those from the covert couldn't help themselves."

Selena blushed and turned away; she did her best to follow Silver's movements; they held hands, spun around, and stepped back into their starting positions. Fighting through her nervousness, she finally understood the direction and flow. Yet, Selena noticed that as their exchange continued, Silver grew more uneasy. "May I ask what troubles you?" she asked.

"Nothing of interest, my dear. Rather, I would remark on the room's grandeur or the number of couples dancing with us this evening."

"You're avoiding the subject entirely," Selena observed, "surely you must be nervous if you're that quick to dismiss its cause."

He gave a nervous chuckle. "If anything, I was reminiscing over our first meeting when we had the pleasure of forming a new acquaintance." He paused for a moment but laughed. "I know Thor has been teasing you."

Her face burned. "How could you possibly know that?"

"I pay attention to your reactions and Thor's body language: you two may share a telepathic link, but others can see from the outside when you're communicating. Remember, I've been studying dragons for thousands of years." It was as if Silver knew her deep affections, and he was trying to get her to confess; she refused to fall for his trap.

She saw that Azrael hadn't moved and thought to perhaps change the subject without jeopardizing her position. "I'm surprised by Azrael's sudden character change. I'm rather impressed by his civility and stunning humility."

Silver grinned. "He's not all bad, and I'm glad you're beginning to see his good intentions. I pray that he still hasn't been a nuisance to you."

"Not anymore, but before, I never preferred his company."

The two then stepped in rhythm side by side, and though Selena had tried, Silver brought their conversation back to the topic she wanted to avoid. "And yet, you don't mind mine, even when I first kissed you."

Her face burned when he inched closer. "Were you regretting that?"

"Not at all. However, judging from your response and reaction, I can now safely assume your affections have indeed deepened since your initial confession."

They circled each other once more, and Selena swallowed hard. "I neither confirmed nor denied the accusation."

"You don't have to."

Their dance finished, and everyone applauded. Both Silver and Selena shared eye contact for a brief moment before she turned away and clapped for the other dancers. She couldn't find the strength to return his gaze, unsure of what to do; walk away? Stay?

"Pardon me, Admiral." She gave him a quick bow before hastily dismissing herself, leaving the defeated Silver behind.

CHAPTER 9: THE MASKED DRAGONS

As if he watched their awkward exchange, Azrael made his way through the familiar crowd and joined her by the punch bowl, Selena looking undone. "I think I understand now."

Selena reached past him and poured herself a glass. "I'm honestly trying to make out his character."

"What have you found out?"

She sipped her brandy spiked punch. "I think I may have been mistaken: I don't believe Silver to be indifferent."

Azrael sighed and scoffed. "It should be obvious: the admiral is in love with you. Pray the Council doesn't find out, but you look as though you've seen a ghost."

"I'll be fine." Yet, she was unsure how to proceed or how she could face Silver again after that display.

"I think you're in danger of making him fall even more in love with you. I still don't understand it." Azrael took another drink and was about to walk away but stopped. "Admiral Altessa is heading this way."

When she saw Azrael was correct, Selena immediately set her glass down and made her way through the sea of guests, growing anxious with every step she took. Silver, waylaid by the number of attendants, approached as she vanished. His eyes then searched for her, and Selena slipped outside.

She walked outside and made her way past the water fountain, deep in thought; her face grew pale when she heard Silver calling out her name. The gentle rain clouds began to weep, and Selena rushed to a nearby bench beside the decorative trees and sat down. Her heart throbbed in her throat when Silver hastily yelled, "Liongod."

She looked up to see the admiral sprinting towards her, sodden and breathless as the torrential rain worsened. Selena immediately stood up and saluted out of reflex, but he dismissed it. "Sir, what's wrong?"

Caught in a state of agitation, Silver stopped and breathed deep. "I've tried my best, but I can't take it any longer. Since you've joined the Air Force, the last few months have been nothing but torture."

Selena stared at him in astonishment. "I'm not understanding."

Silver continued. "I didn't realize it until after Kain and I confronted Azrael for what he did to you. When I heard that the Council discovered who you were, I panicked—I thought I would lose you.

"You are perfect in every way possible. I hated and despised everyone I've met in my life, but you were different. I love everything about you, but aside from your brilliant mind, I admire your willingness to fight for what you believe in, and you never give up on anyone. Even if the whole world is against you, you never stop fighting. I come to you now because I need you to end my pain."

"I-I still don't understand."

"Damn and blast," Silver looked down at his tapping foot but blurted out with passion, "I love you. Please, do me the honor of accepting my hand."

Selena stared at him in utter shock as she struggled through her feelings. It was as if the world fell away, drained of all color; they were the only ones to exist, save for the pitter-patter of rain. When she finally recovered, she said, "Sir, I'm honored by your proposal, but I don't believe this is the proper time."

"Why not?"

Selena chose her following words as carefully as she could. "We're fighting a war, and everything is uncertain. I don't know if we could have a future together with the way everything is going."

Silver's expression changed as if she slapped him. "Are you rejecting me?"

"No, that's not it, I swear to you."

"So, then, are you saying yes?" he asked with more optimism. Selena wanted to run over and embrace him, but she didn't want to put him through any pain if the worst should happen. She shared her thoughts, but Silver reached out and pulled her into an embrace before replying, "It would hurt more if you reject me now and a tragic event affected us later: there would be no closure. I would rather enjoy the time I had being with you and knowing that you loved me too."

She returned the gesture and buried her face into his jacket. "The last thing I want to do is to hurt you."

He tightened his hold. "I love you, and I wish never to be separated from you again. Please, let me hear you say yes."

She tightened her grip on his jacket as her lips trembled to say the words back. "Yes. A hundred times—yes."

Silver brushed her face with his fingers and leaned in to kiss her; Selena wrapped her arms around his neck and deepened it, their affections turning passionate.

"Ahem." The couple immediately pulled apart and looked over to see Azrael gazing at them with a judgmental stare, hiding from the rain under a steel-ribbed brolly. "You're lucky Vidar didn't come out just now."

"How long have you been standing there?" Silver demanded.

"Long enough to know that you two will be court-martialed if the Council catches you. I highly recommend coming back inside before the others start to wonder." Azrael gestured for them to follow and offered them the umbrella.

Silver scoffed and swatted it away but escorted Selena back inside Dragonstone. "Such impeccable timing, as always. Let's get you warm and something to eat, my dear." Azrael scowled but hastily rejoined the booming party.

After Azrael vanished, the two trekked inside, and Thor prodded at her thoughts. **Did Silver ask you?**

Wait a moment, my dear. Did you know about this?

Of course. Silver asked me for my blessing after you left the beach—he had already spoken with your parents, though he said your father showed some reluctance.

Why would he oppose the marriage?

Perhaps for the same reasons as I; Phantom Dust also needed convincing.

As they passed by a row of soldiers, Selena immediately recognized the Steelmane brothers, Gromm and Beck. Gromm was the muscle of the two due to his size and bulk compared to Beck's leaner frame. Yet, the two shared the same brown hair and blue eyes, connecting them as brothers. They nervously approached her and Silver through widened eyes and immediately saluted the admiral.

Gromm then dropped to his knees, followed by Beck. "Oi, it's damn good to see you, Admiral, and you, Your Highness."

Selena smiled at the two, but Silver watched them like a hawk. Before she could ask about his silently rude welcome, Beck interrupted. "Thank the Divines that you and Thor made it through all right."

Yet, she noticed that the brothers continued exchanging troubled glances, looking as though they saw a ghost. "What's wrong? You're both acting strangely."

Before Gromm and Beck could formulate an answer, Silver said coldly, "It's been a while since I've seen you two around. Tell us, how has former Captain Bel been?"

Beck bit his bottom lip and shook his head. "Oh, buggery—damn and blast it all."

Selena finally understood, and her face turned pale like a porcelain vase. "You told him everything."

The flustered brothers turned away to avoid her wrath, but Selena was surprisingly calm. Once he noticed her indifferent demeanor, Beck said quickly, "You don't know what that git is like. We were damn close to reporting him to General Araneus, but…." His voice trailed off.

Gromm quietly finished for him, "Vidar was involved and had granted that arsehole amnesty. Ashur and Jade threatened to hang us for conspiring against the Council when we refused; he somehow had obtained proof, but he needed our confession."

The Steelmane brothers were struck dumb, while Silver gazed upon her in admiration for her forgiving nature when Selena said gently, "I'm not mad at either of you. It's already been addressed, and luckily everything worked out for the better."

After Gromm and Beck had amended their mistakes, Silver escorted her past the sea of guests to a locked parlor; he assured her that "we shall not be disturbed here" and provided her towels, but Selena declined. Much like the breathing techniques to help keep warm, she exhaled steam, drying her hair and silk dress, exhibiting caution for her delicate fabric. "My dear, you never cease to amaze me." Silver smiled to see her limitless magical talent.

Yet, Thor's answer still stung. *Why were you against it?*

It sounded strange to me. I find your concept of marriage more like an obsession: asking someone to be with you forever and making it legally binding? Bah, mortals are rather dull.

What about the bond you and I share? It's very different than marrying someone, but you still pledge your loyalty to another.

What we share is for mortals and dragons, not for those of physical pleasure. For instance, we dragons may take many mates, but we choose to connect with only one rider.

Though dragons could live for hundreds, if not thousands, of years, those they've bound themselves to didn't share their longevity, save for elves and dwarves; a healthy human could live up to two hundred at most, having the shortest lifespan of the races. When a handler passes, dragons may choose to live in solitude for the rest of their days or allow their spirit to transcend into Niflheim and join the Aether streams that gifted life to their world.

Thor assured her he approved of their union, but Selena was daunted by how this marriage would affect him. It would prove difficult, as she and Thor were two halves of the same whole. Their connection was on the same level that one's self was above all else, followed by the spouse, then children if she and Silver ever decided to expand their family. Riders and handlers had families, but it was neither typical nor practical.

My dear one, we are linked in both mind and spirit. If you're happy, I'm content.

If only there were a lady dragon for you.

I haven't been keen on finding a mate for myself. Dragons sexually matured between four to six months, so she had expected a different answer. Still, Thor insisted and sighed. **Enjoy your evening. I know you two must be happy and will want to spend time together and celebrate.**

His distant reply was poisoned with jealousy. *Pray don't assume that I would cast you away, my dear.* He only huffed in response.

When Selena wished to steer clear from the crowd, Silver offered her tea and punch before calling for refreshments from the buffet. As her head swirled from the brandy, she couldn't help but ask how her parents took to asking permission to seek her hand.

As she expected from her mother, the Empress wholeheartedly agreed without much persuasion. However, true to Thor's word, her father presented disinclination. "His Imperial Majesty wasn't wholly against my proposal—rather, I believe it's the same for any father asking to give away his daughter. I cannot blame him after what he's endured, but I had to ensure my argument was stronger than his." Silver laughed after sipping his earl grey tea.

Selena grinned when stirring the honey into her steeping green brew, but her lit expression extinguished like a snuffed-out flame. "I'm assuming Thor had his reasons for opposing our union."

Tight-lipped, Silver cleared his throat. "It wasn't easy subduing his temper."

Her eyes shimmered like a frozen lake. "What do you mean?"

"I assume he wasn't happy with the idea of sharing you, my dear." He squinted at her. "Didn't he mention that to you?"

"Only a little." Yet, Selena couldn't stop her face from fuming in anger that Thor withheld his true thoughts and emotions; she poked and tugged at their mental link, but all Thor could say was that **I ultimately gave him my blessing.**

Sensing her growing agitation, Silver changed the subject while the two indulged in the platter brought to them by the chambermaid. Selena had never eaten so much food; she couldn't deny it was a delicious banquet despite feeling miserably full.

Silver said, "I suppose not all the men from the covert are bad. Most, if not all by now, have already taken your side. I daresay Vidar isn't handling that well, as his directive in defaming you had backfired." He sighed. "Though I'll admit, some still question your role: you being the Crown Princess isn't as surprising as a woman joining their ranks."

Selena set her plate down and wiped her mouth. "Stiff poppycocks, from what I've seen."

Silver laughed, but their evening of solace was wholly interrupted when the ground suddenly started shaking; the dishware rattled, and books fell from their shelves. Selena and Silver jolted from the couch as a loud crash roared outside the city's walls, and blood-curdled screams shattered the already tense atmosphere.

"What's happening?" Selena asked. Silver grabbed her arm, and the two rushed outside the parlor to find the estate in complete panic and disarray.

While Alfheim's citizens rushed to find shelter, the red-faced general shouted, "Move your arses," as their now battle-ready and fully harnessed dragons had soared across the lake. Captain Faelar Allendreth led the innocents to Venerius and Zidragos—a heavy-weight Cerulean Iceclaw companion to Commodore Rhys Harlequin—and the two dragons ferried everyone away to the bunkers hidden near the crystal catacombs, transporting about a hundred per carrier.

Vidar and the Council, however, strolled through the pell-mell crowd in single file, without the slightest concern by the threat looming over the city; they casually climbed aboard Zidragos' saddle and sneered when making eye contact with Selena. The last to mount was the Empress, only leaving after Selena and Silver begged her to seek shelter. Yet, to Selena's dismay, Rahim and Niamh were nowhere to be found.

Venerius and Zidragos zipped towards the Fire Temple when an ear-shattering screech made the earth quake. As Aracania zoomed overhead, leading her readied formation already harnessed—with Thor and Doragon in position—Thor warned as he landed briefly to meet Selena and Silver rushing past, **I see a flight of dragons near the edge of the city.**

Fearing the Lich sprung another surprise attack, Selena and Silver exchanged glances as Thor scooped them with his claws and assisted them in the saddle. The ground quaked again, and Azrael rushed through as Doragon joined near the water fountain. In under five minutes, all of Her Imperial Majesty's dragons had snatched their riders, and the Force was airborne, ready to meet with the rogue dragons that had reached the city limits.

The Force met its overwhelming opposition of twenty-five against hundreds, but when Selena pulled out a spyglass, she gasped upon noticing their grisly differences. Hides as black as the void and claws the size of two long swords combined, these strange dragons had a set of three metallic razor-bladed wings about twice the length of their massive and thick slimy bodies. Their faces and snouts were distorted and twisted behind a chilling ivory bone mask with holes for their smoldering, glowing eyes. Yet, the rider-less creatures somehow resembled Thor, and Selena couldn't quite shake the familiar and unnerving feeling.

They're unlike any dragon I've ever seen.

Thor roared, his eyes fixated on the beasts of death. **They reek of black magic—unholy and unnatural abominations.**

As Aracania commanded her unit through chirps, clicks, and growls, General Araneus sent up two flag signals: *Engage the enemy close* and *fire at will.*

The guards on top of the wall readied the catapults and trebuchets, but the creatures zoomed past before launching a single strike, and the masked dragons began laying waste to the city. They swooped down, avoiding the allied dragons' deadly volley display of breath attacks spewing relentlessly.

Thor abruptly swiveled in mid-flight and roared as the masked dragons unleashed their deadly inferno of black and yellow flames, strafing the streets among the Market and Imperial Districts. Their blasts as hot as the sun's surface, their ensuing cataclysmic devastation destroyed all in their path, leaving no survivors from those caught within their inferno. Denizens fleeing for safety were snatched and skewered by the blood-thirsty beasts; Selena grimaced when she saw the innocents being ripped apart and devoured like a snack.

General Araneus gave the flag signal orders to regroup and focus on coordinated attacks as the grisly creatures flocked to Alfheim like a murder of crows circling their site. However, as the Force dragons engaged in melee combat of claws and fangs, the masked behemoths went unscathed, their slimy scales like impenetrable armor.

Playing on the defensive instead, Cyres and Onyxria baited the masked dragons away before they could overwhelm the general and Aracania. Though Onyxria outweighed many from the enemy flight, she had to exhibit extreme caution without being overpowered herself. Yet, she avoided and dodged when her opposition had attempted to slash at her exposed flanks and underbelly. Cyres sent up a distress signal: *Flank to the port side.* Before Thor could answer, Vulcan's crimson gleam sparkled through the smoke as he rushed to Onyxria's aid with Gromm and Beck wrestling with the reins. Giving her the needed relief, Onyxria successfully drew most away from Aracania, leaving her a brief window to escape.

Selena hissed through her teeth, but her eyes went back to searching the streets for Rahim and Niamh. Thor whipped his head around to the sound of his voice echoing below. **There, I see him.**

Rahim was among the fleeing crowd near the Fire Temple, calling out Niamh's name. Selena's face turned pale when she assumed the worst; as Thor launched himself through the air to snatch Rahim away to safety, Selena looked up at the grotesque scene above. To her horror, she couldn't rescue those singled out and eaten by the masked dragons; their ghostly white masks stained crimson. The dark creatures would soon easily overwhelm Her Imperial Majesty's dragons by their sheer force alone, giving the allies no chance of victory.

When Silver made the same conclusion, he snarled. "We'll have to leave the city while we still can—we can't stay here and fight them or risk them killing us all."

Selena shook her head. "We can't just abandon the city, and I still need to save Rahim and Niamh."

One of the masked dragons landed before Rahim like a meteor striking the ground, the demonic fire blazing across the city, the flames illuminated against its ebony hide. Thor flew as fast as his wings could carry him, but the dragon struck at Rahim with its massive claws.

Selena's face immediately flooded, but she and Silver watched when its bladed claws were pushed away from the cowering Rahim. As the masked dragon recoiled and flinched, Azrael was there with a drawn sword, having saved Rahim's life by countering the deadly attack. Parts of the dragon's mask crumbled away, and it squealed and roared in pain; through a golden flurry of scales and wings, Doragon dashed from circling overhead and pinned down the flailing creature before ripping the rest of its mask clean off its bloodied face. Though nearly outweighing Doragon, the colossus couldn't fight back, and it quivered before growing limp.

Thor landed near the three, and Rahim quickly rushed to his extended paw while shouting praises and gratitude for Azrael's saving grace. Yet, Azrael and Doragon ushered Thor and his party to flee before joining the skies again. Sodden and breathless, Rahim asked, "Have you seen Niamh? She fled down here before the dragons could ferry us to safety."

Selena gritted her teeth, wanting to chastise him for not staying at Dragonstone, but suddenly, two middle-weight masked dragons appeared before them, readying to unleash their deadly inferno. However, Thor was much faster; he reared his head back and spewed a terrifying fire breath, incinerating their masks, but their hide remained untouched. However, similar to the one Doragon killed, the two dragon beasts backed away to recover, leaving Thor to escape.

Yet, he spun mid-flight, and his chest expanded its size thrice; when Selena realized what Thor was doing, she quickly sent a flag signal to her nearby allies: *Take cover.*

General Araneus and Aracania caught her warning; Thor held his breath thirty seconds longer while they signaled for the others to pull back. Once she, Rahim, and Silver ducked down with hands over their ears, opening his maw wide, Thor exhaled a screaming typhoon that made the surrounding void-like behemoths recoil. With the power to move the sky, his piercing and devastating wind storm cracked their masks, and they retreated through painful roars and growls.

When his furious gale storm lessened, and Thor clamped shut his maw, he snorted when he saw that much of their opposition had dwindled to a few stragglers left behind, recovering from his windy squall. Once deemed safe, their allies returned to the battlefield, and both Silver and Selena signaled to Aracania and the rest of her formation: *Regroup and engage at close range.*

Silver announced, "Thanks to Thor, the tables have turned in our favor. I will join the others and ensure that they concentrate on coordinated attacks on their masks; it's our only chance at bringing them down." Selena wholly agreed, and Silver transformed into a wingless, serpent-like white dragon once he stepped off Thor's harness; his snow-white smooth scales gleamed, even amidst the smoke-filled air.

Absolutely fantastic, my dear. Do you see Niamh anywhere?

Thor glowed from her compliment and resumed his search with Rahim; Thor's eyes scanned through rubble and flames and quickly spotted Niamh as she ran down an undestroyed path behind Rune Citadel's mountain. He roared when he noticed a heavy-weight close to his size that had escaped his gale storm was in pursuit.

As Thor launched to rescue Niamh, another heavy-weight masked dragon zipped across and blocked his path; soon, the two dragons were caught in a flurry of claws and fangs. Before Thor could unleash another attack, Doragon rushed to his aide; Azrael had already unbuckled himself from the harness—sword and Aether pistol at the ready. He ran along Doragon's spine and fired a few bullets that struck the dragon's face, leaving smoldering holes. The creature recoiled and pushed itself away from Thor, but Azrael leapt off Doragon's head, propelling straight for the beast. Selena was amazed at how fast he moved and his power to take the creature down himself, but what happened next stunned the trio.

Azrael became shrouded in shadow and darkness, and different elements clashed together through the cloud of magic: fire, lightning, ice, earth, poison, all intertwined in a dance of attacks that destroyed the beast. Seven dragon heads—the main head marked with four horns while the rest had one—emerged from the plumes of shadow and tore the behemoth asunder with different breath abilities. The wafting clouds dissipated, and Doragon caught Azrael in his talons as he fell back.

Rahim couldn't help but remark, "I've never seen magic like that before."

Selena was utterly dumbfounded as the shadows looked like the Divine of Death. Doragon landed, watching Thor soar past; Selena and Azrael locked gazes, and she immediately knew. *He's Death.*

Thor turned a deaf ear to her spine-chilling discovery and dove towards the masked dragon that cornered Niamh behind a nearby building. As the colossus was nearly upon her, Rahim leaned over the saddle's edge and called her name. She looked over for a brief moment before the creature stepped forward, and in one fell swoop, it sliced its front claws through her chest.

Rahim cried for her name as he watched her body fall into its talons, but Selena's eyes started to glow as she boiled with rage. Looking to avenge their fallen friend, she ran along Thor's spine. Thor snarled and reached up to snatch her away, but she had already leapt off and fell through the air as she grew consumed by an orb of brilliant Divine light.

No, don't!

Ignoring Thor's pleas and cries, she slipped through his claws, blinding the battlefield with her glow. He and Rahim watched in absolute horror through growls and snarls as she yielded to her fury and wrath; Selena transformed into her Divinity Dragon state, a spectral and celestial being of pure and terrifying Aether energy.

She unfurled her massive ethereal wings, celestial mist wafting from her membranes; her crown-shaped horns gave her a regal appearance, like an empress or a queen. Gleaming like the twinkling stars was an enormous smoldering ruby emblazoned upon her chest, shimmering from her Divine light. The dragon's piercing, glowing emerald eyes that were unmistakably Selena's fixated on the monster that killed Niamh, and she unleashed a thundering roar. The allies and enemy fighters stopped and looked upon the ethereal dragon in awe and dismay; the masked dragons began pulling back, but the one that struck Niamh remained behind and hissed.

Unfolding her massive wings, she summoned gusts and shockwaves of energy, pushing back the behemoth. Before it could recover, Selena arched her neck like a snake ready to strike, and she spewed forth a white and azure flame that erupted into a dazzling and deadly torrent, blasting off half its mask and singing most of its body.

Though its mask crumbled away with blood dripping down its snout, Thor and Rahim flinched upon seeing its black skull dipped in acid hidden behind. The creature eerily grinned through serrated fangs and frayed pieces of its mask and suddenly departed the city with its nearby comrades.

Yet, Selena hadn't finished her onslaught. Turning a deaf ear to Thor's cries, her eyes shimmered when the monster carried Niamh's body away from the burning buildings. She steered herself around and chased the other creatures lingering behind; one flung itself at her, but Selena unleashed another deadly torrent, consuming the beast, leaving only a trail of ash. Upon seeing her Divine power, the remaining masked dragons fled the city.

With her rage replaced with grief, Selena released her magic and returned to human. Her head throbbed and ears ringing, Selena nearly lost consciousness as she fell through the air. Even Thor's words escaped her as he dove underneath and caught her in his paws before landing in the smoldering wreckage, mourning their loss.

CHAPTER 10: THE SHEPHERD OF SOULS

Thor immediately landed upon his haunches, wings still extended, and reluctantly relinquished his protective hold as Selena stumbled from his paw. The moment her foot made contact with the ground, the growling Thor immediately whipped over and pinned her down with his claws while exerting caution not to crush her under his weight.

His voice rumbled in her mind as he bared his large teeth, his hot and stinky breath making her near gag. **What were you thinking?**

Selena was still a little dazed and confused. She had remained somewhat sensible throughout the ordeal this time: her first transformation rendered her unconscious and not in control, and she considered it a small victory.

I was angry, and I was trying to—

You could have gotten yourself killed! What is the matter with you?

Pray forgive me, for I don't know what overcame me.

Sorry isn't going to bring you back if you had gotten killed. Promise me that you won't do that again

until you have more control. When Selena wouldn't answer right away, Thor roared. **Swear it to me!**

I swear to you, my dear. I won't do that again unless I have more control.

Thor lowered his growling snout to her face before giving her a huff in satisfaction. He lifted his paws and let her get to her feet, just as Doragon circled overhead and landed beside them. Rahim, meanwhile, kept pointing a shaking finger at Azrael and Selena while exclaiming, "I've never seen that kind of magic before from either of you."

While Selena was looking at Azrael full of questions, she answered: "Right now is not the best of times, but just know that I found the power to become a dragon."

Rahim's eyes widened. "By the Divines, you really are a dragon, but how?"

"I said not now. Azrael, you're not human, are you?" When he didn't reply, overcome with fear, Selena pulled out one of her loaded concealed pistols strapped to Thor's harness and pointed it at his head. Ignoring Rahim's protests, she demanded again, "Answer me—what in Oblivion are you?"

The firearm shook in her hands, but Azrael remained calm and collective; even Doragon was unfazed by her threat. Instead, the gold and silver dragon lowered his head and gently pushed Azrael forward, giving a series of chirps and clicks that made Thor's eyes widen in shock.

Thor kept his wings unfurled, and his growls grew in intensity as he pulled Selena back. **Don't do anything rash, my dear. If I understand Doragon correctly, Azrael is—**

Azrael merely raised a brow and pinched the bridge of his nose. "You know, yet you're holding a gun to Death's head."

Both Rahim and Selena were at a loss for words when Azrael nonchalantly confirmed who he was; Doragon stretched out his claws and licked his chops, relaxing after hiding their guises for so long. Hissing and bristling, Thor wrapped Selena and Rahim within his wings, shielding them from the disguised Divine.

Yet, Rahim's misery grew, and he grieved for Niamh, but his sobbing display infuriated Azrael. "Your darling isn't dead," he finally said.

Selena lowered her gun. "We just saw her—"

Azrael's dark blue eyes burned with vicious intent. "Are you mocking me? Niamh isn't dead—badly hurt, yes, but still alive," he groaned when they still looked at him in disbelief, "let's help the survivors before it's too late for them." Selena couldn't move the gun away as he walked back to Doragon, yet Azrael peered over his shoulder. "You can put that away, by the way—I'm not your enemy."

While Doragon and Azrael busied themselves with finding survivors from the attack, Thor and Selena circled the burning city and summoned gentle rain clouds to extinguish the dark flames. As they gazed in despair at the grey, rain-lashed landscape, Rahim kept asking if she or Thor knew what those masked dragons were, but they were just as confused.

Selena said, "Whatever they were, they're not natural." Her eyes remained fixed on Azrael as he and Doragon gathered around fifty confirmed survivors; she and Rahim watched in amazement as Death healed everyone before ferrying them to the Fire Temple to reunite with family and friends.

Silver slithered by and gave them a firm nod when confirming they were unharmed. He and Thor joined the rescue operation when Azrael and Doragon made another round, searching for more injured innocents. Between them and the Air Force dragons, within hours, they had saved over a few thousand trapped under the debris and close to death. Exhausted by their valiant endeavor, Silver led Thor and Doragon to the Fire Temple as the rest of Aracania's formation took over.

However, Selena couldn't ignore the officers' terrified expressions after seeing her Divine dragon state in full grandeur; they feared she would retaliate against the Force, and she couldn't deny the threat she posed. The sooner she could leave for the Snowhaven mission, the better.

Silver asked after transforming back to his usual form, "Is everyone all right?" Rahim's upper lip twitched, and he pointed at Azrael, who still had yet to explain his Divine identity. Unsurprised, Silver gestured to Azrael and "to get on with it, then. I believe my betrothed and," he pointed at Rahim, "her nit-wit deserve to know."

Rahim raised a fist. "Oh, sod off, why don't you? Selena wouldn't be so daft in accepting your hand." When she didn't deny it, there was a sudden crease in his brow.

Instead of dealing with an interrogation, Selena demanded a proper explanation from "a god in our midst," to which Azrael ruefully and reluctantly agreed.

"I wouldn't call myself a god anymore," he sighed, "Xyaxon told you what happened ten thousand years ago when the Day of Eternal Darkness was last upon us: that's when it all began for Doragon and me.

"Like the Divines, Venexus is a primordial being older than existence itself, coming from a time before there was nothing. When Doragon and I held the throne to Oblivion, at that time, Venexus served as my right hand. Over time, I grew arrogant and selfish while he gathered his strength and forces to overpower me. That necromancer convinced and lied to me that I deserved more than the other two Divines, and I gave in to temptation, trying to take all the power for myself." He briefly paused when Doragon whimpered, and his dragon snaked his head around to comfort him.

Rahim hung his head. "What happened after that?"

"Through his manipulation and new power, he dethroned me, and I faced judgment for my crimes. I was banished, and they took away my abilities, leaving me in the mortal realm for eternity, but with Doragon's help, I can still be the Shepherd of Souls. Xyaxon struck my true name from history, so nobody knew who I was: I've hidden behind the name 'Azrael' for so long that I don't even remember anymore.

"Before Xyaxon and Ulrich knew what had happened, Venexus had used the eclipse and taken over Oblivion. That's why Doragon and I must reclaim the throne so we can restore balance and peace to your world. I know it may sound selfish, but it must happen to protect everyone."

"Xyaxon told me this story before when he first warned us about the winter solstice." Selena gestured to Doragon. "Are you not a dragon, then?"

He dipped his head in a heavy bow, and Azrael confirmed. "Doragon is a Spirit Beast and my companion. He can take on the form of anything he wishes, but he chose to be a Sunbeam Shieldtail dragon so we could continue our work with Silver and your father in the Air Force."

Selena said, "I suspected you weren't human. You prattled on as if you knew our final hour." She paused. "Did General Araneus know?"

"The general understood I could see everyone's lifespan, but he didn't know our actual nature—he and Silver officiated me a coroner."

Selena leaned against Thor's forearm as if a club had struck her. "If you can see how much time we all have left, why didn't you warn us about tonight or the Battle of Alfheim?"

Azrael's face turned red. "I'm not a damn fortune-teller. Oh, blast it all—I can't tell you how much time you have left. It violates the natural code and law established since the beginning of time."

Silver sneered. "That's not what you and Doragon said when you two agreed to help me with the Well of Souls."

Azrael crossed his arms and muttered, "Only because Liongod wasn't supposed to be stillborn." Their group grew quiet, and he made an uncomfortable noise. "Since Doragon and I lost the throne, the world has been thrown off balance, including mortals dying before their time." Azrael gestured to the dumbstruck Selena. "I can say that you were supposed to live a long and normal life. We agreed to help Silver because we believed it could help reconcile what we've done; otherwise, I'm forbidden to go to the Soul Gate and bring the dead back, but his project was a way around it."

"What is the Soul Gate?" Rahim asked.

"I can't tell you what it is, but you and everyone else who has lived will eventually stand before it." When Azrael noticed Selena and Rahim trembling in their boots, he whipped around. "I don't understand why everyone is afraid of me; I'm not a murderer but a shepherd for souls, guiding them from this world to the next." He stopped when he realized he lashed out in anger again. "I-I'm sorry. I think I understand why you would be afraid of me, for I'm the promise that everyone has to keep."

Smirking, Silver chanted, "Except me."

"Rahim is right; why don't you sod off?"

Yet, Selena was the only one not laughing. She and Thor exchanged gloomy glances as Doragon pulled Azrael back from lashing out at Silver. Rahim withdrew, however, and finally confronted her if what Silver said was true, to which she confirmed. Rahim's eyes widened, and his mouth dropped to his feet. "Engaged? Do you actually mean to be married?"

"Yes, Rahim, what else could that possibly mean?" When he refused to laugh, Selena's gaze turned stone-cold. "Please don't look at me like that. There is no reason why I shouldn't be happy with him."

Rahim only grumbled and turned away, still unsatisfied by her choice; only when he had a few moments to ponder did he finally say, "I always did call that Genesis Altessa fellow your beloved, but…." His voice trailed off before turning around and giving a firm, jerky nod at the quizzical Silver. "I ought to welcome you to the family, I suppose." However, Azrael couldn't prepare for when Rahim marched straight to him and demanded to know more about Niamh's whereabouts. "We must find her," he pleaded.

Azrael maintained his calm demeanor. "But how, if we have no idea where those creatures came from or where they're going?"

Selena looked at Silver, who grabbed his chin and fell deep in thought. "I'm not sure, and I pray not to seem insensitive, but if you truly wish to save Niamh, the only choice we have is to leave for Snowhaven now with the

Mythic Flight eggs. If these masked dragons are a new threat, we can only stand against them by having the guardians on our side."

Azrael's eyes darted to Selena, and an uncomfortable noise escaped his mouth, but the others paid him no attention. Doragon snorted and clawed at the nearby pile of rocks, but Azrael stomped away with his arms crossed.

Thor lowered his head and nudged Selena's shoulder with his snout. **I don't understand why they didn't kill Niamh like the rest.**

I don't know, but I'm afraid Silver's right: if we want to save her, we must leave for Snowhaven now.

Of course, but allow us to rest a little before we do—I want to snatch up what remained from the feast. Thor stretched out his wings and yawned before he and Doragon launched themselves skyward towards Dragonstone.

As the two dragons disappeared over the horizon, the bell on top of the Pyre rang; its tolls were to remember the sacrifices made this evening. Selena listened to the grisly chimes as she and Azrael trudged up the stairs, answering General Araneus' summons for a private meeting, leaving Rahim and Silver waiting impatiently outside.

Lining both sides of the temple were more injured survivors sitting and laying on blankets, tended to by the frantic Force healers moving from one patient to the next. Many were missing limbs and bloodied, and others grew ill as the fever settled; Selena's eyes shimmered when she saw their pain and heard their agony. Yet, she heard Azrael mutter a chant in, what she assumed, was the demonic language, miraculously healing the survivors; even those missing appendages had healed stumps as they passed by, leaving her wholly impressed.

"It's the least I can do," Azrael whispered when he finished his prayer, and Selena smiled.

Standing near Xyaxon's statues were Vidar and his Council members, eyes closed and hands folded in silent prayer. The pale and ill-stricken Empress stood to Vidar's right, but some color had returned to her face to see her daughter safe.

Aracania, as small and dainty as she was compared to Thor and Doragon, slithered through the Fire Temple with plenty of room to unfurl her wings. She wrapped General Araneus within her protective coils with one big, purple eye fixed on the approaching pair. She clicked her nails in approval to see them again, and the general acknowledged their heroic deeds in assisting with the rescue operation.

"I understand it may not seem ideal given this sudden attack," Araneus carefully continued, "but I need you and Azrael to leave immediately instead of waiting until morning."

Selena nodded. "Sir, of course, but Thor and Doragon wish to rest a little before our journey, and given recent events—"

"Absolutely not—I will expect to see you gone within the hour."

When Thor overheard, he scoffed but said, **Doragon and I are almost finished eating. We'll leave well within the allotted time.**

Even General Araneus should know better than to rush a dragon. Thor laughed at her witticism.

Araneus sternly said, "As Admiral Altessa mentioned previously, the eggs are close to hatching, and the sooner you arrive in Snowhaven, the better. You four must leave immediately to stay on schedule for meeting with Justiciar Holland by the end of next month.

"We're already expecting supplies and shipments from Rhumbek to prepare for war against the Lich before the eclipse. We will move forward once we receive word that you four safely delivered the Mythic Flight eggs." General Araneus cleared his throat as he glared at Vidar, who squinted at Selena with sinister interest. She met his scowl with equal vehemence, but the general added, "If for any reason, you deem Snowhaven unsafe, you are to report back to Nuvak at once and wait there until further orders."

Araneus turned away as Aracania snaked her head around to a sealed wooden chest ensconced within her tail; he clicked open the lid, and inside were the dragon eggs from the Mythic Flight.

Each unborn hatchling was placed within a clay mold covered in silk and unicorn hair fabric. Their smooth shells revealed the full luster of deep-colored gemstones: ruby, sapphire, emerald, and topaz. Within the dragon eggs swirled a developing consciousness that Selena could sense without touching, yet the general granted her permission when she asked to hold one. Surprised by the fire guardian egg's feather-light weight, the soon-to-be youngling vibrated within her hands as if it were already alive.

She gave a small smile. "It feels like a little heartbeat."

Aracania chirped and chattered in approval when Selena set it back in its soft case. Araneus clicked the chest shut, ensuring he locked it tight and securely before granting Selena and Azrael permission to carry the weightless trunk away from Aracania's protective hold.

Vidar spoke instead of Araneus; he stood on his toes and cleared his throat. "I cannot tell you two how sensitive this mission is. Time is against us if we are to find proper handlers before the Day of Eternal Darkness, and you two are Armageddon's last hope. I pray for your safe journey to Snowhaven and the trip back. Dismissed."

Once Selena and Azrael hastily exited the Fire Temple with the dragon eggs in hand, Rahim explained that Silver had left to check on his estate and planned to meet them back at the covert before embarking on their mission. Yet, he couldn't wait any longer and asked what General Araneus said about him joining their trip to see his mother in Nuvak. Selena shamefully admitted she forgot, but she extended permission after peering over her shoulder to ensure no one was eavesdropping.

"I'm the Crown Princess," she declared, "and if the issue arose, the general could take it up with my mother for all I care."

Rahim laughed after sharing his gratitude and added, "I believe you mean Divine Crown Princess."

When Thor and Doragon returned with what remained from their feast—a boar in each foreclaw that they gobbled in mid-flight—they ferried the three back to the training courtyard after packing and strapping the eggs to the harness. Selena affirmed, "For now, we'll leave them with Thor," and Azrael agreed.

Meanwhile, Thor busied himself in polishing his bracelets and necklace until the diamonds and rubies gleamed to his liking; Doragon admired his trinkets through the glimmer in his eyes. **I appreciate that my jewelry is suitable for everyday wear and tear, including if I should choose to dress in battle.**

As they tugged and checked the straps and carabiners, locking the trunk safely in place, Thor shook and flapped his wings to ensure all was snug as he often did before taking flight; Selena assured the eggs were well in place.

Silver soared towards them with haste and purpose in his wingless dragon form, his golden horns gleaming against his smooth, white scales and azure mane flowing like a horse's in Divine's wind. He landed before Thor and Doragon and bowed in respect as he shapeshifted to his human facade, carrying Rahim's bag and a small, wrapped bundle of clothes.

"I pray Dragonstone Estate isn't in disrepair from the attack," Selena said, and Thor groaned; his treasure horde from the dwarven ruin hid within Silver's vault on the property, and his anticipation grew with every twitch his tail made.

Luckily, Silver was in high spirits to make his delivery. "My manor is still in one piece—including everything inside." He nodded to Thor, who snorted and dipped his head; after handing Rahim's bag over, Silver carefully gave Selena a folded sleeveless navy blue dress clad in golden buckles and trimmings, wrapped together by a long, charcoal grey scarf. Underneath the gown was a pair of matching dark blue elbow-length gloves with gilt-tinted edges. Silver smiled. "I've been working on these since the Battle of Alfheim, although I had hoped to gift them on our wedding day."

Azrael scowled, and Rahim gagged; the two stopped when Selena gave them a menacing glare, and she examined the presents with curiosity and interest. "Thank you, they're lovely."

Silver randomly changed the topic by asking, "My dear, do you know why I like wearing my white tailcoat jacket?"

Before Selena could answer, Rahim scoffed at him. "What does that have to do with—?" but Silver interrupted him.

"It took me over four hundred years to make it, all on gathering the appropriate materials to make it damn near indestructible. Upon confronting and killing the spider woman named Arachne from Runefell years ago, I harvested and used her silk for the thread before lining the outside with dragon scales from a shedding Imperial Pearlscale."

Thor and Doragon tilted their heads in interest, and Selena ran her fingers across the dress, only to find that the fabric bore a similar texture to a snake's skin.

Silver continued: "The feathers from my chain were gifted to me from an incredibly rare white and blue phoenix, though they serve no purpose other than for beautiful decoration. I had saved the unused silk from Arachne, and I used it for your new attire—gown, gloves, and scarf—with scales from a shedding Royal Tidalwalker. Neither weapon nor magic can penetrate the spider's silk and dragon scales; not only will you be safe, but this will keep you warm regardless of how cold it gets. The best part is the dress also has pockets on both the inside and out."

Overwhelmed by his generous gifts, she wrapped her arms around his neck and hugged him tightly. "Thank you—I will always wear and cherish them."

While Silver ensured Thor and Doragon were well for the long flight by offering them a stamina restoration elixir, Selena and Azrael rushed to their room to change and grab their readied provisions. As the barracks were still empty, Azrael offered Selena the courtesy to use the steam baths first, but she declined.

Instead, she asked him to wait outside the room for a few seconds while she undressed and used extreme heat to clean her body of dirt and bacteria. She briefly burst into flames, remaining unharmed, before releasing the energy; once she donned her undergarments and the blue dress, Selena declared she was decent, and Azrael came in smelling the air, remarking, "You smell singed as if you've been near a volcano." When she explained her technique, Azrael's eyes widened. "That's incredible—your abilities astound me."

Selena fastened her gold buckles after clad in the scarf and gloves—the spider's soft silk comfortable against her copper skin—and re-polished her hessian boots before belting Dragonheart and strapping her shield over her back. She grabbed her bags packed with emergency supplies containing nonperishable foods, flares, a map, her Air Force issued Winclock revolver, and several water canteens.

After changing out of his formal wear, Azrael slipped on a steel chain mail over his faded, red shirt and steel greaves over his trousers; he had already packed away the rest of his armor in Doragon's harness. When the two were satisfied, they met with Rahim and Silver again in the courtyard, and Silver grinned to see Selena wearing the gifts he made for her.

Thor and Doragon clicked their claws in approval through chittering, and Thor commented, **Now, you are the Crown Princess of Dragons.**

"Azrael, promise me that they will all return from Snowhaven in one piece," Silver demanded through the furrow in his brow, his ice-blue eyes piercing through his spectacles.

Azrael's eyes widened as he caught Silver's hostile glare. He ruefully peered at Selena, hiding that his hands were trembling. Azrael bit his cheeks so hard that Selena swore he could taste blood as he closed his eyes and nodded. "I promise."

"You swear it?"

"Blast it; I already promised—I'm always true to my word."

Thor helped Rahim board the harness, and Rahim strapped and secured his bag next to the Mythic Flight chest. "We have Death with us—what can happen?"

Azrael dug his nails into his palm and rubbed his temples. "I pray you know that you can't go around and tell others who we are," he nodded to Doragon and pointed at himself, "the only reason I mentioned anything is that you and Selena had figured it out."

Thor arched his neck and opened his mouth, releasing a loud groan that made them flinch, but he relaxed when Selena patted his foreleg. As Doragon plucked Azrael from the ground and helped him board his saddle, Silver gave Selena a few extra vials of his rejuvenating potions for the trip, and the two hugged once more. He whispered in her ear, "If you need anything, I'll be here. Send a courier falcon if you must—we anxiously await your word." He pulled her into a kiss and said, "I love you."

"I promise; I love you too."

Rahim grumbled upon seeing their romantic display and leaned against the saddle with arms crossed. "I hope we'll find Niamh on the way to Snowhaven."

Azrael overheard him and rolled his eyes. "Your beloved will be fine—she'll survive."

Yet, even after Thor and Doragon launched themselves over the fortress wall once Selena had strapped herself into the harness, she couldn't help but think about the masked dragons that attacked Alfheim and kidnapped poor Niamh.

*****

CHAPTER 11: RAHIM'S TEACHER

Once Thor and Doragon had embarked on their mission to Snowhaven, Silver returned to Dragonstone; he found Vulduin Xyrrion and Kain Vanguard—with his coffin-shaped case propped against the august couch—waiting for him inside the drawing room, courtesy of the footman. Vulduin donned his Phantom Dust disguise by wearing a black and white mask bearing the black fox symbol of Gundisalvus; yet, he still sported his regal red frock tailcoat embellished with gold buckles and trimmings.

Kain peered at him with his crimson eyes and gave Silver a toothy grin, his fangs and eye color giving away his vampiric nature. A white stripe parted his jet-black hair, intensely contrasting a scarlet cloth wrapped around his neck and stuffed into a black collared gentleman's shirt. Yet, he looked like a wild man with no concern for following a formal dress code: shirt untucked with dirtied black breeches and boots. However, his chiseled face gleamed from a fresh shave.

Silver dug his nails into his palm until his fingers turned white. "Who do you two think you are, letting yourselves freely into my house—?"

The Shadow Emperor lifted his mask; his expressionless pale, sculpted face unnerving his companions upon removing the veil. His deep blue eyes were an empty abyss, piercing the tense air lingering between the two. "Still your Emperor and now your future father-in-law, so might I suggest you sit down and join us, Genesis."

Silver scowled. "I've told you before, Your Imperial Majesty, to call me Silver. Don't tell me what I can't and cannot do, especially in my home."

Kain interrupted before Vulduin could, "Sit your arse down—you're not making any sense," but Silver scoffed as he made himself clear that Vulduin had no right to command his actions.

Vulduin sighed and ran his fingers through his raven feathered hair when Silver begrudgingly offered them tea and refreshments. "Green tea and honey for me, please."

Silver sneered as he wandered into the kitchen. "Like father, like daughter."

When he returned with their drinks of choice—black coffee for Kain—and biscuits, Kain gruffly remarked, "I still believe you're too old to be with her, but I suppose I will never understand what the Crown Princess sees in you."

A pained and twisted look appeared on Silver's face. He lost his stance and almost fell face-first to the floor, but he caught himself and fixed his glasses. Yet, Silver recoiled when Vulduin said through peering over his glass, "But he still has the heart and mind of a child." Yet, the actual reason behind their surprising visit quickly grew apparent. Silver rubbed his temples as he paced about the drawing room when their topic of discussion changed to the unexpected attack on Alfheim; their already tense atmosphere steeped from the grim conversation. Vulduin set his cup down. "What do you make of this, Genesis?"

Growling under his breath, Silver sighed when he paused and held his hands behind his back, contemplatively staring at the roaring fireplace. "From what I've gathered, I believe those creatures used to be normal dragons. However, I highly suspect their alteration is the Lich's work—I have no doubts." He turned around to meet Vulduin's and Kain's terrified gazes. "I fear that necromancer might have used my old research notes from the Well of Souls when he destroyed my laboratory. If so, I believe that these creatures are the result."

Vulduin squinted at him before taking another drink. "This is all based on assumption. It seems that your line of thinking might be improbable, Genesis. After all, the Well was only to bring the dead back. Am I correct?"

"Yes, you are." Silver spun on his heels and lifted his chin. "However, if that magic and research were to fall into the wrong hands—"

A low rumble escaped from Kain's throat when he wholly interrupted. "Wait, are you saying that the Lich recreated the Well?"

"I-I dunno for sure, but—"

Kain bolted from his set and grabbed the collar of Silver's jacket; though he stood to Silver's shoulders, Kain was strong enough to lift the admiral off his feet. "How could you have been so bloody careless?"

Vulduin snarled like an angry wolf when he stood up, and Kain immediately released his grip. "That's enough, now please, sit down. Kain, we don't know for sure, as I've said; this is all based on his hypothesis." Kain and Silver gave each other a firm nod and rejoined the Shadow Emperor in civilized company. "This whole ordeal has been too much for my liking."

Kain watched Silver like a predator eyeing its prey. "Especially after that trial, I would assume so. I would advise *Genesis* to tread carefully across these dangerous waters."

Vulduin's eyes darted between the two, but he sighed and said, "It's difficult giving away and parting with one's child," he nodded to Silver, "I wouldn't have parted with her to anyone less deserving." The three relished in the heartfelt moment, and before Kain could engage in playful banter, Vulduin added, "If I didn't know any better, I see that you have taken quite an interest in someone as well, Captain Vanguard."

Kain snorted as he took another drink. "I don't know what you're talking about."

"I've seen how you looked at her when escorting her out of Alfheim to meet with Lord Godfrey's sentries. Oh, take care, my old friend; Godfrey will ensure her safety at Winterguard. What was her name, Maria?"

Kain looked away and closed his eyes, but he didn't deny it; Vulduin sneered but then warned, "I pray we haven't drawn too much attention to ourselves—Vidar has been off his rocker."

Silver scowled. "If only Aydin Jormungand were still here. The Council had never been in such disarray before."

Vulduin cringed at the mention of Aydin's name, but he agreed. "You're right, but alas, he's not here anymore." He pulled out a sealed parcel and handed it to Kain. "Please, deliver this and give my regards to Lord Vincent Godfrey in Dark Blood Hold, as I believe the next time he and I meet will be under different circumstances." He then turned to Silver and bowed. "Thank you for the tea, but I'm afraid I must take my leave."

Silver raised a brow. "So soon, and when I was getting used to having your company?"

Vulduin scoffed and donned his mask. "I must reach Snowhaven and then Starsong. Farewell." Before stepping out the door, he had transformed into a massive, red dire wolf in mid-spring down the stairs, his sleek and glossy pelt shining in dawn's light. His claws clicked against the rocks, crimson fur bristling along his spine and tail.

When Silver and Kain approached the door, Vulduin had vanished beyond the lake as he soared across the ground in gigantic leaps, traveling at Divine's speed.

*****

Soaring through Armageddon's arctic skies was a freeing, exhilarated rush that reminded Selena of what it meant to be a dragon. Maintaining a steady speed of about fifty kilometers calculated by Azrael, Thor and Doragon flew beside each other, sailing across the breath of the Divines as their favorable wind gently ushered them away from Alfheim. The rejuvenated dragons had spent a few hours in flight, fresh like the new rising sun now peering over the horizon. Though Armageddon was always icy due to the continent's proximity to the far north, Selena was wholly warm, courtesy of Silver's gift.

Her stomach rumbled with hunger when Rahim rummaged through one bag and pulled out bread and cheese. To her shock, Rahim broke off pieces to hand them to her. "I have plenty to share."

"I'm surprised by your sudden generosity, as you never share."

The offended Rahim stuck up his nose, but he asked about her dragon abilities, seeing as they finally had time for a proper discussion. Owing him the truth, Selena regaled him of her discovery, as Kain had rescued Rahim before witnessing her initial transformation. He grinned, and all he could say was, "Wicked."

Selena's mind raced to what the other provinces would compare to the Fire Kingdom as the two indulged in food, and she shared her thoughts with Thor. *I can't wait to see Rhumbek.*

They heard the Eaglewater Express from a distance below, traveling full speed from the dwarven city with the promised shipments General Araneus had mentioned.

Neither can I. I wonder if the city is full of technology like what we found before.

That would be wonderful, but now I wonder why they haven't shared their knowledge with the world.

As Thor and Doragon continued coasting throughout the following hours, Azrael worked more with Selena on learning about Aether and understanding what each of the elements represented, as they had plenty of time. Yet, Rahim shuddered while remarking, "Why do you want Death to teach you?"

"Death and time are good teachers."

Azrael made an uncomfortable noise and shifted in his place. "I'm not a good teacher. Please stop saying that," but Selena continued insisting otherwise. He sighed. "I suppose I'll do what I can. However, please bear in mind that I don't know everything—I thought I did, being a Divine. If any good came from my banishment, it was that I learned more about what magic was."

Doragon inched close enough to Thor for Azrael to hop across his wings and jump into Thor's saddle, joining Selena and Rahim. He sat down cross-legged and began sharing his wisdom. "The more you can understand, the more powerful you'll become as a Divinity Dragon—Thor, you should pay attention, too." Thor snaked his head around, and his forked tongue slithered from his serrated fangs.

As they headed towards the Earth Kingdom Province, Selena requested to learn more about the earth itself; during Azrael's education, Rahim groaned, but he listened in on the lesson. "All magic came from dragons until mortals learned how to harness the surrounding energy. As the basis of all other elements, the earth is mighty, stable, and the heart of life itself, only achievable to those in tune with nature. Everything comes from the earth, providing shelter for the creatures inhabiting it. When you touch the dirt, you can feel its vitality and strength. And when we die, our bodies become part of the ground. This energy thrives within and around us: we can't exist without it."

Selena nodded and took a solid and steady stance, rigid and stable, powerful and unmovable; her heartbeat turned into a steady drum, and her body relaxed. Selena maintained a calm mind and imagined a still pool of water; she was tranquil and peaceful.

Though Thor was high in the sky, when she slammed her hand down, the earth quaked with seismic tremors giving way to her will. Azrael and Rahim backed away, afraid she would strike them down from the air; however, Thor and Doragon watched Selena's performance with great interest. The cracks below spread in all directions, and Selena summoned rock spikes shooting skyward into towering spires. Thor and Doragon weaved through the sudden peaks and towers, dodging her rocky maze; Selena fixed her mistakes by leveling out the earth with Thor's help, and the landscape resumed its shape.

When all was clear again, Azrael swore under his breath as he stood up, panting. "Confound it all; that damn Xyaxon and Ulrich ought to reconsider creating something as powerful as Divinity Dragons. Perhaps we should focus our education elsewhere before destroying the world ourselves."

Selena laughed, but she immediately thought of learning how to dual-wield weapons as the Lich had during the Battle of Alfheim. Azrael squinted at her when she made the request. "Dual-wielding Aether pistols isn't the same as using two swords."

"I believe I'll grow proficient with your wisdom."

When night descended upon the land, the two dragons landed through the soft flail of tired and burning wings between some hills outside Moonridge. After Selena, Rahim, and Azrael dismounted, unpacked, and removed their dragons' harnesses, Thor stretched out his wings before declaring, **I'm going hunting.**

He launched himself skyward, followed by Doragon, and the dragons flew away as quickly as they had arrived, their combined weight making the earth rumble. Yet, shortly after making the campfire and setting up their tents, Selena and Rahim fell into a deep stupor before Thor and Doragon returned from their evening hunt, clean of the gore. Thor wrapped around Selena and Rahim, bringing them within his protective wings, shielding them from the cold as the flames died out. Azrael, however, leaned against Doragon's foreleg and watched the stars drift overhead.

Selena awoke the following day just as the sun's rays lanced through the heavens, but Rahim looked as though he had been up for a while; he watched Azrael like a hawk, exhibiting similar distrust he had in Silver upon their first meeting. He glared as Azrael bent over to grab a stick and slashed the air with it like a sword. "He hasn't slept at all last night."

Selena looked between the indifferent Azrael, then back to him. "Why are you always suspicious of everyone?"

Rahim held a pained expression. "Have you forgotten what he did to you?"

Selena rummaged through her pack for a used rag and a vial of oil for Thor's scales. "No, I haven't, but I forgave him and made my peace."

"You made peace with Death."

Selena raised an eyebrow. "Is that bad?"

"Damn—yes? No? I dunno. Why am I the only one who is uncomfortable?" Rahim threw his hands up in the air and kicked the dirt.

Selena sighed and went to wash Thor down with oil; he opened one eye when she asked his permission to unfasten his jewelry. Although he was hesitant at first, Thor eventually agreed for her to remove his trinkets. *Just for a little while, my dear one. Your scales need to gleam like your gold and gems.*

Thor snorted, his pupiled-slits fixated on his treasures, anxiously ensuring they were safe and sound. As soon as Selena was done oiling his wrists, neck, and back to prevent his hide from chaffing, she assisted in fastening his trinkets back in their rightful places, and Thor was delighted.

Thank you, my dear. He snaked his head around to examine his shimmering scales compared to his dazzling jewels. Yet, Rahim's continued grumbles and mumbles added to his agitation; Thor stood up, tail sweeping across the ground, and released a low roar upon the ignorant Rahim. He stumbled and fell backwards, and Thor snorted in satisfaction. **It's too early in the morning for this headache.**

Doragon jerked awake from the startling sound, but he groaned, stretching out his claws and taking clumps of dirt with each pass he made. Azrael spun around with a furrow in his brow, and Rahim whimpered and hurried back. Selena approached to talk, but he sniffled as he dusted himself off, held up his hand, and marched away.

"What's wrong with him?" Azrael asked, moving towards the scene.

Overcome with remorse, Selena excused herself from Azrael and called for Rahim's return. "Please, talk to me."

Even though he ignored her, she rushed to his side. After several minutes of walking, he eventually sat on a boulder and gave a huff in defeat. When she drew near, he finally said, "Sometimes I wish you would listen to me. You always seem to know what to do, and you're certain of who you are, but I feel like I don't always have a voice— I'm not anyone special."

Selena knelt beside him and placed a hand on his shoulder. "I'm sorry to make you feel like that, but I don't want you to worry when there isn't anything to worry about."

Rahim's face turned red, and he fumed. "That's what I'm talking about. You don't understand, and I'm still uneasy; sometimes, I hate that you only see from your perspective."

"Then explain it to me so I can understand," Selena said again, "why don't you trust Azrael?"

"I dunno—maybe because he isn't the first person I want to see after I die, or perhaps I don't know what lies beyond life." Rahim sighed. "I'm sorry. You said you've made your peace with him, but I haven't."

Selena hung her head in defeat and shame. "Death isn't the end. It may be for this world, but it's only a gateway to the next—a beginning of a new journey. But that doesn't mean that life isn't precious. We should make the most of the time we have left."

Rahim sniffed but nodded in agreement. "You're right, but then I want to feel useful. Azrael and Doragon have their Divine magic, and you and Thor are powerful Divinity Dragons, but I don't have anything—I'm just plain and ordinary."

"That's not true. You're the mastermind behind our plans who handles the map and guides us; we'd be lost without you. Not to mention, but Thor and I wouldn't have been able to join the Force if you hadn't helped us."

"I appreciate your effort to help me feel better, but I want to be useful when fighting. I saw how brilliant you were against the Lich, and I was jealous—I felt like I couldn't do anything."

When Selena recalled her feelings of inadequacy and self-loathing, she had no idea Rahim suffered the same; she suddenly realized he had attempted to confess his hidden sentiments before finding Ragnarok. It pained her to know she wholly dismissed them without a second thought. "Pray forgive me for not seeing it before, and I want to help you. What is it that you've always wanted to do?"

Rahim's expression lit up. "Well, I can't use magic, but maybe I can learn how to use a weapon."

Thor's voice rumbled in the back of her mind. **Maybe we can take him shopping in the town nearby.**

I think he'll appreciate that.

Selena relayed Thor's suggestion, and a huge grin appeared on Rahim's face; he jumped up to hug her, then ran over to embrace Thor. "Thank you."

That's a fantastic suggestion, my dear, and I know he will never forget it.

I know how much it means to you. I would rather see Rahim happy than have all the jewels and gold in the world.

Shortly after, both Thor and Doragon went out hunting. Meanwhile, Selena, Azrael, and Rahim hiked a short distance over to the blacksmith shop in Moonridge. Azrael stood back while Rahim eagerly searched through the shop's merchandise.

The blacksmith set up most of the weapons outside with a practice dummy in the corner, with two wooden racks filled with swords and daggers hoisted behind. A forge was nestled to the side under the opened ceiling, smoke wafting skyward. Empty wooden plaques covered the middle wall behind the lined, heavily armored mannequins. Beside them was a metal safe filled with firearms of different sizes and calibers, covered in rust with age and use, but a few appeared brand new. Selena immediately knew that she would have to help him pick one out no matter which weapon Rahim chose.

"Maybe this?" Rahim picked up a longbow hanging from the first rack.

"Be careful, as the draw is a bit heavy," the blacksmith warned. Rahim ignored his caution and walked to the practice dummy but, to his dismay, couldn't draw it back.

Azrael groaned and pinched the bridge of his nose. "Are you sure that this is a good idea?"

Selena shrugged. "Why wouldn't it be?"

"Are we forgetting that we're supposed to reach Snowhaven? We don't have time for this nonsense."

"We'll be fine, and look how happy he is." Selena pointed to him as he picked up a firearm hanging in the safe, completely ignoring their conversation.

"He shouldn't even be coming with us in the first place. Why in Oblivion—?"

Selena whipped her head around, and Azrael tightened his lip. "It's my mother's Air Force, and I extended him the invitation, if you happen to recall. You'll learn how we work together as a team as we travel. And besides, since Rahim is coming with us, he will need to be armed so he can help us fight if the situation arises."

Selena knew that Azrael was still unhappy with her answer, but he stopped arguing. "Fine. I'm going to restock on supplies—let's meet back with Thor and Doragon in an hour."

As Azrael left, Rahim ran over and grabbed Selena's arm. "I want to learn how to shoot a gun. Can you show me?"

He brought her inside, and the blacksmith immediately burst into laughter. "She's a woman and doesn't know anything about weapons. Her place is in the kitchen, scrubbing the floors and cooking meals for any man willing to tolerate her."

Selena suddenly felt vulnerable, but Rahim rushed to her defense. "That's not true. I bet you she knows more about weapons and fighting than you do."

The blacksmith continued bellowing with laughter and wiped his eyes from a joke he only found funny. "Why don't you go back into the kitchen where you belong, *housewife?*"

Selena paid no mind to the blacksmith's sexist remarks; when Rahim showed her the weapon, she wasn't sure how to explain that he would make a terrible decision. She pointed at his choice and said bluntly, "That's a harpoon gun."

"So? Imagine getting shot by one of these."

"They're not practical. You would prefer something that could carry more ammo as you would only get one shot from this, and reloading is a pain."

Rahim's smile disappeared. "Oh."

Selena redirected him over to the other available firearm selections. "What about this revolver? It's a Winclock too: the same model we use in the Air Force." She whipped out the one holstered to her belt so she could compare, and she sneered when the blacksmith's eyes widened, shocked by her knowledge. "It can hold at least six rounds, and you can fire a series of shots without reloading. These are very accurate: they're designed for aerial combat with the dragon rider in mind." She held it up delicately as she inspected its design. The blued barrel was short and thick, closer to the grip; the dwarves who built the Winclocks in Alfheim figured out how to design for better accuracy and faster shooting. "This was well taken care of and fairly clean, too. I can show you how to load it. It's reliable, steady, and easy to shoot, making it the ideal gun for dragonback."

Both Selena and Rahim looked up to see the blacksmith staring at her, utterly dumbstruck. "May I buy this with a holster and ammunition, or should I return to the kitchen?" She smirked and tossed fifty gold pieces on the countertop.

Selena ensured they walked away with enough bullets to practice with and use in actual combat. As they left with their purchases, Rahim turned to the baffled blacksmith, raising a fist in victory for Selena's win. Yet, she yanked him by the collar when he was about to blurt out her imperial connection, whispering, "You can't tell other people that," but Rahim only shrugged.

The trek back was filled with questions Rahim kept firing; she was a little exhausted and grew weary of his curiosity, but she was happy to see his enthusiasm. Selena attempted to answer them all, but eventually, she said: "How about I show you? It'll be much easier."

Thor and Doragon had returned with their latest catch, an elk dangling from each foreclaw; they gulped them down in seconds, save for their horns. Azrael, however, was busy firing shots with his Aether pistols at his self-made stone targets, blasting them into Oblivion. When he noticed they had returned, Azrael said, "It's about bloody time. We need to get moving soon."

Doragon licked his chops and let out a long groan, and Azrael flinched when Doragon swept his tail across the dirt, destroying his rock dummies in dust billows.

"I think he wants to rest," Selena observed.

Rahim bounced in his spot. "Besides, she was going to show me how to shoot."

"Oh, buggery—if you two want to waste more time, fine." Azrael shot down his last standing target before walking away; even Doragon moaned and snorted, blowing smoke rings flaring with embers that singed his shirt. After extinguishing the flames, Azrael swore under his breath and stomped towards Doragon in mumbles and grumbles before marching over the hill.

"Ignore him. Here, I'll help you." Selena explained how the gun worked, how to handle it properly, how to load, and so on; Rahim remained intrigued with each piece of wisdom she had to offer. She worked with him on placement and had Rahim practice shooting it with one of Azrael's stone targets while warning that "unless you intend to kill, as a safety measure, you must always keep her finger off the trigger." Starting at a short distance away, Rahim was able to get used to shooting after a few misses. Yet, Selena cheered him on. "You're doing great."

"Do you think so?"

"I know you'll make a great sharpshooter yet. Make sure you shoot with both eyes open: it will help you move on to your next target more quickly."

Despite Azrael's wishes, Selena spent the remainder of the afternoon and early evening shooting with Rahim, his fingers getting loose after growing used to the trigger's feel. Copying Azrael's practice regimen, Selena summoned stone targets shaped like the robed zealots from the Obsidian Order. She and Rahim worked together on quickly firing down each dummy until the two could clear a group of ten within five seconds, rapidly and accurately engaging their targets.

Soon, she had him practice from more than twenty meters away. After tweaking his sights slightly, Rahim quickly adjusted to the distance change, and, true to Selena's predicted praise, he was slowly growing to be a perfectly able gunslinger. When Thor and Doragon were ready to leave, Rahim still wished to keep practicing; while airborne, Selena accommodated him by summoning rock disks she launched in the air, and Rahim focused on shooting them down. He missed more than he blasted, but Selena was satisfied by his prowess.

Yet, among all the gunfire, Thor asked her as he and Doragon cruised side by side, **How do thunder and lightning bother you, but these other loud noises have no effect? Is your fear truly more psychological?**

Selena suddenly cringed and recoiled when her past nightmares from the Lich resurfaced; Thor was right, as she had associated the loud storm noises with the dark spells tormenting her dreamland; her lack of response was more than enough confirmation for Thor.

Please forgive me, my dearest one. I didn't mean to bring it up, but I was curious.

You have no reason to apologize; I would rather have you understand than assume.

Of course, and now I understand more clearly.

Thor and Doragon insisted on flying nonstop for a few days in hopes of reaching Rhumbek soon. As fast and steady as their flight was, even though they had made it into the Earth Kingdom Province yesterday, they were still two—perhaps three—days away from arriving at the capital. Selena hoped they would make it to the dwarven city by now, but Rahim reassured her they were still making good time.

"With Thor's and Doragon's endurance, they're very swift fliers; I'd reckon we'll reach Snowhaven in less than a month," Rahim soothed. When he ran his calculations by Azrael, he agreed, though he still grumbled that they needed to arrive and leave the Water Kingdom capital as soon as possible. Selena couldn't understand why Azrael was so keen on finishing this mission quickly when they were making good time.

Yet, by the fourth evening of continuous flying since leaving Moonridge, Thor announced: **I'm growing weary, and I believe Doragon is in the same state.**

You two are amazing. Pray, find us some shelter closer to the Hinterlands' border, my dear.

When the two dragons decided on a location closer to the Hinterlands, they made their graceful descent. The trees bent and yielded to the might of their wings, their membranes like sails stretched tautly. Once Selena and her group unpacked and unstrapped their harnesses, Thor and Doragon collapsed, wrapping themselves within their coils before falling into a deep slumber. Their wings laid loosely on the ground, too exhausted to fold.

The trio relaxed by the fire Selena ignited, yet they were too awake to fall asleep. Selena expected Azrael didn't need to, but she was surprised to see Rahim's tenacity. She yawned but leaned against Thor's limp wing, the membranes catching her body like a hammock. The curiosity getting the best of her, she asked, "Azrael, have you ever been to Rhumbek?"

His eyes widened with shock, but he looked down at his feet. "I have, but it's been a very long time."

Rahim fed her curiosity by asking, "What was the city like?"

"It's been many years, but the Emerald Dragon, Ulrich, destroyed Rhumbek the last time I was there."

Selena squinted at him. "Why would he do such a thing?"

"The Earth Kingdom is his territory—he watches over the dwarves and decides their fate. Ulrich is a cursed mad god; I pray for those who are unlucky enough to cross his path."

"Can I say that it's both incredible and scary at the same time that you're one of the Divines we worship?" Rahim asked in nervousness.

"I told you, I'm not a god anymore—I'm just the Shepherd of Souls."

"You're still Death." Selena corrected.

"That may be so, but I still have to earn the Divine title and status," Azrael growled. "I don't want to keep talking about this anymore."

"Okay, I'm sorry." Selena held up her hands in defense. "I didn't mean to offend you, but that leaves me to wonder: did any of their old technology survive Ulrich's onslaught?"

"No," Azrael confirmed, "the dwarves abandoned everything in ruins scattered across the Empire."

It greatly pained Selena to think that their most significant discoveries were wasted somewhere underground; if only Ulrich left the dwarves be. "I thought it would be fascinating since Thor and I discovered their mechanism that can read starlight to tell the past, present, and future."

"When was this?" Azrael asked. "I don't remember hearing about anything that can do that."

Selena stared at him, unsure of how to explain. However, she cleared her throat to try. "It was at the time when the Lich attacked Alfheim when we were chasing after the legend of Ragnarok."

"Legends don't destroy cities." Azrael barked, but he sighed when Selena continued with her tale. "I believe you, but I'm surprised that the dwarves were able to reach that kind of power," he growled, "who knows what could be waiting for us in Rhumbek?"

*****

CHAPTER 12: THE FOREST

A light, crisp, and cool evening breeze blew through the Hinterlands. The chilling clouds scattered across the twilight sky, and the trees sang their grisly melody as the moon rose. Kiba ran through the ancient forest, quiet as a mouse; her bristling white fur kept her warm against the unforgiving terrain. Her large paws patted softly against the earth. The landscape donned its white fleece, concealing the She-Wolf and her hunting party of five, making it nearly impossible to be tracked down.

Kiba was in hot pursuit of two dwarf thieves who desecrated Artio's shrine and stole their paragon that kept the Hinterlands alive. Yet, she paused and sniffed the ground and air; when the delectable scent graced her nostrils, she howled, gathering the rest of her group. *We must be careful—I sense three nearby, and they could overwhelm us if we're not cautious.*

Her members nodded, and they willingly followed; Kiba sprang through trees, dodging the twists and turns within the forest's thick embrace. A sea of stars flowed across the sky, and she snarled through her teeth, picking up the pace, the soft pitter-patter of paws thumping against the ground.

They immediately paused their pursuit when a massive red and yellow dragon soared above them, donning a harness large enough to carry a crew of more than fifty. Kiba held her breath, but the behemoth flew past, and the hunting party silently withdrew and continued their chase.

Kiba's heart raced as she slowly approached a glowing campfire roaring near the forest boundary. As if allured by these new, weary trespassers, she and her party halted their pursuit of the thieves, for their scent was still fresh. The She-Wolf swiveled her head, meeting her pack's intent gazes. She crouched behind the thick bushes, her ears ticking to the noises ahead, staying clear from the glimmering colossus golden dragon lying beside the Raging River. Its stained-glass silver wing membranes shimmered in the moonlight, matching its armor-plated scales; its tail wrapped around a basket full of freshly caught catfish. Ensconced within the dragon's forearms was a young human boy with a scar slashed over his right eye and a voluminous, black cloak draped over his shoulders, protecting him from the cold night.

Kiba immediately ordered her party to back away, as they would have been no match against the god-like creature; even the Aynu knew of the dragon riders from Alfheim. She would need the strength of the entire pack, but even then, their chances of actually winning and taking one down were very slim.

The boy looked as though he had barely reached adulthood; his messy black hair covered his dirty face as his empty eyes focused on the blazing fire. Kiba's brilliant white fur bristled when she sensed his grim appearance and posture; he barely moved a muscle.

His dragon lowered his head to look at him and nudged his shoulder, and the boy snorted. "You're now well-rested—right, Doragon?" The golden dragon chattered and groaned. "They'll be fine. Selena and Rahim are more than capable, and Thor is only circling the area. That's what these are for." He pulled out a half-full vial of blue liquid. "I suppose that Admiral Altessa is useful after all. Besides, I don't exactly see how it's our responsibility to look after the Crown Princess and her dragon. Selena and Thor are more than capable of completing this mission themselves."

Doragon snarled and unfurled his wings as his tail whipped around in place; his head snaked around, but the boy shook his head. "It's okay—no one can hear me. You know how chaotic my thoughts can be, and it helps drown out the other voices when I talk aloud," he sighed, "It isn't easy being the Shepherd of Souls."

Kiba lowered her head and bared her fangs as if she were about to spring an attack, but she remained hidden. The other five wolves slowly approached from both sides, but they obeyed their alpha's command, yet their eyes fixated on the dragon, hoping it didn't notice their presence. Doragon remained ignorant, or perhaps he knew the wolves were there but only waited patiently if they struck first. Either way, he didn't raise the alarm, but the golden dragon continued pestering the boy about what Kiba could only assume.

"I know what the Empress said," the boy snapped but stopped. Kiba squinted at him, wondering if he was arguing with himself or the dragon. "I'm sorry," the boy ruefully said, "It frustrates me. I'm trying to be better, and I've been doing what I can to help, but then I'm forced into these situations I have neither say nor control over." He waved his hand in the fire; the flames under his palm changed from yellow and orange to blue and purple.

Kiba was taken by surprise by his sorcery and growled. *What is this magic?*

He spat on the ground. "Selena confuses me by trying so hard to protect everyone when most of the world has already accepted its fate. I've admitted mine, but why can't she?"

Kiba crept closer but held her breath when she stepped on a small twig, snapping it. Her heart raced, ticking and thumping in her ears; ensuring her party escaped, she ran as fast as she could, feeling frightened for the first time. Both Doragon and the boy immediately looked in her direction, but Kiba and her hunters fled deeper into the forest before they were seen.

*****

Hours had passed before Thor returned from making his rounds with Selena and Rahim, but he took a slight detour and caught two large wild boars; he ate one in mid-flight before returning to camp but saved the other until he landed.

Doragon gorged on a pile of trout and catfish after finishing off the basket while Azrael busied in fishing for more. Selena and Rahim joined him as Thor tore into his catch and licked his chops when he finished devouring the pig in two bites. He snorted before taking several large mouthfuls of river water, gathering fish in every swallow.

Selena sat beside him and watched before her stomach growled; Azrael groaned and pulled his empty line away. "Soon, there won't be any fish left."

Thor backed away from the riverbank and gave him a long, irritated groan. The putrid air from his throat made him gag, and Azrael fell on his back, coughing. Grumbling, he approached Doragon, who nudged the rest of his untouched food towards him, and prepared their meals to roast over the open fire.

Yet, Rahim dug through their remaining supplies, searching for jerky, while Azrael seasoned the meat with salt and pepper; Selena looked at him in disbelief and said, "We just restocked. Please don't tell me that you've been eating it all."

Rahim was about to bite into a piece of cured pork before setting it down. "I-I haven't; there's more in here. I'm sorry, but I get so hungry on long trips."

"Azrael is making our food—you can wait."

Rahim grumbled and reluctantly packed away the rest and crouched beside the fire, arms crossed. Once he placed their fish over the fire to cook, Azrael pulled out a map from his nearby bag. "We should be right around here," he said after placing a finger where it read 'Hinterlands' and moving it across the parchment, "I'm hoping that we'll get to Rhumbek by tomorrow, but there's no telling."

"That's what I'm good for," Rahim called out and attempted to snatch it away, but Azrael was faster; he rolled it up before Rahim could get close.

When assured that Rahim retreated, Azrael announced, "Since the Council forced Doragon and me to go on this assignment, I might as well keep us on track."

Rahim's nostrils flared; flames would have erupted if he possessed the aptitude. "I don't care. I'm always the map guy. Besides, I know your mission is critical, but we still need to track down those monsters that took Niamh."

"Our assignment is more important," Azrael snapped. "Niamh will be fine for a while, and we may even run into those creatures, but we still need to focus on the eggs. I think preparing for this upcoming war is more important than rescuing one person."

Rahim's lips trembled, and he slumped his shoulders. "Yeah, but to Niamh, it would mean everything. All you think about is completing the job and that saving one person won't make a difference compared to protecting the world, but it will matter to Niamh."

Rahim's words hit harder than being shot by a pistol. Selena walked over and placed a hand on his shoulder. "I understand, and I promise we will find a way to save her—"

Azrael interrupted. "Does my indication of her survival mean nothing?"

"Of course, it means everything, but that doesn't mean she deserves to be tortured or worse," Rahim growled, but he withdrew any harsh remark when Selena tightened her grip.

"I dunno how we'll track down those masked dragons that kidnapped her, but I promise we will find a way to save her as soon as we're able," Selena glared at Azrael, "isn't that right?"

Azrael looked between them and sighed. "Fine, we will work on finding and saving Niamh, but only after we complete our assignment. Agreed?"

Selena nodded, but Rahim sniffled before saying, "Agreed."

Selena and Rahim ate their meals in silence when Azrael finished cooking, but Azrael withheld consumption. "I don't need to eat. It's better to save the supplies for you two."

Yet, Rahim inched away and turned his back on them once he finished his fish. Selena joined him, lying on the soft grass and staring at the swirling, twinkling diamond stars overhead. When he noted her presence, Rahim grabbed his blanket from his sleeping bag and threw it over her shoulders. "Thank you," he said quietly.

Selena smiled. "It's the right thing to do."

"I don't think you understand how much that meant to me. I won't lie; I like Niamh very much, and I wish I could have told her before those weird dragons attacked us. Now, I may never get to."

Selena placed an arm around his back and brought him into a side hug. "That's not true. Azrael said she's still alive, and we will save her."

When Thor finished his fill, Selena and Rahim worked together in unstrapping his harness and, with much persuasion, removing his jewelry. *We will keep them together by your saddle, my dear one. It won't do your scales any good to keep wearing your trinkets.*

I know, but still.

Yet, Thor appreciated being naked and free, stretching his neck and wings before laying beside them, spreading out his bat-like wing like a blanket shielding the two from the outside elements, his jeweled harness and treasures well within sight near his paws. Selena and Rahim leaned against his stomach, concealed within his coils.

Thor grunted as he laid his head down, fixing one smoldering eye on her. **I understand Azrael's argument, but saving Niamh does matter.**

Rahim bade the two good night, and Thor lifted his tail, allowing him to reach his sleeping bag. Selena repositioned herself into the crook in his forearm until she was comfortable.

I pray we can save her, but I wouldn't know where to begin, even after completing the mission. She sighed and watched Azrael extinguish their campfire and join Doragon's side. *I wish I knew why those masked dragons attacked us.*

Selena heard a growl rumble within Thor's throat. **No matter the reason—we will destroy them and put an end to this.**

I suppose, but I don't know how to fight back if I'm not proficient enough. You nearly wiped out hundreds with a single attack, but I didn't stand a chance against two. I'm not strong enough.

Thor snarled, and his tail flickered in agitation. **You're a Divinity Dragon, are you not? You will withdraw any harsh remarks about yourself; otherwise, you will never shine. We will retaliate with a god's wrath and fury.**

As their group finally settled into slumber, Selena heard the faint rustling of bushes behind them. Although Thor assured her they were alone, she couldn't help but feel they were being watched with warm, yellow eyes taunting them.

As the sun rose, Selena awoke before the others. Her body ached, and her mind raced as she paced around their campsite, unable to sleep last night, searching for any signs that they were being followed. Looking over at her friends, they seemed not to be bothered by the eerie ambiance surrounding them; even Azrael had fallen into a deep torpor with Doragon coiled around him as if guarding a pile of gold and jewels. She smiled when she noted how peaceful Thor was as he slept. Sometimes, she wondered what kind of dreams he had—possibly of excitement, adventure, and perhaps treasure.

Thor stirred slightly and opened his beautiful amber eyes when she patted his neck. *Good morning.*

It took Thor a moment to respond; he stretched and uncurled his neck. **Good morning, my dear one. When do you suppose everyone will be ready to make way for Rhumbek?**

I take it soon, but Azrael and Rahim are still sleeping.

Black smoke plumed from Thor's nostrils. **Shall I roar to wake them up?**

Selena declined, snapping on Thor's bracelets and fixing his heavy ruby chain around his neck. Thor snaked his head down to examine them when she finished, humming in delight and satisfaction to have his jewelry.

Selena ran her fingers through her hair and noticed how it tickled her shoulders. It had been more than a week since deciding to let it flourish; she hadn't given herself a proper trim since before her arrest, but the rate at which her hair grew was surprisingly fast. She knelt beside the riverbed and examined her wild hair; she pulled out a brush once she cleaned herself of dirt and filth with extreme heat and combed the knots and tangles. Yet, after finishing her morning routine, Selena abruptly whipped her head around when a couple of rustling bushes caught her attention, but they stopped moving.

She snarled. *I think something is watching us.*

Thor looked up and growled. **I don't see anything, but please stay away. It's already risky enough that we're near these dangerous woods.**

The bushes shifted again, ever so slightly, and Selena caught a faint shadow dancing through the trees in the distance, followed by childish laughter. *I think someone is there, maybe a little girl, but why would she be wandering in the forest all alone?*

What do you mean? There's nothing there. I'm begging you, please stay here, Thor pleaded again, **the forest will play tricks on you.**

Although Selena knew he was right, she couldn't help but feel the undeniable lure tugging at her subconscious; the Hinterlands wanted to take her. A cold breeze blew past, leading into the void spaces between the trees. It was as if the forest was calling out to her, whispering her name.

The wind is pulling me In.

My dear, please, no. You're beginning to scare me.

Her dragon's voice drifted away as Selena ventured deeper within, no longer in control of her steps. Thor attempted to grab her with his claws, but he suddenly disappeared as the Hinterlands welcomed her with a cold and loving embrace.

The primitive forest beckoned her as she plunged into the tree's knotted arms, their massive roots twisting across the ground, and the foliage grew thick and lust. She followed the laughter from the enveloping darkness, muffled by the wickedly woven leaves. Every tree she passed looked like an ancient guardian watching over the endless grove.

Though she had no light to guide her path, Selena followed the child's giggles ringing through the air as if she knew the forest well. The sounds danced around her, continuously moving in different directions, captivating her as if she were under a spell. The forest's eerie song was enthralling, playing with her curiosity, toying with her desires.

Selena suddenly stopped and regained her senses, fighting back the urge to continue following what she thought to be a child. Her head whipped around when realizing how far she had wandered away from camp; Thor's voice was lost to her, and her anxiety grew with the ticking sounds of her beating heart.

My dear one, where are you?

The realization of her utter isolation settled in: Selena and Thor were separated mentally. It shook her to her core when she could neither hear nor feel his presence.

Selena turned around to look for an escape but was unsure of the direction from which she came. Her paranoia rose as she trembled in absolute fear; Selena's heart nearly exploded from her chest.

She attempted to find any familiar landmark during the trek back to camp, but her surroundings grew thick, pulling her deeper into the mysterious land. It was as if the trees were changing.

"How can this be?" Selena asked out loud. "But that can't be possible…." Her voice failed, and once again, she heard the child's laughter taunt her. Selena spun around and backed away. "Hello? Please, can you help me? How can I leave this place?"

The ghostly laugh continued mocking her. Selena turned around and got into the position to perform magic in case of an unexpected attack, but the giggles faded away. "Please, I wish to leave," she whispered in fear, "I mean no harm unless provoked."

She heard the colorful sound once more; Selena twirled around and saw a young girl around her age standing on a large bolder with a white bird in her hands. Despite Selena's petite height, she nearly dwarfed the stranger; her tangled and dirty long, white hair practically glistened with the same iridescence as her mother's. Yet, Selena had to avert her eyes, as her only piece of clothing was a white wolf mask with red markings. She ignored Selena's intrusion and stroked the bird while grinning and snickering.

"Hello? Who are you?" Selena asked the little girl, but she only giggled. "Are you lost too? Do you need help?"

The girl turned around, peering through her messy hair with brilliant yellow eyes burning from the mask. The white bird flew away, displaying an eerie and perpetual grin. Selena immediately backed away, hands raised in defense, but the wolf girl perched on the boulder.

Suddenly, Selena's thoughts thundered from Thor's panicked roars, and the wolf girl vanished within an eye blink. A cold wind stirred in the air, pushing her away until she saw the bright sun peeking through the trees. Her heart fluttered like the white bird flying overhead, Selena dashed towards the opening, and Thor's voice drew her from the darkness.

As soon as she reached the open field, Selena returned to camp; she looked back at the forest and heard the thick trees whisper as if they were sharing secrets. The Hinterlands played a macabre song as Selena made haste to reach her friends, but she only saw Rahim and Thor staring at her dumb.

Was it all just an illusion?

Satisfied that she had finally returned, Thor rushed over and pinned her down with his paws without warning. He lowered his head to hers, opened his mouth wide, and roared; it was a long-winded, bellowing thunder that made the birds in the trees scatter.

"Is this always going to be a thing with you?" Selena asked when he finished.

How could you leave me again like that? You were gone like you didn't exist.

My dear, I don't know—

Thor lowered his smoldering red-tinted amber eyes until she was a reflection against his irises, and his voice blasted deep within her consciousness. **This happened when the Obsidian Order first attacked you. You promised me this would never happen again.**

Please, my dear, forgive me.

You will never leave my side again, Thor said, still bristling, **Azrael and Doragon went out looking for**

you when you didn't return. I was about to tear apart the damn trees and mountains to find you.

Rahim ran over when Thor finally let Selena go. She stumbled to her feet as he brought her into a tight embrace. "We heard Thor making a ruckus hours ago when you disappeared."

"Hours ago?" Selena asked in bafflement, "But I've only been gone for a few minutes." Both Thor and Rahim exchanged confused glances, thinking she was babbling utter nonsense. Yet, she saw the sun was close to setting over the horizon, and her face drained of all color when she realized the day had passed.

From the sky, Selena saw the silhouette of Azrael and Doragon flying back towards their camp, sailing across the ghastly emerald sea. Doragon's massive, silver wings engulfed the heavens. The air rumbled around them with each flap, the membranes holding taut like firm sails from a ship.

As they got closer, Azrael started swearing when seeing she had returned. Azrael didn't wait for assistance, climbing and jumping down Doragon's forearm as the golden dragon landed upon his haunches and approached her with heavy steps. He grabbed the hem of Selena's blue dress and hoisted her up, making her stand on her toes. "What in Oblivion is wrong with you?"

"I don't know—"

"You don't know? We thought something terrible had happened." His hand trembled, but when Doragon snorted and chirped, Azrael swallowed hard, slowly brought her down, and released her dress. "When Thor told Doragon you disappeared, we've been searching for you all day. Because of you, we lost precious time; we're now a day behind in our journey when we could have been on our way to Rhumbek."

It wasn't possible: how could she have been gone for so long? Selena hung her head in shame when everyone waited for an apology. "I'm sorry to have worried you all."

Azrael grimaced at her words, but he nodded and stepped back. Without another word, he walked over to Doragon and packed their campsite, grumbling. Rahim looked between him and her before joining Azrael to help.

She gave Thor a pleading stare, wanting him to forgive her desperately. She could handle Rahim and Azrael being angry with her, but not him. *I don't know what else to say, my dear. I'm so sorry, and I don't know what I can do to make it up to you.*

Thor snorted and turned away for a moment before finally saying, **Don't ever do that to me again. That's the second time you've wandered away from me, and it will be the last.**

I never wanted to be parted from you.

Ember shards exhaled from his nostrils, and his tail swept across the ground while he helped Selena strap his harness. **I didn't know if you were dead or alive. If something had happened to you in the forest, I don't know what I would do. What if you were killed?**

Selena peered at Azrael from over her shoulder, but he gave neither inclination nor indication of her fate if she hadn't found her way back. *I'm certain Azrael and Doragon wouldn't allow that to happen, my dear. I promise you; I don't plan on meeting my untimely end.*

Once satisfied that Thor's harness was secure, she busied herself with packing her bags; however, Selena couldn't help but take one last look at the haunting forest, wondering if the young girl in the wolf mask was the spirit of the Hinterlands.

The grove felt alive; she paused when she saw a silhouette of a magnificent white wolf glaring at her with the girl's same blazing yellow eyes hiding behind the verdant brush. Yet, the chilling evening wind blew through the leaves, and the wolf's image vanished.

CHAPTER 13: THE KING OF RHUMBEK

Selena's group had been traveling all evening until the grey clouds drifted close to the ground as the sun rose, bringing life to the new day. Yet, Thor and Doragon groaned when Azrael mumbled and swore every time he looked at the map, continuously pushing them to keep moving. Eventually, Doragon had enough, and when Azrael least expected it, he made a whole aerial spin. Azrael wasn't buckled, but Doragon was fast enough to resume position without losing his rider, and Azrael floated freely for a few seconds before thumping back into the saddle.

The only one who wasn't amused was Selena. She leaned against the Mythic Flight egg crate, and Thor bombarded her with more questions about what had happened in the Hinterlands. When Selena gave him the same answers as before, Thor grunted, and smoke wafted from his nostrils. **Are you sure of what you saw? All of this is because of a child you claimed to have seen.**

Selena tightened her grip around the trunk's handles and fingered the wood finish. *You know I wouldn't lie about this.*

Thor didn't answer at first, and Selena felt uneasy by his silence. **I don't know what to say,** he finally said, **I don't think you're lying, but I was frightened. You understand how dangerous it is to wander the Hinterlands.**

I was afraid I'd lost you and the others forever. Do you forgive me?

Of course, I forgive you.

I thought you said before that dragons don't have fear.

Thor grumbled and swiveled his head away in shame. **I misspoke,** he said after a long while, **I was afraid when you first encountered the Order and when the Marcupo and the Lich almost killed you; I don't want to lose you.**

My dear one, you won't lose me.

Something always happens whenever we're separated. Imagine if Silver were here—we would never hear the end of it.

Selena sighed, for she knew Thor was right. Though Silver believed in her abilities, he would have reacted similarly, if not worse. *Perhaps it's a good thing he didn't join us on this assignment.*

She brought her bag close, pulled out a few books Apollo had gifted her before their departure, and offered to read to Thor as they resumed course; Thor heartily accepted. She shared with him the tale of Epoch: the first known Divinity Dragon Silver had the pleasure of meeting.

Epoch existed over twelve thousand years ago and was a Regal Flamescale blessed by the Divines to commune and coexist with mortals. Not realizing he was granted god-like power, Epoch wanted the ability to save the dragons from extinction as the war between them and mortals took a drastic turn. He spent hundreds of years seeking out the original guardians—the ancestors from the Mythic Flight—and asked for the magic to help him save his race.

Though no dragon had ever possessed two elements before, Epoch insisted he could learn to do so. Each of the guardians agreed but held on to their magic until Epoch could master the energies. Once he trained, eventually, the masters passed on their secrets and knowledge; within a year, Epoch became the first dragon to master all magic. Working with Xyaxon, he learned how to use Aether, thus allowing him to save the dragons from utter annihilation.

Yet, wielding all this power put him in mortal danger, and Epoch lost his life protecting the dragons. However, before dying, Epoch apologized for not ending the conflict, but Xyaxon promised that his quest would continue through the next Divinity Dragon, beginning the Divine cycle through Epoch's prayer.

When Selena continued through the stories, she and Thor learned there were six other Divinity Dragons before them. Their dragon mother, Yggdrasil, a Crimson Deathwing able to wield earth and fire, finished Epoch's quest by finally ending the war between mortals and dragons almost sixteen hundred years ago. The Empire used 'Enno etem Drvanis' or 'Year of the Dragon' to mark the new age since Yggdrasil peacefully resolved the conflict.

She must have been an extraordinary dragon to accomplish this feat, Selena remarked, and Thor chittered in agreement.

While Selena and Thor were engrossed in the stories, Azrael walked across Doragon's wing and leapt towards Thor's harness. They faintly overheard Azrael coaching Rahim on how to behave and address His Majesty, King Dionysus Goldthane of Rhumbek. Yet, Rahim couldn't help but roll his eyes as he continued mentioning his already Divine imperial company by pointing at Selena, but Azrael wasn't amused. "You shouldn't misbehave around her," he leered at Selena, "the dwarf king isn't as carefree as the Crown Princess."

Selena snapped her book shut. "Should I act like those pompous peacocks in Rune Citadel, then? We will respect His Majesty, but King Dionysus will remember that I am the Crown Princess—he should worry about offending Her Imperial Majesty."

Azrael glared at her from near Thor's tail; though there was a considerable distance between them, his piercing eyes shattering the tense air. "Remember that the kings serve the Council, not the Empress—King Dionysus Goldthane may scoff at your imperial connection." Exhibiting his way to defend Selena's honor, Rahim made an unfriendly gesture as Azrael pulled out their map and said, "We should arrive by this time tomorrow—be on the lookout."

Steadfast by Azrael's calculations, the large, metallic city of Rhumbek was well within their aerial view by the next day. Built into the very foundation of the Mustang Mountains, the metropolis of copper and stone was surrounded by a thick wall of marble, its massive metal door guarded by two heavily-armored giant, green mountain trolls. Their tusks curved over their underbites, revealing horrendously serrated teeth sharp enough to tear flesh from bone. Etched into the walls were mirrored images of Ulrich amidst his fiery fury and destruction; Ulrich had gifted the dwarves technology since they initially didn't favor magic. "However, I believe the dwarves have been slowly learning to harness earth energy," Azrael briefly explained.

The three donned hooded cloaks upon Azrael's instruction, exerting caution as the troll guards lifted their spears upon seeing the dragons. Doragon and Thor gracefully descended before the gate, wings unfurled, prickling in anticipation as the guards stepped forward.

Azrael warned, "I'll do most of the talking, so please, don't speak unless you're spoken to, both of you. I don't think I need to remind you two that the dwarves hate the Fire Kingdom."

Selena ruefully nodded; she knew their animosity stemmed from the elves' rebellion, as Alfheim was built after fleeing the Earth Kingdom. Though the dwarves still displayed resentment against the elves—they could hold a grudge forever—time slowly healed their wounds when Alfheim opened its doors to the dwarves wishing for a truce. The two capitals established a mutual alliance and business arrangement still honored today.

While Doragon and Thor remained behind, Selena, Rahim, and Azrael approached the metal door, but the guards slammed their steel spears together, forming an 'x' to prevent the trio from passing. "No one may enter His Majesty's domain."

Azrael cleared his throat and pulled back his hood. "We graciously ask that you please let us through, for we wish to meet with King Dionysus Goldthane."

One troll held out his spear and pointed it at Azrael's chest. "State yer business for needing tae see the king."

"We're dragon riders from the Imperial Air Force, currently on assignment, weary from traveling. I pray it wouldn't be considered paltry to ask for hospitality—"

The two guards snorted, and Azrael held his tongue; they looked at each other and grunted. One firmly nodded and pushed open the gates with his massive hands. Thinking that it was their queue to follow, the group made their way in, but the second guard held up his weapon to keep them in place.

The trio flinched when someone from beyond the wall yelled, "What be goin' on here?"

The troll guard returned with a dwarf dressed in steel armor covered in amber fur draped over his shoulders. His red eyes blazed from his long, dark red beard tied in a neat braid decorated in gold chains and tiny jewels. Thor and Doragon snaked their heads closer, allured by the trinkets embellished upon the dwarf.

He was of short stature, barely reaching the height of Selena's waist. "What be goin' on here?" the dwarf repeated. His expression drew blank when his eyes landed on Selena and her sword. He then looked at Thor and her companions. "Dragon riders? About bloody time—King Goldthane has been waitin' for damn near a week since Vidar sent word."

Selena knelt before the dwarf and bowed. Before Azrael could get in a word, she said: "Please, accept our apologies for our delay."

Azrael and Rahim followed her example, and when the dwarf was satisfied by the regal address, he lifted his chin high and said, "Great tae meet ya. I be the King's Hand, Dormrir Stronghorn, and I serve His Majesty."

Through low grumbles and groans, Thor and Doragon lowered their heads in respect after folding in their wings. Dormrir nodded when he got the respect he deserved and looked up at his troll guards. "Let them through—they may pass. I welcome ya tae Rhumbek. Now, follow me: I will take ye three tae meet His Majesty."

Dormrir beckoned them to follow and gave clearance for Thor and Doragon to fly towards the keep, stating that "they be allowed tae stay in the city near the caves. Yer dragons may hunt outside Rhumbek, but please mind yer manners and don't be snatchin' our cattle."

Doragon and Thor snorted but wholly agreed before sweeping themselves off the ground and making their way towards Rhumbek's keep. **We will meet you there—the city is stunning from up here.**

Azrael gestured for Rahim to follow, who had been quiet the entire time, and both he and Selena marched through as the guards resumed their watch. Dormrir led them through the sea of dwarves up the steep incline, passing by the bronze and steel buildings built along the slopes. They strolled through the breathtaking Rhumbek along the cold, red-brick pavement, staring in wonder at the intricate structures as Thor and Doragon circled overhead, ensuring their safety. Pipes were constructed along the walls, spewing hot steam, the vaporous spires wafting skyward. Signs made of bronze and wood were strewed outside the shops; the stores near the gate sold weapons and armor. The one across was a general goods merchant, and next door was the Rose and Crown Inn.

They passed by a few open stands with fresh food and fish on display when Selena heard someone cry out randomly, drawing many civilians: a priest clad in black robes, too tall to be a dwarf. "The end is nigh. Come now and repent for your sins—the Divine of Death shall have mercy over your souls if you give in to him willingly."

Azrael scowled and walked away from the scene, ignoring those gathered around the dark priest shouting angrily. Selena was appalled by their violently growing protest against the sermon—even Rahim was alarmed.

However, what disturbed her the most was that Dormrir neither stopped nor intervened but ignored them. Violence was never the answer to settling conflicting religious views, and she respected everyone, even those whose opinions differed from hers; she wanted to object but held her tongue. Selena knew she had to show His Majesty respect as they were visitors, no, ambassadors from Alfheim.

Instead, she reached out and pulled Azrael back. "Isn't there something you can do?" she whispered.

Azrael's eyebrow twitched and pulled away. "We can't intervene."

"But he's one of your priests."

It looked like Azrael wanted to strangle her. "I don't care, and hush—that's enough from you."

Selena wanted to argue further; she knew Azrael was right, but the situation was wrong. Selena looked over at Rahim, who kept himself distracted, preserving the mindset not to impede. Her stomach tightened into knots, watching in disgust as the locals drove the dark priest out of the city.

Dormrir led the group past the scene and towards the giant temple-like structure made of metal constructed into the mountainside. Once the four marched up the steps, Thor and Doragon gracefully landed beside the stunning keep, observing and marveling at the city's splendor. Dormrir paused while Selena, Rahim, and Azrael unpacked their bags and unstrapped Thor's and Doragon's harnesses. Once Selena picked up the egg chest, the two dragons grabbed their saddles before bidding the group a brief farewell.

Mind your manners to His Majesty. I don't think he'll appreciate the stubborn Crown Princess.

Yet, Thor stuck his tongue out, jesting to Azrael's previous warning, and Selena smirked.

Doragon nudged his snout against Azrael's open palm, and he and Thor followed Dormrir's instructions for the caves. When everyone was ready, the King's Hand ordered the mountain troll guards standing on post to lower their weapons as he pushed open the doors. The inside was a sight of beauty—the stained glass ceiling of various colors from the rainbow, set against the gold-streaked stone and copper walls, catching the sunlight painting the building like an oil canvas. Fur rugs draped before their feet, stretching across the floor, decorating the already lovely marble foundation.

Dormrir turned to them and noticed they were admiring the work. "This temple was built a thousand years ago," he said, "we carved it out of rock and stone before those damn elves were here—more trouble than they were worth if ya asked me. They haven't been seen in these parts since, except for the Empress. This structure has stood tall and proud through the test of time against war and destruction."

A large, metal throne covered in deer hide sat ahead with a pair of antlers perched above, seating a giant and heavily-built dwarf clad in ebony armor and a puzzled-together sable pelt. Like Dormrir's, his thick, dark red braided beard was embellished with jeweled chains. A solid gold crown set with rubies rested upon his head, magnifying his amber-pooled eyes.

King's Hand Dormrir paused and bowed before His Majesty; the trio followed his example and bent the knee as King Dionysus Goldthane stood from his throne. "It's about bloody time ye three arrived—I was beginning tae grow impatient." When the King of Rhumbek bade them permission to stand, he pointed directly at Selena.

"Vidar told me of ya and that I should pay special attention tae ya."

Selena's lips trembled when she wasn't sure how to address his near-accusatory remark; Rahim and Azrael turned to her, eyes wide, but King Dionysus grinned. "It's an honor for tae Crown Princess herself tae be here in me city. Pray don't disappoint me, Yer Imperial Highness."

Though it would have been more respectable for the king to bow before the Crown Princess first, Selena had broken tradition upon kneeling before the king and said, "Your Majesty, thank you for your hospitality. My mother and I appreciate the kindness."

Azrael and Rahim followed her example, and King Dionysus nodded. When Dormrir crossed a single fist over his chest, the king asked, "Are the guestrooms ready?"

Selena was surprised, as she thought they had to stay at the local inn; Dormrir confirmed and said, "Aye, Yer Highness."

"Yer welcome tae stay here and rest, and I pray ye three outsiders won't be causin' trouble. Dormrir will take care of the details later. Well? Off with ye."

Dormrir ordered them to follow him down the halls towards their apartments. "It's great tae meet ya, Yer Imperial Highness. Who are ye two?"

"The pleasure is ours." Azrael and Dormrir shook hands. "I'm Azrael, at your service."

Dormrir nodded, but then his eyes landed on Rahim, who kept to himself during the meeting with the dwarf king, not wishing to drive a wedge between the diplomatic exchange. "And who be he?"

Azrael and Selena swallowed hard; they couldn't validate why Rahim was their companion since he was not part of the Force, but Selena said, "this is Rahim. He joined us for my protection, as his skills exceed those from the Force.”

The beaming Rahim shook his hand as well. Dormrir stared at him and nodded, accepting the introduction. “Very good, and this way.”

The King’s Hand led the group through the great hall, where long banquet tables covered in silver dishware and lit by candles lined the keep. “The king’s high lords join His Majesty in a feast every night,” Dormrir explained, “they cannot touch the food ’til the king himself takes the first bite—it’s out of respect. Since ye three are guests here, ye will join us later for a feast held in her honor.”

“We’re honored by his generous hospitality.” Yet, Selena and Rahim exchanged glances; she was unsure why, but she could tell by the look on his face that the situation seemed unsettling.

Rahim whispered when Dormrir was out of earshot, “I feel like something bad will happen.”

“What do you mean?”

“I don’t know, but I know you feel it too.” Rahim hastened his steps to chase after Azrael and Dormrir. Selena shuddered, for she knew he was right; perhaps this overwhelming sense warned her of an uncertain fate.

The King’s Hand steered them down the hall with lit torches perched along the walls, their flickering flames illuminated against the stone. Dormrir pointed to the first available room. “This be yers, Yer Imperial Highness.” He then mentioned Azrael and Rahim to follow him to their quarters.

Her august apartment’s copper ceiling and stone walls were painted by the stained glass window illustration of the Emerald Dragon jolting out of a body of water in a thunderstorm. Selena sat upon the velvet-cushioned window seats and ran her fingers across the gem-like glass. She immediately recognized Thor's horn design mirrored Ulrich's, and she smiled when realizing that Thor was made in his image.

She immediately collapsed on her bed, her muscles melting into the crimson blankets and pillows as she drifted into a temporary stupor.

When Azrael and Rahim had settled into their rooms, Azrael asked Selena to bring Dragonheart and join him outside the city so he could attempt his dual-wielding teaching. "I brought my sword so you can use it with yours." Azrael held up his blade, dangling in his right hand.

"Is Rahim coming with us or not?"

Azrael jeered at her question. "Is he needed? He passed out as soon as we unpacked."

Selena requested to stop at the Rose and Crown Inn to find a courier; before Azrael asked her to join him, she had written a letter to Silver and General Araneus, so far detailing their trip up to current events, keeping them informed. They were welcomed by a bard, singing in front of the fire pit, with a few local drunks sitting on the ground, listening. The innkeeper watched Selena and Azrael like a hawk as he cleaned his countertop. "Ye two be outsiders, then?" he barked.

"Yes, we're soldiers from the Force," Azrael answered before Selena could, "is there a courier nearby?"

The keeper grunted and nodded to a young human boy in leather armor sitting at the bar with a drink; a gorgeous-looking brown falcon perched on his shoulder. He looked up and raised his hand to signal them over.

Selena pulled out a letter from her dress front pocket and flashed it in the courier's face, along with a gold piece for postage. Upon seeing the address, the boy grunted and nodded before grabbing the parcel and gold, gulping down the last bit of his drink, and he held the letter before the bird's face. At first, the falcon ruffled its wings but stopped and eyed the parcel fiercely. The boy didn't say a word, tied the letter to the falcon's talon, and pointed to the door; with one screech, the bird darted out at such incredible speed.

Selena was always amazed to see courier falcons at work, as they were bred to read and be more intelligent than their wild brothers. After sending the letter, the two went outside the city gates and found an enclosure nearby within the emerald forest, a location Azrael deemed perfect for training. "This should be big enough to practice." Azrael paused when Thor and Doragon flew over, the wind and trees billowing from their slow flapping wings, and landed nearby to watch and observe. The ground shook when the two dragons laid down on their bellies, their tails twitching in anticipation.

I thought you and Doragon would be resting, Selena anxiously said.

We're still resting, but we wanted to watch you and Azrael train. Thor swiveled his head around, and through a few head bobs and chirps, Doragon dipped his head in agreement.

There was a slight furrow in Azrael's brow, but he sighed when Thor and Doragon made no inclination to move. "As I said before, dual-wielding is not common. Usually, it's for those who have already mastered traditional swordsmanship because using two weapons will split your attention. To keep up with that, you'll need rigorous training and quick thinking because until you get used to it, you could be giving up leverage, acceleration, cutting, and parrying. It's not very practical unless you truly know what you're doing."

Selena nodded. "I'm sure it can be a deadly force once I master it. Wasn't it hard when you first learned how to dual-wield pistols? They're different weapons, and it wouldn't be fair for me to compare them. I could only imagine that using two guns hindered your accuracy before getting used to it."

Azrael agreed and tossed his sword by the hilt for her to catch; he created two rock training dummies that erupted from the ground by lowering and raising his hands. He stepped back to summon his Aether pistols and demonstrated his dual-wielding skill by shooting down his targets with speed and accuracy, blasting them to rubble within seconds.

Thor and Doragon chittered and clicked their nails on the rocks in approval. Azrael lowered his spirit guns and stepped forward; his targets rebuilt themselves, ready for Selena and her swords. "The first part I learned about using two weapons is preparing and introducing the other hand practices. Are you left or right-handed?"

"I'm ambidextrous, but I'm used to wielding Dragonheart in my right," Selena answered.

"Then I need you to use left-handed practices and some two-handed ones. For the two-handed techniques, I want you to do them with dominant left swings to build up the strength the same way you did with your right. You must develop a special sense of awareness centered around that both of your arms will be capable of hurting yourself and others." Selena breathed in deeply, and Azrael asked, "Nervous?"

"I'm more anxious than anything."

"I think you can handle it. You're good with the standard techniques. It will feel awkward, so don't worry about getting the force in your cuts now—focus on these basic slashes. We'll start with the first one, so get your blade ready." Selena nodded and unsheathed Dragonheart after setting aside Azrael's sword. Although she was ambidextrous, the grip felt alien in her left hand. "Now, hold your sword forward and bring it up as your hand is above your shoulder. Cut forward, and snap the blade's end forward a little. Then, immediately stop as you reach your neck's level."

Selena did as he instructed. Her arm strained a little, and she felt embarrassed by her lack of strength. However, Azrael seemed pleased with her progress. "Very good. You will want to repeat this as many times as you need to, for it will build up your strength and help you control the blade."

Throughout the next couple of hours, Selena practiced that same simple technique repeatedly. Azrael had to intervene and rest her arm on a few occasions, preventing injury and strain, but Selena insisted she was okay, wanting to push herself to do better. "I know that you said this can be very impractical, but I want this to be my technique," Selena said. "No one would expect it, and maybe I can catch my enemies off guard."

Azrael shrugged. "No argument there. Do you feel a little bit more confident?"

"Yes, and faster, too."

"Good—that's what you want. Now, let's try the next step. Take that sword in both hands." Selena did. She held a stern, steady gaze as she eagerly waited to do more. "Bring your hands and blade back so they're in front of your chest, and keep the weapon parallel to the ground. Doing this will help you get a feel for where your blade is."

She did her best to follow Azrael's instructions to the letter, but he had to correct her first. He made her swing the blade with both arms, first with her right, then left. Each time, Selena made a calm cutting motion by adding the snap at the end of the cut with her wrist, careful not to snap too hard. Once she gained control with one arm, she switched to the other until, eventually, the motions felt familiar. Thor and Doragon watched intently. The two looked like statues, taciturn and still; Selena wasn't sure if they had even moved since they landed.

Eventually, Azrael had her twist her waist and told her to move her body's weight back onto the opposite foot to help the momentum. Doing this, he explained, would also take some of the work away from her arms, simplifying her technique. "The more you do this, the more proficient you'll be at dual-wielding. Now, again."

*****

CHAPTER 14: THE DRAGON AND THE WOLF

The Hinterlands grew restless under the fading sun as two warhorses galloped through the twisted trees with a ball of blue light guiding their path—the first rider tightly held on to a leather satchel concealing the stolen paragon. Kiba had been hunting the dwarf thieves like a stealthy assassin for a week since they robbed Artio's shrine. After almost encountering the dragon rider, she ordered her unit to return home; she wouldn't risk her pack members on this mission.

When the She-Wolf reached a reasonable distance ahead of the robbers, she switched to her human form, carrying her self-made bow and a few crafted arrows dipped in Marcupo venom resting in her quiver. Giving a toothy grin, she quietly jumped up the branches of a nearby tree, using the shadows to hide her murderous intentions before drawing an arrow and holding her bow taut, aiming it at the rider holding the egg. Yet, Kiba suddenly felt a gush of wind brush against her backside. The hair on her neck and spine stood up on end when a large shadow drifted over the earth.

The two horseback riders stopped when a massive green dragon soared overhead, its thundering roar making the Mustang Mountains and Hinterlands tremble in fear. Its bat-like wings caught the evening sun like stained glass windows, glimmering against its brilliant scales like sparkling emeralds. Its crown of horns gave it a regal appearance as if it were the god of all dragons, as it was proper for Ulrich, the Divine of destruction, war, and technology.

Ulrich swooped down and belched out a torrent of green fire with tendrils of lightning striking the earth nearby; Kiba hissed and roared as she lost her footing, and the two horseriders escaped her wrath and fury. Yet, the Emerald Dragon's destruction knew no bounds, as his fire quickly blazed across the land, consuming the Hinterlands within seconds.

Kiba jumped out of her tree to avoid his emerald inferno, but now she lost the thieves as they made their hasty return to Rhumbek, not far from there. Without Artio's golden egg, she couldn't regrow the forest or stop the dragon god's cataclysm from scarring the landscape. Instead, she ran after Ulrich. Kiba readied her makeshift longbow and nocked three poisoned arrows, aiming at the rampaging Divine, but he was too quick for her; Ulrich disappeared behind the sea of trees through his thundering roars.

Kiba growled and swore under her breath before rushing after the green dragon, frustrated with how it toyed with her. *Artio will not be pleased.*

Kiba looked up at the skies and saw the outline of the Emerald Dragon flying overhead once more, its wings translucent against the twilight sky. She readied her arrows and aimed again at the dragon as he continued dancing above her. Her shots whistled upon release, but they missed as he swerved. Kiba growled and pulled out another arrow while she ran, chasing the dragon's shadow.

She fired with a deep breath and careful aiming when the timing seemed right. This time, it hit.

The Emerald Dragon cried in pain as her poisoned projectile pierced his armored hide, but he withheld further destruction to the forest as he fled; Kiba howled in agony as the blazes burned before resuming her hunt for the bandits.

Kiba traveled a few hours more until she reached the outskirts of Rhumbek; when she stumbled upon a meadow outside the dwarven city, she caught the familiar scent of the boy and his dragon named Doragon from her previous encounter, plus two more. Kiba slowly approached the clearing, staying well hidden within the bushes, but flinched upon seeing a lovely maiden accompanying the young man.

The She-Wolf sniffed and growled; the copper-kissed-skin lady smelled and looked familiar and yet, different. At first, Kiba believed she was a former member of the pack, but she knew it couldn't have been possible: the Betrayer left the Aynu to remain behind in Alfheim shortly after the elves rebelled.

Though she was tempted to jump out and attack, she withheld after noting the two dragons taking guard. The humans were armed and equipped with weapons of their own, and they were close to the city limits; these two dragon riders would destroy the entire pack.

The Emerald Dragon circled above them before fleeing towards the mountains yet again; the man, woman, and their two dragons looked up to see it roar in anguish and pain, and Kiba withdrew back into the forest.

*****

Selena had begun growing more proficient in practicing with both swords, but she and Azrael immediately spun around to see the Emerald Dragon rushing overhead, his roars echoing across the trees and mountains. Selena squinted at the distraught Divine, wondering what in Oblivion disturbed him.

Thor and Doragon rushed to all fours, growling and snarling through half-furled wings, flames boiling within their clamped maws. They circled their meadow, inspecting every tree, rock, and bush, tearing through leaf and limb with their mighty paws, but the two dragons agreed that whatever was there had fled.

As they ought—Doragon and I would have torn them to shreds.

What was it?

Thor arched his neck and sniffed the ground, and growled. **We believe it was another predator, but they're too small and weak to handle our combined strength.**

Doragon had relayed this information to Azrael, who said, "I'm not as worried about woodland creatures and other predators. If Ulrich is already here, that means —never mind. I'm getting uncomfortable. It's already evening, and I think we're done."

Satisfied and comforted by Thor that the four were once again alone, Selena sheathed both swords and handed Azrael his blade, puzzled by his concerns regarding Ulrich's return. Yet, she faintly recalled his story about Ulrich's mad god curse, and her face became pale as if she had seen a ghost.

Her head whipped up to the echoed howling bouncing between the trees, and she assumed that either wolves or the Aynu pack were nearby. Selena's skin crawled from thinking of their name. Rahim had told her rumors and stories before about the natives, and she wondered if the white wolf she saw earlier was one of the forest guardians. Besides Thor's power, the Aynu truly frightened her as they were intelligent and deadly.

Azrael shared her fear; he shivered. "Last time, Doragon and I interrupted one of their kills and scared them off. Their victim's souls torment me." Doragon chirped and chattered in agreement, and Thor snorted through tail flickers, but he relaxed and allowed his wings to draw back into his sides.

When Selena wrapped her hand around Dragonheart's hilt, her wrists and hands burned like they were on fire, sore from the constant dual-wielding practice, but she was determined to keep up the training. When Selena expressed her desire to continue in the future after Azrael asked if she still wished to learn, he muttered, "it's not that you need to practice. You're talented, but you can't give up."

Selena stopped and stared at him in shock. "You complimented me."

"Oh, blast it all. Don't twist your mind around it." Thor and Doragon grunted, and their lips twisted back as they tried grinning, amused by Azrael's now flushed expression. They extended their paws and ferried the two back over the city walls towards Castle Rhumbek.

Selena and Azrael enjoyed the evening sky as they soared above the city of copper and stone. A small ball of green light—a fairy after Selena's discovery—fluttered down the streets and lit the gas lampposts for the guards patrolling at night. The residents headed inside their homes and shops for the evening, only to prepare for the next day.

Azrael explained: "Fairies are only found in forests, as they usually like to stay away from mortals. I'm surprised that they're here in the city and working with the dwarves, no doubt—I've never seen one up close before."

"Me, neither. They're beautiful." Selena stared in appreciation and awe as the blue sprite's crystal-cut wings quivered as fast as a hummingbird's, leaving a trail of sparkling dust illuminating the darkened streets.

Doragon and Thor circled the grand temple standing proud and tall, casting large shadows blending in the evening. They landed before the marble steps, ignoring the mountain troll guards' quizzical brows when they released Selena and Azrael from their clawed cages.

Enjoy your feast, my dear. Thor dipped his head before swinging his whole body around, launching skyward, and diving into the ancient grove. When he assured Azrael was well, Doragon followed suit for the evening hunt.

Yet, Selena paused when the trees whispered, sharing secrets as they had before luring her within its twisted embrace. Wolf howls whistled in her ears; her skin crawled, and her breaths quickened, but she pulled her attention away when Azrael called her name. However, the two paused when Rahim stood at the entrance, tapping his foot and arms crossed. "There you are. We need to start getting ready for the feast."

Azrael's eyes burned when he stared at Rahim. "That's why we headed back."

"Great, but did you two see that huge green dragon earlier?"

Azrael raised a brow in confusion. "Yes, why?"

Rahim bit his bottom lip as his eyes darted between Selena and him. "That was Ulrich, wasn't it?" He swallowed hard when Azrael ruefully nodded. "I've never seen him out in the open before. You don't suppose...." His voice faded.

Selena and Azrael exchanged glances, and Azrael squinted at him. "What are you getting at?"

Selena's eyes widened when she understood Rahim's concern. "Do you think he has returned to destroy Rhumbek again?"

Azrael's expression changed. He looked up at the sky as if trying to spot the dragon. "I-I dunno. Ulrich has always been strange, but perhaps his curse has returned."

"I think we should talk to His Majesty about this. He would know." Although she tried not to show it, Selena was mortified that Ulrich would catch them in the middle of his rampage. As the three made their way down the great hall, she couldn't help but believe fate to be so unkind. *Why wouldn't Xyaxon help them?*

They passed by King Dionysus Goldthane, speaking with two hooded members of his court; one handed him a leather satchel hiding what Selena could only assume. The happy monarch wrapped his muscular arms around the prize before paying the two a hefty exchange. Satisfied, the two fled the keep with their gold while Dionysus retreated to the stairs behind the throne, caressing his unknown prize like a newborn babe.

Azrael and Rahim were confused by the transaction, but they remained tight-lipped, as they didn't wish to get involved with the king's secret affairs. Yet, when Selena persisted in speaking with His Majesty either during or after the feast, Azrael grew flustered as they had no right to interfere with Rhumbek's fate. "We're to leave first thing in the morning," he declared as they approached their apartments, "If Ulrich wants to destroy Rhumbek, let him—it's his city."

Selena's anger rose. "That doesn't give him the right to annihilate everyone."

Azrael's eyebrow twitched as he inhaled deeply. "Yes, it does. This cycle is how it's always been."

Selena saw the confusion in Rahim's eyes as he spoke in her stead. "What do you mean it's always been this way? I've never heard of this curse before until now."

Azrael pointed a shaking finger at them, but he withdrew heated remarks and inhaled deeply, now thinking more rationally. "There has always been a reason for Rhumbek's isolation. We don't have time to discuss this, but I need you two to trust me—pray don't interfere with the Divines."

Through his agitation, Azrael kept redirecting their focus to their assignment, but Selena knew she had to force Azrael to sit down and explain. Despite his warning to not meddle in such affairs, she resolved they would have to do what they could to protect Rhumbek from the Divine's wrath, whether Azrael was for or against it.

"I think I understand why the dwarves left behind their technology," Selena began, "Their civilization was destroyed and re-created many times. The dwarves here don't recall what their prior generations have built." While she worked through her reasoning, Azrael's eyes grew wider by the second, and he swore under his breath. Yet, Selena continued: "Even now, the dwarves were always hundreds of years ahead of everyone else in technological advances. Is that why Ulrich is always destroying and rebuilding their society?"

Azrael turned away from hers and Rahim's heated gazes. "There's more to it than that."

"There has to be something—"

"I already said there's nothing we can do."

Their discussion was wholly interrupted when King's Hand Dormrir marched down the hall with purpose. He bowed as he approached their company, and the three returned the gesture. "Hey there. Ye three are expected in the great hall in an hour. Wear somethin' nice: His Majesty put together a ball in yer honor."

"That is very kind of His Majesty, but a ball?" Selena asked in astonishment, "I thought it was only a feast."

"It was, 'til His Majesty changed his mind. Everyone in Rhumbek will be there. See ya soon." Dormrir bid each of them farewell and left.

Azrael scrunched his nose. "Even if the whole world ends, everyone wants to celebrate and have parties."

Selena sighed. "I don't like it any more than you do, but it seems we don't have a choice. Let's meet back here after getting ready. I want to talk to the king beforehand."

Azrael's face fumed as his rage boiled. "It won't make a difference."

Selena's fists trembled at her sides, and she declared: "We still have the right to decide our fate and future. You will help us save Rhumbek, whether you like it or not. You said you wanted to redeem yourself, and you can do that by helping us protect the innocents."

Rahim gave a thumbs up. "She's right—I stand by her."

Azrael bared his teeth and looked like he wanted to throw blows, but he kept his composure. When he calmed down, he said, "I don't understand. Why do you try so hard to change something if you know it won't make a difference?"

Selena held her head high and tightened her shoulders, not backing down. "Thinking that harshly and not taking action won't change our future. We have to embrace that power ourselves, and it begins with us."

Rahim chuckled and rubbed his forehead. "Let's see how we can stop a mad dragon god."

Looking beat and undone, Azrael hung his head in defeat. "You're both insane, but it looks like I don't have a choice. Fine, I'll talk to Doragon tonight after speaking with the king. I don't think Ulrich will be happy with our interference."

After they briefly retired to their separate rooms, Selena started preparing for the ball. Once she undressed and cleaned her body of the dirt and bacteria with controlled flames, she made her way to the bathing room, wishing to wash her hair with soap and water. Folded towels sat on the washstand underneath a large basket filled with soft soaps made from mutton fat, wood ash, and natural soda, scented with sweet flowers and herb oils. Although most lavished homes in Alfheim began using indoor plumbing, every building in Rhumbek was equipped with hot piped water, a bathtub, and a shower.

As she washed her hair, Selena kept thinking about how they would stop Ulrich from destroying the city. Her first idea was to evacuate the citizens, but she feared that wouldn't stop the dragon from hunting and killing them. If they were his devoted followers, they would return to face his rage and fury. Perhaps she, Thor, Azrael, and Doragon could overpower the Divine—no, they couldn't possibly; even with Azrael's former status and power, they couldn't hope to defeat Ulrich.

Glumly after finishing washing her hair, she went through her bag and pulled out the extravagant evening ivory gown she wore to Silver's ball. She remembered how to appropriately decorate the dress with the light pink laces, but her face immediately burned crimson when the red rose was still pinned to her neckline. Once she donned the white silk elbow-length gloves, she gingerly touched the petals, surprised by how they withstood the ravages of time.

Perhaps Silver enchanted the flower never to wilt. Thinking of him made her heart ache as she slipped on her now polished hessian boots, uncaring if the others considered her improperly dressed.

Ensuring her hair was dry, she was delighted to see it had grown long enough for her to pin it together in the back and embellish it like a proper lady ready for the evening. *My dear one, are you and Doragon busy?*

After a few moments, she heard his deep and soothing voice echo within her consciousness. **We just finished our evening hunt. Are you well?**

She briefly went over her conversation with Azrael, to which Thor confirmed he overheard. *Did you two see Ulrich earlier?* Thor didn't immediately respond. *My dear?*

Pray forgive me; I was deep in thought, but we saw him. Doragon and I sought cover, but he was fleeing from something.

That was not an answer she was expecting; she couldn't imagine what would frighten a Divine dragon. *It must have been something too terrible to describe.*

I'm not sure what that could be, as dragons have little fear. Let anyone be brave enough to come and try to strike me down.

That's not what you told me before.

Thor was not amused. **You know what I mean.** Yet, the two shared a lighthearted laugh, but Selena reaffirmed her plan to speak with King Dionysus personally, and Thor agreed. **Keep me informed, my dear.**

When Selena finished decorating her hair with pearls, she heard a knock on her door and Azrael calling from the other side, "Are you decent?"

When she opened the door, Azrael stood there dressed in his best black suit embellished with gold buckles and trimmings, matching his breeches and boots. His face was fresh from a clean shave, his jet-black hair neatly slicked and combed back. When he saw her in a more formal gown, Azrael's face turned cherry red before looking away. "Glad to see you're ready," he said quietly. "Do you want my honest opinion?"

"What is it?"

"I hate social gatherings and parties," Azrael admitted. "This is getting ridiculous. I want to leave as soon as possible."

Selena smoothed out the wrinkles from her hem. "They're not all bad. Where is Rahim?"

"He's already at the great hall. We should join him." His face still flustered and unable to meet her gaze, Azrael instinctively held out his arm for her to take and escorted her down the corridor like a civilized gentleman.

They met the royal subscription dance as it was in full swing, an enthusiastic affair, complimenting the august keep's splendor and decoration. At the end of the great hall, the musicians began their next piece, and another dance was underway as new partners got in position. The kitchen maids were busy setting the food while the keep echoed from His Majesty's steward clad in fancy garments, reading from a long list and calling out the names of the invited nobles and citizens stepping into the king's court.

King Dionysus Goldthane occupied his fur-covered metal throne, watching the dazzling merriment and twirling, graceful dance with King's Hand Dormir Stronghorn standing to his right. The two had swapped their armors for regal furs and robes, yet their faces were already flustered from the heavily spiked punch, reeking of spiced rum. Selena couldn't imagine what to say to His Majesty now that he was in a drunken stupor.

Azrael led her into the blitz of the king's company. She faced forward, trembling as her hand clutched tightly onto his arm when they approached King Dionysus and bowed. "Please, enjoy yerselves, dragon riders," Dionysus announced, spitting from nearly every word he said.

Azrael almost snarled, and he forced his answer. "You're too kind, Your Highness."

"Your Majesty," Selena began, "may I have a word in private?"

"Not now. Go, and have fun—be good." The dwarf king waved them away, and Selena and Azrael both bowed once more before taking their leave of his presence.

Selena grumbled under her breath but dismissed the king's rude behavior as she looked around to find Rahim. "Do you plan on dancing at least?"

"Probably not," Azrael muttered. "I don't know about you, but I think I will have some punch."

Selena glared at him. "Why not? Last time you didn't dance with anyone at all. Why not at least enjoy the moment?"

Azrael scowled. "I've already told you, I don't like dancing and hate parties. Besides, I don't know anyone else here."

"Oh, like no one can be introduced at a party? I don't know anyone here either, but that doesn't mean we should sit it out and not have fun." Selena grabbed Azrael's arm to bring him over, but he resented her touch.

"I don't like dancing," he repeated.

"Have you ever danced before?" He was about to object but stopped. Selena smirked. "Just one dance, and I promise I will leave you alone."

He didn't object. Instead, he moaned and reluctantly followed Selena to the dance floor and joined the other couples when the music began again; beginning the folk dance, he and the others from his line stepped up, and, together, they swirled around their partners.

Selena admired the general splendor and said, "Even though this is the second affair I've attended, I enjoy the music."

Azrael avoided eye contact, remaining focused on his footwork. They held hands and spun around before stepping back in place. Yet, Selena could sense his awkwardness as Azrael kept looking from side to side as if someone would catch him dancing. "I won't lie. I am a little nervous," he admitted.

"Because this is your first dance?" Selena asked when she passed by him, and they swayed down the line beside each other.

Azrael groaned. "I told you before how I detest it."

"Honestly, I can't fault you," Selena responded, "I assumed this is more appropriate and suitable to those who fancy one another."

"That's what makes this alarming."

His response left her feeling confused. "I'm well enough familiar with you that I couldn't shock you even if I wanted."

Azrael rolled his eyes but still averted his embarrassed gaze. "Dancing is to encourage affection, which I have no interest in—" he stopped as he looked around the dance floor. "Though you are very agreeable, I find this puts me in a rather uncomfortable situation. You had recently altered your opinions of me, though I deserved to be repulsed."

It was Selena's turn to blush from his unprovoked compliments. "If I'm not mistaken," she began, "you had wished to become acquainted since Thor and I arrived in Alfheim."

His eyes widened when she caught on to his meaning, but he didn't say another word about the subject. As the night continued, Selena noticed a slight change in Azrael's demeanor. He wasn't just going through the motions like when it began; he briefly shared the sentiment when she smiled before turning away again. "Tell me, do you always find it easy to talk to strangers?" Azrael noted. "You seem to be much more confident than when I first met you."

The two spun around each other as she worked on an answer. "Not nearly as easy as you seem to think, but it is always interesting to meet new people."

"Maybe I need to take your example and practice." When the dance ended, the musicians stopped playing, and everyone applauded the performance. Selena and Azrael bowed before she politely left the dance floor to find Rahim near the food table.

Her cheeks flushed when Thor noted her behavior. **Be careful. Otherwise, your soon-to-be husband will be jealous.**

There's no reason for Silver to be. Besides, it will do Azrael some good to enjoy the affair.

By dancing with Death? You're strange.

I may be so.

Doragon said he hadn't seen him this happy in a long time. Maybe he needed a mutual companion.

The dancing stopped, and everyone sat at the tables graced with green lace tablecloths and gold trimmings. Silver platters with food lay open across the tops.

The banquet table was laden with delicacies lying in wait. Whole roasted cows and pigs were served on their spits, coated in extravagant spices and sauces, while the cooks presented large platters of stuffed fowl with fruits and charred vegetables. Many cheese wheels and loaves of bread lay before steamy, savory soups, surrounding a perfectly cooked boar on its back on top of a silver platter, all drizzled in a special honey sauce. Decorating the edges of the plate were different herb garnishes.

King Dionysus sat at the very end of the mid-table with a goblet full of punch next to him that he drank heavily. When Selena took her seat, Rahim came with a few meat-filled biscuits stuffed away in his robes. He paused when she caught him, ignoring her smoldering stare as he sat next to her and started munching on his treats. On the other hand, Azrael sat across from them; head hung low as he displayed no interest in the upcoming feast.

Dionysus first served himself before anyone else did. He took a bite, smiled, and announced: "Eat. Get to it."

The guests did not wait for a second longer and did as their king commanded. Selena watched as Rahim eagerly cut himself some portions from the boar. She followed suit, but she wasn't famished. Food was the last thought on her mind, but she still served herself without insulting His Majesty. King Dionysus was definitely in a festive spirit. He had already gone through several bowls of punch and still wanted more before stuffing his face with the roasted game hen.

Azrael leaned in and asked, "Did you still want to talk to him?"

Selena scowled and looked back at her plate. "Of course I do. I'm not changing my mind, though perhaps I'll wait until he's sober."

*****

Determined to retrieve Artio's paragon from the greedy and thieving dwarf king, Kiba hid in the bushes just as she reached the gates of Rhumbek. She peeked through and found that the entire city was deserted.

Gritting her teeth to see mountain trolls standing guard outside, Kiba slowly climbed up a tree close to the wall. Once she reached a reasonable height, she shapeshifted into her wolf form and gracefully jumped from the branches, clearing the high gate, and landed softly behind a building. Upon checking to ensure she remained undetected, the She-Wolf emerged from the shadows and dashed towards the castle straight ahead.

The soft pitter-patter of her large paws was as gentle as the evening breeze, but she dove behind the nearby dragon statues by the citadel doors when she saw a lingering and formidable shadow approaching. One mountain troll guard walked up the castle steps, gripping its large spear as its eyes scanned the area. The armored behemoth stopped and turned its head in Kiba's direction, and she froze as the troll's yellow eyes glared into hers, but it didn't see her. The shadows hid her well.

The guard grunted into the night and marched to the entrance. Ensuring no other surprises were waiting for her by scouring the landscape, Kiba followed closely behind in absolute silence, keeping herself concealed in the dark as the two walked through the massive doors. The troll began its rounds and disappeared into an empty room; Kiba was as quiet as a giant cat hunting its prey as she darted down the corridor, ears twitching to random noises as she sniffed for the golden egg.

However, she halted just as she heard footfalls thumping in her direction. She was careful not to be caught, slipping into another empty apartment beside her as two more mountain trolls trekked down the halls, weapons held high. They stopped when passing by Kiba's hiding place; she held her breath, fur bristling down her spine, but the king's sentries continued their patrol, their enormous footsteps making the floor shake.

When they were out of sight, Kiba abandoned her hiding place and continued her pursuit until she reached a large, circular room with four different paths. Kiba sniffed around, and a smile formed on her furry lips when she decided on the corridor to her far right. *It's nearby—I can smell it.*

However, her stomach growled when Kiba smelled food, making her mouth water, but she focused on her task. She made her way to the dining hall entrance, and she nestled her snout in between the cracks of the door.

The dwarf king sat at the table, already intoxicated and full of merriment, as were the rest of his guests. Ignoring the delectable smells from the feast, Kiba allowed her nose to direct her to the passageway behind the empty throne. She had to act fast to get to the vault before being spotted, but a familiar voice from the forest held her back. She shifted her weight on her left leg and pressed her ear against the door, discovering the same young man and maiden in attendance.

The She-Wolf silently snarled, but she ignored them and inhaled deeply. She was close, anticipating what she had to do next; Kiba quickly and silently slipped through the door while everyone was distracted and traveled along the edge of the wall like a stealthy assassin. Her ivory fangs gleamed in the shadows as she smiled from the sheer thought of returning her pack's paragon. *That foul and fat old king will learn not to steal from me. I will make quick work of him once I retrieve Artio's artifact.*

However, a cloaked man—no, a dwarf by the smell, walked away from the feast. Kiba pressed herself against the shadowed wall beneath the red tapestries, but the dwarf official was oblivious; he marched to the corridor behind the throne. Kiba followed him, tiptoeing across the hall undetected until she reached past the throne. She dashed down the descending staircase and reached a deserted hallway until she found a large, metal safe built into the castle with a locked door. Two massive, heavily armored trolls stood guard.

The dwarf stood before them and fumbled through his robes until he found two keys. He inserted both into the door, and it creaked open. Treasure chests filled with gold coins and gemstones sparkled inside as thousands of gold bullions lined the walls. Strongboxes filled shelves with unfinished pieces of jewelry and even more gems glimmering like the stars in the evening sky. However, the golden egg sitting on a pedestal in the middle of the treasure trove caught Kiba's eye; her anger and wrath boiled to see her stolen idol.

As the dwarf walked inside the vault, Kiba switched to her human form and reached for her bow. Before the trolls could react, she aimed at their exposed necks and shot a poisoned arrow at both; their bodies fell heavy to the floor, shaking the castle's foundation. The startled dwarf was about to pull out a weapon, but Kiba was faster than he was, drawing another arrow and letting it fly through his chest.

*****

The formalities came to a screeching halt when the ground shook, followed by Dormrir's screams echoing across the keep from the corridor behind the empty throne. Everyone within the hall panicked and scattered for the exit. Selena, Rahim, and Azrael exchanged glances before following Dormrir's ear-shattering cries, fighting through the pell-mell crowd.

"What is the meanin' of this? No, me vault!" The red-faced King Dionysus immediately pushed and shoved his way through. The trio followed His Majesty to the vault room and caught up to a young girl wearing only a wolf mask holding a bow, standing over the fallen guards and Domrir. The masked girl stowed away her weapons and ran towards the displayed golden egg, snatching it from the pedestal. As she escaped, the dwarf king approached with heavy steps; though still drunk, he performed magic flawlessly, moving his hands and making the ground ripple like water, turning the tides into waves. The ground slammed the thief against the wall and away from his treasure.

The wolf girl dropped the golden egg, and the trinket slid across the floor as the king's troll guards marched down the stairs to the vault corridor, rushing for the girl with weapons ready. The egg danced around their massive feet, sliding in every direction as the armed behemoths trampled past, but the artifact remained unharmed.

Rahim whipped out his revolver belted to his waist and joined in on the action; Azrael summoned his Aether pistols and, with Rahim, began shooting at the girl, but she dodged with lightning speed. Selena gritted her teeth for leaving Dragonheart behind, but she got into a position to use magic. Among Azrael's and Rahim's volley of bullets, Selena reacted like a dragon and exhaled a torrent of fire that made everyone back away.

The wolf girl sidestepped their attacks, and as the trolls approached her with their spears, she waved her hands; the ground rose above the trolls' heads and crashed on them, swallowing the king's guards within its depths. Selena was amazed at the girl's ability to summon the earth with grace and ease, but she gasped upon seeing her wolf mask, realizing she was the lost child from the Hinterlands. Her ragged white hair covered up parts of her dirty face; the dragon and the wolf locked gazes for a moment, and the thief gave her an eerie smile as her yellow eyes sent chills down her spine.

"It's her," Selena gasped to Rahim, "I've seen her before."

Rahim shuddered, and he pointed out her mask. "She's one of the Aynu. They wear wolf masks, giving them the ability to transform into wolves."

The girl pulled out more arrows from her quiver and aimed them at Dionysus, but the dwarf king waved his hands above his head when she released them. The ground erupted, shielding him from the attack as the arrows bounced off the rock and landed by the king's feet.

The girl stuffed her bow away and stomped on the ground, sending a shockwave exploding in Selena's direction. Selena, out of reflex, rolled on the ground away from the attack, and when she recovered, she summoned a sword made entirely of fire with a flicker of her hand. She slashed at the air, and flaming waves blasted in the masked girl's direction, but the wolf dodged it. The girl gathered the stones from the temple structure, and upon flicking her wrists, the rock broke into tiny pieces, shooting through the air like bullets.

Selena and Dionysus worked together and created a massive rock shield protecting everyone, the projectiles breaking and crumbling through their earth barrier; the king called out again: "Where are the rest of me guards? Arrest her, kill her—I don't care, but I want her captured!"

The double doors that led out of the dining hall burst open, and a great line of more trolls ran at the young girl with their weapons at hand; the wolf summoned the earth beneath her feet, projecting her upwards to avoid the storming battalion. She landed right beside Selena, pursuing the golden egg. As the thief got closer, Selena darted in front of her. The girl hissed, "You're wasting your time with me, *dragon rider*." Selena was shocked to hear she knew and spoke their language.

Yet, the wolf ignored her as she focused all her attacks on the dwarf king; she summoned a large boulder and hurled it in His Majesty's direction. Before Dionysus could react, Selena immediately intervened by creating a barrier made of fire around him, absorbing the attack like a meteor flung into the sun, protecting the dwarf king. Selena looked over at him to ensure he wasn't injured, and His Majesty gave her a firm nod, acknowledging her deed.

When Selena withdrew her molten shield, the dwarf king extended his arms and clenched his hands. Mounds of earth erupted from underneath the thief girl and encased her feet. King Dionysus lowered his hands down, and the girl sank to the ground, trapping her from the waist down.

"Let me go," she shouted, struggling and waving her hands around to force the earth to release her, but Selena extinguished her flame sword and joined the king's efforts, the two keeping firm and steady grips. When the king's troll guards surrounded the lone wolf, the king and Selena released the girl's earth bindings, and the guards grabbed the wolf's arms before she could retaliate. The girl fought against their grasp but couldn't escape.

King Dionysus walked up to her; his face beat red with anger. "Take her away. Get her out of me sight." The dwarf king scanned her head to toe and said again: "Take that mask off her."

The girl spat at the king, "You can't remove it, you swine," but the guards still attempted; she squirmed to avoid them.

"Forget it—take her to the dungeons, now." Once his guards dragged the masked girl away, King Dionysus returned to Dormrir's corpse, whose body was already free of the arrow and covered in a white blanket, courtesy of the royal court healers. They escorted his body out of the treasure catacombs and through the now-vacant dining hall.

Selena reached for the fallen King's Hand, but Azrael gripped her shoulder and shook his head. Muttering a quick prayer for Dormrir's soul, she picked up the golden egg and held it in the light. She examined it to ensure it wasn't damaged; it was still as flawless as ever, yet the trinket felt alive, like the dragon eggs.

Rahim and Azrael joined her after putting their weapons away, and Rahim asked, nodding to the treasure, "Why was she after that?"

"I don't know, but it's lovely."

The king walked over to the group after dusting off his royal robes. "Thanks. I owe ya me life. I'll be takin' that back now." He snatched the egg from her hands and returned it to the destroyed vault. The king was surprisingly calm after getting the egg back; Selena watched him use magic to clean up his treasure scattered about from the commotion. His gleaming pile returned to its previous, neat state before King Dionysus was satisfied and shut the vault door. Yet, Selena couldn't understand why the wolf girl ignored the rest of the king's treasure, only for the golden egg. Her eyes fixated on the happy monarch, suspecting possible foul play.

CHAPTER 15: IMPRISONED

Once the prisoner had been dealt with, the dwarf king dismissed Selena's group for the evening. However, before leaving, one of the king's servants advised that His Majesty invited a proper conversation in the morning. Selena's spirits lifted; she would finally have her chance to speak with him about Ulrich's return.

Azrael warned when Selena expressed her content, "Remember, we don't have forever."

The three separated and went to their rooms for the rest of the night, though Selena couldn't ignore Thor as he poked and prodded her thoughts until she answered his burning questions. *I swear to you and Doragon, we're all well.*

I hope so because we were about to destroy the castle ourselves.

We're thrilled you didn't. I don't think His Majesty would have appreciated that.

We don't care. I serve neither god nor king.

Yet, her dreams swirled around the lone wolf as she gave in to the evening's torpor. Her visions of the girl haunted her; Selena watched as Ulrich swept through the Hinterlands, spewing his emerald lightning mixed inferno, strafing the ancient grove in one pass. His deadly conflagration engulfed the masked girl within the firestorm, spreading to the surrounding trees and consuming the forest in a torrent of fire and ash. However, what awoke her was a woman's voice gently pulling her from the nightmare, urging her to seek out the Aynu.

Thor expressed confusion about her vision when Selena jolted from the bed and rushed to her mirror, washing her face, tired from the lack of sleep. She looked at her reflection and almost panicked when she saw the wolf mask blaring from the surface. The glowing yellow eyes continued staring into her deep emeralds, but her image returned to normal when she blinked.

My dearest one, I don't believe that voice was from your dream, Thor carefully said. **I feel a presence surrounding you, but it's not like before.**

Thor was right; Selena shivered when she realized the aura, too. *Perhaps a warning that the Aynu need help—I believe it has to do with Ulrich and the golden stone in the king's vault.*

Hmm. I wonder.

Selena's heart raced when she heard a knock on her door, and Rahim asked, "Are you decent?"

She hurried to find her robes, draped them over her nightclothes, and fixed her hair before opening the door. "I am now."

Rahim trudged through when she gestured to a nearby chair with dark and heavy eyes. He stretched and yawned before sitting down, and Selena called for some morning tea and coffee. "How are you feeling?" he asked her. "I heard you scream a little while ago."

"I'm sorry you heard that. I'm afraid night terrors are quite common for me."

"I wonder how you ever get any sleep." Yet, Rahim was sighing tiredly; one of the chambermaids arrived with the requested refreshments but apologized for not having Selena's usual choice of green tea. Selena groaned, but she made do with earl grey and lemon while Rahim gulped down his coffee and cream.

"I pray that the dwarf king won't judge the Aynu girl too harshly," she whispered between sips, but Rahim nearly choked on his drink.

"You can't be serious. She's a thief who attempted to murder His Majesty."

"I'm beginning to wonder why she extended this effort to steal from the dwarf king. It doesn't make sense why she was explicitly after that egg, and she ignored attacking me." Selena paused when Rahim squinted at her. "Do you understand what I'm getting at?"

"Yes, and that is interesting, but maybe Azrael is right; we should leave Rhumbek as soon as possible before things get worse—I don't want us getting mixed up in all of this political nonsense."

Selena rubbed her chin and set her tea down, leaving Rahim bemused and dumbfounded; she regaled him of her nightmares, leaving him even more bamboozled than before. "Something's telling me we're not getting the whole story. Why would a lone wolf risk her life to steal from the dwarf king?" When Rahim couldn't give her an answer, Selena went as far as assuming that "I believe King Dionysus stole that from them."

"Now that's far-fetched, wouldn't you agree?"

"I don't believe so. Remember when we were returning to our rooms before the ball? He paid two mercenaries for that egg, and someone from the Aynu has come to reclaim what's rightfully theirs."

Thor listened intently to their conversation, and he snarled when now convinced the king was a thief and liar. **If he had stolen from me, I would eat him. You say**

the word, my dear, and Doragon and I will tear his vault apart piece by piece.

Pray let's not jump to that.

Rahim's freckled face turned pale when he realized Selena was right. He clasped his hands over his lap and hung his head in defeat. "Perhaps the forest gave you a vision when you disappeared for that whole day," he whispered.

"What do you mean?"

"I dunno. Maybe you two were supposed to meet. The Hinterlands is cursed to lure travelers to their deaths, but perhaps the ancient grove is seeking your help—yours and Thor's." Rahim gobbled down another biscuit before saying, "If you genuinely believe King Dionysus stole their valuable trinket, I think you should go and talk to her."

Rahim excused himself from her room after the two shared morning tea and coffee, and Selena dressed in her dragonscale dress, ready for whatever awaited. As soon as she ventured outside the keep for some fresh air to help awaken her senses, Thor circled overhead, his jewelry gleaming against his blood-diamond scales, casting red and purple flecks across the ground. He descended through the soft flail of wings, hovering briefly before gracefully landing upon his haunches.

Thor wrapped his long tail around his legs, keeping it out of the public's way, and gently folded his wings as he wrapped a protective arm around her, herding her close. **I know you're still thinking about her. You're terrified and curious about your visions, but I believe Rahim is right. I'm not sure who this girl is or how she's connected to you, but perhaps your destinies are somehow intertwined.**

What makes you believe that?

The vision you had of her in the Hinterlands, the events from last night, and now this. It is more than just a coincidence. Thor gnashed his fangs together. **I still believe we should make the dwarf king pay. If he had stolen from me, I would devour him like the fat pig he is.**

No, please don't, but I want to rectify the mistakes. I don't even know her, but I fear the worst.

Thor ruffled his wings. **You should do what Rahim suggested and meet her, or you will regret it forever.**

She wasn't sure what gave her the courage to march into the dungeons before meeting with His Majesty, but Selena followed her instincts. She asked for directions from the troll guards standing post outside the main doors, and they pointed to a set of steps leading underground beside the castle.

Once Selena walked through a decrepit wooden door leading to the vaulted undercroft, her skin crawled from the horrible state in which the king kept the dungeons. Cold air carried the festering smell of rotting corpses, sending chills along her spine. The dark and damp prison corridor sent her the eerie message that she from the brightened world wasn't welcome.

She passed by the cells screaming for death; skeletons sat in one corner with their bony wrists chained, blood smeared across the walls, while others hung by what was once the neck from the arched ceiling. Yet, she stomached through the horrible place until approaching the last barred chamber, graced with one window catching a tiny ray of sunlight. Her pounding heart nearly exploded as she gazed into the box cell and cringed when she heard a small and crackled voice from the corner. "Yes?" Selena swallowed hard but couldn't reply. "I know you're there—you can't fool me."

Selena's throat nearly cracked when she reached out and grabbed the bars; the wolf girl shifted in her corner, but she didn't move from the shadows. "Please, listen to me. I just want to talk to you."

"Why do you care? I'm only a savage to you, yet you want to talk. Don't make me laugh." The girl tried, but her parched throat wouldn't allow her so much as a cackle.

Selena squinted at her, trying to make out her outline in the darkness, but the wolf kept her back turned. She pulled out a pocket-sized flask filled with water she always carried in case of emergencies and offered it; the girl was reluctant to drink at first, but eventually, she moved closer to the bars and reached out, snatching it from Selena's hands. She sniffed it and gulped it down within seconds before tossing it back. "Thanks," was all the girl could muster, and Selena took her flask back. "Why did you find me?"

"I had a couple of visions of you in the Hinterlands and last night after the king captured you—I want to understand why." The girl only shrugged, but Selena carefully added, "I think I realize why you wanted the golden egg. It belonged to you and your people, didn't it?"

The girl snorted, but she peered over her shoulder, her blazing yellow eyes burning from her mask. "That stupid fat king stole that golden egg from us, and I've been tracking down the thieves for the past week. Our goddess, Artio, gave us the egg to protect and regrow the forest."

Selena shared her resentment, and she tightened her grip on the cell bars. "I saw them. He paid them a hefty sum in exchange."

The girl hissed and slammed her fists against her metal floors, and Selena saw them ripple and give way to her fury. "I don't want to destroy this damn city if I don't have to, but I will if it means getting that artifact back."

"We shouldn't resort to that. What if we helped you?"

The girl slowly turned around, peering at her through her messy long white hair. "Why would you want to help me when I tried to kill you?"

"You weren't trying to kill me," Selena clarified, "you could have attacked me at any point, but you were going after the dwarf king, and rightfully so, I might add."

Silence lingered between them for almost an eternity, but the wolf inched closer to the cell bars and sniffed the air. "You're Selena, aren't you?" the girl said lazily, "And I remember your dragon's name was Thor. I heard about you from another dragon rider I saw in the forest while I was tracking the thieves. They were talking about you, Doragon or something, and—"

"Azrael," Selena interrupted, "You've been tracking us."

"Not really—you and your friends were always near whenever I was hunting those thieves. Honestly, it would be stupid of me to pick a fight I know I would have no chance at winning."

Selena glared at her, but the Aynu wouldn't last against two Divinity Dragons and Death. "You know our names, but what's yours?" she asked.

The girl approached close, her mask's nose poking through the bars. "Kiba," she finally said.

"It's a pleasure to meet you, Kiba of the Aynu."

Yet, Kiba still didn't seem wholly convinced of Selena's true intentions. "You said you had visions of me, and I feel like I know you from somewhere; you remind me of someone I used to know." She hung her head and clicked her nails against the metal bars. "I don't even understand the forest, but sometimes it can lead to death, or it can reveal the path and destiny of others. No one can escape it."

You were right.

Thor hummed in delight. **Of course, I'm right.**

Selena sat down beside the cell, and she and Kiba spoke to great lengths about the history of the Aynu. "We lived among you before being outcasts," she explained, "But we were banished from your lands because we didn't believe in what you call the 'Divines.' We believe in the old ways, in Artio. We were forced out of our homes and out of what you now call Alfheim."

That was the first Selena had heard of this. "I thought the elves built the city after they rebelled against the dwarves."

"Kind of, but there's more to it. After the Aynu fled the Earth Kingdom, we sought refuge in what is now known as Alfheim. However, elf outsiders came, but we allowed them sanctuary. Artio blessed us with our wolf powers during our brief and peaceful union.

"We established and owned all the gold mines in the area after we took them back from the dwarves, and our city was the richest among the land, but we soon became blinded by our greed. At first, we planned to unify our races through an arranged marriage between the alpha's daughter and an outsider. They soon took advantage of our generosity, outnumbering us three to one, and eventually drove us out of our land in the name of the Divines. We've been in exile ever since.

"The alpha's daughter betrayed us and joined the interlopers with a few others. Like them, she was an elf, so it was easy to accept her. She and those who followed her lost their masks, but they still retained their powers to transform into wolves. I wouldn't have believed it if I hadn't witnessed their renouncing Artio's oath and still retaining their abilities. I wonder if they're still alive."

Selena bit her bottom lip. "Do you remember their names?"

Kiba shook her head. "She was only known as the Silver Wolf, and her betrothed was the Red Wolf. I still remember the Betrayer's scent, but not her actual name." She examined Selena a little more closely. "It's so strange—you remind me of her." Selena was left dumb, but she didn't think any of it; she reiterated her wish to help Kiba escape, and this time, Kiba agreed to the assistance.

Meanwhile, Thor listened the entire time, and he finally said, **Be sure to run this plan by Azrael and Rahim. I shared our discovery with Doragon, but he warned that Azrael wasn't too happy.**

Shortly after visiting Kiba, Selena met with Rahim and Azrael in the king's throne room. Ignoring Azrael's heated gaze, she immediately bowed before the king, doing her best to hide her scowls.

King Dionysus lifted his hands and ordered her to stand. "Thanks for yer patience, Yer Highness. I remember ye three wanted a private meetin' with me—it's the least I can do after what ya did for me last night. Now, spit it out; I don't have all mornin'."

Selena did her best not to take the king's rudeness personally, but she secretly scoffed at his blatant disrespect for not acknowledging her imperial authority. "Your Highness, on our way over here, we saw a giant green dragon circling Rhumbek. We fear that you and your city are in danger," she carefully explained, keeping her wrath in check.

Instead of showing concern, the dwarf king laughed at the news. Selena, Rahim, and Azrael exchanged glances. "Ya mean good ol' Ulrich? That means it's about time," King Dionysus explained.

"Time for what?" Rahim asked.

"Haven't ye ever heard of the stories? At the end of an era, every era, Ulrich grows mad and lays waste tae Rhumbek. After the destruction, the great Emerald Dragon grows sane and rebuilds the city. I be a survivor from the last time it happened. I watched me kingdom burn, but this—this temple has stood time and time again."

Selena realized that many she met on her travels were always much older than she initially thought. "Amazingly, dwarves can live that long," she said.

"Aye. I'm in the prime of me time: two hundred and fifty years. We dwarves are too stubborn, refusing tae kneel before Death." King Dionysus bellowed in laughter, but Azrael wasn't amused; his lips curled into a snarl.

Selena was displeased by his explanation. "That doesn't make any sense. How did the rest of the Empire not know of Rhumbek's destruction when this last happened?"

"We share in Ulrich's curse: the Empire doesn't know because of it. Everyone suddenly forgets we exist durin' his rampage, and when Ulrich rebuilds our realm, it's like nothin' had ever happened. The Divines punished us for bein' years ahead of our time." Surprisingly, there was neither hint of sadness nor remorse in the king's voice.

"You mean the technology left behind, like in the ancient dwarven ruins."

"Now that I remember. Yes, and our curse hasn't stopped us from continuin' where we left off. We recently started usin' these lights without magic and gas." The king beckoned them to follow when seeing their bewildered faces, leading Selena's group to an outside patio upstairs. High poles were covered with copper plates and glass bulbs underneath the covering, connected by copper wires.

"What are these?" Selena asked.

A huge grin spread across the king's face. "These are our first arc lamps—better than gas and oil. They last for hours, and we just got 'em up and workin'; they'll be on the streets soon. We call it electricity. Electrical generators fer our lamps are bein' built as we speak."

Azrael and Rahim looked at His Majesty in wonder, and Selena remarked, "That's amazing."

"Aye, it be a matter of time before we can finally get these contraptions goin' in every city."

Selena eyed the new inventions with bafflement, the dark realization that Armageddon may never see them. "But what about when Ulrich comes through here again? Since there are usually survivors from the destruction, I could only imagine there are secret tunnels or some escape system put in place."

"Aye, that we do, but if Ulrich catches ya, he will kill ya. But first, he must catch ya!" King Dionysus' laugh roared like thunder.

Selena felt relieved to hear that the dwarf king had a plan in place, but she noticed Azrael tapping his foot impatiently and growing fidgety. She wasn't sure if he wanted to leave right now or if he anticipated an unforeseeable deadly event, and she believed Ulrich would soon make his grand appearance. "Would there be anything we could do to help you, Your Majesty?" she asked.

"Nothin' that we can't do. Now, off with ya." Dionysus shooed them away with a wave of his hands.

The three returned to their rooms in silence, but Azrael mumbled and complained about his and Doragon's discussion while casting dirty glances in Selena's direction; yet, her determined and headstrong stare made Azrael recoil.

To say Azrael is angry is putting it lightly.

Thor grumbled when Selena packed her bag and slung it over her shoulder. **Doragon is doing his best to ease his frustration, but Azrael detests being manipulated.**

I'm not controlling him but using his assistance to save someone from a fate they don't deserve.

That sounds like a form of manipulation, my dear.

The three shuffled out of the castle with their bags and dragon eggs in hand under the mountain troll guards' watchful eye; Thor and Doragon patiently waited for them, their saddles dangling from their claws. The dragons assisted the three in harnessing properly before strapping down the eggs and their supplies and provisions. Selena polished Thor's ruby from his harness until it gleamed like his donned jewels.

Regardless of purchasing a new weapon for Rahim, Selena still had enough gold and banknotes for necessities to last for the remainder of their trip. She, Azrael, and Rahim separated briefly and returned to Thor and Doragon with food, water, and ammunition boxes—bullets to replace Rahim's practice rounds. When they finished their shopping and buckling their supplies to the harnesses, Azrael asked the two to follow him inside the Rose and Crown Inn, while Thor and Doragon agreed to wait outside Rhumbek until they decided on a plan.

The dwarf innkeeper snorted when the three approached his counter. "What can I get for ya?" The three gave him a few silver coins and ordered mead and bread before sitting next to the roaring fire, music blaring from the bard singing songs about Ulrich's return to the mortal world.

Selena slouched her shoulders as Azrael mumbled about Thor's and Doragon's current topic of discussion. "Now, they have this insane notion of taking out the dwarf king themselves. I swear either Ulrich or they will destroy this Divine forsaken city," he pointed at Selena with a shaky finger, "because you can't leave things well enough alone."

When Rahim raised a brow in confusion, Selena admitted her fault by explaining what she had learned from Kiba and her resolve to help her. "Now, Thor is ready to, and I quote, 'eat him like the fat pig he is' for stealing from the Aynu." Rahim spat out his mead and laughed, but Selena peered over her shoulder, ensuring their conversation remained safe; the Divines forbade if one of the citizens overheard her speaking ill of His Majesty, regardless of her imperial status. However, only Azrael was unamused.

Rahim took another gulp and set his bottle down beside the stone hearth. "I'm glad you finally spoke with that wolf girl, but I don't think there's anything you can do to help her."

Selena looked over at Azrael, who only shrugged before drinking. "Are you bothered whenever someone passes away?"

Shocked, he choked on his mead. "Why would you ask that?"

"Do you feel uneasy, knowing that Kiba is about to suffer and die alone? You were tormented by those killed from her pack—"

Azrael interrupted her. "You're asking questions you shouldn't be asking."

"How is it wrong for me to wonder if mortals dying disturbs you?"

Azrael sighed and explained with caution, "It's complicated, but yes. I detest feeling their last moments—it's always fear before finally accepting the end. I must bring them peace, but it's difficult."

Tight-lipped, Selena gently asked, "What about Kiba? Will she continue to suffer?"

He muttered, "I don't know."

Azrael looked away and bit his inner cheek before scowling, but his head swiveled back when Selena sneered. "That's all I needed to hear."

Thor snickered upon eavesdropping. **My dear, I would advise against manipulating Death in the future.**

He knows it's not her time yet because we're supposed to take action.

Azrael gritted his teeth. "I must learn not to answer you when you do that. You're meddling in affairs you shouldn't be involved in."

Selena ignored his warning and took a long swig of her mead before bolting towards the front door, but Azrael swore and snatched the hem of her dress, pulling her back. "What are you planning to do? You can't waltz into the dungeons and save her."

Selena sat down on the closest chair, the seat covered in an abundance of furs. "I think I will, along with reclaiming their paragon."

Both Azrael and Rahim gasped. "You're mad as a hatter."

"I assure you, I'm not mad. I will do what I have to on my own, so none of you are involved."

After making herself clear, Selena stood up and scoffed as she marched away, but Azrael grabbed her arm and glared at her before saying, "You will be wasting your time trying to get her out. You need to trust me if you want to help her." Selena squinted at him, but Azrael spun around and pointed at Rahim. "You've seen the vault: can you break into it and collect the egg?"

Rahim grunted but gave a quick nod. "Aye, I think I can manage, but you'll have to buy me some time."

Azrael released his grip when Selena was satisfied with his cooperation. "Take care, for you'll get your chance soon."

Selena crossed her arms, staring at him as if he were a fascinating creature. "How soon?"

Their heads whipped around before Azrael could answer when the city fell into an uproar; the innkeeper and his patrons suddenly rushed outside to the growing mob yelling for bloodshed: His Majesty was about to hang Kiba. Azrael gave Selena and Rahim a sly smile. "About now."

CHAPTER 16: THE MAD GOD

Azrael led Selena and Rahim through the headlong crowd gathering before the keep, screaming and shoving through to the now blocked-off undercroft. His Majesty's troll sentries took their post beside the dungeons with weapons and shields forming a wall, keeping the blood-thirsty locals away. Rahim was about to take off to the palace, but Selena pulled him back. "Please be safe in there. I don't want anything to happen to you."

"I'll be fine. I've gotten out of worse situations." Rahim laughed, but Selena was not amused.

"I'm serious. Please come back if you don't think you can do it. I don't want to see you getting hurt."

"I promise." The two hugged before Rahim broke away with a nod, his silent agreement and cue to begin his heist. As Azrael and Selena continued through the dwarven sea, Thor and Doragon circled overhead, their massive shadows blotching out the late evening sun. They briefly hovered when Selena reiterated the plan.

Why make everything so complicated? I would rather burn the city to the ground and send that foul king to Oblivion myself.

Thor snarled, his flames erupting from his serrated fangs, but Selena intervened with *No, we won't. Whatever happens to the dwarf king is on him.*

Yet, what worried her was the news of their transgressions reaching the Council; she looked to Azrael, who remained stoic, and she hoped that after Ulrich's attack, the Council wouldn't remember they were at the capital. *That also means we won't remember either.*

Precisely. If I decide to make short work of the king myself, what could they possibly do to me?

However, the city paused when a sudden roar echoed through the mountains. Rhumbek's denizens paused to listen, if not admire, the thunder signaling Ulrich's arrival, but they soon resumed their angry mass, ready to storm through the dungeons. Selena and Azrael refused to move with the others when the earth trembled, and suddenly, colossal green crystals erupted from the ground, towering over the buildings; though they signified Ulrich's oncoming destruction and cataclysm, Thor and Doragon couldn't help themselves from appreciating their sparkling and dazzling deep emerald luster.

Miraculously, the residents didn't mind the destruction threatening to render their city or the small earthquakes making way for the crystal clusters sprouting from the earth. Doragon and Thor dove with talons extended, ready to snatch the two, but Selena and Azrael pulled away; more emerald spires exploded among the rocks nearby, blasting them back and out of the dragons' reach.

Perhaps we ought to leave now while we still can.

Once Selena collected her bearings, she said, *Not without Kiba and her treasure.*

The crystal towers stopped growing, and the earth remained still; Azrael's eyes widened when he whispered, "It's the calm before the storm; he's coming. We'll have to keep moving before it's too late."

As they broke away, Selena warned, *Please protect the dragon eggs no matter what happens.*

Thor snorted before snaking his head around, looking at the chest protecting the Mythic Flight clutch. **I pray I wouldn't decide between you and the eggs, but the choice would be obvious: I would rather watch the world burn than see you die.**

Thor and Doragon reluctantly agreed to stay out of the city and flew high towards the heavens before diving into the verdant grove.

The crowd's screams dwindled when they heard the loud and steady beating of drums. Selena spun around to meet Azrael's gaze. "They're starting." Before they could make it through the mob, the two were trapped by the angry dwarves making their way towards the gallows beyond the castle, carrying torches and weapons amidst their shouting. However, they suddenly stopped when the dungeon doors slowly creaked open.

The dwarf king strolled from the undercroft while two sentry trolls followed behind, holding a chain in each thick hand, dragging Kiba up the steps, her neck and hands shackled together. Her wolf mask faced down, ignoring the townspeople encircling her, howling and screaming. Selena watched in horror how they treated her right before her execution, but Kiba growled and snarled, maintaining what little dignity she had left.

Selena whispered, "I hope you're right, Azrael," but his eyes diverted away. Ignoring his nearly grim disposition, she looked around for any signs of Rahim, but he still hadn't returned from his task. Azrael interrupted her search by grabbing her arm, and together, they followed the crowd.

The drums billowed in the distance, ordering their silence. His Majesty parted the gathering with his guards, making their way through with the growling Kiba. Azrael and Selena pushed and shoved their way to the front, and Selena locked gazes with the lone wolf for a moment before the guards kicked her until she moved.

The wind picked up, and the trees sang their haunting ballad; the crowd followed the drum beats bellowing behind the palace. A horrible sight awaited them: a massive wooden platform with a crossbeam on two thick upright poles and three dangling rope nooses. Standing beside the harrowing stage was the executioner donned in black with a mask.

King Dionysus Goldthane marched up the platform steps with his two guards and their prisoner. Selena and Azrael were pulled back and blocked from making their way to the front before the event began; the anxious townspeople held their breaths when the drummers beside the gallows stopped and held up their sticks in an 'x' shape.

"May the Emerald Dragon watch over us," the dwarf king said when all was quiet, "the prisoner can share her last words." When he finished, another dragon roar pierced the air. The crowd looked around to see where it came from but couldn't find the sound source. Selena looked at Azrael, but he only scowled before muttering what she could imagine in the demonic language. The king waved his hand and ordered, "Keep goin'."

His guards pulled hard on the chains and forced Kiba to stand over the trap door. Then, they strung the noose over her neck as she growled, "Get on with it, and don't make a mess."

The king frowned, but another ear-shattering roar made the heavens tremble, but like before, no one could distinguish from which direction it came. "Proceed. Yer offered a last prayer by our priest, as custom." King

Dionysus stepped to the side, and a priest dressed in green robes stepped up, carrying a leather book under his arms.

He knelt beside Kiba and opened his tome. "I commend ye, dear sister, to the almighty Ulrich, and consign ye to the care of Him, that, when ye shall have paid the debt by death, ye may return to thy Maker—"

"I don't believe in your gods," Kiba spat at the priest, "may Artio watch over my soul as I join her pack."

"As ya wish," the priest said, closed his book, and walked away, following the disapproving noises and shouts of "blasphemy" and "may she rot in Oblivion."

"Silence, and carry on," the king ordered, "we don't have much time tae waste. I have another feast ready."

She scowled and hissed, ready to strike him down herself with a dragon's fury; she secretly hoped Ulrich would end him. "I couldn't imagine serving a king like him—he's terrible. But where is Rahim? He should have been back by now, and I don't see him anywhere."

When Selena asked Thor, he said, **We haven't seen him leave the palace, but we'll keep looking.**

I shouldn't have sent Rahim in there by himself.

Azrael swore under his breath and pointed ahead. The color drained from Selena's face when she saw a troll guard exiting the castle holding a chain; it rounded the corner and stomped through the parting crowd, dragging Rahim in shackles in one hand while holding the Aynu's golden paragon with the other. He kept his frightened head down, his face pale as a ghost's, realizing he was about to meet the same fate as Kiba.

Selena was getting ready to run forward, but Azrael held her back. "What are you doing?" Azrael only shook his head, and Selena's eyes shimmered to see Rahim forced to walk up the wooden steps and stand underneath the second noose. The troll muttered to the dwarf king and handed him the golden egg Rahim had under his possession until he was caught.

King Goldthane hissed as he snatched it back, smoldering eyes burning like a dragon's fire. "I made the mistake of letting ya three enter me city," the dwarf king declared, and his eyes searched the crowd as if to find Selena and Azrael.

Thor snarled when he read Selena's thoughts. **My dear, say the word—Doragon and I will take care of it from here.**

Azrael growled when Doragon repeated the same statement. "Not yet."

"Let it be known that all thieves will be punished by death." The dwarf king marched over to Kiba and held up the golden egg, taunting her that she would never lay her hands on it again. "Yer people will never get this back —the power of the forest is mine." Kiba snarled and growled, her blazing yellow eyes fixated on the monarch, a wolf ready to attack her prey; the dwarf king sneered and smirked, believing he had won against her pack.

Rahim trembled as the noose went around his neck, his eyes anxiously scanning the spectators for Selena and Azrael to save him, but Azrael tightened his grip on Selena's shoulder. Thor still offered to swoop down and snatch them within his talons, but she reiterated Azrael's timed appeals, waiting for the perfect moment, whenever that was.

Upon the king's signal, the hangman walked over to the switch that would open the trap door. Selena's heart raced as she looked at Azrael with a pleading eye, but he made no attempt to return her gaze. However, when the executioner grabbed the switch, the thundering roar returned with the ferocity shaking the mountains. He immediately stopped and stepped back when the ground quaked, and emerald spires quickly erupted beside the execution platform; one spiked gem caught the hangman, piercing through his chest. As Ulrich's enormous shadow dashed overhead, Rhumbek's citizens suddenly realized the imminent danger waiting for them, and they scattered like roaches, yelling and screaming in pell-mell chaos.

Azrael muttered, "About bloody time, you useless dragon," as Ulrich circled above them, his emerald hide sparkling with such beautiful radiance in the sunlight. Thor's horns matched his—save for the bone mask— giving the Divine an unmistakable grand, royal appearance. One wing was the size of Thor and Doragon combined, each beat shaking the air and earth. His chest expanded upon unleashing another terrifying roar, summoning more colossal crystal clusters scattering and consuming the city.

He wholly unfurled his bat-like wings, the membranes catching the sunlight like the castle's stained glass windows, and perched on a cliff overlooking Rhumbek, watching the residents flee before his wrath. Azrael grabbed Selena's arm and urged her towards the gallows. "Time's up—we should go."

As he and Selena rushed up the steps to rescue the still-imprisoned Kiba and Rahim, the dwarf king joined the chaotic fray and ordered, "Get to the tunnels. Out of the city, now." However, before His Majesty could join the fleeing populace, Ulrich roared and swooped down from his perch, snatching the thieving king with his talons. The golden egg fell as the Emerald Dragon ate his catch and rolled over to their feet with nary a scratch. Selena grabbed the egg at the foot of the stairs and helped Azrael remove the shackles binding Rahim and Kiba.

"Thanks." Kiba barked when the chains slipped off; Selena pulled Rahim into a hug and frantically apologized for his unfortunate capture.

"Why didn't you help me when you saw me?" Rahim asked, his face still pale.

Azrael pointed at Ulrich as he swiveled and strafed a row of buildings in a devastating green fire and lightning, pieces of rock and stone exploding from his furious torrent. The fleeing locals making their way to the underground escape tunnels caught within his inferno disintegrated into dust and ash piles. "Because we were waiting for your deus ex machina," he scoffed.

Selena then looked at Kiba, and the two froze before offering the golden paragon. "I believe this is yours."

Kiba reached out to grab it but pulled away. "Let's wait until we get out of here first."

Unable to stay any longer, Thor dashed to their aid from the trees like lightning, but he stopped mid-flight as he confronted the Emerald Dragon. However, Doragon was nowhere to be seen, to which Azrael confirmed he remained hidden with the dragon eggs once Thor passed over the chest.

Selena was amazed to see the Divine in the flesh. In awe, she immediately bowed before Ulrich, despite that he was caught in his cursed rampage. The mad god arched his head in her direction, and his pupils turned into slits; he let out another ear-exploding cry, shattering the nearby crystal spires jutting through the stone buildings. Ulrich reared his head like a snake ready to strike and exhaled his deadly green fire mixed with lightning, blasting into the mountainside. He spun around in mid-flight, completely missing Thor and his allies, and continued with Rhumbek's destruction.

Azrael snarled as he forced Selena to her feet, careful to avoid the green flames spreading across the ground and nearby trees. Though Kiba growled, Selena reminded her to let Ulrich be for now with the promise of coming back and repairing the forest. Still exhibiting reluctance, Kiba moved back when Rahim rushed ahead, calling Thor's name and waving his hands.

With eyes still fixated on the circling Ulrich, Thor snarled as flames wafted from his maw, ready to fight Divine fire with fire, but Selena warned, *If you do, the world will go up in smoke from your cataclysm.*

Snorting, Thor backed down, for now, his pupiled-slits still fixated on Ulrich, but the Emerald Dragon flew further away as if to avoid their company altogether. Yet, as another mineral pool jutted from the ground, threatening to pierce them and Thor, Kiba slammed her fist against the growing spires before it was too late, shattering the emerald spikes like glass. When the others looked at her in amazement, Kiba smirked. "Judging how much the ground quakes, this entire city will be encased in crystal."

Selena nodded, and the earth rumbled again from Ulrich's raw power. "You're coming with us."

"How do you know that we can trust her?" Rahim asked, "She's part of the Aynu."

Kiba's yellow eyes flickered, and she laughed. "I'm the alpha female—the *She-Wolf.*"

Their eyes widened upon learning of her feared role, but they hunkered down as Ulrich flew over them with another roar, circling again towards the city. The mad god unleashed a blast of arcane energy at the castle, destroying what King Dionysus Goldthane claimed to be indestructible.

Ignoring their surprised glances, Kiba ushered the group to follow her. "You helped me, and now I will help you and your friends. Let's find shelter in the mountains for now until that dragon leaves." She shuddered when Thor landed and offered to carry them away; to their dismay, Ulrich strafed another row closer to the caves, his flames spreading further out.

When Kiba's plan was now unachievable, Azrael waved them over to Thor's opened paw. "The mountains are out of the question." He and Rahim boarded the clawed carriage, but Selena and Thor were oblivious when Ulrich made another close pass; his massive wings sliced through the nearby building like scissors to paper, sending a pile of rocks that would soon topple her. Kiba, however, was quick to respond; she stomped with her right foot, and a slab of earth erupted from the ground at a slant, extending and covering Selena in a protective barrier. The falling rock hit and slid off the slab.

Breathless and shaken, Selena nodded. "Thank you."

Kiba gave a firm, jerky nod, but she still backed away when Selena mentioned for her to join. "I'm not one for flying, nor do I trust dragons," she said decidedly.

Yet, the ground quivered once again when the thundering Ulrich swiveled and belched another conflagration. As his flames drew close, Kiba had no choice but to accept Selena's outstretched hand and jump on Thor's paw; Thor unfurled his wings like a lady's fan and launched himself away from the smoldering wreckage and wall of flames sweeping in their direction.

Kiba tightly grasped his claw while crouching down as Thor soared over Ulrich's devastation; they reached Doragon's ensconced golden coils within the meadow where Selena and Azrael had practiced dual-wielding, as it was safe enough away from the Divine's devastation. He perked up when Thor made his descent, the Mythic Flight egg chest wrapped in his protective tail, wisps of smoke trailing from his nostrils. Doragon's slitted eyes fixated on the wailing Kiba, even as Thor released his passengers. The earth rumbled when Azrael reunited with Doragon, his mumbles matching his dragon's low pitches and growls as he drew the trunk closer to his body.

Kiba was ecstatic about returning to solid ground, but Rahim ignored her glee; he marched over to Azrael with a raised finger, exclaiming how "terrifying it was, thinking you're about to die."

Selena glared at him intensely as she climbed up Thor's foreleg and packed the golden egg in her bag with Kiba's permission. "I know what that's like."

Rahim shamefully looked away but said to Azrael, "You owe me an explanation since you seemed so blooming calm during our execution: if I wasn't going to die by hanging, when and how will it happen?"

Azrael rubbed his temples. "I already told you I'm not allowed to tell."

"True, but you've always given us hints. Can you give me one?"

Maintaining a stoic expression, Azrael shaped his hand like a pistol, his index finger ready to shoot at Rahim's chest, whose face suddenly turned pale; Azrael drew back his thumb and shouted, his voice carrying across the trees and making the birds scatter: "BANG!"

Everyone flinched, and Rahim immediately cowered down. Yet he looked at his hands, inspected his body, and sighed in relief that he was still alive. Azrael lowered his hand and smirked. "Don't take me seriously."

"That's not funny."

Azrael shrugged and stuffed his hands into his trouser pockets. "It was for me."

It grew uncomfortably silent, and Thor and Doragon snaked their heads upwards, confirming that Ulrich had flown away, not without one final roar. However, Selena was at a crossroads on how to proceed, as she knew Azrael and Rahim would be set against bringing Kiba back to her people. As she expected, Azrael spoke against her idea, "Absolutely not—the Ankoku Pass is in the opposite direction. We must reach Snowhaven by the end of Goldfire and meet with Justiciar Holland."

"But we owe it to Kiba—we will help her return home," Selena argued.

The She-Wolf was displeased by Selena's lack of assertiveness; Azrael scoffed when the alpha approached him with fists to her sides, her nose nearly touching his chin. "I demand you interlopers take me home now."

"You demand—"

"Yes, and you will do what I say exactly, or—"

Azrael squinted at her. "Your threats mean very little to me, wolf," but he recoiled when Selena snapped at him instead; she wondered if, like Silver, he genuinely feared her though it was hard to imagine what could frighten Death.

Rahim, however, shuddered. "How do you suppose the Aynu would allow us, outsiders, to wander through their home unannounced? I don't wish to be hunted by wolves."

Kiba tore her gaze away from Azrael, who had turned away, and scoffed. "When my pack sees you traveling with me, they'll back off unless I give the order." Her smoldering, yellow eyes burned behind Azrael's head, but he maintained his indifferent disposition to her hostilities. Kiba then pointed at Selena to address her directly. "I like you—you've kept your promise to help rescue me and recover our stolen artifact, and now, I swear my loyalty to you."

Selena rubbed Thor's neck before meeting his squinting eye. *What do you and Doragon think about helping Kiba?*

I'm for what you decide, my dear, though you may need to work on convincing Azrael otherwise. He's been in the foulest of moods, according to Doragon.

He's been particularly anxious about our deadline. I don't suppose the dragon eggs would hatch so soon, would they?

They still have some brooding to do, but their time in the shell is running short.

Azrael snarled but finally agreed when Selena and Doragon used cooperative arguments supporting their cause in helping Kiba. "Besides," she added, "the pass is only a few days from here. Doragon and Thor are fast fliers, willing to make this trip. Why are you anxious about Snowhaven?"

Azrael ignored her as he pinched the bridge of his nose, but Doragon assisted him in the saddle as he refused to answer her. "Once we bring Kiba and their treasure back, we will leave immediately. We won't waste any more time."

Before Thor could pluck Rahim and the resistant Kiba from the ground, Doragon had already taken flight towards the Ankoku Pass, soaring straight into the swirling grey clouds.

CHAPTER 17: ARTIO'S BLESSING

Though Ulrich had finished his rampage over Rhumbek, Thor and Doragon maintained a quick but steady pace, flying nonstop for the following few days. As they could choose to go for long periods without food, they were still satiated from their last hunts. However, when the two dragons expressed their extreme thirst, Azrael began instructing Selena how to manipulate water, but, much to his surprise, she had already started her elemental summons. They used magic to quench their dry throats by drawing water from the air and clouds, holding giant orbs that Thor and Doragon swallowed in one gulp.

Azrael mumbled, but he smirked. "I forget I'm teaching a Divinity Dragon."

Selena offered Thor and Doragon more of Silver's stamina elixir, but they declined. **Thank you, but save the rest in case we need it in the future; we are doing well for now.**

Kiba's apprehension slowly eased as time wore on, but she still clutched to Thor's harness handles, not trusting the buckles and carabiners to keep her safe. When Selena asked her about it, Kiba muttered her preferences for solid ground and "I don't understand how you fly all the time."

Rahim had been pale and quiet since they fled Rhumbek, and Selena assumed he was still bothered by his near-death experience. Though Azrael had assured him he was in no imminent danger, Rahim remained agitated and anxious throughout their trip, and Selena grew concerned with his mental health.

The group may have already put a great distance between them and Rhumbek, but they could still see the emerald spires leftover from Ulrich's curse, lancing through the city of stone and copper; Selena wondered how they could still remember, including Kiba. When she asked Azrael about it, he didn't have an answer. "Perhaps we frightened Ulrich because he wasn't expecting us to be there, but I dunno. If you happen to see him again, you should ask."

Rahim shuddered. "Oh buggery, I pray we won't have to see that mad god again."

"Fate is a fickle friend," Azrael said, "and Ulrich isn't all bad when he's sane." He peered over his shoulder and nodded towards the Aurora Peaks. "He lives in Heaven's Tear in seclusion if you ever wish to pay him a visit."

Rahim groaned and leaned against the saddle with his hands propped on his head. "To Oblivion with that," and Kiba growled in agreement.

Selena held her chin; her eyes fixed on the mountain peak. "That doesn't explain his reaction when I bowed in respect."

She looked to Azrael, whose expression turned blank upon thinking of the anomaly, but he said, "As Divinity Dragons, you and Thor are gods among mortals. I think Ulrich realized who you were, even in his madness." Though Selena would rather not compare herself to the Divines, Thor was pleased with Azrael's recognition.

Kiba dismissed their notions about the Divines and scowled at Ulrich, vowing, "I will come back and bring him down for what he's done to our forest."

Selena warned: "Regardless of your beliefs, I ought to remind you of Ulrich's might and power—you'll get yourself killed."

Kiba snorted. "I'll join the great hunt with Artio when my time comes."

As they flew closer to the pass, Kiba went to great lengths to describe their home and how it rivaled cities like Alfheim and Rhumbek. "We made our dwelling in the rock behind the water—wait until you see it."

As the third evening settled upon them, Selena searched through her pack and pulled out a blanket, offering it to Kiba. "You must be freezing; I don't understand how you can't be when you're not wearing anything."

"I have my fur." Kiba changed into her magnificent white wolf form and curled in a ball, falling into sleep's deep torpor. Selena still draped the blanket over her despite her objections, and Kiba snuggled underneath the wool. Satisfied, Selena moved over and leaned against Thor's neck; though Armageddon's arctic winds were nearly unforgiving, she was wholly warm because of her dragonscale dress.

Thor groaned as he swiveled to look at the egg chest still strapped to Doragon's harness. **I pray we'll finish our side trip soon, my dear: the hatchlings are growing anxious. Earlier, the fire guardian said it wanted to come out soon.**

What do you mean?

When we're still in the shell, we're fully conscious and aware of our surroundings. That's how we learn about the world and language, and we can still communicate with unborn hatchlings.

I never knew that—dragons are fascinating.

Thor glowed from her compliment. **Doragon and I can ask them to wait until later.**

Amazed by Thor's words, Selena reiterated the news to Rahim and Azrael, leaving them stunned. "Let's hope they will listen," Azrael sighed.

"Dragons are still such a mystery," Rahim said.

We can only try, but hatchlings are antsy, and they may or may not listen—younglings never do. Thor chuckled.

The flight turned peaceful under the clear evening sky. Kiba and Azrael had already fallen asleep, but Rahim stirred as he stared over the horizon through a spyglass, looking for the Ankoku Pass. He flinched when Selena scooted closer and nudged his shoulder. "I know you went through something traumatic back in the city. How are you feeling now?"

Rahim bit down on his thumbnail and shrugged. "I'm fine. Why?"

Selena looked up at the stars and drew her knees to her chest. "I've been worried about you since leaving Rhumbek. I'm sorry to have sent you in there alone; I should have gone with you and helped."

Rahim closed his glass and dismissed her apology. "I agreed, but being in that noose was terrifying. That bloke would have suggested differently, but—oh, blast it, it's hard to explain, but my life did flash before my eyes."

"I never want to put you through that situation again." Selena reached out and embraced him. "I would rather see myself in that noose than see you or anyone else there."

"I swear, you shouldn't be so harsh on yourself," Rahim pulled away, "though I appreciate the sentiment."

Selena grinned. "That means we will need to work harder and save Niamh."

"Aye. We won't return to Alfheim without her." Rahim wrapped himself in a blanket and fell asleep near his pack, and Selena was content to have made amends for Rahim's ill behavior.

Thor snaked his head around and declared that, when he and Doragon asked, the hatchlings stated they would wait for as long as possible. **It's very dull inside the shell. You're just surrounded by darkness all the time with nothing to do but listen and wait.**

Thank you, my dear.

Of course.

As much as Selena wanted to sleep, she couldn't. Instead, she watched the beautiful northern lights swirl through different marvelous colors. They varied each evening, but tonight, she watched the Divines paint the aurora shades of green and blue. Weak at first, the entire sky burned like the blazing sun. She always wondered what awaited beyond the earth's horizon, but she believed the sky continued forever.

Azrael was the first to spot the pass through his spyglass as the sun began to rise; Doragon growled and picked up the pace, though his wing muscles burned from flying nonstop for four days. Thor exhibited similar weariness, straining as much as his body would allow.

Once Selena, Rahim, and Kiba were alert and ready to meet with the Aynu, Thor and Doragon dove through the clearing close to the mountains. The world quickly transformed, and the group soon entered a winter tundra where the landscape donned a snow coat. A whirring waterfall echoed through the trees; Kiba gripped the saddle's handles until her knuckles turned white, anxious and excited to return home with the stolen paragon.

When the two dragons couldn't fly through the thickened trees, they landed, their massive wings bending the canopy and branches. Kiba jumped off the saddle before Thor could assist her, announcing that "my pack is on their way here to investigate—I want them to see me first."

True to Kiba's warning, the group was surrounded by wolf howls; soon, different colored masks matching the She-Wolf's glimmered through the verdant lush. Slowly, they emerged—as humans and elves—with spears, swords, and bows ready.

Thor and Doragon bared their fangs with flames wafting from their clamped maws and wrapped protective arms around Selena, Rahim, and Azrael, but Kiba stepped forth with her hands held high upon declaring her return. Her wolves immediately dropped their weapons to the ground and ran over to welcome her back.

Selena and her friends watched intently and observed their behavior. Kiba's pack members transformed into their wolf forms and sniffed her; once confirmed she was their She-Wolf, they yipped and howled in their joyful reunion. However, they immediately stopped and backed away when an adolescent boy with a black wolf mask stepped forth. He ran over and held Kiba tightly as the two nuzzled each other.

Assuming he must be her mate, Kiba introduced them to Maru as he eyed them suspiciously. However, once his mate confirmed her alliance with the outsiders,

Maru snarled but gave them a firm nod. "You're welcome among us, outsiders. Join us, and later, we will celebrate our She-Wolf's return."

Kiba said, "Tonight, you will bear the marking of our pack."

"What does that mean?" Selena asked.

"It means you will be one of us, outsider," Maru explained, "the forest will always be your home, and Artio's blessing will follow you wherever your travels may take you."

Rahim crossed his arms over his chest and gave a huge grin. "That's pretty wicked."

Selena smiled and bowed before digging out the golden egg from her pack. "I believe this belongs to you."

"Since you rightfully returned it, you will have the honor of putting it back in Artio's shrine," Maru stated. "She will be most pleased with your efforts." Selena nodded and put it away for later.

Kiba gestured for them to follow her and Maru to their cliff dwellings. "Please, rest easy. Your dragons are free to hunt, so long as they pay their respects to their prey by offering a small prayer to Artio beforehand. Remember: nothing should be wasted from a kill."

"Of course, that is most gracious." Selena bowed once more.

After Thor and Doragon made themselves comfortable and went to sleep from complete exhaustion, Selena and her friends followed Kiba and her pack directly to the waterfall.

The Ankoku Pass was a breathtaking sight to behold. The Aynu built the rock house structures beneath the overhanging cliffs stretching across the base of the mountains. A white blanket draped their hollow valley, with dirt paths like molten gold circling towards the middle. A smooth-edged figurine of a woman wearing a wolf headdress lay beside a black stone slab with cupped hands, perfectly shaped to hold the artifact. Explaining how this was Artio's shrine, Kiba added, "You will place it here."

As the two alphas were well within sight, more pack members came out in the open to investigate the newcomers. Humans and elves living together with wolf masks, Selena was amazed by how many were part of the group; Kiba explained there were more than fifty.

Rahim watched with enthusiasm as some women brought food from their vault in preparation for tonight's celebration. "I'm so hungry."

Selena gave him a smoldering stare. "Rahim, we are the first outsiders ever to step foot here, and all you can think about is food."

"Hey, it's hard for me to enjoy anything on an empty stomach."

"We will eat soon. Our pack prospers from Artio's plentiful bounty," Kiba stated, "We always ensure we have plenty of food stored away to get us through hard times. We use ice blocks from the sea and snow to preserve our supplies."

Throughout the day, Selena observed the Aynu lifestyle from the side; Kiba mentioned that some dens near their food vault were reserved for new mothers. Selena watched a few lower-ranking members go in and out, but they were only permitted entry as long as they carried food. Meanwhile, Azrael and Rahim walked around with Maru, learning of his role as the alpha male; however, he kept his answers short, as Kiba was in charge.

Kiba explained, "Since the mothers cannot leave the den, other pack members will bring food when the pups are born."

"When you say pups, do you mean they are babies born with the wolf mask?" Selena asked.

"Yes, but we are wolves at heart." Kiba thumped her fist against her chest. Selena noticed how social and family-orientated they were; she learned there was order and some ranking within the pack, and the alpha male and female were like parents: nobody won the role of the leader. "Most of my pups have grown and moved on to form other packs elsewhere. Some may still be well within the Hinterlands, while others have moved far south. Unfortunately, we've had fights with other full-blooded wolves over the years. We can communicate with them just as well as I can with you, but it always ends in blood and violence." Kiba lowered her head. "A few weeks ago, we lost one of our members during a hunt—an omega. We still mourn for her."

Selena felt the tug of her heartstrings. "I am sorry for your loss."

"It's all right, but it hasn't been the same. We value every single wolf, no matter their role."

"I hope it's not rude of me to ask, but can the masks ever be taken off? Do you have a face underneath?"

Kiba leaned back against the rock and looked up at the sky. "It's a blessing given to us by Artio," she began explaining, "When we prayed to her for the strength to survive in her lands after the rebellion, she gave us the masks, and no, we can never remove them unless you renounce your oath to Artio. This mask is *my* face, and to us, it's a blessing. We've been stronger because of it."

Selena's eyes widened in wonder. "Will we be given masks too?"

Kiba looked at her. "No, not unless you want them."

"I see. I think, for now, I'll stay the way I am if that's all right." Selena was careful with her words so as not to offend the She-Wolf.

Kiba nodded. "I wouldn't expect you and your friends to join us that way," she squinted at her, "Is it true you're a dragon?"

"It's complicated to explain, but yes."

"Interesting. Regardless, you will always be welcome here."

"Thank you, but what did you mean by bearing the mark of your pack?"

"It will be a small totem symbolizing our pact," Kiba explained. "After we offer a prayer to Artio, you and your friends will each be presented with a specially carved figurine."

"I promise we will carry them always," Selena swore.

Kiba narrowed her eyes. "You better because you'll be fair game to us without them." When she saw the look on Selena's face, Kiba laughed. "Don't take me too seriously; we'd still be able to recognize you by scent alone. The entire pack will be at the ceremony, and everyone will be used to your smells by the time it's over."

Kiba began asking why they traveled through the Hinterlands and how they ended up in Rhumbek. Selena went to great lengths and told their story, from the attack on Alfheim to now. The She-Wolf didn't interrupt and saved her opinions for later.

Selena sighed heavily. "We hope to deliver those dragon eggs to Snowhaven. The Mythic Flight guardians can help us defeat the Lich before the Day of Eternal Darkness."

"Is that when the sun turns black?" Kiba asked, and Selena nodded. "I've only heard stories. Fables of the sun turning black are always interwoven with tales of doom." She then eyeballed Selena up and down, examining her with bewilderment. "Though, I don't understand why you need more dragons. You're strong enough with how well you can use magic—I've never seen anyone who can use earth as well as we can."

Selena hung her head in shame. "I don't believe I'm good or strong enough to face the necromancer."

"See, that's part of your problem right there," Kiba pointed out, "you're so unsure about everything. You're losing focus and drive when you need to face this war head-on. You have to be stubborn and stable with no hesitation." She stood up and dusted off her arms and legs. "I've decided: I will try to do what I can to help you, but it's up to you to go the rest of the way—you can't back down. I need you to promise me that you will see it through."

She nodded and held out her hand to Kiba. "I promise."

"Good. I'll hold you to it." Kiba stared at her in confusion. "But what are you doing?"

"This?" Selena looked down at her hand. "A handshake. It's what we do when we meet someone, or if we agree to do something."

"What's a handshake?"

"I'll show you." Selena reached out and grabbed Kiba's hand to demonstrate the gesture. At first, Kiba was curious but became excited and bounced in her spot as she returned the shake with vigor.

Once the two finalized their pact, Thor had awoken and declared that he wanted to go swimming before the celebrations. **Please, find me by the sea—I want to relax by the water.**

I will be there shortly.

Selena bowed to Kiba and excused herself; the alpha announced as she rushed off: "Come back after dark. Don't be late for the ceremony."

Selena approached the unending teal sea; its surface was clear as glass and lined with pine trees. Heaven's light gave it a golden glow, marking it a place of eldritch beauty.

Thor was already waiting for her by the water's edge, taking huge gulps before meeting her gaze, his crimson gleam reflecting the late afternoon sun's rays. His scales exhibited the same luster as the rubies shining from his gold chain, contrasting the clear diamonds casting rainbow streaks across the ground.

Judging from your mood, I'd say the Aynu are treating you and your friends well.

Yes, they have. The ceremony begins at sunset.

Fine. Thor knelt before her. **Come with me.**

She clambered up his foreleg, and once she was comfortable in the harness, Thor stepped into the sea. He floated like a sailboat, using his wings like oars to row them further out. Selena leaned back against the edge of the saddle and admired the glorious luster of the water, the air laden with pine-sweet smells; the world was quiet there.

I can stay out here forever, though I wish Silver were here.

Hmph.

Selena sat up, expecting a better answer. *Are you feeling all right? What's wrong?*

Nothing. This moment of respite was supposed to be only for you and me.

Please, forgive me.

Don't fret.

She knew he wanted to say more; his short answers made her feel awkward, so Selena steered the conversation. *Aren't you cold?*

Thor perked up. **No, I'm quite warm. Wouldn't it be nice to go diving?**

Selena grabbed the edge of the saddle. She looked over, and her skin crawled with goosebumps. *You're off your rocker; the water must be freezing.*

Thor chuckled. **For a little while? You look sleepy, and besides, your dress should keep you warm.** Suddenly, his thoughts turned sour when he was reminded of Silver again, and Thor turned away.

My dear one—

It's fine. Thor paused before swiveling his head back. **Besides, you keep yourself as warm as I can. Be like a dragon.**

Selena crossed her legs and held her hands together as she breathed in deep. After the first few breaths, smoke emitted from her nostrils; though she had used this trick before, Thor never missed the opportunity to observe her tiny flames. Selena opened her eyes and noticed the embers erupting with each breath. She felt like she was wrapped in several blankets roasting by a fire.

The lining that defined Thor's mouth twisted unusually. It took Selena a while to recognize that he was laughing at her. **Let's go.**

He tucked in his wings and, ignoring Selena's protests, began submerging. She tightened her grip around his reins, but before she knew it, they were both underwater.

The frigid azure sea was a beautiful but different world; various colored fish swam underneath through hidden treasured reefs. She released the reins and floated for an eternity, watching her air bubbles reach the surface as Thor drifted away. Selena thought he looked like a giant sea serpent slithering through tranquil turquoise. On the other hand, Thor dove deeper, chasing the undersea life and devouring them by the mouthful.

As the desperation to catch her breath crept upon her, Selena noted her air bubbles, giving her the idea to enclose her face within a sustainable, breathable globule upon exhaling. Her mouth and nose were graced with fresh air, and her chest relaxed as she swam to join Thor's delightful and serene dance. However, when Selena returned to the surface, she was surprised by how long they had spent underwater, as the sun would soon set.

My dear, we ought to make our return—they'll be sure to begin soon.

Do we have to? I'm having so much fun.

We have a ceremony to attend, and I can't willingly transform into a dragon and fly myself back.

Very well. Thor's words were slow, displaying reluctance, but Selena was delighted to see him resurface; he paddled over and assisted her into the harness. **Did you enjoy our time together, at least?**

That was incredible, but I still don't understand why you were quiet earlier.

I don't know what you mean.

When I wished Silver was here. What's wrong?

Instead of coasting across the water, Thor took to the skies and sailed through the trees upon their return. **I already said before. This moment was supposed to be our time together.**

Are you getting jealous?

No.

Stop lying to me.

Maybe a little.

When they returned, the pack had already begun putting together the ceremony, with Doragon's assistance gathering wood for the bonfire. Meanwhile, Azrael and Rahim helped set up their banquet with the rest of the pack; as soon as Thor and Selena arrived, they aided in the remaining preparations per Kiba's and Maru's instructions.

Rahim huffed and wiped the sweat from his brow. "Good timing as I can't wait to start this thing—I'm starving. I know they said to wait, but I think my stomach is starting to eat itself."

"You're useless," Azrael barked at him, but he sighed. "I want to leave as soon as this thing is over."

Selena nodded. "I swear we will, but I'm glad we helped Kiba and her pack." Azrael didn't seem entirely convinced, gruffing and moaning while muttering complaints. Rahim didn't help when reminding them he still wished to see his mother in Nuvak, and Azrael turned around and punched a tree but didn't say anything; Selena said, "Take care, we will still make it to Snowhaven."

"How, when I don't want to endanger our position? I…." Azrael's voice suddenly trailed off, and his face turned pale. "I fear if we're not quick about completing this assignment, we may risk everything we're fighting to protect." His eyes pierced through her emeralds, but he suddenly turned away; Azrael banged the tree again and placed his forehead against its bark.

Selena slowly walked over and put a hand on his shoulder; he didn't try shoving her away. "I swear we'll make it through."

When the Aynu finished, Kiba asked for Thor and Doragon to stand opposite beside the bonfire while Selena, Rahim, and Azrael followed Maru. She pointed at Selena and said, "Bring the egg and set it within Artio's hands. Afterwards, we will present your totems, and the feast will begin."

"Finally," Rahim moaned, but Selena elbowed him; she climbed up to Thor's harness and pulled out her bag hiding their paragon; when she rejoined Kiba and nodded at Thor, he and Doragon chirped at each other and took their designated places. Maru stood before the shrine, holding a stone bowl with red paint with a drummer to his left and right; the rest of the pack stood in a large circle surrounding the fire and statue. Once Selena unwrapped their artifact from the leather satchel, the drummers began chanting, and Kiba led the trio to the ring in a single line: the She-Wolf first, Selena second, Rahim third, and Azrael last.

Maru stepped forward as the four advanced. "Who approaches this sacred place?"

Kiba held her head high. "I bring you those who wish to join this pack and honor our goddess."

"Goddess Artio has deemed you five worthy. Please enter our sacred circle, and kneel before the shrine," Maru commanded; the trio knelt before the shrine once Thor and Doragon bowed. "Please state your names."

"Selena."

"Rahim."

It took Azrael a few seconds, but he said, "Azrael." Thor and Doragon chirped and clicked, mimicking vocal speech to state theirs.

"By joining this pack, you will become part of our family, our endless kinship, loyalty, and hospitality. Ancestors, please watch over us and guide our newest family members kneeling here before you. May Artio guide you on your travels. Are you willing to uphold the values of our pack?"

"Yes." Selena, Rahim, and Azrael spoke together.

"Do you swear your unwavering and undying loyalty to Artio and us to protect and preserve this land?"

"Yes."

"Are you prepared to be reborn and join your new family as a child of Artio?"

"Yes."

"Then rise and be welcomed into Her light and love." As the three stood up, Maru approached with his bowl. He dipped his thumb into the red paint and drew two lines on their foreheads, including Thor's and Doragon's.

He finished, and Kiba presented them each with personalized stone-carved figurines the size of Selena's thumb. Thor and Doragon received dragon-shaped totems strewed together with leather; Kiba tied Thor's to his golden ruby chain and Doragon's to his index talon like a ring.

Azrael was given a raven; as Kiba draped it around his neck, he inspected it but set it down against his shirt, scoffing at the implied absurdity. Rahim received a fox for his cunning and intelligence, and, to Selena's surprise, she was presented with a wolf. "We made this for you because of your intense loyalty and desire to protect and value everyone," Kiba explained, "from my short time with you, though you're a dragon, you have the heart of the wolf. Please, step forth and present your offering. May you gain Artio's favor."

Selena walked forward with the golden egg, and the drummers stopped chanting and held their sticks up. It grew eerily quiet as she set the artifact back in the statue's hands. Suddenly, time froze, and her world had ceased spinning. A ball of light appeared above the shrine, and a woman's voice as beautiful as the twinkling stars echoed through Selena's timeless prison. "Ah, yes. I was wondering when we would speak, Selena Liongod."

"Who are you?" Selena asked.

"I am the goddess of the wild; We meet again."

"I've never met you before."

Artio continued: "Don't you remember? We have met before. When you first stepped through my forest, you entered my domain. When you prayed for safe passage, I heard your pleas. I've been watching you, mortal, and now, you serve me by bringing back my gift to the Aynu. Now, the dwarf king Goldthane swims in the void, and his soul will endure eternal suffering for angering me—it is fitting. You have proven yourself to me. You and your friends are now one with the Aynu. Go now with my blessing, and I'm sure we will meet again."

The light vanished, and time resumed forward, leaving Selena dumb amidst the victorious howls upon seeing the artifact's return.

CHAPTER 18: UNMOVABLE AND UNSTOPPABLE

The celebration was in full swing as the Aynu were resplendent with dance, food, and merriment. Rahim eyed the meat roasting in their spits over the bonfire, but he had to wait until the two alphas gave the word; Kiba and Maru took their share first, then the new pack members. Rahim graciously and ravenously accepted his food, but Selena and Azrael weren't as enthusiastic.

Thor and Doragon, meanwhile, had already returned from their evening hunt with freshly caught wild boar, but Thor asked if the Aynu could cook his. **I pray neither to be impertinent nor a snob, but I enjoyed how Silver's chefs prepared the meat during the ball.**

Not at all, my dear. You deserve the best, even if that means preparing your meals however you see fit, though that may prove difficult with our journey.

Doragon remained indifferent as he gobbled his catch without a second thought, watching the show as the other wolves howled and danced around the fire. They ate, laughed, and told stories for the remainder of the evening.

Selena twirled her wolf totem between her fingers before returning it to her neck and sought out Azrael; he had just sat beside Doragon with his untouched bowl of food as she approached. "Please forgive me for seeming too forward, but did you know Artio was real?"

"Yes."

Selena wasn't expecting his freely given answer. "Pardon me? I've never heard of her before now. I hope not to sound intolerant, but—"

Azrael rubbed his hands together over his knees. "It's not my place to say which gods are real or fake, as that defies what religion is about and the purpose of believing. Artio exists like the Divines, and she's important to this forest. Did you speak with her?"

"Yes, when I returned the artifact."

"I see. If you must know, Artio is my sister."

"Sister?" Selena took a step back. "I didn't know you had any other family."

Azrael only shrugged, but when he asked her to keep their relationship a secret, Selena agreed. However, she wanted to share with Thor what she had learned but decided against it; Azrael asked her to keep their discussion clandestine on his behalf, and she wanted to honor his wishes.

Yet, she was distracted when Thor lunged forward at her, like a cat attacking its prey. His scaly lips curled into a sneer when his surprise attack made Selena trip over her feet. *Please, be careful next time.*

I don't believe that's my fault that you're not paying attention to me. Thor lowered his massive head, his smoldering eyes almost twice the size of her shield, and his studded eyelids clicked as he blinked. **Could you hold onto this for me?**

Hold on to what? Thor snaked his neck back and lowered his chin to the totem tied to his necklace. *Oh, don't you want to wear it anymore?*

I don't want to lose it when flying or in combat.

Selena's eyes darted down to Thor's bracelets. *But you have no issues with your bracelets or the chain Aracania gave you.*

My treasures are safely clasped on my wrists and neck, but this leather is flimsy. As Thor lowered his neck to her level, Selena untied the stringy necklace from his gold chain. Upon further examination of the crafted piece, Selena believed Thor was right and that it was a matter of time before he lost it. *I'll keep it in my bag for you.*

Thank you, my dear.

The group agreed to spend the evening and rest before setting out towards Starsong and Nuvak, though Selena faced Azrael's opposition. He ultimately changed his mind when Doragon and Thor complained, wishing to rest their wings before setting off again.

"I hope we'll make it because Nuvak is still about a fortnight away, maybe less if the winds are in our favor." Azrael ruefully looked at the map before Rahim snatched it away. "We have a long ways to go before we reach Snowhaven."

Thor groaned as he made himself comfortable close to the shrine. **His insistence on finishing our assignment is putting me in a foul mood. Pray tell Azrael I will ensure my wings will carry us safely to the capital, but I must rest.**

Selena joined him and passed out under Thor's protective wings without saying a proper goodnight to Azrael and Rahim.

Yet, Selena didn't have much time to sleep, as Kiba had awoken her at the crack of dawn; keeping her promise to help Selena in her magical endeavor, the She-Wolf brought her to a large, empty clearing outside the Ankoku Pass.

When Thor and Doragon finally awoke, they pestered Azrael and the lazy Rahim to join them and watch Kiba's training session. Rahim, still half-asleep, grumbled at Thor, who slammed his tail against him, throwing him across the ground. Though Doragon and Azrael were amused, Rahim jumped back to his feet and grumbled at Thor again before protesting the pair and angrily stomping away.

Through their magic duel, Kiba tested Selena on her resolve throughout the day, as she still displayed disinclination and uncertainty. "And it shows. It's not just your magic but also your stance whenever you're communing with the elements." The She-Wolf stood on her toes and pointed at Selena's forehead. "Whatever is going on up here is holding you back. You're a dragon; now fight back like one."

As Kiba resumed their sparring match, she hurled a large boulder at her, and although Selena cleaved it in two, she lost her footing and fell; the alpha began losing her patience. "No, you're supposed to stand your ground. We will keep doing this until you get it right."

Selena's face grew red with embarrassment as Kiba's words echoed in her ears. "I'm sorry—"

"No, don't apologize. Just get back in position—we're starting our duel again."

Even Azrael flinched. "This is coming from me, but that's too far." Thor and Doragon agreed through snarls and growls, but one piercing look from Kiba silenced them.

"Quiet—we're doing it my way."

Selena stood up and dusted herself off. "I'm trying, but—"

"Are you *really* giving it your all? You need to be an unstoppable force, but you're too shallow and weak. You must show the Lich that you're not a coward—he should fear *you*. Don't let him get in your way." Kiba repeated her instructions, but Selena failed in the She-Wolf's eyes.

Selena hung her head in shame and defeat. "I'm sorry."

Kiba was disappointed. "What are you playing at?"

"Maybe I don't like it when you're yelling at me."

"I'm sorry, what?" Kiba asked, leaning her head down to better hear her.

Selena's nostrils flared, and the firestorm within her steeped. "I don't like you pushing me around and putting me in this position." She stomped away towards Thor.

The stubborn Kiba stomped and shattered the nearby pile of rocks like glass. "Fine, go away."

While relaxing within Thor's saddle during their duel, Rahim flinched when he saw Selena storming over, fuming. "Selena, stop—"

"I'm not ready to hear it, Rahim. I want to leave right now."

He had attempted to dismount, but he was caught in the mess of belts and buckles; he dangled from a carabiner tied to his leg. Yet, Selena climbed up Thor's foreleg and, through her frustration, ordered Thor to take flight. Thor, too, was somewhat wrapped in her fury and hadn't paid attention to Rahim; unfortunately, Rahim's yells and pleas were drowned by the whoosh of Thor's wings, and he was left dangling off the side for dear life.

Selena's eyes widened with shock when she realized what she had done and, with Thor's assistance, helped him board the saddle and untied the carabiner that tore through his pants and bruised his leg.

"I'm sorry." Selena turned away as Rahim mumbled and pulled out another pair of trousers to change.

"You're sorry? You tried to kill me."

I know you're angry, but you need to pay more attention to your surroundings. Selena ignored Thor and sat in the corner with her legs up to her chest. **If he had fallen, I would have been able to grab him, but that's beside my point. Where do you want to go?**

I don't know.

Thor snorted. **Then I'm not straying far; I'll circle the valley until you decide.**

Once Rahim recovered from his second near-death experience after slipping into new pants, he asked, "Why is this frustrating you?"

"Nothing is upsetting me."

"You're full of it. Is it Kiba, or is it because you're not as good as you thought you were? How does this make you feel?"

His words cut deep. "Do you really want to know how I feel?"

Rahim nervously backed away to avoid invoking her wrath. "I thought I was quite clear about that,"

Hot tears streamed down her face. "I'm tired of failing. Every time I think I can do something, it turns out I'm not good enough, and it blows up in my face like everything else. I can't fail, not with the eclipse drawing near. I'm not strong enough to face the Lich again, not after what happened with Ragnarok." Selena looked at

Thor, who had swiveled his head back and fixated a single smoldering eye on her.

Why do you always believe you have to do this alone?

That's not it, my dear. I'm not strong like you.

Not yet, he corrected. **When your time comes, you will be a force to be reckoned with, and your fire will make the Divines kneel.**

The three flew in silence under the late afternoon sun as Selena allowed Thor's words to soak. However, she curled herself into a ball the longer she remained alone with her shrouded thoughts.

Eventually, Rahim broke the tense air. "You put so much on your shoulders, and it's not fair. You just found out who you were not long ago, and everyone forced you into this situation. You didn't ask for any of this, but the Divines still chose you and Thor."

Selena looked up at him and wiped her tears away. "I don't know what to do, Rahim."

"Yes, you do. You've never given up." Rahim's eyes brightened upon discovering this revelation. "I believe I now understand your resolve. You never give up— unmovable and unstoppable. That's your hard-headed attitude. Maybe when Kiba pushes you around again, that's what you need to focus on."

Thor dipped his head in agreement and released a few loose ember streams. **Rahim is wise, and he's right. Now, fight back like the Divinity Dragon you are.**

Selena appreciated the small reminders of what she was capable of, and upon recognizing she was a Divine miracle, she smiled and agreed. When Thor circled back and made his graceful descent, Kiba approached, snarling and arms crossed; she taunted, "I knew you would be back. Are you going to run away again?"

As Thor helped Selena dismount, she growled back at the She-Wolf. "I'm done dealing with you."

Kiba's eyes narrowed. "What did you say?"

"I said I'm done dealing with you," Selena declared, "Now, I want a rematch."

Kiba scoffed. "A rematch against the She-Wolf—are you going to leave and cry to your dragon again?"

Selena held her head up high and took her stance, ready to begin; she became mentally and emotionally unmovable, eager to fight back with the strength of a hundred dragons. Instead of arguing, Kiba smiled and began their duel; she stomped, and a boulder erupted before her, and when she believed Selena was ill-prepared, she launched it.

As she focused on her restored resolve, Selena maintained her firm stance and cleaved the massive boulder in two, her hand slicing through like a knife in butter. The rock split apart, the halves flung behind her. Breathing deeply, she saw Kiba lunging forward at her with an unstoppable force. Selena whipped her arm around and blocked the She-Wolf's attack, leaving the two in an awkward stare-down. Selena knew what Kiba was attempting; the Alpha Female wanted submission, but Selena was a dragon refusing to back down.

I serve neither god nor king.

Flames wafted from Thor's and Doragon's mouths from this delightful display of raw power. Rahim and Azrael fidgeted as they anxiously looked at the dragon and the wolf locked in a silent battle, wondering who would back down first.

When Selena squinted down upon the alpha, a huge grin spread across Kiba's face. "It's impressive to stand up to the She-Wolf; I think you have what it takes to face that necromancer, dragon."

Thor and Doragon clicked their nails against the rocks in approval; Kiba and Selena backed away and bowed, but the alpha wasn't finished and transformed into the white wolf. As she barked and growled, Selena heard her voice ring within her thoughts; she asked the alpha of her telepathic abilities, as she had only known dragons to develop that link with mortals.

I share this telepathic bond with my pack members through Artio's blessing, Kiba explained, *Now that you're part of the Aynu, you can hear me as long as you're nearby.* She looked at Thor and Doragon, listening to her explanation; they watched her with keen interest. *Unlike you and your dragons, we can't communicate with you if you leave this forest, but the link will return if you do. Before I continue, you must tell your dragon that he cannot interfere no matter what happens.*

Thor snarled when he overheard; Selena didn't feel comfortable. *Is something terrible going to happen?*

Perhaps. Accidents happen all the time, but Thor cannot always be there to save you.

As reluctant as she was, Selena concurred, but Thor wasn't as willing when she pleaded. **Silver took it too far the last time I agreed to something like this.**

I trust her.

Thor fixated his fiery gaze on the white wolf; she met with equal intensity. **Very well; I'll stand by for now, but I will take action if Kiba takes it too far.**

That's not what I'm asking. Kiba has a point—I must be able to help myself. I can't count on you to always be there to save me. Swear it.

Thor gnashed his fangs and flickered his tail. **Fine. I swear it.**

Thank you.

Once receiving his consent, Kiba warned her to ready her weapon. Reluctantly unsheathing Dragonheart, Selena asked: *Why would I need it?*

I believe you should always be armed. Think fast. Selena's face turned white when Kiba gave her a toothy grin; the alpha jumped, and as soon as her paws touched the ground again, the dirt beneath Selena's feet crumbled away, swallowed into the abyss.

Azrael and Rahim protested as they rushed to the edge with Thor and Doragon peering over, but Kiba reminded them of their agreement; Selena struck her blade into the earth, slowing her fall until she was left dangling. The pit in her stomach sank to see her bottomless chasm, and she growled when she heard Kiba's howls from the surface. Before she could brace herself, a large boulder formed over her hole, shrouding her in absolute darkness. The earth rumbled, and her sword trembled as the giant rock slowly lowered down, threatening to crush her. Small rocks fell on her head from the stone scraping against the abyss walls.

Though she didn't have her wings, Selena had an idea; she withdrew Dragonheart from the rock as she concentrated on summoning flames erupting from the soles of her boots and left fist. She sighed in relief to see herself levitating, wobbling in mid-flight but successfully kept herself aloft. Steering herself with the fire from her fist, Selena focused on the lingering threat still making its descent as it increased its fall speed. Stubborn and steady, the flames from her feet grew, and Selena propelled herself forward with Dragonheart at the ready. As the boulder was upon her, she slashed through with one slice and used her free hand to blast the rubble out of the hole with a whipping gale storm.

When they saw an eruption of shattered rocks bursting from Kiba's abyss, Thor and Doragon whisked the She-Wolf, Azrael, and Rahim away, protecting them from the raining stone and debris. Seconds later, Selena flew out of the hole with Dragonheart hanging from her side and flames blazing from her feet. She maneuvered her graceful landing and extinguished her fire as she stepped back onto solid ground and crossed her arms over her chest.

Thor snaked his head around to examine her newfound prowess. **You certainly know how to triumph with flair.**

Kiba, Azrael, and Rahim looked in awe as Selena made her grand entrance; though sodden and breathless, she stood her ground when the She-Wolf approached, grinning ear to ear as she shapeshifted back to human. "I will never underestimate you again," she said.

"Pray don't try to kill me again."

"I make no promises."

While Thor and Doragon made their final hunt to ensure they would be satiated for the long trip to Nuvak, Selena and Kiba were locked in a magic contest, keeping her awake and alert for any threat lurking around every corner. Amidst Kiba's repeated test of resilience, the alpha explained as she and Selena broke more boulders apart, "My pack and I can all use earth magic because of Artio, and the dwarves learned by watching us. Before that dragon destroyed them, they were almost as good as we were, but from what you saw, they favored that weird magic over the old teachings."

"By weird magic, I'm assuming you mean technology."

"I don't know what technology means unless you're talking about those unnatural things made of metal, then yes. I don't like your firesticks, either."

"Firesticks? Oh, I think you mean our guns."

"Meh. Whatever you call them." Kiba clapped her hands together and summoned a stone disk. "Think fast." She waved her hands, and the rock lunged for Selena's head. Selena held out both her arms without time to analyze the situation, and two large stone pillars erupted from the ground beside her. She then moved her arms together, and the spires followed. They positioned themselves before her, and Kiba's attack crumbled upon impact with her block.

"You've done well to keep up with me," Kiba reached up and knocked on Selena's forehead, "Don't lose your drive and keep thinking stubborn thoughts. Make that necromancer fear you, dragon."

When Thor and Doragon returned within the twilight hours, freshly fed and bathed from swimming in the North Sea, Selena and Azrael wasted no time harnessing and packing. The Aynu members brought out baskets of food and woven furs used to line Thor's and Doragon's saddles, making them more comfortable for the long trip.

Though Rahim expressed excitement to see his mother again, Selena was afraid of what she would think of her and Thor for running away. However, Thor maintained an optimistic attitude towards their reunion. **I'm sure she's both worried and proud.**

Do you believe she's mad at me?

What reason would there be? I think she misses you and Rahim dearly, and she would love to see all of us again.

Amidst their packing, Kiba and her wolves froze and began snarling for no apparent reason. Azrael and Rahim shared Selena's confusion, but Thor's and Doragon's lips curled back, revealing their serrated fangs at an unknown looming threat that Selena had yet to see.

My dear, stay close to me. Thor's growls turned to thundering roars as he and Doragon unfurled their wings and wrapped shielding arms around the trio while the bristling wolves scattered in pell-mell fashion. They looked to the trees, and hovering in absolute silence was one of the masked dragons that had attacked Alfheim.

No, it couldn't be. Selena's hands trembled at her side, and her breaths turned ragged and harsh, her heart nearly bursting from her chest. The dragon's black silhouette taunted her.

Yet, even amid the wolf pack's battle preparations, the twisted dragon didn't retaliate. Instead, it glided down as gentle as a breeze brushing against a tree and landed near the forest's edge, its razor wings unfolding like a graceful swan in full grandeur. Upon further examination, Selena noted its partially damaged mask and realized it was the same creature that withstood her Divine might and took Niamh.

"Must I use this foul tongue of yours?" it hissed at them. Selena was appalled to hear it speak; its voice was slow and sounded like guttural shrieks. "Your pursuit will be your undoing; it would only serve to strengthen us. We will be waiting for you, but you better hurry. The one you call Niamh misses you." Before Thor, Doragon, and the pack could attack, the masked dragon flew away and left as quickly as it came.

"Get back here and fight," Rahim pushed Thor's wing aside and pulled out his gun to shoot it down, but Selena intervened and pushed his firearm away. His eyes shimmered as he watched the goading behemoth flee, and Rahim was undone.

Selena warned, "Now is not the time. It's only taunting us."

"But Niamh…." Rahim's voice turned hoarse as he gripped the barrel of his Winclock.

"We will get her back. I swear it."

"If you want to save her, we need to leave now and deliver the eggs," Azrael announced as he strapped himself into the harness; Doragon grunted, stretching his wings and nodding to Thor, indicating he was ready for take-off. "We can't afford any more delays."

Kiba and Maru stepped forward while their pack circled the two dragons; they gave her a firm but jumpy handshake in farewell. "Thank you for everything, but be careful if you're going after that dragon. If you ever need us, you know where we are—you're all welcome here."

Maru grunted and placed a fist to his chest. "You're one of us now."

Selena bowed to the alphas, and the trio clutched their totem necklaces. "Thank you, and I know we will meet again."

Once they were ready and the trio belted, Thor and Doragon launched skyward in one massive leap, their wings sweeping across the ground; the Aynu made a great deal of noise, howling in a unified and beautiful farewell.

CHAPTER 19: A SHADOW OVER NUVAK

Twilight faded into blackness freckled by specks of light, glowing like a million fireflies. For the rest of the evening, Thor and Doragon were quick and silent. It started as a race between them to see who could fly faster, but Selena and Azrael reminded them to pace themselves. The wind was to their backs, and the two dragons relaxed while coasting.

Over the following few days, Selena rode with Doragon—against Thor's wishes until she successfully convinced him otherwise—and Azrael resumed teaching her how to dual-wield swords using his blade and Dragonheart. She quickly grew accustomed to fighting with both her left and right hands through relentless bitter work; Azrael forewent his Aether pistols for the time being and practiced sparring with her using two ethereal broadswords. Though he was a gunslinger, Azrael still exhibited more experience and skill than she did, easily beating her in every match they had. Yet, Selena remained determined to improve.

They would practice firing shots with Rahim between their dual-wielding matches, warming up their trigger fingers. Azrael would summon stone disks and launch them heavenward for both Rahim and Selena to train their aim; although Selena was proficient enough, she never gave up her chance for drilling exercises. The two spent countless grueling hours perfecting their talents; Rahim had proven his worth behind a firearm after their contest, blasting more targets than she had within the allotted time.

Other than stopping to relieve themselves occasionally, they flew nonstop; by the fourth night, the group flew over a giant statue of Ulrich lit with candles, his shrine, outside the ruins of Rhumbek. Azrael explained, "Usually, his most devout followers preach or perform rituals with a priest. Sometimes if you leave an offering, he might talk to you."

Selena knew Xyaxon's was closer to Alfheim, but when she asked about Azrael's, he ruefully said, "I don't know if mine still stands, but it was on a cliff overlooking the Turquoise Ocean."

"What kind of offering would I have to leave at the shrines if I wanted to commune with the Divines?"

"For mine, it was gold, but it may be different for Ulrich's and Xyaxon's. I wouldn't expect an answer—they may or may not choose to speak, as I often did."

Selena secretly scowled. *He's always so bitter.*

The chill breeze made her spine crawl; she wrapped herself in her scarf before leaning against the egg trunk. Selena forced herself to stay awake and enjoy the brisk wind blowing across her face. It was a beautiful night, with the stars shining brightly through some drifting clouds.

Rahim swore he saw the masked dragon creatures flying ahead of them on several occasions, though they were far away. Azrael joked that they could be birds instead, but Rahim was persistent. He watched them through his eyeglass over the next several hours, and the only way Selena could make him take a break was by bribing him with food. Even then, Rahim was still reluctant. "We're not going to find Niamh any faster." Rahim ignored her and went back to his watch after a few mouthfuls of jerky. Eventually, he grew weary and stopped looking; he sulked in the corner before resting on the bundle of furs gifted from the Aynu.

By the fifth evening, Selena could tell that Thor was straining his wings; despite his objections, she offered him a few drops of the stamina potion, and Thor begrudgingly accepted. She extended the civility to Azrael and Doragon, but the pair declined. "As a Spirit Beast, Doragon's stamina is limitless, though he likes to partake in earthly pleasures from time to time, such as eating and resting." Doragon groaned, confirming that he was only insistent on joining and giving Thor the rest he needed since they first set out on their journey, for which he and Selena were grateful.

Before Rahim went to sleep, he and Azrael had rechecked the map and their calculations based on Thor's and Doragon's speed of about sixty kilometers—courtesy of the blistering yet favorable winds. The two were happy to announce they would soon arrive in Starsong within the next couple of days.

Thor was delighted to hear the news, as he slowly grew famished since his last meal; Silver's elixir could only do so much for a hungry dragon. After Selena and Azrael drew water from the clouds to quench Thor's and Doragon's thirsts, Thor assured her that **I will be fine until we can make it to Starsong.**

Selena smiled and rubbed his neck. *I'm glad you and Doragon are working together.*

I'm happy you and Azrael are too.

Azrael interrupted, "I'll stay awake and watch if you want to get some sleep. Rahim is already resting, and you should too."

Selena didn't want to admit that he was right, but she drifted off again. Eventually, she conceded defeat, "All right," and grabbed a bundle of fur, using it as a pillow before collapsing.

The trio spent the next couple of days in anticipation, anxious to finally reach the village before making way for Nuvak. As much as Selena loved flying, she didn't appreciate the developing saddle sores; if only she could freely transform into a dragon herself and soar like Thor and Doragon, she wouldn't mind the long flight nearly so much.

Soon, their patience paid off when Azrael spotted an inn behind fenced-off fields of horses, cows, and pigs through his eyeglass: they made it to Starsong within a week. The satisfied Azrael still grumbled, "That puts us back on schedule."

Starsong was a small settlement similar to Helshire; besides the few houses and shops behind the inn connected by a rocky road, the village wasn't impressive, but it was enough. Once Thor and Doragon made their descent, Thor couldn't wait for Selena and Rahim to dismount; he immediately collapsed, his massive weight making the ground shake. The penned animals panicked upon seeing the two dragons and fled to their wooden stalls.

After unbuckling their bags, Selena climbed down Thor's forelegs, sighing from Thor's ill-timed laziness. *My dear, can you help me with unloading first before you drift off?*

He snorted and wobbled as he reluctantly stood up; reaching his back, Thor scooped up their bags and the dragon egg chest before dumping them on the ground, giving Selena and Rahim enough time to unstrap his harness. Once it slid off, Thor swung his body around and collapsed again with his eyes fixed on the scared animals.

I could eat them all in one bite. Thor's pupils turned to slits, and he flexed out his claws, ready to pounce.

I'm afraid you'll eat them out of house and home, my dear. I will see how many their owner is willing to part with.

Thor groaned and flickered his tail when she and Rahim helped Azrael unharness Doragon; he stretched his wings and joined Thor in his lethargic stupor.

Selena and her group walked inside the tattered inn, barren and empty. The only company was the innkeeper behind the counter and a local donning a cloak in the corner with a drink; the table's lantern illuminated the man's molded jaw, but his face remained hidden under the cowl. Beside the barhop was a staircase leading to the rooms for rent.

"Welcome to Starsong," the innkeeper greeted, "we don't get many visitors here except for merchants traveling between the cities. Are you travelers?"

"Yes," Selena said and inquired about the price of the livestock for Thor; meanwhile, Azrael kept his eyes fixed on the cloaked stranger but withheld his opinions.

"Ah, dragon riders. I haven't seen any here in years."

Thor interrupted her conversation. **I want at least four cows and perhaps two pigs—I'll hunt later when I've rested.**

When Selena repeated Thor's order, the innkeeper's eyes widened, but he gruffed when giving his price of one hundred twenty gold pieces for all six animals. When he believed that a young woman wouldn't have been able to afford a hefty price, Selena pulled out her coin pouch and set the agreed amount on the tabletop. Yet, she noticed the stranger shift, but she quickly turned away.

I'm starving. Pray tell me I'm ready to make my selections.

Of course, my dear. Please, take your order and complete the transaction.

Her ears prickled at the sound of the chair sliding back, and Selena instinctively pulled out Dragonheart when the man suddenly approached. The cloaked stranger retaliated by summoning one chain, its shackles wrapping around her blade like a snake about to strangle its prey, pushing her sword back. Selena's eyes widened when she realized it was her father, but he pressed his finger to his lips.

Selena sheathed Dragonheart, and the Shadow Emperor gestured for them to follow him upstairs into the first room on the right, housing a small bed in the lonely corner. He beckoned the trio to sit down at his small table with a candle and a plate of fruit, bread, and cheese next to a wine bottle; he lifted the cowl, revealing his black and white mask that he removed and left hanging over his pointed ear.

Selena rushed over to hug him. "It's so good to see you."

Phantom Dust smiled and returned the embrace. "It's great to see you again too, and I've been expecting all of you."

Yet, when the trembling Rahim realized who he was, he immediately dropped to his knees. "Please, forgive me, Your Imperial Majesty—I had no idea."

Dust's stoic tone was unmoved by Rahim's groveling. Instead, he offered him wine and food, but Rahim quickly declined and sat on the bed, twiddling his thumbs while Selena and Azrael sat at the table. Dust squinted at the trio when he noticed their totem necklaces, but he looked away and went silent when Selena and Azrael asked him the matter.

Grumbling, Azrael asked, "What are you doing in Starsong?"

"I've been waiting for you five to arrive. I recently returned from Snowhaven after meeting with His Majesty, King Boreas Tristan, and Justiciar Holland."

Selena squinted at him. "How did you make it to Snowhaven?"

Dust nodded to the small window, and the trio saw an airship tethered to boulders behind the inn. "I arrived earlier this morning after flying over the Turquoise Ocean for almost two weeks, though I should imagine Thor and Doragon would be faster than my zeppelin."

Selena and Azrael exchanged glances, wondering how Phantom Dust had beaten them to Snowhaven. Yet, they shamefully looked down when realizing how much time they had wasted in Rhumbek and backtracking to the Ankoku Pass. However, Azrael confirmed they were back on schedule, and Selena grew puzzled by her father's swift trip across the Empire; when she asked him how that was possible, Dust said, "I travel and hide within the shadows —I can cross Armageddon faster than most."

While Selena and Azrael drank and ate, Dust regaled them on his trip to the Water Kingdom capital, confirming that the king and justiciar were expecting their arrival. However, Selena was confused at how her father could request a meeting with King Boreas Tristan without his disguise. "His Majesty serves not the Council but the imperial family. He is willing to aid us in this war, and has been building a covert for new dragon riders, hence the hefty sum for the Mythic Flight clutch." Dust nodded to the egg chest resting by Selena's feet; he stopped and sighed. "I must warn you, Selena, that General Araneus, your mother, and I have been keeping a close watch on Vidar and the Council since you five have embarked on your journey, as they've been holding secret meetings almost every night and funds have gone missing. All of this began after those masked dragons attacked Alfheim—that's all I know."

Selena's throat suddenly turned dry, and not even the wine could quench her discomfort. "What do you suppose this means?"

Dust rubbed his temples, hesitant to answer. "We believe they're planning something, but it's too soon to assume. After you leave Starsong, I will return to Alfheim, and we'll find out more." He met her concerned emerald gaze. "Selena, I want you and your friends to be on your guard. If you suspect your mission is compromised and Snowhaven is no longer safe, I want you to leave immediately and wait in Nuvak. I will neither risk your lives nor the dragon eggs; if the Mythic Flight hatchlings fall into the wrong hands, someone could use their magic for malicious purposes."

Selena's throat constricted; overhearing their conversation, Thor said, **As the Lich intended when he had my egg.**

Dust continued: "Otherwise, I will provide safety while you five rest. If you need directions for Nuvak and Snowhaven, I will be more than happy to accommodate you, but I recommend leaving first thing in the morning. Pardon me, and please, help yourselves." The Shadow Emperor excused himself and left the room; the two rested and ate after sharing the wine bottle, but Azrael continued glaring at the door.

Overcoming the awkward exchange, Rahim scooted off the bed and joined in food and drink, and he and Selena indulged in light conversation. However, Selena sighed after taking a bite of cheese and bread. "Will we defeat the Lich before the Day of Eternal Darkness?"

"We have to," Rahim's tone turned grim, "including finding Niamh."

"We will find her. I'm sure Azrael would have warned us if we couldn't." Selena looked up at him for reassurance, but he didn't stir; she sighed and looked out the window to see her father checking his zeppelin.

She flinched when Azrael broke from his trance, scowling and scoffing. "Really now? You honestly believe that I will bow to your every whim by warning you ahead of time. How could someone like you understand me? You don't know anything about me."

"I believe I'm well enough acquainted with you to know—" Before Selena could react, Azrael pushed the table aside, drew a knife he kept hidden in his sash, and held it to her throat, ignoring Rahim's alarmed protests.

"You know nothing," Azrael growled through gritted teeth, "do you think I wouldn't do it?"

The calm Selena knew he wouldn't harm her, and his eyes widened from her relaxed demeanor. "I believe you're a kind soul."

Azrael hissed and swore as he lowered his knife. "Don't say that. I am not a good person."

"Yes, you are. You showed me what you're capable of, but I saw it in your eyes: you're teaching me always to keep my guard up."

"Even facing death, you don't cower down," Azrael commented, putting his knife away, "interesting and astounding."

Yet, Rahim was the only one still objecting; he glared at Death. "Oh, blast it all—that's enough threats, fights, and whatnot."

The jaded Azrael rolled his eyes. "I wasn't going to kill her."

Dust's voice rumbled over their heads as he quietly returned. "Don't you dare, or else I will kill you."

Azrael scowled but refused to meet the Shadow Emperor's heated glare. "You can't kill me."

"A god can still be killed." Azrael glared at Dust and mumbled, but he didn't argue. However, the Shadow Emperor hastily explained, "Unfortunately, I need to leave earlier than planned as I have other matters requiring my attention. See that you five leave by morning to stay on schedule."

"Wait, I thought you would stay with us for a while?" Selena asked, the feeling of abandonment creeping upon her.

"My plans have changed, and I must return to Alfheim as soon as possible."

"When will we see you again?"

"In due time, I assure you. Pray that the next time we meet, it'll be under better circumstances. Safe travels, and farewell." Dust offered her one last hug. "May the spirit of the wolf guide you." The two broke away, and when Selena raised a brow, he pointed at her necklace before donning his mask and disappearing, leaving her and her friends dumb. A stone sank in her stomach, and Selena had to watch her father vanish again. However, she held her tongue and prayed in silence to herself for a hopeful future.

The three took Dust's advice and rested until morning. The rejuvenated Thor confirmed he was well enough for the flight to Nuvak, though Selena still bought him an extra two pigs for breakfast.

While packing, Rahim quietly asked her, "That Phantom Dust fellow is the true emperor of Armageddon, then?" Selena nodded, and Rahim ruefully said, "I couldn't imagine all that you and your family have gone through, and it's all because of the Council and the Lich."

"The Council and the Lich," Selena repeated, "I don't like the sound of that."

When Rahim saw the horror on her face, he said: "Wait, do you think there's a connection?"

"No, it can't be," Selena quickly dismissed, "Let's be off soon." She failed to convince herself, as she suspected Rahim was right. This revelation was like tumbling into darkness after missing a step on the stairs, and Selena questioned the Council's disposition; even her father expressed doubts about their allegiance.

The group finished packing, and they spoke of their plans for Nuvak; the innkeeper overheard and asked, "Why on earth would you want to go there?"

Selena looked at him strangely. "We have official business at the capital. Why?"

"Oh, well," the innkeeper stuttered, "His Majesty, King Camulus Urileth, isn't allowing any visitors in or out at the moment."

"What do you mean?"

"Haven't you heard? A disease spreads, and everyone inside the city is dropping like flies. The king closed the borders, but the illness had already infected most of the denizens of Nuvak. The king still forbids opening the city gates."

"Bullocks—let's be off." Azrael scoffed and grabbed Selena's arm, pulling her away. However, Rahim's face turned cherry red, but he quietly followed the two with trembling fists.

"Be careful," the innkeeper shouted, "you can never leave once you enter the city."

After gobbling his breakfast, Thor waited near the pens, cleaning his claws and scales from the blood and gore. When he finished, and with Rahim's assistance, Selena applied a fresh coat of oil, cleaning his hide until his blood-diamond scales sparkled like his jewelry before harnessing. Meanwhile, as Doragon stretched his claws, Azrael approached and snapped his fingers; Doragon's lusterless golden scales suddenly gleamed like the morning sun from his magic. He unfurled his wings, the silver membranes catching the sunlight, casting grey and gold specs across the ground.

Once Selena and Rahim strapped on Thor's harness and buckled the egg chest and their bags, Selena squinted at Azrael, unnerved by how calm he remained by the innkeeper's warning. Yet, Rahim climbed down Thor's foreleg, and he approached the apathetic Azrael, grabbing the hem of his shirt and spinning him around. "What are you playing at?"

Azrael snarled and pushed himself away. "I don't understand—"

Selena came to Rahim's defense and demanded, "You know what he means: we must save *Matu*."

Azrael pinched the bridge of his nose; Doragon slithered his head across the ground and nudged his back, chirping and chittering. "I can say this for sure: Chaliss is safe."

She and Rahim relaxed their shoulders, but they still weren't satisfied; Selena declared, "If what the innkeeper says is true, we will save Nuvak from this disease before it's too late." Azrael groaned and muttered profanities, but Doragon spun his head around and snapped his fangs, making him flinch, confirming that they would help.

Once their riders were safe and strapped in, Thor and Doragon stretched and moved, ensuring their passengers and cargo remained buckled. The trio confirmed they were well, and the two dragons launched themselves skyward in one leap.

They traveled for the next two days, but the floating city of Nuvak could be seen hours prior; Selena was amazed by the hovering capital, noting the hot air balloons and airships tethered to docks, allowing the citizens to leave and travel. She crinkled her nose at the foul, disgusting odor plaguing the air, and she spotted a misty green cloud polluting the gilded city.

Selena cringed upon seeing metal-hued clouds circling over Nuvak, her skin prickling when lightning cracked the sky. She had been grateful for the clear summer days, but a cold shiver ran down her spine to think that a brewing storm waited for her. She squeaked when thunder rumbled softly in the distance, leaving Azrael and Doragon confused; Thor and Rahim, however, grew concerned, for they understood her fear of thunder and lightning.

Night settled upon the land; as they soared closer to the shadow over Nuvak, Azrael noted the vortex of green poison swirling behind the king's marble palace streaked with gold and purple. Selena and Rahim glared at Death, resolving they would do what they could to protect Chaliss and the other innocents; Azrael gritted his teeth and swore. "There's no way for me to convince you two otherwise, is there?"

Rahim raised a fist at Azrael. "No, we will help mum."

Azrael groaned but said when Doragon swiveled his head around and snapped his fangs, "Liongod, follow my example to avoid falling ill." He held his hand to his mouth, creating an air bubble encasing his nose and lower face. Selena agreed and summoned breathable globules for herself and Rahim; Thor and Doragon did the same for themselves as they flew above the city gates.

Selena scanned swaths of streets, and to her dismay, the entire city was deserted; they made their way to the grim and desolate cathedral standing tall in the middle of the poisoned town. Thor and Doragon gracefully landed before the marble stairs at the crossroad where the path split in a 'v' shape: the right side led towards the blacksmith with a string of other shops, whereas the left steered into the residential district.

Two sickly guards toppled over the church steps, groaning softly, "My chest hurts. Please, help," and they heaved a pile of mucus and blood. Azrael and Selena summoned an air bubble for the sentries; they inhaled deeply and quickly stood up amidst endless gratitude. "At first, I thought I was looking into the face of Death."

Both Rahim and Selena looked at Azrael but didn't say a word. "Where is everyone?" Selena asked. "The city looks completely abandoned."

The first guard said: "Once the plague settled in, His Majesty ordered everyone to take refuge inside the castle, locking them within."

The second woefully added, "We've been ordered to stand guard and ensure no one leaves or enters the city, but thank the Divines you lot showed up. It's been about three days since the disease spread."

Selena glared at Azrael, who only shrugged, and she said, "We ought to meet with His Majesty and help the citizens." Thor and Doragon clicked and chattered in agreement with unfurled wings.

Yet, the two guards straightened up and slammed the butts of their spears into the pavement, announcing, "His Majesty isn't allowing visitors."

Selena growled, and although she hated playing this card, she revealed her imperial connection. "Will His Majesty grant an audience with the Crown Princess, Selena Liongod?" The sentries' eyes examined her through their helm visors when Selena indicated herself. Hoping that Nuvak would recognize her family's mark, she slipped off her left glove and revealed the imperial family sigil etched into her palm; to her delight, the guards identified the symbol and nearly toppled.

They dropped to their knees and stumbled through ill-rehearsed apologies. "Forgive us, Your Imperial Highness, for we had no idea."

Azrael and Rahim sneered. Thor snorted and gruffed at the sudden change in treatment, but Selena ruefully slipped on her glove. "We understand you're following orders, and you two are doing a marvelous job, but given the city's state, we hope to assist in cleansing this disease."

Rahim interjected and said, "Perhaps His Majesty can provide us some insight into what's causing this mist."

The two guards looked down and sighed, as they knew they couldn't insult the Crown Princess and her company; the second guard said, "Very well. Your Highness, follow the road here, and it will lead you to the king's castle."

"Thank you." Selena bowed, but the guards looked at her strangely, wondering why someone from the imperial family would lower themselves before the common rabble. She ignored their flabbergasted expressions, for she neither considered herself above nor lower than anyone else.

"Be warned," the first guard began. "The king isn't like anyone else you've met before."

"Do you mean he's mental?" Rahim asked.

"You've been warned." The guards then resumed their post.

Not accounting for the poison mist, Selena shuddered when realizing the city seemed odd like Rhumbek; she wondered how any of the provinces could operate and function under such terrible monarchs, but she understood they served the Council, not her family.

Thor and Doragon lowered their paws and carried their riders towards the ivory keep; the dark green maelstrom swirled heavenward as the growing black and emerald squall billowed overhead. Selena cowered down and wrapped her arms around Thor's ivory talon, staying grounded; Thor and Rahim did their best to ease her anxiety and fear while Azrael and Doragon observed her, perplexed.

The two dragons circled the cathedral and ascended above the city wall over a long bridge that separated the king's castle from the lower class. Selena peered at the blackened sky above the fortress of darkness, and she gasped when it seemed she was looking straight into an abyss leading to Oblivion itself.

Thor's voice twinkled against her stormy thoughts: **Be well, my dear one.**

I-I can't.

As Thor and Doragon made their downward spiral, cautioning when dropping off their passengers, Selena tumbled to her hands and knees when thunder rumbled overhead. Rahim rushed to her aid and held her upright, leaving Azrael more confused. Now understanding Selena's predicament, Doragon growled and nudged him forward.

Yet, Azrael was still the only one who didn't understand. "What's the matter with you?" Lightning tore through the sky, followed by thunder's ear-shattering roar. Selena broke away from Rahim's grip and immediately ran to the door, slamming her fists to get inside. The door slightly opened, and she scurried within, hiding and quivering in a shadowed corner.

Azrael squinted at her, but Rahim yelled as the torrential rain fell. "You're a thick-headed nit-wit, aren't you? She's terrified of thunder and lightning; whenever Selena hears a storm, she gets so scared that she can't move."

His eyes widened. "How in Oblivion was I supposed to know that?" Thor and Doragon roared at him, and Azrael trembled as he dashed inside the keep to go after her. "She's not afraid to die, but she's terrified of thunder and lightning."

Rahim swore and followed him, leaving Thor and Doragon hovering in the rain, waiting for confirmation that Selena was well. Azrael found her hiding underneath a small, wooden table with hands clamped over her ears, whimpering and fighting back the tears with her eyes shut. "Liongod."

Selena opened her eyes and glanced up at him. "A-Azr—" The thunder shattered the already stormy atmosphere, and she closed her eyes again.

When the drenched Rahim approached, Azrael knelt before her and placed a hand on her forehead; he whispered a few words from the demonic language, and suddenly, the terrifying sounds drowned from her ears. All Selena heard now was the soft and gentle pitter-patter of rain, soothed by its therapeutic effects.

He sat next to her and pulled her to his side. "I'm sorry for not understanding."

Selena gasped when he tugged her close, and she accepted his friendly warmth. "Thank you, Azrael."

Thor's loving thoughts wrapped around hers when her fears subsided, and Rahim wiped his brow in relief. When he assured Selena was doing well mentally, Azrael stood up and announced, "I will speak with His Majesty in her stead."

Yet, they paused when a large glass chandelier sparkled in the dark suite, lifting the shadows; the main hall was densely crowded with the overly dressed upper-class, wearing extravagant suits and gowns, and embellished embroidered masks. The full-swing party abruptly stopped when His Majesty's guests screamed and squealed that someone had opened the castle's door.

Yet, a loud voice echoed from the throne, and the king's company quickly fell into silence. "Who dares to barge in here? What is the meaning of this intrusion?"

CHAPTER 20: DEATH'S MASQUERADE

His Majesty, King Camulus Urileth of Nuvak, stood from his golden throne and parted his way through the crowd. He was the first human of power they had met, dressed in robes of deep purple accentuated with gilt trimmings. A thick, golden crown set with rubies rested upon his balding head, magnifying his deep crimson eyes blazing at the trio for barging into his castle, uninvited and unannounced.

"What is the meaning of this intrusion?" His Majesty repeated, "You're ruining our masquerade ball."

"Masquerade ball?" Selena's group asked in unison and noted each guest's unique, colorful, enchanting mask, embellished with feathers and jewels.

"Yes, and you're quite rude, barging in here without an invitation. Who is important enough to think they can come inside my castle unannounced? I've had enough—Guards!" the king ordered, and his armored sentries took up weapons and shields before stampeding towards Selena and her friends.

Azrael stepped forth with his arms extended; the guests, too afraid to confront them, backed away and allowed him to walk through. "Please, Your Majesty, we mean you and your guests no harm. We're dragon riders from the Imperial Air Force, accompanied by the Crown Princess herself."

The keep gasped at the sudden news; the guards immediately halted when Selena stood up and revealed the imperial sigil on her hand, and the assembly bowed. Yet, the king of Nuvak was the only one unwilling to show Selena the proper respect, but he recoiled and stepped back. "The Crown Princess herself, you say? And dragon riders—well, then I suppose you could stay. But how do we know that you aren't bringers of the plague?"

Selena stepped forward and marched down the guest-made aisle towards His Majesty. "We've just arrived here, Your Highness, and we've come to assist you in cleansing your city."

"Well, isn't this a hoot? A princess and her mere soldiers from the Force want to help out old King Camulus." The king bellowed in laughter to mock her; his guests, hesitant at first, followed his example.

The trio growled in anger from this insult; Thor's roars shattered and disrupted her thoughts. **Shall Doragon and I intervene and strike fear into this king's heart?**

No, that's not how politics ought to work, my dear. We must convince His Majesty that we are on his side.

The king continued. "Isn't that hilarious? Vidar and the rest of the Council have never bothered to care about my kingdom. Why should I think that this time will be any different? Well, what do you have to say? Speak before I get bored—you won't like me when I'm bored."

Selena growled and snarled like an angry dragon, but she reeled back her wrath when Rahim gripped her shoulder. "Your Majesty, perhaps we ought to speak in private—"

"Absolutely not," the king interrupted, "Either speak with me here and now or leave at once and never return, *Your Highness.*"

Selena's fists trembled at her sides, already infuriated by his lack of respect, but she trod carefully through these dangerous waters. "We're currently on our way to deliver powerful dragon eggs to the Water Kingdom capital that will aid us in the upcoming war against the Lich."

"Your war doesn't concern me—"

"I believe the end of the world concerns everyone, *Your Majesty.*"

King Camulus' upper lip twitched, and he ordered his guards to escort Selena and her friends out, but they refused to show disrespect to the Crown Princess. "You obey me, not some possible imposter—"

Azrael snarled. "You obey your princess and empress, or need I report you to the Council and Her Imperial Highness?" The guests and guards took another trembling step back, and the king growled, but he withheld any further disrespectful remark. "We've grown weary, and while we rest for the evening, we promise to assist in cleansing Nuvak. What say you, Your Majesty?"

The king laughed. "Why should I accommodate you?"

Azrael rubbed his forehead and groaned. "We are soldiers accompanying the Crown Princess, after all. Why do you find any of this humorous?"

His Majesty waved them away before turning his back on them. "Return outside to that filthy mist. How do we know you haven't brought the disease in with you? You've probably contaminated us all, yet you're here asking me to provide for you and your comrades?"

"I'm curious how you think you're safe from the plague," Selena gritted her teeth, "How do you know you're not already infected?"

The king's assembly nervously whispered to each other, but Camulus barked. "Enough. If you don't leave, Crown Princess or not, I'll have my guards escort you out. Death will not find me here, no sir." Azrael and Rahim looked at each other with dumbfounded expressions; Rahim was about to object, but Azrael held up his hand and shook his head.

Azrael cleared his throat before the king issued another order. "Why refuse our aid? We'll figure out how to purge the city in exchange for one evening stay before we make our way to Snowhaven."

The king ordered his guards to stop and put his hand to his chin. "Hmm. If you can find a way to dispel this poison looming over my city, I suppose you could stay for the night. Very well then—there is no time like the present. Get to it, and don't return until the city is clean."

King Camulus clapped his hands, and his guards hastily approached the trio to escort them outside while whispering, "Please forgive us, Your Imperial Highness." Once they were out, the guards locked the front door.

The lightning and thunder had ceased, and the torrential rain turned into a drizzle. Thor and Doragon were no longer by the entrance, but their shadows loomed across the marble steps as they circled the castle, investigating the source of the poisoned mist. The three exchanged puzzled and dismayed glances, but before deciding on a plan to cleanse Nuvak, Thor announced, **The poison vortex is within the castle courtyard—Doragon and I will meet you there.**

Be wary, my dear.

Thor snorted as their gold and red glimmers vanished behind the ivory towers. **Nothing can withstand the might of two gods.**

Selena relayed Thor's news to the group, and Rahim asked, "How did the king not notice the poison coming from behind his palace?"

"The king is a madman," Azrael replied, "and I thought the dwarf king was terrible."

The three followed the amber pathway arcing around the gold-streaked marble towers, leading them to an unguarded gateway. The group walked into a large courtyard separated into two sections by a mossy flagstone path, with rain-pearled lawns covering both sides. A large and shaggy willow tree stood drooping in the middle, hiding the cause of the mist's maelstrom.

A tiny wail—like from a crying dragon hatchling—echoed across the air. Thor and Doragon had already landed, backs turned and arched like angry cats, hissing and growling at the source of the disease. When the confused Selena asked for the reasons behind their hostility, Thor warned: **I think you'll want to have your sword ready.**

My dear, please stand down and let us through.

The two dragons reluctantly moved away, revealing a tiny baby dragon with its head tilted back, spewing forth the toxic mist. However, Azrael and Rahim quickly readied their weapons when they recognized it as a masked dragon hatchling. Yet, it ignored them as it continued its lamented wails, displaying its black, jagged teeth; stubs, where its bladed wings began growing, prickled across its back. Black ooze dripped from its slimy ebony hide and ivory bone mask.

"It's one of them," Rahim announced, "Let's kill it and be done with it."

Thor growled through his braced fangs while slowly backing away; his protective wings unfurled and shielded Selena and Rahim from the creature. Doragon's pupiled-slits fixated on the hatchling, but he slightly relaxed when Azrael stroked his neck. Selena grimaced at the sight of it and pulled out Dragonheart hanging from Thor's saddle. She kept her eyes on the creature, preparing for a possible attack, but the baby was oblivious to their company.

Rahim peeked underneath Thor's wing with a furrowed brow. "Why is it crying like that?"

The creature stopped when hearing Rahim's voice and cowered away through whines and whimpers; the vortex disappeared as soon as it shut its tiny maw. Selena's hand quivered around Dragonheart's grip when she observed, "It's afraid of us, and it only spews this poison when it cries."

"How did it get here, and why is it crying?" Azrael asked.

Rahim growled, his revolver shaking in his grasp. "What do you mean why? What are you waiting for? Kill it."

Selena swallowed hard when she noticed the claw marks across the creature's dark hide with purple blood oozing from its wounds; she couldn't do it. "No, I can't—this isn't right."

Rahim pushed past Thor's protective barrier and pointed at it; the creature recoiled and whined as tears shimmered down its mask. "What is wrong with you? That *thing* is one of those monsters that attacked Alfheim and took Niamh. It's killing all those people in Nuvak, including mum. We must destroy it." Selena and Azrael looked over at the hatchling as it curled itself into a ball and sobbed; even Thor and Doragon seemed swayed by the creature's innocence and charm, but Rahim was adamant about his prejudice and indifferent disposition.

"There must be a better way." Selena put her sword away and got down on her hands and knees; she slowly extended her hand, but it avoided her touch and grew ensconced within its oily coils.

"What are you doing?" Rahim asked, but Azrael elbowed him in the ribs.

Selena ignored them and reached out to pet it, reassuring through the calm and gentle tone in her voice. "We're not here to hurt you."

Drawn to her aura, the creature lifted its head and sniffed her fingers. Thor snorted, and flames sparked from his nostrils. **Why are you doing this?**

It's only a baby that's been hurt, and it's alone. It won't hurt anyone.

Thor bared his fangs but didn't interfere; he swung his body around to avoid seeing her showing affection for another creature besides him, but Doragon urged him to stay through clicks and chirps. Selena ignored the dragons and spoke to the hatchling as if it were another intellectual. The whelpling slowly uncurled itself and limped to her hand, its lowered head touching her palm.

Rahim grumbled as he belted his revolver. "Pray don't tell me you'll want to keep it and tame it; I beg you not to name it."

"You know what? I believe I will," Selena grinned, "For a name, how about—?"

Rahim pleaded under his breath, "Don't do it, don't do it, don't do it—"

"Tiamat," Selena declared, and the whelpling chattered and chirped like a curious baby dragon.

Rahim hung his head in defeat. "And you named it."

She picked Tiamat up and held the whelpling in her arms with great care. It wailed and screeched, but Selena's voice calmed it down, and it purred within her embrace.

Azrael put his hands on his hips and looked up. "What will we tell His Majesty? The creature stopped crying, but the mist is still here."

"I think it will clear soon. See, a breeze is already taking some of it away." Selena pointed at the leaves blowing in the wind. Tiamat curled up and fell asleep, and when Thor finally accepted the hatchling, he leaned down and sniffed it. Snorting, he backed away, but Doragon gestured for him to follow before his sky-bound leap.

As if conceding defeat, Thor lowered his head until his nose touched the ground. **Doragon and I will see if we can help clear this poison faster.**

He launched himself towards the heavens and joined Doragon's side, fanning their massive wings to help blow the fog away. Yet, a slow and deep shudder passed along their bodies as Thor and Doragon drew breath, their sides swelling thrice the size of their rib cages; the trio from ground level could feel the dragons' power to move the sky itself, the air echoing and resonating from their enormous lungs.

Their tremendous shudder was similar to Thor's powerful display to fend off and defeat an entire armada of masked dragons from the attack on Alfheim. He and Doragon opened their maws and released a terrible wave of noise and wind, their furious typhoon screaming like a banshee as their gale storm cleared the city's poison. The trees writhed and flailed as their limbs ripped away, and within moments, the diseased mist finally cleared. Thor and Doragon looked more shocked than pleased, and Azrael looked upon them in awe. "Well, I'll be damned."

Selena shared her sentiments once she recovered from her brief haze; the masked hatchling cowered in her arms but relaxed when she stroked its sides. *Let's allow nature to take care of the rest, my dear. Otherwise, I fear you'll blow the whole city down.*

Thor held his head high, proud of his feat, but he grew cumbersome to see Selena's shared affections; through much persuasion, he and Doragon agreed to wait in the courtyard while the trio trekked back to the castle doors. However, Azrael and Rahim paused when the storm clouds rumbled again, ready to unleash its next turbulent squall, but they were surprised to see Selena not reacting.

Azrael noted, "The storm isn't bothering you."

"I believe not." Although Azrael's spell wore off a while ago, the wrathful thunder faded and drowned away, leaving her at peace during a storm for the first time. Selena looked up from the whelpling and gazed at the swirling maelstrom ensuing above them.

Azrael asked, "Do you need me to place the enchantment on you again?"

She smiled at them. "No, I think I'll be fine."

Rahim gazes after Azrael in surprise. "What on earth have you done to her?"

"I have no idea."

The three knocked on the door; a small wooden slide near the top opened, and a pair of eyes looked at them. "You are not permitted to enter Castle Nuvak until the mist clears, per His Majesty's orders," the guard said.

Azrael stepped forward. "We have come to report to His Majesty: we cleared the disease from his city."

Selena did her best to wrap the dragonet in a shroud without risking exposing it to the nobles while the guard's eyes squinted at the trio, suspecting lies. However, he shut the slide, and the doors cranked open, permitting them entry.

The king's masquerade ball halted once more, and the guests, still too afraid, allowed the group to pass and meet with His Majesty. King Camulus hadn't moved after jolting from his throne previously, and Selena wondered if he had meandered far at all since he had them escorted out.

Nuvak's king looked upon them with disgust on his beat red face. "Well? Out with it—I'm on a rather busy schedule here."

Azrael looked like he wanted to deck the king, but he kept his temper in check. "Your Majesty, we come bearing good news: we cleansed your city." The three knelt before the king, but Selena watched him like a dragon ready to strike.

He didn't show the Crown Princess the same courtesy. "Oh, did you now? I suppose that's good news, and I'm assuming you're here for a reward?"

Azrael's eyes widened, and his breaths became quick. "Will you allow us to rest here for the evening?" he asked, though it sounded more demanding.

"Oh, yes, about that: I've changed my mind," Camulus said with a wave of his hand.

"What?" the three asked simultaneously.

"Did you think I would just let you stay here in my castle or city? I'm the king."

"You're a raging madman," Azrael shot at him. "We saved your people from the plague; the least you could do is offer us and your princess refuge."

"This is my city: my kingdom, my rules. I've had enough of you, and we're done here. Begone!" King Camulus shooed them away like pests, but Tiamat suddenly woke up and wriggled itself out of the shroud, hissing at His Majesty. The king and his court were appalled and backed away. "What is that horrible thing? Get it out of my palace at once." King Camulus shouted, but Tiamat squirmed out of Selena's arms and spat black and green acid blobs at the king's feet, burning through his royal red rugs.

Rahim took a few steps back and nodded to the door. "I think we overstayed our welcome. Let's get that thing and run out of here."

Selena reached out to grab the whelpling, but Tiamat turned around to hiss at her before darting down the hallway behind the king's throne. Amidst the pell-mell chaos within His Majesty's keep, Azrael ran ahead before the king's men took up arms to give chase.

The castle was a magnificent structure, explicitly made for the king's august taste. Azrael followed Tiamat, zig-zagging from the sharp and irregular turns, running through different rooms of various colors with the ornamentation and stained-glass windows to match. Each apartment entertained more of His Majesty's guests, allowing Azrael and Tiamat to pass through the six chambers. The first one was blue; the second was purple, the third green, the fourth orange, the fifth white, and the sixth violet.

The whelpling was surprisingly fast. It dashed into the seventh and last apartment and disappeared behind the black tapestries near the giant ebony clock. The windows in this room were the only ones that didn't match; instead, the panes were a deep blood color, the chilling pair of shades deterring the king's company. Azrael stumbled inside and found Tiamat hiding in a corner, ignoring the similar grim and ominous chimes that reminded him of the Pyre; the ebony clock struck midnight.

Azrael picked up the frightened Tiamat before King Camulus and his men marched through the room, sodden and breathless. "That is quite enough. Out—out now, before I have you chained and thrown in prison."

Azrael's blood boiled with rage; he muttered a few words in the demonic language before taking his leave with Tiamat curled in his arms; upon the clock's final strike and as soon as he crossed the threshold, the king began sweating profusely. Both he and his guards heaved over in sharp pain, and the sneering Azrael waltzed through as the noble guests pushed their way to His Majesty, screaming in horror at the scene.

He walked by Rahim and Selena, beckoning for them to leave Castle Nuvak; Selena asked, "What's happening?"

Azrael grabbed her shoulders and kept her moving forward, and a wicked grin spread across his face, Death's masquerade holding infinite dominance over all. "I think His Majesty succumbed to the plague."

*****

CHAPTER 21: TIAMAT

General Araneus paced about his office before Admiral Silver Altessa, looking out his window with hands clasped behind his back. "I will say, the new captain is excelling thanks to you, Admiral. Captain Allendreth and Venerius are performing admirably, and we'll assign their recruits to their dragons within a month. You are well on becoming a seasoned admiral yourself."

"Sir, you're too kind," Silver smiled, "Of course, I only want to see the success of the riders and what's best for the Empire."

"Yes, of course. How is your Aether line project coming along?"

Silver paused for a moment and nodded to the general's office window. "I'm afraid it had its setbacks, sir."

"What do you mean by that?"

Silver raised his left hand and moved his pinkie finger. "It was fun re-growing this. Harnessing this power for transportation isn't as easy as it seems." Though he could use portals for shorter crossings, Silver could never replicate that for traveling far distances, such as from Alfheim to Snowhaven—doing so required a tremendous amount of magic. Silver figured he could harness Aether through many conductor elements; he found that great power lines crisscrossed Armageddon—like blood vessels of spirit energy coursing through the earth—and could use them to create portals. However, it grew challenging for him to control the flow, and his latest experiment was a disaster. Silver would be walking around with missing limbs if it weren't for him being a shapeshifter.

"That's why I put my best minds to work. However, there is something I need to talk to you about in private. Please, close the door and take a seat." General Araneus sat behind his mahogany desk while Silver bowed and did as he asked. "Now then, the first matter is regarding Liongod and Thor. I recently received word of their travels, and they should be on their way to Nuvak as we speak. They're making excellent time, and I reckon they should return to Alfheim by the end of Stardusk— I've already approved her time off."

Silver's heart raced, but he remained calm and collected before the general. "Sir, of course."

"Very good. I'm sure that you of all people would appreciate it."

Silver was afraid to offer more to the conversation. "I'm sorry?"

"I'm well aware of the relationship. Need I say more?"

Silver swallowed hard; General Araneus knew of their engagement. "Sir, I don't understand how you could accept it if it's against the law."

"It is if I say it is. Right now, I think that this matter stays between us. As far as I'm concerned, this conversation never happened." The general winked, and Silver let out a sigh of relief. "There is, however, an urgent matter that we need to address. I will warn you: it is disturbing." General Araneus opened his desk drawer and pulled out a large book listing all the transactions that the Council had approved over the last year. "My order to you is that whatever is discussed within my office stays in my office. Do I make myself clear, Admiral?"

"Absolutely, sir."

"Very good. Now, I want you to look over these dated documents from within the last six months and tell me if you see anything unusual."

Slightly confused by the general's request, Silver agreed and grabbed the book. Silver's eyes widened after shuffling through the pages when he realized what Araneus meant and said, "Vidar told us that Justiciar Holland had approved a hefty sum of one million for the Mythic Flight eggs."

"Yes."

Silver looked through the book again. "I don't see anything about this exchange, but these numbers don't add up. That means—"

"The Council hasn't received any form of payment from Snowhaven," Araneus ruefully announced. "Not only that, but if you go back further in the records, you will see that a large sum of money was sent to an unknown organization for weapons and other supplies for war *after* the Battle of Alfheim." Their faces drained of all color, and the general broke their tense atmosphere. "Something isn't right. I need to follow up with this and find out more if I can. In the meantime, you will say nothing. Let me deal with this."

"Sir, of course."

"Very good. Please return to your duties, and I will let you know if I find out more."

*****

As the trio trekked through the clean streets, Azrael ignored Selena's pestering questions about what happened to King Camulus; all he said was, "I believe he fell ill to the disease." Yet, he confirmed Chaliss wasn't in the castle and agreed to help Rahim find her. Selena, however, wished to stay behind with Thor and Tiamat near the airship docks, afraid to face Chaliss. Her chest ached when she felt the worst, but Azrael agreed without hesitation.

Thor emerged from the courtyard and ferried Selena and Tiamat to the piers once Azrael and Rahim parted; Doragon had already left the floating isle to hunt while waiting for them to finish business with the king. Thor, however, insisted he wasn't hungry and wished to stay with Selena and the masked dragon hatchling. After climbing into Thor's harness, Selena did her best to sex Tiamat; noting the lack of defined groves under the base of its tail, she assumed Tiamat to be female.

Tiamat nipped at her arm a few times; more surprised than hurt, Selena grabbed a sack full of lettuce and potatoes to offer some to the whelpling as Thor launched himself skyward, soaring towards the hot air balloons and zeppelins.

The creature sniffed her gift and hissed like a cat. "Stop; it's food." Selena took a bite before offering them again. Intrigued, Tiamat mimicked her actions and licked her lips, bobbing her head up and down through chirping noises. "Do you want some more?" Selena offered a piece of beef jerky, and the whelpling gobbled it in delight.

Thor snorted, jealous of not receiving her affections. **That's interesting. Maybe you can train these beasts not to be killers.**

They are not beasts. Please, don't treat them like they're monsters. Thor turned away, but Selena gently added, *I want to take care of Tiamat until she's big enough to survive on her own. Will you help me, my friend?*

Thor growled. **If that is your wish.**

Why are you acting like this?

Thor landed and tucked in his wings before curling up on the pier. He ruefully helped Selena and Tiamat dismount his harness and grumbled. **I'm supposed to be the only one to receive your affections.**

Though Selena couldn't help it, she grew furious at his obsessive behavior. *What will happen when I get married? I will also have to care for Silver; I don't think you're as ready for this as you said you were.*

Thor bared his fangs and flickered his tail. **You're supposed to be my handler, my rider. I thought I was, but I honestly can't stand the thought of you being with anyone else. Why must I share you?**

That's not going to change—

Yes, it will. You will soon forget about me, won't you?

No, Please—

I've seen how happy Silver makes you, and soon, you will forget about me.

I could never forget about you. Thor hissed and turned away; Selena extended a gentle hand to his neck. *My dear, I wish I could help you understand. I'm confident if you had a companion, you would see the difference. I love you, and you're my brother. But—*

I know. It's different compared to your love for Silver.

And yet, you're still not satisfied?

No, and I don't know if I ever will be. I love you too, my sister, but I don't like seeing you care for anything or anyone else.

Selena sat down and leaned against Thor's warm stomach. The whelpling ran around, spewing blotches of acid all over the ground before calling her over. Tail twitching, Tiamat prodded over like a happy cat before curling up beside her legs, wisps of black smoke wafting from her nostrils.

I need to figure out how to help you because mine and Silver's future isn't going to change. I want you to be happy too.

Selena rested her head against his stomach while Thor continued sulking in silence; yet, he snaked his head around, the warm steam from his nostrils touseling her shoulder-length chocolate hair. **Maybe you're right, and I'm sorry. It's always been about us and no one else. It's so hard to imagine someone coming between us.**

No one will drive a wedge between you and me, and I don't want this continuing to be an issue. I need to ensure both you and Silver will be happy by being a companion to you and a wife to him.

Thor hung his head low in shame. **I know I haven't made this easy for you; pray forgive me for my outburst earlier.**

My dear, there is nothing to forgive. Please, give me a chance to show you that I won't forget you. Selena paused when she considered Silver's feelings. *I hope Silver doesn't feel excluded and that he understands; he's never shown to be jealous of our bond.*

I know you'll talk to him if he does, just as you've spoken with me.

She smiled when Tiamat suddenly clawed at her dress and crawled on her lap; she curled up and went to sleep. Thor wrapped the two within his protective wing and held them close as the three dozed off for a few hours, waiting for Azrael, Rahim, and Doragon to return.

Selena woke to the soft flail of wings; Doragon returned with Azrael, but Rahim wasn't with them. As Doragon landed beside Thor, he lowered his paw; Azrael stepped from his clawed carriage and explained: "He's spending the night at his mother's house to catch up on lost time."

Selena's eyes lit up, but she looked down at her feet. "Did *Matu* want to see me too?"

"I'm sure she did, but I didn't get a chance to speak to her." Chaliss was the only mother figure she had ever known; she felt like Thor, wanting parental affection. "What are you going to do what that thing?" Azrael asked, interrupting her train of thought.

Selena placed her hand on the twitching whelpling still lying on her lap. "Tiamat is a she, and I want to care for her until she's old enough to survive on her own."

Azrael shivered. "I don't care what she is; those monsters only bring chaos and death. I don't like it."

"But aren't you the Divine of chaos and death?"

Azrael made an uncomfortable noise. "Yes, but this is different. What I do is natural and needed, but these creatures are violent abominations that shouldn't exist. Looking at that monster is making me nauseous."

Selena scowled at him. "Tiamat isn't a monster; she acts like any dragon I've ever met."

Thor nipped his fangs and flickered his tail in agreement; Azrael yielded defeat and held his hands up in defense before declaring their plans to immediately leave after Selena had a chance to meet with Chaliss. However, the whelpling woke up, interrupting their discussion, and randomly hissed again. Selena panicked as Tiamat nipped at her and jolted from her lap. Thor got on all fours and started growling back, and Tiamat scuffled away in fear, but Selena ran after her. *My dear, we startled her.*

Thor's smoldering amber eyes flickered to a shade of red. **That thing keeps trying to attack you.**

She, Selena sternly corrected, *and Tiamat doesn't know any better.*

Selena knelt before the trembling hatchling and extended her hand, allowing Tiamat to sniff her fingers. Satisfied, she reached into her pack and pulled out another piece of jerky to feed the whelpling. When she deemed her surroundings safe, Tiamat curled into Selena's arms, allowing her to bring her back to Thor and Doragon.

While relaxing with the two dragons by the nearby lit brazier, Azrael arranged a few small sticks over a large, flat stone to cook a salted slab of pork Chaliss had given him. He cut a few pieces to offer Selena for Tiamat, who snatched each slice with ravenous enthusiasm. While Tiamat ate, Selena ran her hand over her hide and shuddered when she felt the open, crusted wounds. "Azrael, can you show me how to heal them?"

He froze but nodded; Azrael knelt beside her and grabbed her hand without warning. Selena immediately withdrew it back, but he explained: "I'm about to show you how."

"But I've never healed before."

Azrael refused her answer. "I know you can do it. You're talented, and you always figure everything out." When she permitted him to do so, Azrael moved her hand to touch Tiamat's wounds. While he instructed her to breathe deeply and imagine a tranquil pool before her, Selena closed her eyes as she felt a burn erupt from her palm. The pain intensified, but then she felt relief; her eyes fluttered open in surprise to see her hand glowing white over Tiamat's injuries. The wounds were gone when the light disappeared, and the hatchling was wholly healed; Tiamat chirped and twittered as she sniffed her stomach and scratched her sides with her hind claw.

Are you and Doragon able to communicate with her?

Thor shook his head. **I don't know how, but her mind is so twisted. We tried to before when you announced you wanted to keep her.**

When Tiamat curled up beside Thor's foreclaw, Azrael offered to continue his teachings behind the elements. He bent over and picked up a stick from the brasier to draw with the charcoals on the pier. "Pray don't knock the city from the sky, but air magic is more about freedom."

Thor's eyes glimmered. **Like how a dragon feels in the sky,** he commented.

"When you breathe in deeply, you feel the energy of the air and reflect that you have this energy within yourself. It's the power of the mind and intellect, and it's considered a vital spirit that passes through all living things, giving life: air magic binds all things together." When he stopped, Selena saw that he drew curvy lines that depicted a wind storm. "Before starting anything, you should meditate first and let your mind be free."

Tiamat worked her way to crawl back into Selena's lap, but Azrael reached down and picked her up. Thor and Doragon nodded and left the pier through a flutter of wings. **We shall not disturb you, my dearest one. Doragon and I will go hunting, and we'll return soon.**

Thank you.

As the two dragons soared away from the floating city, Selena closed her eyes and drew in a lung full of fresh air. The night was calm and relaxing, like her mind drowning out the thunder and lightning from Azrael's enchantment; the sound of the breeze filled her ears until her muscles melted. Her arms and shoulders fell loose, and her head tilted forward. At first, her thoughts drifted over to Thor, but she did her best to resist the temptation to speak with him. Instead, she didn't think at all.

An hour passed in silence; the serenity brought her mind and spirit into a sweet surrender, free of all worries and cares of the world. She finally opened her eyes as if awakening from a deep sleep, her gaze steady to the horizon, and her face lambent with faint starlight.

She stood up, her eyes narrowed, and she punched forward. However, a blast of air sent her backwards and slammed into the pole before falling face-first. Azrael laughed but stopped when she glared at him from the ground. Feeling agitated, Selena regained her posture and dusted herself off. She inhaled deeply before trying again, and this time, when she punched forward, her summoned gusts followed. "It's almost like fire," Selena observed as she made another air blast skyward.

Azrael nodded. "Air and fire mix in harmony—for instance, fire needs air to burn. Then, there are the opposites, like fire and water, and air and earth." He paused when Selena inquired about light and dark Aether and scratched his head. "Light and dark are utterly different, opposites on the spectrum of Aether magic.

"Channeling dark energy is black magic, involving the manipulation of free will and necromancy. However, this can be deadly if it backfires; hence it's outlawed in Armageddon. Its opposite, light, is the energy permeating the natural world, usually as either lightning or a light beam. Light Aether is in tune with our world, so knowing the primary magic is essential. Once you understand the main four, you can fully grasp light Aether —my energy pistols are an example.

"If you could master both light and dark Aether, think of all you could do: stop time, prevent natural disasters, create a new world—the possibilities are endless.

It's only limited by what you're capable of and how much of a strain your body can take. As a conduit, you're channeling so much energy through your body. You're guiding the magic to where it needs to go, so be careful not to muck it all up."

Selena asked through widened eyes, "Has anyone accomplished mastering light and dark Aether?"

"To be honest, I don't think so—not even Silver. I don't know how to use it, nor have I seen the other two Divines."

Selena's face turned pale, and her blood ran ice cold. "Silver has. On our way to Alfheim, he showed us that he could manipulate Rahim's free will and forced him to reveal hidden secrets subconsciously."

"I'll be damned; that old bastard never ceases to amaze me. He probably has other tricks hidden up his sleeve, but I wouldn't recommend it."

Selena bit her cheek. "I don't plan to, but why wouldn't the Divines know how to use both?"

"Because it wasn't until the time of Venexus that we knew there was such thing as both: he discovered and experimented with it. Even after what happened in Oblivion, we decided never to attempt the deviant art, as it would only lead to destruction."

"I see. Perhaps Silver was right in showing me. Maybe I should learn—"

Azrael immediately interrupted her. "You shouldn't mess around with dark Aether—you could get yourself killed."

"Even if it means to defend myself?"

"I said no. I know your heart is in the right place, but dark Aether could easily corrupt you. Besides, I know you have other things that you need to do, like figuring out how to control your dragon state. Have you thought about how you're going to do that yet?"

Selena shook her head. "I was hoping to when we returned to Alfheim and see what Silver thinks." She was surprised by Azrael's reaction, wondering why he would care if harm befell her. "You never cease to amaze me."

Azrael narrowed his eyes at her. "What do you mean?"

"Your concern for me—I don't think I've ever seen that side of you before." Without warning, Azrael's face flushed, and he turned away. "What was that for?"

"Nothing."

Selena said: "Don't say that. Why can't you tell me how you feel?"

"I don't feel anything," Azrael snapped. Tiamat squirmed in his arms, and he hung his head. "Forgive me. I'm so used to letting my anger control me." He looked up and met her concerned gaze. "Yours and Thor's existence means we have a chance at changing our future, and I'm ashamed to admit that it took me a while to realize it. After traveling with you, I'm starting to understand your ways. I still struggle," he nodded to Tiamat, "but I'm trying. Doragon and I had accepted the world's fate for the longest time. It may sound strange coming from me, but we won't have a reason to exist if everyone dies. The Lich's new world would be one without the Divines. You've given us hope, and I don't want to see you do anything reckless."

Instead of words, Selena reached out and brought him into a hug. It was an unexpected gesture, but Azrael wrapped one arm around her back. However, their silent communion was interrupted when Tiamat squirmed in Azrael's other arm, jumping down and hissing as she had done before.

Selena pulled away, but Azrael pointed to the full-grown monstrosity flying in their direction. Upon closer examination, it was a lonely masked dragon; they believed it was the same gauding creature from the Ankoku Pass, but it screeched as it soared above the floating city, its metallic wings shimmering in the moonlight.

When Selena called out for Thor of the imminent danger lurking above them, his and Doragon's roars could be heard from a great distance; yet, she was afraid the two dragons wouldn't arrive in time as the masked behemoth circled overhead. It withheld his devastating breath attacks that could reduce Nuvak to cinders in moments, but its smoldering eyes burned from its mask, fixated on her, Azrael, and Tiamat.

Tiamat spat out acid globs and exhaled its poisoned mist while backing away, quivering in fear. Ignoring the hatchling, Azrael took his defensive stance after summoning his Aether pistols; Selena prepared to use magic, though she suspected her attacks to be folly against the creature. However, Selena's attention remained on subduing Tiamat when she circled them, attacking blindly.

Azrael swore and fired a quick shot at the alarmed hatchling; his bullets missed, and the creature spat acid in his direction. "Blast it; Rahim and I warned you that this would happen."

Selena's emerald eyes shimmered as she stood in between him and Tiamat. "Please, stop—she didn't mean to."

Meanwhile, the masked dragon drew close, its claws battle-ready. It tucked in its metal wings and dropped into a deep, swift dive like a falcon about to snatch its prey.

Yet, Selena remained oblivious to the looming danger; she knelt before Tiamat with tears and held out her arms. "I know you're not a monster." She leaned down and reached out to pet Tiamat, but she nipped and hissed. Ignoring the small gashes the hatchling made into her arms, Selena pulled Tiamat close; she finally calmed down and rubbed her head against hers.

Azrael looked confused and nearly dropped his pistols, but his eyes widened when he saw the diving dragon almost upon them; he made haste to her side. Before Selena could react, Tiamat forcefully headbutted her out of the way as the masked dragon swooped in and skewered Tiamat with its sharp talons before taking off with her body.

"No!" Selena cried and tried running after it, but Azrael grabbed her shoulders, holding her in place. The masked dragon carried Tiamat's lifeless body away before vanishing over the dark horizon.

CHAPTER 22: FIRE AND WATER

Armageddon's cold and nippy air brushed against Selena's cheek. The Turquoise Ocean mirrored the dangling crescent moon as the clouds drifted above, glowing silver and blue. Thor and Doragon had arrived after Tiamat was killed and shared their grief upon learning of her sacrifice. Selena finished making a small grave for Tiamat, setting up a wooden cross embellished with flowers and vines staked in a pile of rocks, and wiped her tears. "Azrael, can you offer a prayer?"

He cleared his throat, held his hands, and bowed his head. "Lord Xyaxon, we bring before you those with the devastating experience of having someone close to them they knew and loved suffer a sudden, violent and needless death. We grieve for those who have to experience this right now, and we pray that you would look down with pity and mercy and meet them right at their point of need in your grace.

"As we lift in prayer those who have to come to terms with the sudden and violent death of a loved one—we pray for Tiamat, who gave her life to save another, that you will welcome this whelpling with open arms. May she find peace and happiness in the afterlife."

"Thank you."

Both Thor and Doragon stood on their haunches, wings unfurled, as they released a lamenting roar echoing across the heavens; they spewed a single torrent of fire shooting overhead like falling stars. Azrael reached out and patted Selena on the shoulder. "Maybe there is hope for the others."

Selena tried to smile through her tears but couldn't bring herself to do it; she knelt before the grave. "You saved me, Tiamat. Maybe one day I can try to save your kind."

Azrael bit his tongue. "Even with this tragic end, I think you made Tiamat happy."

Selena wiped her face on her sleeve. "What do you mean by that?" Azrael shrugged; he stuffed his hands in his pockets and walked away. Her eyes darted between him and the sky, and she smiled. "Thank you."

Keeping the promise she made to herself, she and Thor left to find Chaliss and Rahim once the first hint of light appeared in the sky. With the mist gone, the city was bustling with activity as if the disease never existed. However, the pair overheard gossip among the townspeople that Nuvak needed to find a successor to the throne, and Selena scowled when reminded that Azrael had cursed King Camulus with the plague.

Thor found a spot to land by the water fountain and assisted Selena in dismounting. She followed Azrael's written directions to Chaliss' house while she and Thor ignored the strange looks they received from passersby as they strolled down the widened streets. Selena guessed the residents weren't used to seeing dragons walking around freely.

Chaliss' small house flaunted a small yet dainty garden near the entrance. When they arrived, Selena hesitated. *What if she doesn't want to see me?*

Thor nudged her closer to the door. **That's not true. Knock, and you'll see.**

Selena sighed and tapped the door three times. It opened a few moments later, and Chaliss stood in the doorway, her face covered in tears. She rushed over and embraced Selena in a tight hug, offering for her to come inside. Thor, as he was too big, was only able to slip his snout through the doorway.

Chaliss had three fancy bedrooms with the master bath on one side and the other two apartments on the opposite end. Rahim sat on the couch in front of the welcoming fireplace within the elegant parlor attached to a stylish dining room. Translucent curtains adorned the windows, and the entire house shimmered in a light cream tint. Rahim joined them, and the three fell into a group hug. Chaliss offered to make them some tea while Rahim asked about the whelpling and her training, but Selena gave him the grave news. Rahim's face turned pale. "I'm very sorry to hear that, but maybe you were right."

"We must keep trying."

Chaliss returned with a tray full of earl grey with lemon, scones, and Selena's choice of drink. "I never forgot," she grinned, "Before the mist, life has been kind to me here."

Selena smiled and sipped her perfectly sweetened green tea. When Thor groaned, she offered him a scone, and he slurped it with delight. "We were afraid the Order killed you in the fire."

Chaliss set the tray on top of her coffee table before sitting down. "Loki saved my life and brought me here."

Selena set her cup down. "I wanted to ask you something. Before I do, please understand that I know who I am and have reconnected with my parents."

The color drained from Chaliss' face. "I pray that you're not angry with me."

Selena's eyes widened. "Why would I be angry? Did you already know?"

Chaliss sighed. "The day Flying Officers Gromm and Beck brought you and Thor to my house, Her Imperial Majesty gave them a parcel addressed to me explaining everything. It read that you were her daughter and that the Council was to never find out about you or Thor. The Empress even gave you a different surname so that the Council couldn't trace you back to her. Your parents said they would compensate me well for taking care of you, and they did. Even being here, your mother and father ensured that I would live well and be safe."

"That's wonderful that they've been kind to you, and that was what I wanted to ask. Unfortunately, the Council found out." When she saw the look on Chaliss' face, Selena hastily continued. "They agreed to allow me and Thor to remain in the Imperial Air Force; we're currently on a mission for the Council as we speak."

Tears glistened in Chaliss' eyes. "Rahim told me of your adventures, and I couldn't be more proud of all three of you."

Selena spent the next few hours catching up with Chaliss on all the lost time. While going through her story, she felt silly for how she had behaved earlier. Selena captured moments of hers and Thor's training, how she found out about who she was, and so on. Chaliss eagerly listened to every detail, illuminating that she had missed them dearly. Even as it was time to leave, Chaliss offered to let them sleep in her spare rooms.

Selena declined. "Unfortunately, we have to be in Snowhaven soon as we're already behind schedule. Let's meet again under better circumstances." She gave Chaliss one final hug before Thor pulled his snout away, allowing them to walk outside.

Chaliss followed and patted his nose. "It's wonderful to see you again, Thor. I can't believe how big you've gotten since I last saw you. How much does he weigh now?"

"I believe he was last measured at fifteen tons."

Thor snorted and groaned. **You make that seem like it's a bad thing.**

Not at all; rather, you're growing to the size of a mountain.

"I'm going with you too," Rahim announced, and he, too, marched outside.

"Wait, you're not staying?" Chaliss asked through glistening eyes.

"There is something I must do first, but I promise to return soon."

Chaliss embraced her son one last time with tears streaming down her face. "I'll be waiting here."

After their reunion, they made their way to the local inn to find a courier falcon. Selena gripped her letter to Silver and General Araneus and coin as she delivered them to the handler. When she and Rahim were satisfied as the falcon zipped towards Alfheim, they left the inn and bought the necessities before going to Snowhaven. Selena pulled out the vials with what little remained of Silver's stamina potion and agreed to save them for Thor and Doragon if they needed the extra vigor.

When Selena and Rahim returned with small boxes of food and water, Thor set the supplies within his harness, and the two strapped their provisions near the dragon egg chest. Yet, Selena poked her head up when she thought she heard whispers coming from the trunk, but the sounds quickly faded; Thor confirmed he heard them too. **The hatchlings are growing anxious by the day,** he said.

Upon Selena's and Azrael's marks, Thor and Doragon launched from the zeppelin piers and sailed through the heavens as the winds carried them towards Snowhaven.

The hours had passed by in silence during the dragons' flight to the Purewater Fishery off the coast. While Selena leaned against the dragon egg trunk, Rahim had his arms crossed, facing opposite with his head hung in defeat; he had been this way since they left Nuvak.

"How are you feeling?" Selena asked him.

Rahim stirred and shrugged his shoulders. "Just a little anxious—I'm glad I got to see mum, but I can't stop thinking about Niamh," he sighed, "I want to get some rest before we land in Snowhaven."

"I understand."

Rahim snorted as he leaned up against the bundle of furs, his eyes drooping. "I'll be better once we find her." He peered over at the Mythic Flight egg chest. "I pray the dragons will help us."

Thor and Doragon dipped their heads in concurrence; with the guardians and two Divinity Dragons, Selena knew the Lich must be growing apprehensive to know his adversaries planned on fighting back before the eclipse. However, she couldn't shake away the gut-wrenching sense that their efforts were folly, and Selena began questioning the Council's gambit. Instead, she imagined Snowhaven's icy glory as they soared closer to the Water Kingdom Province.

The azure ocean was as calm as the clear blue sky, the water's surface as still as glass. Down below was the Purewater Fishery laboring on the black sandy beaches; workers moved boxed equipment and goods in and out of the warehouse along the docks, emptying the returning ships from the fishing grounds.

Thor and Doragon made their graceful descent near the piers, ignoring the strange looks from the workers, resting their wings before the nonstop flight to the capital. However, Thor suggested that he could easily float along the water if he grew too weary, but Selena reassured him she still had enough of Silver's elixir to rejuvenate his muscles if needed. *I would rather ensure that you and Doragon were well fed before we embarked across the ocean.*

As she and Azrael inquired about purchasing their freshly caught fish for Thor and Doragon, the curious clerk couldn't help but ask, "Where are you dragon riders heading?" His eyes widened when they answered Snowhaven. "I wouldn't recommend going out there. It's too dangerous—a storm is coming and you don't want to be caught in the squall, not with the Kraken lurking beneath those depths."

Selena had heard stories of the primordial creature slumbering at the bottom of the ocean, for the colossal cephalopod was known to terrorize sailors. She reassured him that they were well-armed and protected by two behemoth dragons, but the worker shook his head. "The Kraken is larger than any creature you've seen, taking down entire fleets of more than ten ships in minutes; there are some things too terrifying in this world that not even dragons dare to face."

When Selena and Azrael returned with two large boxes filled with fish, Thor overheard the warning, and he growled through clenched fangs. **The Kraken is only a sailor's legend. I'm not afraid of the ocean.**

Selena popped open the box and watched as Thor thrust his head inside, gulping down the tunnies by the mouthful. Yet, she anxiously looked over the water's horizon and shuddered; the world's oceans were the greatest mysteries, and Selena feared what could be lurking beneath the surface.

Let's still use extreme caution when crossing, my dear.

She examined the clear sky once more, and when she reiterated the storm warning to Rahim, he laughed. "He's out of his mind; there isn't a cloud in sight."

Selena, however, grabbed the edge of the box until her knuckles turned white. "Perhaps we ought to consider his alert and seek shelter until it's safe."

Rahim looked up and held up his hands. "From what? The weather is perfect." He and Selena looked over at Azrael, who only shrugged. "See? He says we'll be fine, and that's good enough to assure me."

Yet, the workers passing by scoffed, "It's your funeral. Don't say we didn't warn ya," and resumed their duties.

Doragon let out a huge groan and ruffled his wings, and Azrael nodded. However, he nervously peered up at the suspiciously clear sky. "I hope I'm not wrong."

While the two dragons finished their fish boxes, the trio busied themselves, wiping their scales with oil, washing away the gore as best as possible. Selena ensured to clean underneath Thor's jewelry and wiped his gemstones until they sparkled in the sun; Thor chittered in satisfaction as he inspected her handiwork. Whatever mess they couldn't clean, Thor and Doragon stepped into the water and rinsed off in the ocean.

We're ready to make haste, my dear. These waters won't deter us. Thor growled as he lowered his nose to the calm surface, but Selena was still wary of the possible danger.

When everyone was safely buckled within the harness, Thor and Doragon took flight, creating huge water spouts like a volcanic eruption. They maintained steady wing beats, a reasonable pace that would quickly and safely carry them to Snowhaven. Yet, not even an hour had passed since they resumed their journey, and black storm clouds brewed on the cold horizon; the coming early-afternoon darkness and damp smell laded the air. Thunder roared in the distance, and a bolt of lightning cracked the charcoal sky in two. The rocking waves grew violent as Thor and Doragon soared higher into the darkened heavens; there was no warning for the torrential rain—it was merciless.

The three passengers had finished pitching their harness tarps as the storm struck, the rain droplets slamming against their tents, threatening to shred the fabric. Surprisingly, Selena wasn't affected by the thunder and lightning; even Azrael took note of her change and acceptance. "Will you be okay?" he asked her. She looked around and shivered slightly, but she didn't cower down. She looked at Azrael and gave him a thumbs up.

Thor swiveled his head around, his smoldering amber eyes glowing in the darkness. **It's the first time I've seen you this calm during a storm, not counting Nuvak.**

I promise I'm much more relaxed.

However, even in the sky, Selena felt the earth tremble beneath the water; concentric rings rippled across the violent waves. Quivering, Selena stumbled backwards, her eyes darting back and forth as the desperation to run crept closer. "Did any of you feel that?" she asked.

Rahim shook his head as he examined the stormy horizon. Doragon snaked around and nuzzled Azrael's shoulder; he groaned and said, "We need to be careful and keep moving. I feel like we're being watched."

Thor, however, snarled as flames wafted from his chops, lighting their way through the black storm. Selena froze when she felt the vibrations from the water again. *Pray tell me that was you, my dear.*

For once, I wish it was.

Doragon's wings flapped in a frenzy like a hummingbird's as he examined the swirling whirlpool forming below. Azrael's eyes suddenly widened, and he jumped up from his spot, "We need to fly, now. Go!"

Both Thor and Doragon spread their wings and beat them as fast as possible; the steep incline made their buckles and carabiners creak, and Selena and Rahim looped their arms through the saddle's handles. Azrael looked down at the icy waters to see a titanic black mass underneath the ocean's depths; a massive yellow eye with a diameter of Thor's length glowed in the darkness.

A large jet of water erupted from the deep that reached for the two dragons, and a tentacle lined with sharp, jagged spikes on its suction cups lunged towards Thor's underbelly, its thickness comparable to his body. Thor flapped furiously and dodged it; the black, slimy tip barely touched his tail, but Thor escaped unscathed. A few more tendrils plunged through the surface and wildly thrashed about, lunging straight for Azrael and Doragon. Yet, the pair evaded swiftly, using the stormy turbulence to their advantage, allowing them to avoid and break away.

Selena wrestled with Thor's reins to hold herself steady, and both dragons moved sharply from one side to the next, ducking the monster's attacks through quick swerves. The trio trusted Thor's and Doragon's instincts far better than their own; if there was a chance for escape, they were sure the dragons would see it.

Answering through mighty wing-strokes, Thor and Doragon struck out immediately, exhaling fiery torrents illuminating against the turbulent tempest, blasting through the tentacle-filled sky. Thor waged war with gravity and the blistering winds; he and Doragon flew straight down between the erupting tangled mess of spikes and suction cups. However, Rahim's belts and carabiners strained from Thor's twists and turns, and they snapped apart one by one.

Rahim frantically grabbed hold of the saddle's handles. "I'm slipping," he shouted, and before Selena could help him, Thor bucked, and Rahim was thrown from the harness, screaming as he disappeared beneath the swirling clouds.

Selena had been dreading this possibility as she desperately screamed his name and pulled hard on Thor's reins, steering him through the pell-mell tentacle battlefield. Thor locked his pupiled-slits on Rahim plunging for the ocean; he cupped his wings and dove after him in a speedy descent.

Nothing was more unpleasant than watching Rahim making his terrifying fall as she remained safely buckled. Thor's vigor proved superior to the storm's; he made his way beneath Rahim, and Selena reached out, caught his hand, and pulled him aboard. Upon Rahim's rescue, Thor smacked the water and used his legs to push up from the ocean's surface, beginning his ascent once more.

The mass of tentacles let loose another barrage of attacks, and Doragon and Thor veered back and forth as more shot from the watery abyss. Selena, however, remained entirely concentrated on avoiding the onslaught. *You can do this—I believe in you, my dear.* A look of obstinate determination overcame her when a single tendril went straight for Thor. He tried to dodge it, but Selena knew he wouldn't evade it in time: they were headed for a collision course.

With a determined look on her face, she quickly unbuckled herself and assumed the position of using fire magic, but she widened her stance and breathed deep. Without considering her actions, she challenged the ancient creature in a contest of fire and water; unleashing the mighty dragon within, she breathed out a torrent of fire, obliterating the tendril and blasting the pieces of flesh around them. After the Kraken had suffered enough damage, its surviving tentacles slammed against the ocean's surface before slipping into the depths.

When the Kraken withdrew to recover and lick its wounds, the screaming storm lessened, and the rain turned into a drizzle. Selena collapsed into her seat as Doragon and Thor flew away as fast as possible; meanwhile, the gasping Rahim continued sharing praises and gratitude, saying, "Thanks for saving me."

"Don't mention it." Selena leaned against the saddle and looked at the dissipating squall, ignoring Azrael's and Doragon's confused and bemused looks. Doragon nodded in approval at Thor's impressive aerial maneuvers, clicking and chirping.

Thor snorted before his head swiveled back, ensuring his passengers and cargo were safe. **My dear, you're becoming more and more like a dragon each day. Soon, you and I will conquer the skies.**

Selena grinned, though she didn't want to admit her envy. *Niflheim will illuminate from our blazes as fully realized Divinity Dragons.*

CHAPTER 23: CITY OF SECRETS

The days following their encounter with the Kraken were peaceful and serene; their flight was blessed with clear weather as a golden light cracked through the sky, illuminating the monochromatic background. The impatient Selena continued practicing dual-wielding techniques with Azrael, growing faster and more agile during their sparring matches. She had worked up enough strength in her left hand that she could easily switch in the heat of battle.

In between their duels, the trio continued their shooting practices. Rahim had become a proficient gunslinger with Azrael's and Selena's instructions, developing a sharp and cunning eye matching his quick draw. In Selena's opinion, Rahim was more accomplished than the Force's trained snipers; she spared no expense in sharing her jubilation over his prowess, and his face lit up from the endless compliments.

As they soared over the undisturbed crystal clear waters for a week straight, Selena offered Thor the last of the stamina elixir, easing his burning and trembling muscles. He licked his lips and stretched his wings, confirming all was well.

Unable to further contain her excitement, Selena grabbed Thor's horns and leaned forward to spot the islands with the naked eye. To her dismay, she only saw fog dancing across the ocean's surface in the far distance. *Do you see anything?*

Thor groaned and uncurled his neck. **Hmm. I see beautiful waterfalls and marble towers shooting skyward with gold patterns across their gateways.**

You're not funny. Selena grunted, crossing her arms over her chest.

If you knew I couldn't, why did you ask?

You're supposed to have much better eyesight than me. I'm very disappointed in you.

Thor huffed; though Selena was teasing, she knew she slightly wounded his pride. **Be that as it may, I cannot see anything yet, but we will bask in the glory soon.**

I'm just a little impatient. Selena looked over at the dragon egg case. *I wonder who will be chosen as handlers.*

Let the king and his justiciar figure that out. I'm confident they will host ceremonies for those they would deem worthy.

Selena grinned, disregarding possible complications with the Council's disposition; she relaxed beside a bundle of furs and watched as the sky swirled into the beckoning evening. She counted the stars flickering like candles, eased by the slow, deep rushing of Thor's heartbeat like the ocean's infinite song.

Their bags, boxes, and trunks crusted over with frost from the icy air. Though Rahim had already fallen asleep after spending the last two hours training and keeping watch for the capital, Selena rummaged through her pack, pulled out a wool blanket, and draped it over him. It didn't take long for her to give in, and she fell asleep while Azrael stayed awake and took charge.

By the morning of the twenty-eighth of Goldfire —about a month since the group had left Alfheim— Snowhaven's icy stone fortress became a beautiful sight waiting to greet them.

Small little lights could be seen through the clearing fog, illuminating the glacial walls protecting the Water Kingdom capital collected in three isles. Thor and Doragon soared by four towers reaching the heavens, guarded by an enormous archway. Selena and her friends were greeted by the largest snow-covered island exhibiting a massive crown-shaped castle of ice and stone. Two islets were connected to the main by a thick ice bridge as lights shone from the windows strung across the stone buildings.

The group was stunned by the city's glory, but Rahim bolted from his spot and leaned over the saddle; he opened his eyeglass, examining the capital with admiration and determination. "We'll be coming for you soon, Niamh."

Selena was taken aback by the sudden bustle and noise arising explosively from Snowhaven's shore. Thor and Doragon landed softly and carefully on the ice island with much caution needed by their unwanted new company as both men and women waved them down, drawing attention.

Thor observed their behaviors with great interest, snorting in amusement at some of the denizens pushing forward and waving them in their direction, tail twitching as he strutted by. Selena was confused and overwhelmed; she was never given this much attention, even back home at Alfheim. She looked over at Azrael and saw that he wasn't taking the welcome well, keeping his hands over his belted revolver—the one issued to him from the Force. Doragon shared his contempt for the crowd, avoiding them like Nuvak's plague, and followed Thor closely. Rahim, on the other hand, returned their waves, enjoying being the center of attention.

The crowd's cheers and chants were interrupted when a robed official parted through the enthusiastic audience, shouting for everyone to move away. "Pardon me—make way for His Majesty's justiciar. Ah, you must be the anticipated riders from the Force. Welcome to Snowhaven."

Justiciar William Holland was a stout middle-aged man dressed in a high-necked blue coat of silk and unicorn hair lined in gold and furs, matching his golden breeches. A pair of round spectacles perched on the bridge of his nose set against his beat red face beaded with sweat that he wiped away with a handkerchief. As the justiciar had approached, the crowd circled him in with Thor and Doragon, but the dragons finally had enough; they unfurled their tired wings and roared—not loudly out of intimidation, but their growls were enough to deter the spectators.

Once she confirmed the ground was clear, Selena climbed down Thor's foreleg and politely greeted Justiciar Holland, who knelt before her, recognizing her imperial status before Rahim and Azrael had a chance for introductions. "It's a pleasure to meet the Crown Princess herself. Not long before your arrival, your father, His Imperial Majesty, had sought an audience with King Boreas Tristan regarding the Mythic Flight clutch. You and your allies are very welcome, Your Imperial Highness; you five have traveled a great distance, so please, follow me, and you shall be housed in the castle at once. His Majesty has made quarters ready for you and a stone garden for your dragons."

Selena and Rahim had unstrapped the egg chest, which Thor scooped within his claws and set it before the justiciar, who eyed it greedily but withheld grabbing the trunk. Azrael, meanwhile, remained mounted on Doragon, looking at the dispersing crowd with a suspicious glare; Doragon's tail flickered from side to side, sharing his apprehension.

Satisfied, Holland gestured for the group to follow him towards Snowhaven's citadel; Selena and Rahim trodded beside Thor and Doragon with the dragon eggs, taking in the icy city's grandeur as the justiciar gave them the grand tour.

Snowhaven's castle was magnificently large enough to accommodate Thor and Doragon, granting them easy passage for dragons of Ulrich's mass. Selena's steps echoed across the polished black stone and never-melting ice, the stained glass windows reflecting small, shimmering sunlight. They passed through the vaulted keep, its braziers lit by blue flames, but Selena noticed the empty throne and asked where His Majesty was. Holland briefly explained, "King Boreas Tristan is very busy running one of the finest cities in the Empire. If you wish an audience with the king, Your Highness, I may be able to make the arrangements if time permits."

"I beg your pardon, Justiciar, but we pray that the capital has been safe since the recent assault on Alfheim," Selena said; Holland paused his tour and looked at her strangely. "I'm sure you've heard of the news."

Holland readjusted his glasses. "Yes, indeed. We received the news from Vidar's falcon, and your father reaffirmed the importance of our providing aid in the upcoming war. Take care, Your Highness; you and your friends are safe here as we construct our covert of dragon riders, beginning with the Mythic Flight."

Rahim suddenly grew impatient. "You haven't seen the strange creatures that attacked Alfheim, then? They look like dragons but reek of death and decay, and now the Empire is in danger—"

"Danger? Snowhaven is a fortress—we could never be in peril. Please follow me," Holland said, speeding ahead before gesturing down a nearby corridor. Selena and Rahim exchanged glances, for Holland purposefully avoided the subject altogether. "The heated stone gardens are this way for your dragons; His Majesty's cooks are preparing for their dinner as we speak."

Thor's eyes flickered to a shade of red and chittered in delight; Doragon shared his glee but waited until Azrael dismounted before joining Thor in their quarters. With the two dragons taking the lead, Holland escorted the trio to the dragons' sanctuary, a crystal chamber decorated with rainbow gemstones growing beside heated pools. The gardens were fairytale-lovely, Thor's and Doragon's nails clicking against the ebony tile contrasting the gilt-painted ceiling, the onyx walls streaked with gold and mother-of-pearl.

The vast crystal garden was laded with mouth-watering smells. True to Holland's word, three chefs from the king's kitchen were busy roasting swordfish and marlins on massive spits over the open fire pit; once the first fish was properly cooked and seasoned, one chef sliced the marlin in half and mentioned for Thor and Doragon to partake. They gobbled the delicacy in seconds and licked their chops, ready for more.

My dear, you must try this, Thor eagerly stated, **it's so delicious.** Doragon hastily agreed through chirps and approving nail clicks, his slits fixating on the soon-to-be-ready swordfish. When the cooks finished roasting the last marlin fillet, Thor and Doragon lay drowsy after their substantial meals, leaving half of the fish unfinished.

Wholly satisfied by the royal treatment compared to Rhumbek and Nuvak, Selena smiled. She, Rahim, and Azrael unstrapped Thor's and Doragon's harnesses and watched as the two dragons stretched and submerged themselves in the water, washing away the dirt and pieces of fish scales stuck to their mouths.

When Holland reconfirmed all was well, he gestured for the trio to follow him back the way they came to their readied apartments once they gathered their belongings. "Your quarters are just down this hallway, Your Imperial Highness—not far from your dragons."

After a short trek and passing by a heavily guarded grand staircase, the justiciar led them to a set of extravagantly prepared rooms with velvet-cushioned chairs and window seats, thick carpets lined with the finest furs heaped over the stone floors, and in the center of their rooms was a roasting fireplace with blue flames. The first apartment was designated for Selena, connecting to Azrael's and Rahim's through a closed closet door.

As the trio unpacked, Holland suddenly grew impatient when his eyes landed on the treasured egg chest Selena had set on her bed, but she shielded it from his view by spreading her arms. "We ought to wait and meet with His Majesty before we finalize this exchange," she declared.

Holland's eyes suddenly gleamed with murderous intent, but as soon as Selena noticed, he recovered his previously agreeable facade. "I signed the agreement on His Majesty's behalf upon arranging the delivery of payment. Therefore, I implore you to seek an audience with the king, who will only confirm my part in the exchange."

Selena squinted at him. "Very well. I wish to meet with King Boreas as soon as he can grant the Crown Princess a meeting." However, she grew increasingly reluctant to hand over the eggs when her gut-wrenching sense returned. Once she was reminded that her father assured her all was well in Snowhaven, Selena finally handed over the dragon egg trunk to the suddenly gleaming justiciar.

Holland nodded in approval as he snatched the chest. "Your trust is well-placed, Your Highness. Take care and rest easy, for I will ensure His Majesty receives the eggs. Otherwise, King Boreas will grant an audience with you three later—I will return to let you know when." Holland swiftly carried the eggs away before any other objections could be made and disappeared down the corridor.

Azrael broke the tense atmosphere lingering once the smiling justiciar had hastily vanished. "I don't believe a word that foul-smelling git says—I'm not sure if any of you have noticed, but everyone is acting fake."

"You're right, and this is absurd," Selena said; for all of Holland's genial welcome, he had left them without another word as soon as he had his greedy hands on the dragon eggs. After seeing the empty throne, Selena highly suspected that Holland didn't want them to see the king, steeping her distrust in the Council for arranging this delivery.

Not long after Holland's departure, the cooks from the stone gardens arrived with gourmet fish dishes and steaming cups of tea, serving Selena first before Azrael and Rahim. They offered her strange looks when she requested green tea and honey, and Selena sighed, accepting the strong black tea served with milk instead. It seemed as though green tea wasn't a popular drink of choice outside of Alfheim after visiting the other provinces, and Selena had to make due.

Rahim was the only one eagerly eating his food, but Selena and Azrael picked at their roasted salmon and boiled potatoes before pushing their plates away, their appetites lost. Minutes turned to hours, and they still hadn't seen an inkling of Holland since he ferried the dragon eggs; Selena began doubting if they would meet the justiciar that day or if their time had been wasted in vain.

Thor, in the meantime, attempted to steer her angry thoughts to more pleasant matters. **My dear, why not join Doragon and me by the mineral pools while you wait?**

I don't wish to miss our chance to see Holland again. I want to speak with King Boreas myself and ensure the safety of the dragon eggs.

While they sat and waited on the window seats, Selena and Rahim played a card game while Azrael sat and sulked in the corner, grumbling and muttering about what Selena could only assume. The two ignored Death and Rahim complained and groaned when Selena won their next game; he threw his cards down and protested as Selena gathered them together and shuffled.

Yet, she looked up at said, "Azrael, come over and play a game with us."

He growled and sunk further into his dreary attitude. "I don't want to play. I want to talk to the king and go home."

Rahim snorted and leaned against the windowpane, noting the late hour as the sun began setting over the horizon. The black and grey clouds swirled over the capital, preparing a fresh bounty of snow. "I wish I knew where Niamh was," he whispered.

Azrael quickly peered over his shoulder when the revelation suddenly struck him. "You two won't believe me, but I feel she's here." Rahim's ears perked up from the news, and he shuffled over, begging for a more concise explanation. "I'm not sure how to describe it, but it was a sudden shudder: there was nothing one moment, and the next—" His eyes widened when he met Selena's and Rahim's confused gazes. "Niamh and those masked dragons are hiding somewhere within the city."

"Where?" Rahim asked, but Azrael stared down the hall in a confused daze.

Their conversation was interrupted by echoing footsteps, and the trio flinched when Holland finally returned, this time with a parcel in hand. "I have great news," he shouted. "Your request to meet with the king is pending approval: it should take eight weeks."

Selena snarled. "Eight weeks? But we don't have that long."

"That's much more quickly than usual. Normally it's about four months, but you're in luck. In the meantime, feel free to enjoy your time here in the city." Holland closed his eyes and smiled when Selena snatched the parcel from his hand and scanned the approved request.

"I think we'll all feel much better once we see His Majesty," Selena said, "is there any way we can see the king sooner?"

"As I've said before, King Boreas Tristan is extremely busy—"

Selena scowled and vainly clarified, "Too busy to grant an audience with the Crown Princess, but not with the Shadow Emperor."

Justiciar Holland grinned, ignoring their annoyed expressions. "Only if time allows—the king has no time to get involved with your petty squabbles."

"Where did you bring the dragon eggs?"

"I can assure you that they're safe." His eyes narrowed on Rahim, whose face was already cherry red. "I understand you're looking for your friend. It would be a shame if you failed in finding her."

Rahim was already about to explode when Azrael announced that Niamh was still somewhere within the city, and he unleashed his pent-up fury. "Where is Niamh?" Holland sneered before turning around; Rahim's fists trembled, and he launched for the justiciar, but Selena and Azrael held him back. "This whole city is mad—what is going on here?" Rahim asked.

"The less you know, the better," Holland said, his eerie tone making the hair on the back of their necks prickle before taking his leave.

Unable to subdue Rahim's anger, Selena marched over to the stone gardens, the crystal decorations losing their luster in this city of secrets. Thor and Doragon overhead that unpleasant exchange as they were in growls and snarls when Selena approached. Thor demanded to know, **Where did Holland take the dragon eggs?**

We don't know for sure, and we can't see the king, Selena grabbed Thor's harness and dragged it over to his stomach, *But Niamh is in the city, and we must find her and leave.*

My dear, it's already unsafe, and I will take you away. I don't care what happens, for I will not let you fall to harm.

Selena paused and set his saddle against the hearth. *We're not leaving without Niamh.*

I pray never to repeat this, but I don't care what you think; to Oblivion with Niamh, the king, and even the dragon eggs. I'll bring you back to Silver if I must.

Their argument was drowned out by Azrael's and Rahim's heated discussion on how to pursue their next course of action. Regardless of Rahim's insistence on staying to find Niamh, Azrael suddenly grew apprehensive about spending more unwarranted time within the capital, confirming that "Niamh will be fine even if we leave her here."

Rahim remained utterly unconvinced about Niamh's safety, and Selena agreed after glaring at Thor, who shamefully looked away, distracting himself by staring at the mineral pools. "We will find out what's happening in this ersatz city once we save Niamh, see the king, and reclaim the dragon eggs."

Concurring with their new resolve, the trio marched outside the castle and crossed the icy bridge to reach Snowhaven's market district, asking every local they passed by if they had seen Niamh by offering a physical description of her character. Unfortunately, their search always led to a dead-end, for everyone gave the same answers, "I'm sorry, but I haven't seen your friend anywhere," and "we haven't received visitors from the Fire Kingdom Province in years."

However, the nearby stall clerk selling vegetables gestured for Selena and Azrael while Rahim was busy asking the townspeople across the road. "I heard the Crown Princess was here visiting. It's great to meet you, Your Highness—James Hockley, at your service."

Selena bowed. "It's a pleasure to meet you, Mr. Hockley."

Azrael, however, squinted at the shopkeeper, questioning his possible motives. "Can you tell us what's going on in this city?"

When James trembled, Selena changed the subject. "He means that we're looking for a friend who may be here, but we can't find her, and the justiciar won't tell us anything nor allow us to see the king. Do you know anything about that?"

He held up his hands in defense, his eyes scanning the crowd to ensure he wasn't seen. "You didn't hear this from me, but everything changed when these strange creatures appeared three months ago. They looked like dragons, but different—"

"The masked dragons," Azrael stated, and James nodded.

"Please, Your Highness, heed this warning: stay away from the justiciar and leave while you still can." James then hastily unloaded his stall and brought his produce inside his house across the street.

Rahim ruefully returned, hanging his head in defeat upon hearing the same dismal answers; as he was about to admit defeat, their ears perked up when a familiar voice called out from behind: "Selena? Rahim? Is that you?"

The trio wheeled around with startled gasps when Niamh emerged from the shadows behind one of the shops, and Rahim ran over to hug her. As Azrael promised, Niamh was alive and well, clean and devoid of any scars or wounds. Selena joined the happy reunion, leaving Azrael confused and skeptical of the sudden gathering. When Selena and Rahim bombarded her with questions about her well-being and how she survived the masked dragons that kidnapped her, the shocked and confused Niamh asked, "Monsters? What are you talking about?"

Both Rahim and Selena took a step back and exchanged glances; Rahim placed his hands on her shoulders before making direct eye contact. "Do you not remember anything? You were attacked and taken by these strange dragons."

Niamh shook her head. "No, I traveled here with my family."

Azrael scowled and pointed at her. "Something doesn't seem right—I think she's been brainwashed."

Niamh seemed as surprised as they were as she exclaimed in defense, "No, that's insane. I can't be."

"Why would they do this to Niamh?" Selena asked.

Azrael growled and glanced to the sides, ensuring no one was eavesdropping. "I bet you anything that this is a trap."

While Rahim and Azrael talked to Niamh to see if they could help trigger her memory, Selena reached out to the still-distraught Thor. *We found Niamh, but she doesn't remember anything.*

He kept his answers short and blunt. **We can help her remember on the way back to Alfheim.**

We're not finished in Snowhaven yet. She paused when realizing Thor still felt ashamed and added, *My dear, I know you want to protect me, but remember our duty is to the Empire and the world. We have to try and help.*

I would rather watch the world burn than see you hurt or killed.

Selena's throat tightened. *Pray it won't come to that, my twin flame.*

Azrael suddenly growled and pulled Selena close, away from Rahim's and Niamh's earshot. "If you want to see the king and find out where Holland took the eggs, we must find King Boreas *now*."

Selena's eyes widened when she caught his meaning: King Boreas was in danger, but they still had a chance to change his fate. "Where can we find him?"

Azrael spun on his toes and eyeballed the citadel's towers. "He must be within the castle not far from Holland's control. If I had to guess, he's probably somewhere upstairs where he can still overlook the city, but we must be careful: I'm assuming Holland warned His Majesty that we're coming."

The four dashed back to the castle and up the slippery steps, but a sudden ice shard twice the size of a fully grown human erupted from the ground near their feet. To their horror, a myriad of crystal spikes jutted from the castle floor, and the group zig-zagged across, avoiding the deadly traps.

Suddenly, an entourage of heavily-armed and armored castle guards rushed from the keep, but Selena and Azrael stomped with one foot, generating a massive stone wave, knocking back the stampeding sentries. Meanwhile, Rahim kept the confused Niamh close, his revolver drawn, picking off the straggling guards that Selena and Azrael had missed before they could summon more icicle spears.

As they continued inside, they paused when they finally saw His Majesty, King Boreas Tristan, clad in royal furred robes, walking towards the throne from the grand staircase with Holland following him. However, before the king could turn around and address Selena's company, a cloaked figure appeared behind the throne, pulling out a glistening dagger hiding underneath the sleeves. Azrael warned His Majesty while he, Selena, and Rahim loaded and readied their firearms, but the stranger struck swiftly and silently like a deadly snake, dragging their blade under the king's exposed throat, leaving the group to watch in horror as his body fell into his crimson pool.

CHAPTER 24: THE WOMAN WITH THE COBRA TATTOOS

"This ends now." Holland sneered at the group as the hooded stranger stepped over the king's bloodied corpse and sat on the throne, crossing their legs. Long platinum blonde locks flowed from underneath their cowl, and though Selena assumed them to be a woman, the figure didn't unmask their identity.

Azrael and Selena slowly backed away when a whole battalion of soldiers and guards encircled them—about fifty in all—but Rahim's hands trembled as he aimed his Winclock at the stranger's head. The conspirators displayed no reaction, but Selena whispered for him to back down while her eyes darted down the corridor for Thor and Doragon, but the dragons had yet to make their appearance.

My dear, where are you? Her heart sank when she received no reply; Thor's thoughts had vanished, leaving her isolated within her tempestuous mind.

Selena growled like an angry dragon ready to strike and retaliate but heard a pitiful cry squealing from behind. With great care, she glanced back and saw Rahim was already in chains with a black hood draped over his face, and the guards circling them revealed themselves to be the dreaded members of the Obsidian Order, their silver dragon-head masks glowing in the faint, eerie moonlight. What terrified her the most was how fast and quiet they were in detaining poor Rahim, for she and Azrael were oblivious to his sudden capture.

She unexpectedly felt freezing metal pressing against the side of her cheek. Her heart stopped, and she didn't have to turn around to see that Niamh stood behind her with a loaded revolver. Selena did her best to stay calm, even facing her possible imminent fate. Instantly, she understood their meeting with Niamh was a trap and that their brainwashed friend had betrayed them.

Niamh's stoic tone unnerved the trio as she said, "Don't do anything so rash, for you're surrounded. If you look back, I will pull the trigger." Azrael growled but neither objected nor attempted to fight back as Niamh pressed the barrel deeper into Selena's cheek.

"Well done, Niamh," Holland said, clapping, "Medusa should be quite pleased." The cloaked stranger laughed in amusement, and given their feminine pitch, Selena assumed they were a woman and possibly Medusa herself. The justiciar straightened his spectacles until they gleamed in Selena's eye. "Please forgive our sudden rudeness, Your Highness, but I tried to warn you," he nodded to the silent cultists, "Bind them."

Selena didn't struggle when bound in ropes and chains, nor when Niamh forced her to her knees, liberating her, Azrael, and Rahim of their weapons. She hunched forward, holding her head in defeat while snarling under her breath, swearing to seek vengeance upon these traitors. Azrael, unwillingly at first, soon followed her example, not without muttering and grumbling.

Selena knew she would be risking her life by speaking up, but she swallowed her fear. "How could you do this?" she quietly asked Niamh. She ignored Selena's question without a reaction, and the painful realization that Niamh was brainwashed made her heart sink further.

Her eyes scanned the castle, wondering if the Lich was somewhere hiding within, waiting to unveil himself. However, she couldn't sense his demonic presence or the masked dragons lurking within the city's shadows. *How is that possible? Thor and I were always able to detect their auras.*

Selena continued to reach for Thor's consciousness in desperation, but he remained in the dark. Looking at Azrael, he exhibited the same frustration, and she assumed he couldn't contact Doragon either.

Pleased in exposing them to the world's censure and its derision of disillusioned hopes and dreams, Holland smirked, enjoying the fruits of his victory. "Your dragons cannot hear you—the crystals from the stone gardens are enchanted to trap them within their gilt-painted prison and block all telepathic communication, courtesy of the Dark Master's magic. They activated once we captured you."

Selena scowled, disdainfully remembering the Silent Vow necklaces that former Captain Ashur Bel designed. This black magic was the work of the Lich himself, and Ashur used the dark Aether enchantments for the Council, thus further proving Vidar's betrayed alliance with the necromancer. She and her friends fell for the Council's gambit, and now the Lich possessed the Mythic Flight dragon eggs—like harnessing the power of a Divinity Dragon.

"This is a dangerous move, Justiciar," Selena said, "kidnapping the Crown Princess and dragon riders from the Imperial Air Force. You and His Majesty swore allegiance to the imperial family." Yet, regardless of her building wrath, Selena couldn't bring herself to call upon her dragon state. She didn't wish to risk her friends' safety or the dragon eggs, wherever Holland hid them.

Holland turned to the stranger, who nodded, approving him to continue. "My apologies, Your Highness, but the king pledged loyalty, not I. Your father was blissfully unaware of our coup. Snowhaven fell long before he came, and even His Majesty, King Boreas, was oblivious, but he served his purpose."

The howling winds screamed behind them through the open doors, delivering a thick white fleece over the darkened city. Footfalls marched up the stone steps, revealing the locals who had greeted them upon arrival; they morphed into soldiers wearing sinister spiked armor of black and red. Selena scowled to see that the Lich's army disposed of and replaced themselves as Snowhaven's citizens, avoiding detection from the outside world.

The ice isle shifted as waves spewed and rippled across the violent ocean, and hundreds of masked dragons burst from the dark depths like an erupting volcano and circled the citadel like a murder of crows. Selena clenched her teeth as her eyes watched their every move from the opened doors like a hungry wolf anticipating the dragons' raid upon the city as they had done with Alfheim. However, they withheld any possible attack and perched along the floating icebergs, their smoldering crimson eyes glowing in the shadowed fog, watching and waiting.

The stranger finally stood up from the throne and removed her cloak: a charming woman of beauty with an eerie physical resemblance to Selena, save for her long, strikingly blonde hair and purple eyes sparkling against her copper-toned skin. Donning a prestigious sleeve-less military uniform and polished hessian boots, the woman —Selena presumed to be Medusa—stepped down the throne's steps, the blue flames illuminating the cobra tattoos on both shoulders.

Azrael scowled with disgust, and Selena assumed he was familiar with her, judging from his hostile reaction. The woman with the cobra tattoos ignored them and looked at Niamh. "Well done, my pet," she said, her voice sinister. She then looked at Selena and sneered. "It was about time that we met. I've been looking forward to this moment. Oh? You look so confused and depressed; we might as well get acquainted, though you've probably figured it out by now: I am Medusa."

Selena almost didn't care what her name was, as it didn't matter. Instead, she recognized her from the Grand Exchange, hiding underneath the ridiculous attire. "You were with the Lich, pretending to be his sister when he disguised himself as Myrrdin. I'm surprised we couldn't detect the evil looming over this fake city."

Medusa had a gleam in her eye, and her wicked grin stretched across her face. "You're not so daft, after all. You and Thor couldn't sense us because we masked our essences," she held up a gold necklace with a jeweled pendant, "this enchanted piece is enough to hide us from you and Thor for leagues—I didn't want you to spoil our fun."

Rahim struggled in his bindings and growled through his hood, "What have you done to Niamh?"

Medusa sneered and put a hand over Niamh's shoulder. "As soon as my children, the Nidhoggr, brought her here, it didn't take long to convince her to side with us. After all, Niamh is the honored guest of His Dark

Majesty." In response, Niamh tightened her grip on the revolver.

"Why did you need Niamh?" Selena asked.

"We didn't *need* her. My Nidhoggr believed her useful, so they brought her to me instead of killing her. So far, I have not been disappointed—I've even allowed her to keep the same one that brought her here."

"I am honored, lady Medusa." Niamh's voice was monotone and almost mechanical. The ground suddenly rumbled when one of the masked dragons landed before the castle stairs, poking its head through the doorway. It stretched its blade wings during its slow walk, the tips brazing and scraping along the castle walls; Selena recognized its damaged mask and its lips curled as it imitated their speech through guttural shrieks, "Niamh belongs to me," the same goading creature from the Ankoku Pass.

The trio growled and snarled as the Nidhoggr walked inside, the castle trembling from the weight of its massive steps; it lowered its head and rubbed its slimy snout against Niamh's side, purring and chittering in a display of affection.

Medusa sneered and scoffed when noting their close bond, but she returned Selena's paled face with scorn. "Don't fret, *Your Highness*, for Thor is safe and alive. As long as the Dark Master wishes it, we will treat his dragon like royalty as he is not your house pet. Soon, the dragon will join His Dark Majesty and be by his side at the rise of the eclipse. You may be lucky enough to witness the dawn of a new age." Medusa then turned to Azrael. "And welcome back, Azrael. Oh, the Dark Master so longed to see you again."

Azrael grunted and turned away. "I'm all tied up at the moment. Maybe I'll return another time."

Medusa wasn't amused; she moved with inhuman speed like a striking snake and punched him right in his stomach. Azrael doubled over in pain and spat out blood but cursed and swore her name; Selena tried to move to help him, but Niamh held her in place. "Ashur and I knew of your betrayal for months, but it no longer matters," her eyes shimmered with murderous intent, "for we have the Crown Princess to thank for her part in our scheme." Medusa held out her hands to present her to everyone standing there as if to mock her.

Holland and the malevolently smiling Medusa turned, and there stood the former Captain Ashur Bel, strutting forward from the shadows with his hands clasped behind his back. His pointed chin and gaunt cheekbones brushed against the wide collar of his dark red frock coat with black and gold trimmings and buckles, black breeches, and polished hessian boots. His black hair slicked past his pointed ears, accentuating his thick slanted eyebrows, giving him this intimidating aura as if he were always angry. Around his neck, Ashur still wore an obsidian dragon tooth necklace, and Selena assumed it carried the same enchantment as Medusa's.

A ghostly white shadow slithered around him, and Selena recognized it was his dragon, a rare Imperial Pearlscale with venom and acid abilities named Jade. His ivory nails clicked against the stone as he stepped forward in the light, his translucent scales smooth like a python's hide. Relatively small compared to Thor and Doragon, Jade was shockingly pure white, like fresh snow. Two long tendrils the length of his neck flowed in the blizzard breeze. He folded in his great wings and gazed upon them with piercing, emerald eyes. Adorned around the base of his neck was a heavy golden torque set with sapphires; the deep color magnified the hue of his sea-green eyes.

Though Jade presented the same venomous personality as his handler, Selena believed him a lovely breed, beautiful like a viper.

Ashur smiled wickedly. "It is a pleasure to see you again, Liongod," he said sarcastically, "I pray the Council didn't trouble you too much when discovering yours and Captain Altessa's secret."

"He's an admiral now and doing much better since you're no longer there."

Defending his rider, Jade hissed and snarled at Selena; he nudged Ashur's side, his tongue slithering from his clamped serrated fangs as the frill along his jawline trembled and flared. "Now, now, Jade. I told you that we must play nice." Although Ashur spoke to his dragon, he didn't dare tear his gaze away from Selena and her friends.

"For some reason, I am not surprised by you, *Captain*." The words tasted vile in Selena's mouth. "I wouldn't even spit in your direction. I swear by the Divines, if I weren't in these chains, I would—"

Niamh used the butt of her revolver and smacked her in the head, and Medusa smirked. "Thank you, pet. I thought you would have figured it out by now, Liongod, but I'm disappointed by your lack of intelligence and cleverness."

"I figured out this was a ploy before you made your grand appearance, *snake*," Selena said, "allow me to guess the rest: you and Vidar negotiated the terms where you get the dragon eggs, and you send him an army of Nidhoggr." Medusa's lips curled into a sinister sneer, and Selena grimaced, ignoring Azrael's disapproving glances, and continued, "Quite frankly, I'm flattered you would consider taking on my form but may I suggest finding a unique look next time? It's rather dull when mimicking someone else far greater than you."

Medusa's smile vanished, and her subordinates took a step back; however, she held her tongue. "Ashur and Jade warned me you were headstrong and foolish, but I find it entertaining." She looked down the hall and jeered at Thor and Doragon locked away in the crystal gardens. "It was a risky and bold move, needing you and the necromancer's dragon to deliver the Mythic Flight eggs to us, but we had no choice. As Divinity Dragons, you two were the only ones strong enough to stand against my children, as Vidar notified us by the courier falcon." Her purple eyes fixated on Azrael. "But you brought us Azrael, and he's the key to making everything happen."

He squirmed and grumbled, but Medusa continued. "What you've done was technically treason, as you aided our Dark Master in the war effort. You're now labeled an enemy of the Empire, and of course, the Council will have no record of their part in this, so the Crown Princess is the one to blame."

Medusa strutted and knelt before Selena, forcing her to see her evil reflection. "I think you will also love this one. His Dark Majesty utilized your beloved's research from the Well of Souls and replicated the project in his lair at Mount Blackrock. It can do so much more than resurrect the dead." She nodded to the Nidhoggr, wrapping the brainwashed Niamh within its protective coils. "The Nidhoggr were dragons until the Dark Master killed and brought them back through the new Well as powerful, undead alterations—they only obey me."

No....

Medusa's eyes sparkled when she saw the hope leave Selena's face. "However, they weren't the new Well's first success. You helped the Dark Master too. Don't you remember? I was made from your blood when His Dark

Majesty had you locked up before those buffoons rescued you. Isn't that amazing? I am your clone, but perfect."

Selena refused to hear more, having enough of what Medusa had to say. Yet, Azrael grunted and asked, "What other plan does the Lich have up his sleeve this time?"

Medusa gave him a sinister smile. "You'll see soon. Your usefulness will redeem you of your sins."

"Why is Azrael part of your plans?" Selena asked quietly.

Medusa snickered as she stood up and dusted off her uniform. "I won't ruin that little surprise for you just yet." Before Selena could brace for it, Medusa acted with lightning speed, punching her in the stomach as she had done to Azrael. The pain was unbearable; she tasted blood in her mouth and heaved over, gasping for air.

Medusa looked to Holland and ordered: "Take these prisoners to the dungeons and keep their dragons locked in the crystal gardens. If they so much as fight back, their riders will be the first to die, but do not touch the necromancer's dragon."

Niamh backed away and joined her Nidhoggr companion, allowing Medusa's subordinates through. Followed by Holland, three cultists of the Order led the bound trio behind the throne and down the hidden stairway, spiraling downwards before reaching a stone wall lit by two torches with flickering blue flames. Holland grabbed one and pressed a switch, and the wall crumbled and lowered itself down into the depths. Selena was frightened, though her face lacked emotion, recognizing their solemn hour.

As the former justiciar continued his victorious march, Selena recalled Xyaxon's warning that the Lich would still find a way to succeed in destroying their world by the winter solstice, and he planned on using the dragon eggs to do so. As for Azrael's role in finishing his plans, she could only guess.

Holland led them past a few empty, decrepit rooms, the damp air smelling most foul. A slight noise escaped her lips when she noticed blood smeared across the narrow walls, but Azrael grunted. Rahim, meanwhile, still couldn't see from his hood and dragged his feet, but he was forced to walk faster with a tug of the cold chain.

Holland and his associates brought the trio to their designated cell—hollow by design as a stone cube with no windows—equipped with dangling chains and piled burnt corpses. Once the Order removed Rahim's hood, the three were locked in separate suspended metal cages with shadow locks. Selena felt disorientated by the prison's layout, her stomach churning from the smell of scorched, rotten flesh and the blood-coated table in the corner, covered in filthy rags. When the justiciar and the Order sealed the dungeon doors with magic and left, Selena touched the lock, but electrical pulses surged through her fingers. She recoiled back and cradled her stinging hand.

While Selena and Azrael sighed and leaned against their bars, Rahim squealed and panicked until Azrael barked at him. "I can't hear myself think—just be grateful that Medusa kept us alive. She's not known for her mercy."

Selena snorted as she continued reaching out to Thor's thoughts, hoping to circumvent the enchantment, but the crystals within their beautiful prison severed their connection. "We can't sit and rot in here while Medusa and those gits run amok."

Azrael bit his bottom lip. "We don't have a choice right now, but eventually, we'll find the right opportunity.

At least we're warm, dry, and alive." He shrugged and stretched.

Rahim finally relaxed when understanding Azrael's point and let out a long sigh before whispering, "I'm sorry, Niamh."

Selena gripped the steel bars and wondered if she could melt them with dragon fire, but even if she did, she knew they wouldn't break past the dark enchantment Holland and his associates placed on the dungeon door. She scoffed when Azrael confirmed to sit and wait for now, for they had no way of dispelling the dark Aether, but her thoughts steeped with the fiery passion that Medusa could never extinguish. Selena wrapped her hand around her wolf necklace, reminding herself that she was headstrong, stubborn, and born to fight, and no matter what it took, she resolved that, for her friends, she would never quit.

CHAPTER 25: THE DRAGON AND THE SNAKE

Time was an illusion, and their existence slowly unwound from the arbitrary construct as Selena, Rahim, and Azrael dangled in chains within their windowless prison cell. Hours turned to days, but an eternity had passed since Medusa captured them; as Selena began questioning her sanity, she wondered if the concept of time was correct or even relevant.

Yet, the trio cringed and recoiled when they heard footsteps approaching their cell, and two of Medusa's heavily armored soldiers wielding bloody spears came inside their dungeon. One lifted their gloved hand without saying a word, and the lock to Selena's cage disappeared. Selena squinted at them, almost ready to lash out, but Azrael grunted, disfavoring her contemplated decision as she was in no condition to fight her way out alone.

The soldiers swung open her cage and watched as Selena carefully stepped out, ready to attack if she retaliated; instead, she quietly and obediently followed as they grabbed her shackles and led her out of their cell. She slowly sauntered down the ghastly corridor with one sentry to her front and the other behind.

However, Selena tripped and fell, and she suddenly felt the crack of a whip—cat-o'-nine-tails—snapping at her backside, the stings quick and sharp. Her resilient dress absorbed most of the brutal attack, but a few thongs still caught her bare skin; she tried not to scream but couldn't contain herself at the second set of lashes; the guards finished delivering their punishment and forced her to stand up and continue the march.

They led her to a vast stone room where Medusa stood in the middle, waiting underneath the rusty chains hanging from the ceiling over a stone table covered with blood and tools; cages lined up against the wall behind her with shackled skeletons in tattered clothes. When Selena was hesitant to walk inside, her captor whipped her again, but she swallowed her screams and stood her ground, her smoldering eyes fixated on the sneering snake.

"That's enough for now." Medusa raised her hand and nodded at the two soldiers in satisfaction; they vanished in a plume of smoke where they stood. "You look dirty and uncomfortable in that pretty little dress of yours."

Selena snarled and brought her chained hands to her chest, stepping back. "I swear I will rip you apart if you lay one hand on me, you treacherous snake."

Accepting this dragon's challenge, Medusa moved like a lightning bolt and ripped her dress off before Selena could so much react, leaving her clad in only undergarments. Selena's blood boiled, though Medusa was too busy examining the fabric, jeering at the possible materials used to create it. "I knew you used dragon scales, but we can't have that. I want you to feel *everything*."

Before Selena could retaliate, she felt a strange, involuntary force that shoved her to the ceiling shackles when Medusa raised a hand. The chains that bound Selena disappeared in a puff of smoke, and her arms were forced upwards, slamming into the stone. The bonds closed shut around her wrists and ankles, stretching her across the wall as she stood on her toes.

Medusa smirked and lowered her hand as she tossed the blue and gold dress aside. "There we are; that's much better." Selena snorted and turned away. "Are you ignoring me? Won't you say thank you for not killing you when I had the chance?" Medusa mocked her again, but Selena gave her the cold shoulder. "I want you to answer me when I speak to you."

Selena quietly smirked when she heard Medusa swear, but the snake lifted her hand, and Selena suddenly felt a jolt surging down her spine. Sharp pain lanced through her body, and she saw blurred spots flashing before her eyes. Her body tore itself from the inside; her muscles and bones throbbed and quivered from the tiny eviscerations appearing everywhere, from her feet to her head.

Medusa didn't stop, and Selena knew she wanted submission, but like her contest with the She-Wolf, she refused to concede. Even as tiny cuts slashed across her cheeks, the dragon and the snake remained locked in an unyielding standoff; though it was a matter of time before her torment became unbearable, Selena was willing to hold on for as long as possible. However, the pain only grew worse, and the cuts deepened, her lacerations like a hot knife carving into her flesh.

Only when tears trickled down her bloodied face did the torture finally end. Content to receive some form of surrender, Medusa slowly walked over and made eye contact. "I always get what I want—you will obey me." Selena only snarled through trembling lips, sweat beading her torn skin, but Medusa scoffed. "The Dark Master doesn't want me to kill you, for he wants to do that himself. However, I can make you beg for death." Medusa then waved her right hand, and a whip appeared in her grasp; Selena spat at the ground near where she stood, willing to accept her dragon state transformation to strike her down. "You will be my little experiment until the Dark Master returns; let's see how much of this you can take before dying. We will start slow."

Without another moment's hesitation, Medusa lashed at Selena with sharp rocks tied at the ends of the knotted thongs, digging into her skin with every flog. Her wounds seared; they were intensifying and brutal. Medusa stopped and waited for a few seconds before she delivered another blow. Selena screamed and tightened her fists to brace herself, but the pain worsened when she clenched. Each lash amplified as her muscles quivered.

Medusa scourged her again and again. Selena lost count after ten, her mind swirling into a black haze, drawing her into Oblivion. She was covered in blood by the end of her beatings, and Medusa's whip ripped her undergarments to shreds until the fabric could no longer hold, leaving her completely naked and covered in crimson gouges.

"I hope this was as much fun for you as it was for me, but I don't want to see you again for a while." Medusa grew bored of her methodical experimentation, and her whip disappeared as she walked out of the torture chamber, leaving Selena chained to the ceiling. Warm sanguine fluid oozed down her copper skin, but Selena winced from the black bruises forming around her wrists and the new wounds opening over the scars on her legs from her first flight with Thor.

Thor.... Saying his name hurt more than the lashes; only the Divines knew what Medusa did to him and Doragon. *I'm so sorry.*

The dark, damp room trickled with water dripping from the ceiling, matching Selena's beating heart. Each tortured second that had passed grew challenging for her to draw a single breath; Selena slowly suffocated with the weight of her body pulling down on her arms. Although it was a few minutes, she was trapped in her timeless prison, waiting for eternity since Medusa left.

When Selena believed herself to be wholly alone with her tormented thoughts, the dungeon doors swung open. She clenched her fists as Medusa waltzed inside, weaponless this time. "We have much to accomplish, dragon," she hissed and raised a single hand as it glowed red, "Tell me: does this hurt more or less than the whip?"

Before Selena could give her a rude gesture, her organs and bones suddenly burned as if she were engulfed in flames. Surprised by this agonizing fiery pain—as a caster's summoned fire did not affect her—she screamed and howled from Medusa's new form of torture, her insides melting as if tossed into a lake of magma.

Medusa then withdrew for a few seconds, allowing Selena a moment of respite. "Very interesting, but don't worry if you die—the Dark Master will bring you back to life himself." However, her smile faded when she waved her hand, and a sudden cooling and refreshing wave washed over Selena, healing every cut and laceration she had received previously. She finally exhaled in relief, and she flexed her restored limbs.

Medusa interchanged different forms of torture throughout the day, both physically and magically, watching and commenting on Selena's endurance and tolerance to her methods as she switched. "Is this too much? Please, tell me your pain level on a scale of one to ten." Medusa would graciously heal her between experiments, as her uninterrupted trials would have proven too much for Selena to handle.

After hours of these sadistic tests, Medusa finally finished for the day; she raised her hand, and the chains around Selena's wrists disappeared. Her legs gave out, and she collapsed onto the stone floor, but shackles reappeared, keeping her bound to ground level.

"Everyone's threshold for pain is different, I see. I had considered letting you hang until you suffocated and died, but the Dark Master has other plans for you." Medusa flickered her hand, and Selena was forced to sit against the wall, her body giving way, and she leaned to the side while gasping for air. "Thank you for your assistance, as you've given me much to consider for my research. We will begin anew tomorrow." Medusa then reluctantly healed her wounds before leaving.

Hours after she left, her guards arrived with water and bread, throwing down the dirty, metal tray by Selena's feet; the water splattered over the floor, and the loaf was hard as stone, but she was grateful for any nourishment. Once the guards left in synced silence, ignoring her stiff muscles from the barbaric torture, Selena curled her fingers, drawing the spilt water from the floor, and poured the drops into her mouth.

Satisfying her thirst some, she breathed hard and heavily until flames erupted from her nostrils, creating steam to moisten the stale bread for consumption. As she finally relaxed her quivering and aching muscles and welcomed the sweet call of slumber, Selena remained determined to survive.

Selena endured the same repeated torture day after day, week after week. Medusa would walk in, no words exchanged, and she continued with her inhumane trials while Selena remained chained to the ceiling. Between experiments, she would be healed, and Medusa began anew.

Her sadistic experiments ranged from draining her body of blood before she passed out to confining her in a cage within viewing distance of a chained ravenous starving hound the guards brought on Medusa's command. "Your presence has increased its ferocity and has a particular thirst for your Divine blood—perhaps I ought to let you and this creature simmer awhile in each other's vicinity."

Yet, when Medusa stepped out and released the two from their confines and battle, Selena destroyed the beast with a single fire breath blazing as hot as the sun, thus ruining Medusa's trial. Before Selena could focus her magic attacks on Medusa, the snake had chained her arms and legs again to the wall as she walked through her torrent unscathed. Frowning, Medusa remarked, "I came well prepared against your magic, dragon, but I see: I am making you fight harder for your life."

As the weeks passed, Selena's body slowly grew tired and weak, her once beautiful brown hair now long and messy; she hadn't seen Azrael or Rahim since Medusa moved her to the new torture chamber, not knowing if they or Thor and Doragon were still alive. She wondered if anyone knew she and her allies were missing or that their lack of communication was amiss. Her days jumbled together, and time was just a blur; Selena remained headstrong and determined to escape, but she had a terrible feeling that she would die there.

*****

Since Medusa's guards escorted Selena away, Medusa freed Azrael and Rahim from their cages, shackled to the floor by their ankles. Rahim grunted when Azrael announced his plans to help rescue Selena, Thor, and Doragon, but he concurred. However, Azrael quickly discovered that Medusa had their entire prison cell enchanted to prevent using magic as a means to escape, and he hissed at her deception.

Not willing to give up, he clapped his hands and touched the floor and walls, leaving Rahim confused and asking, "What in Oblivion are you doing?"

"I'm looking for a weak spot in Medusa's curse. If I can dispel it, we can escape."

Rahim squinted at him. "Could you not have done that before when we were first imprisoned?"

Azrael snarled, making Rahim recoil. "It takes time, as I'm not familiar with her dark magic." Medusa's imprisoning wards were steady and strong, and Azrael doubted his abilities. He cursed and swore, slamming his fists against the stone floor, his faith in his abilities hanging by a thread.

It had been weeks since the guards checked on Azrael and Rahim, only delivering food by shoving the trays through an opening from the prison door's bottom chute. When Azrael and Rahim finished, they would stack the trays near where the guards could take them. Because of their cell's disorientating design, Azrael was the only one who knew how many days had passed; he kept track by drawing tally marks on the wall behind them, counting to thirty.

Though Rahim was tired and weary, Azrael remained vigilant, standing watch over their door. He had the routine down; right before the guards came, he ensured to return their food trays to their familiar spots without arising suspicion, thus keeping the guards away from checking on them. Azrael refused to eat since he didn't need to and offered his share to Rahim, blessing his stale bread to give him back his strength. Meanwhile, Azrael continued figuring out how to dispel Medusa's black magic between his watches. Here and there, he could locate a few vulnerable spots in the barrier. He broke through them while muttering in the demonic language, and the magic gradually grew weaker, though this contest lasted longer than he would have preferred.

Rahim grew depressed at his efforts and groaned. "I feel like we're going to die here. I miss the sun, the cold —"

"We'll make it through," Azrael said, focusing.

"You keep saying that, yet Selena is still gone, and I'm imagining the worst."

Azrael slammed his fists against the floor. "She's still alive." He swallowed hard but didn't allow Rahim to see his festering doubt.

Luckily, Rahim hadn't. "Why hasn't Her Imperial Majesty sent out a search party for us yet?" He swiveled his head around. "How long has it been?"

Azrael hesitated before answering: "One month."

Rahim grimaced and hissed through his teeth. "One month—we've been trapped here in this Divine forsaken city for a bloody month, yet neither the Empress nor the general has done anything about it."

Azrael's eyes narrowed at the spot in the corner he had slowly and steadily been dispelling; Rahim was right, of course, and he was as frustrated that Her Imperial Majesty hadn't taken action to rescue them. He snarled, his face paler than usual. Azrael hastened his operation while muttering, "the Council must be covering up our imprisonment, possibly lying to the Empress that we're assisting King Boreas or waiting in Nuvak—it could be anything." He roared, his eyes shimmering in frustration when realizing that today was the evening of the thirty-first of Stardusk. "I'll rip Vidar apart myself if I ever get my hands on him."

Yet, Azrael's heart raced when he found the curse's breaking point, and he uttered one final demonic spell. To his relief, he felt the magic barrier shatter like glass from his touch: he finally succeeded, and they were free of Medusa's sorcery. He and Rahim celebrated their well-earned victory, with Rahim uttering silent prayers to the Divines for Azrael's success.

Azrael dusted off his hands and pointed at the door. "The guards are gone until morning. Stay here while I get out and find where Medusa took Selena. Once I find her, we'll rescue Thor and Doragon."

Rahim perked up. "So, she is still alive then?" Azrael nodded. "Thank you. I hope this works."

Azrael gave him a small smile, but it quickly vanished when Rahim didn't return it. "What's the matter?"

Rahim's eyes glazed over. "Am I a bad person for wanting to leave Niamh behind?"

Azrael gasped, shocked by his question, but he sighed. "We must if we're to escape—she's one of them now. We can't do anything for Niamh right now, but please accept my promise: no harm will befall her as long as you don't give up on her."

His spirits somewhat restored, Rahim nodded; Azrael clutched his shackles, and the restraints cracked open upon tightening his fists over the links; he did the same for Rahim. Once Azrael freed them both, he approached the cell door and held his hand before the lock; a shadow ball pluming with black smoke appeared above his palm, transforming into a smokey key he used in the keyhole; the lock clicked, and the cell door flew open.

Azrael strolled free for the first time in a month while Rahim willingly remained behind, but he couldn't shake the terrible overwhelming hunches; Medusa could have assumed his actions. Her curse was challenging to dispel, and Azrael might have underestimated how powerful she became, but there was no turning back now: Selena needed to be rescued.

Azrael hurried down the corridor until he made his way to a room illuminated by torches containing shelves full of helmets, shoulder pads, armor, and boots. He took advantage of the supplies and dressed in full uniform, disguising himself as one of Medusa's soldiers. Once wholly donned in costume and tucking away his raven totem necklace, it didn't take him long to figure out that Selena's room was a little down the hallway beyond the supply closet. "Let's see if we can change fate."

*****

In the meantime, Medusa shackled Selena's hands and feet, and she left her prisoner alone as she often did after finishing her experiments. Over time, Selena's endurance built from the daily beatings and torture, and she silently sneered at Medusa's continued attempts to subdue her, but nobody could control a dragon. Like Thor, she bowed to no one.

Yet, she went into a daze when she heard footsteps echo down the hall, and she purposefully went limp, as the guards must be making their rounds to bring her food. The door swung open, and instead of the two usual guards she was used to seeing, there was only one this time, and he came with a torch. Selena snorted and shifted to look away, her long and tangled hair covering the murder burning from her piercing eyes, but the guard scowled at her rude disposition. "Is that the respect I'm going to get?"

She growled at his remarks, ignoring the familiar tone, but her eyes widened when the soldier marched over. However, he paused when he pulled off his mask, and Selena's face softened. "Azrael?"

His face burned crimson with embarrassment, and Selena finally realized it was because she was naked. Quickly covering her body, Azrael had already wheeled away before seeing too much; when he found her blue and gold dress tossed aside, he snatched it from the ground and threw it at her. "C-cover yourself up so we can finally get out of here."

Still scowling, Selena held up her chained wrists, silently indicating that she couldn't move to dress. Azrael, still averting his eyes, freed her of the shackles. As Selena cleaned herself from the dirt and grime through extremely controlled heat, she asked, "How did you escape? Where is Rahim? Pray tell me he's alive and well."

With his back turned to give her needed privacy, Azrael hastily recounted his success in removing Medusa's curse. "He's waiting for our return. The guards won't be back to check until morning, so we must escape fast."

Finding her resolve, Selena smiled as she buckled her straps; since their capture, she had grown too thin, the dress now drifting down her bosom; with Azrael's assistance, she had to tie the top of her battle dress with her scarf until Silver could modify it. When she was decent, Selena said, "Let's change our future, for it starts with us; we're not finished yet."

*****

CHAPTER 26: RED RAIN

Black clouds hovered and swirled above the glass towers of Rune Citadel, lightning bolting through the darkness. The wind screamed, and the torrential rain grew merciless over the grim, ivory city of Alfheim as Vidar and the rest of his Council associates stormed through the castle. Heavily armed with swords, firearms, and magic, they blasted their way through the massive double doors with fire.

A crackling fire warming the room for the cold, stormy night welcomed the Council's revolution, the light flickering against the large banners hanging from the vaulted ceiling. Yet, the imperial diamond throne donned in extravagant furs remained empty, and Vidar scowled in disgust.

"Find the Empress," he ordered, "I want her dead or alive. Our coup happens now." His Council colleagues nodded and broke off into two groups to search for the missing Empress, their footsteps echoing throughout the keep. Vidar looked up at the banners and snapped his fingers, immediately setting them ablaze.

Meanwhile, hiding in the august bed-chamber, the Empress—in her white wolf form—and Loki looked out their tall window as a pile of furniture barricaded the locked doors. Their ears caught the sound of footsteps and the smashing of glass and stone.

Her Imperial Majesty, however, remained calm amidst the Council's long-anticipated rebellion; General Araneus brought the fraudulent matters to her attention weeks ago regarding the Mythic Flight clutch exchange. She, Vulduin, and Silver had planned to extract Selena and her allies before they reached Snowhaven and completed their compromised mission, but the Council acted sooner than they had expected.

As the Council pounded on the bedroom doors, the Empress said to Loki, *Thank you for coming to warn me. Now, I have one last order for you.*

"What is that, my Lady?" Loki asked, flinching when the sounds grew suddenly louder with the roaring thunder.

After we jump out the window, we must leave Alfheim immediately. You need to find the Oracles and Neith and get yourselves to Nuvak. I'll hide elsewhere.

"What about you, Your Imperial Majesty?"

Don't worry about me, for Silver is waiting with an airship that will ferry me to safety. He has a zeppelin ready for you and the others near Moonridge. Flee to Nuvak and stay with Chaliss—that is an order. She pawed at the window, and the glass creaked open; she and Loki winced when they heard voices echoing beyond the barricade, followed by a command from Vidar to break in.

Loki whimpered and circled underneath the cushioned window seat, his orange fur bristling. "Please hurry, Your Majesty."

The Empress closed her eyes and concentrated. She didn't have time to act. As the Council blasted through her barrier, her eyes shot open, and the world froze around her. Knowing her spell wouldn't last long, she and Loki made haste and jumped out the window. Although her magic neither froze them nor anyone within their proximity, their movements slowed drastically. Her Imperial Majesty's spell wore off when their paws touched the ground, and the two ran away, disappearing down the shadowed streets.

The Council associates blasted their way through the furniture pile but were disappointed to find that the room was empty. Vidar parted through with his sword ready in one hand and a ball of fire in the other; his eyes darted to the open window, and he swore.

"Sir, shall we give pursuit?" one of his men asked.

Vidar growled and desisted. "We don't have time. The Dark Master has already given us the order to let his troops into the city when they arrive. Today, Alfheim will fall."

His second associate spoke up: "But sir, there are innocents within the city."

Vidar's lip twitched. "If we do nothing, there will be rebellion. It was just as my grandson once said: the Force will eventually rise against the Council." He peered over his shoulder and scowled. "Listen for the bells."

Some of their faces betrayed their trepidation towards Vidar's orders, but they bowed nonetheless. "Err, yes, of course, sir." They left him. Vidar, on the other hand, made his way back to his main quarters; as he reached his office, he surveyed the great capital city. His eyes landed on the bell tower on the Pyre, waiting and listening. It swayed and began to swing.

Vidar closed his eyes; his face remained expressionless; without warning, a blazing fireball crashed through the blood-red sky and struck the dragons' quarters. The alarm around Alfheim's fort shattered the already tense atmosphere as dragons and soldiers were assembled and called for battle. Soon, the Nidhoggr emerged from the blinding sun and dove through the sky towards Alfheim.

It didn't take long for the city to fall into chaos. Vidar opened his eyes and watched as the civilians rushed towards Rune Citadel's protective walls, each carrying supplies on their backs or balancing on their heads. The guards that once swore allegiance to the Empress were now helping Vidar keep the residents from passing through.

Under General Araneus' and Aracania's command, the Force assembled to retaliate and defend the city. The soldiers rushed to the catapults stationed along the wall and wasted no time loading and launching their oil-dipped and flame-lit boulders. Yet, the Nidhoggr evaded and continued with their steep dive. Three broke from their flight and soared above the wall, leveling their trajectory and letting forth an eruption of black fire, decimating the catapults and the Force men. The rest of the Nidhoggr flight flew at unbelievable speed and, one by one, destroyed the slings before arcing away. The undead dragons then belched forth dark Aether destruction, blasting through Alfheim's infrastructure and buildings; the amassed residents fled the scene to avoid incineration.

The bell continued ringing through the flames, alerting the innocents of Alfheim's red rain of Oblivion fire. Another wave of Nidhoggr arrived from the east, ferrying large, metal ships housing the Lich's armored soldiers. Vidar's lips curved into a sneer when he saw that Captain Ashur Bel's army had returned from their mission in Snowhaven.

The ruse went splendidly, arranging the exchange with Medusa and Ashur to hide their ploy and treacherous alliance with the Lich. With Selena and Thor out of this perfect and destructive tableau, hand-delivering the eggs to the Lich's right hand while the Council hid their partnership with the necromancer, the Divinity Dragons couldn't interfere. Yet, Ashur and Jade weren't seen among the flight, and Vidar wondered when they had planned on returning with the Mythic Flight eggs. Jade was a fast flier and could make the return trip within a few weeks, but time was of the essence, for the eclipse was less than two months away.

Meanwhile, General Araneus rallied his officers and ordered his armored men to get to their dragons. The general mounted Aracania, and together, they launched themselves skyward as their other fellow riders followed behind. He held up his sword and shield and ordered his dragon to fly through the fray once he sent the signal to his formation: *Engage closely.* However, he shuddered at the sight of the masked dragon mutations; they were Death.

Aracania dove right down to their first target, and before the Nidhoggr could swipe her away, she bit down hard on its neck, keeping it from going any further. General Araneus jumped off his saddle and, with the thrust of his sword, dug it right in the back of the creature's head, striking the mask as the two dragons thrashed wildly in the air. Its mask shattered, and the pair broke away as they left their foe to crash below. The dismayed general and Aracania turned to see the largest of the creatures and their new platoon of undead monsters closing the distance to their city at tremendous speed.

General Araneus gritted his teeth before facing those operating the remaining catapults and bashed his sword against his shield, gathering the soldiers' attention. "Reload. RELOAD!" The general thrust his sword forward when the boulders were locked in place. "Fire!"

The catapults launched blazing meteors, but they were too late, for the masked dragon flight had already breached the walls, engulfing the Force soldiers in a massive, deadly dust cloud of black poison. General Araneus watched the flesh melt right off the bones of his men.

The Nidhoggr carrying the metal ships landed with their precious cargo. The doors burst open, and thousands of undead soldiers donning black armor twisting like demon horns poured forth into the city, rotten flesh hanging from exposed bones. It didn't matter how many of their limbs were lobbed off or even decapitated, as the horrific power of flesh regeneration kept the enemy going. General Araneus had never seen such relentless fighters, watching in horror and disgust as what remained of his men met the enemy in battle.

Another rider—a young, armored maiden riding a Nidhoggr about the size of two dragons alone—swept through the city as men and women incinerated within the black and orange blazes. The mysterious handler remained enchanted by the growing flames as the sky filled with the creature's metallic flurry of wings; the pair soared high above the destruction and perched on top of Rune Citadel. The creature spread out its bladed wings sweeping the heavens and roared at the city dwellers trapped between its mercy and the oncoming undead battalion.

Once it was satisfied, the behemoth of Death launched for the burning heavens, dodging the Force's combined might, spewing forth more destruction. Together, they made their way back towards the wall and destroyed another part of the battlement, its torrent of flames consuming the unwieldy catapults before they could threaten the pair. The general's soldiers caught in the inferno were obliterated to ash. Vidar watched as his new rider scorched great swaths of Alfheim as the girl shared no qualms while her Nidhoggr laid waste to another street full of innocents.

While the general was distracted by his hopelessness and despair, Aracania leapt upward to avoid them being closed in by the enemy. Instead, she did her best to focus on their next attack. General Araneus had to smack himself in the side of the face to concentrate; however, Aracania abruptly stopped when Onyxria and Colonel Cyres zoomed past, baiting three heavy-weight Nidhoggr away from Venerius and Captain Allendreth.

There came a terrible noise in the general's ears as the masked dragons overwhelmed Onyxria, leaving deep furrows and gashes on her sides. Commodore Rhys Harlequin and his Cerulean Iceclaw, Zidragos, rushed to her aid, clashing with one colossus while Venerius lured the other, granting Onyxria a means to escape and recoup. However, she launched herself at her last pursuer, and Onyxria latched her fangs over the creature's mask and ripped it apart as the enemy sank its teeth deep into her neck.

After tearing its face off, she killed the heavy-weight, but she slowly succumbed to her fatal wounds. Before the colonel accepted their fate with a bullet to his head, Onyxria snatched him from the harness as he unbelted himself and enveloped him within her wings as she crashed to the burning ground, protecting him from the fall as she faded to Oblivion.

The general's soldiers were soon overwhelmed by the enemy's sheer numbers. The pair pulled the same maneuver, bringing the next abomination down with Aracania engaging it in close combat and Araneus plunging his sword through the back of the creature's head. The Nidhoggr screeched as it spiraled downward and dropped its vessel, but unfortunately, many soldiers inside survived and rushed out to join their brethren in the slaughter.

Go down below and unleash your fury. Aracania dove as low as she could get. She opened her mouth and exhaled a foul breath upon the onslaught. As her poisonous mist covered the battlefield, General Araneus relaxed his shoulders and lowered his sword and shield. However, he tightened his grip on the handle until his knuckles turned white as the poison dispersed: Aracania's attack did not affect her enemies. The general looked around in dismay at their failed attempt.

"Sir." He spun around to find Captain Allendreth and Venerius flying in their direction; the Malachite Diamondwing had suffered severe wounds from their rescue attempt, and Araneus feared losing more dragons and officers. To his dismay, he didn't see Commodore Harlequin and Zidragos among the pell-mell blitz.

As if the captain read his expression, Allendreth gravely confirmed that Rhys and Zidragos had fallen in battle upon rescuing Onyxria and Colonel Cyres. "I'm sorry, sir, but we're spread too thin to fight them on land. There are way too many of them—we're estimating over fifty thousand on foot, plus these airborne abominations."

General Araneus swore, wondering how the Council couldn't have known about this attack. "Pray tell me, where are the Empress and Vidar now?"

"I don't know, sir."

I don't understand. The Oracles always alerted the Council to surprise attacks—how did they not foresee this? The general surveyed the destruction as he toned out his pleading officer. He became mesmerized by a low, dull ring that made him feel numb, and at that moment, he didn't hear a word Allendreth said.

Aracania snaked her head around and nuzzled his arm. **What should we do?**

The general shut his eyes. "Evacuate the city. Try and save as many civilians as you can and get out of here. We might be lucky to escape with both the Lich's army and his abominations here. May the Divines watch us all." Captain Allendreth gave a salute, and Venerius gave the two a pitiful roar before returning to what may be their final fight. As Araneus had feared, he and Aracania watched as Venerius and Allendreth, with two officers, baited the Nidhoggr attacking the fleeing civilians, sacrificing themselves so that the others could survive.

The general watched his soldiers face the creatures' might while he sent up the flag signal: *Evacuate the city and retreat.* He placed a hand on Aracania's neck when they understood the battle was lost, a silent communion between a handler and their dragon.

What remained of Her Imperial Majesty's dragons followed through with his command, the surviving heavy-weights rounding up any survivors and ferrying them to safety, carrying more than a hundred apiece. His remaining fighters clashed with the undead creatures, tearing his soldiers and dragons to shreds before devouring their flesh.

General Araneus and Aracania joined the front lines to give his men more time to rescue the innocents. When Aracania was close enough to the masked behemoths, she aimed her venomous acid shots directly at their masks, leaving them squealing in agony as their facial coverings corroded away.

They looked up as more Nidhoggr flew overhead, and they unleashed their deadly black inferno, laying waste to more buildings and consuming the soldiers. The innocents waiting to be ferried out of the city fled, but the

Nidhoggr rose behind, exhaling more of their deadly torrent of dark flame. General Araneus watched as the buildings in the surrounding area collapsed under the raging fire, and the citizens disappeared as the magic consumed them.

The flight split, strafing another street, decimating innocents and buildings alike. Residents huddled together in false security while others attempted to flee the path of destruction amidst those screaming as they died painful deaths. Meanwhile, Vidar continued watching from his big office window, his eyes scanning the lines of fire scarring the city and the vast plumes of smoke rising from the piles of ash and corpses.

As General Araneus and Aracania broke rank below, he looked outward towards Rune Citadel, and the realization set in. The Council planned it all: Liongod's trial, the egg mission, the unaccounted expenses, all of it. General Araneus was stricken with grief, but couldn't believe it, even when delivering the disturbing reports to Her Imperial Majesty. His men, his family, friends—

He clutched his weapon and swore and screamed. *I'm going to kill him. Take me to him, now.* Aracania bared her teeth and fled the battle before her rider could object. *What are you doing?*

We've done all we could, and now, I must protect you and get you to safety.

I will not abandon my men. Aracania didn't answer, creating as much distance between them and the city with incredible speed.

The Pyre chimed the sixth hour. The maiden rider flew to the clock tower, and her companion opened its mouth, spewing out bolts of lightning that struck the clock. Its rings died, and the spire crumbled and exploded.

The heavens wept over the cataclysm, marking the Red Rains of Alfheim on the thirty-first of Stardusk.

The determined Aracania pierced the air like a freshly fired bullet as they made their way over the Hinterlands. The farther they flew away from the fallen city, the more General Araneus became overwhelmed with sorrow when considering all that was lost. His stomach tightened into a knot, and he wanted to vomit. Araneus couldn't bear to move his gaze from the back of her thick neck. *Where are we going?*

Aracania snorted but didn't answer; within a few hours, the two made their way to Moonridge to figure out what to do next. Although the small settlement was not far from Alfheim, the pair felt it was safe for a brief moment. Before Araneus dismounted, Aracania remained vigilant, swiveling and inspecting the area before she deemed the inn clear.

Araneus peered over the burning horizon but quickly announced when he grew distracted by Aracania's hunger snarls, her eyes fixating on the livestock herding away. *Pray allow me to bargain with the owner.*

Her tail flickered as she flexed her claws, ready to snatch them. **Thank you.**

The central tavern was a much better comfort than what he and Aracania had experienced just hours prior. The lit hearth warmed his frosted cheeks, the bard's song about a foolish man named Thaydon tickling a sleeping dragon chiming through his ears, entertaining the local drunks. As soon as General Araneus bought three cows for Aracania, he was immediately greeted by Admiral Altessa. "Sir, I never thought I'd find you here."

The general was at a loss for words, for he was thrilled to see Silver again. The two exchanged hearty handshakes. "It's damned good to see you again, Admiral, but where in bloody blazes have you been?"

Silver's throat constricted. "Helping Her Imperial Majesty escape when the Council stormed Rune Citadel." The two ordered a bottle of gin to share as Silver recounted his mission to ensure the Empress' safety, and Araneus explained what happened in Alfheim. Meanwhile, he kept his eye on Aracania, who happily gobbled her meal down to the hooves. Silver's face turned pale while listening to his harrowing tale, and his lips quivered, unable to grasp the grave news. "No, all of them?"

Though Silver could hold his alcohol, the general's face burned crimson after the two had shared half of the bottle. "Aracania and I couldn't do a damn thing to save them." Araneus slammed his tankard against the table. "We watched them die. I've never seen anything like it, and I will never forgive myself for allowing this to happen."

"How could you have possibly known?"

"If I had acted faster and exposed the Council sooner, I could have saved my men. My duty was to protect them, to lead them."

Araneus went to pour himself more gin, but Silver reached for the bottle. "You're already pissed, sir—"

Before Araneus could protest, they were interrupted when the Shadow Emperor marched inside the tavern, already pulling off his mask as he joined them at their private table. Ignoring the intoxicated general, and before Silver could formerly introduce the two, Vulduin suddenly demanded answers about Her Imperial Majesty's whereabouts.

Silver grinned, which infuriated Vulduin even more. Araneus, however, was confused by how the two were acquainted. "Who are you? I don't believe we've met before."

"Sir, watch who you're speaking to," Silver warned, "This here is the true Emperor of Armageddon."

Araneus spat out his gin and looked at his tankard, believing he had too much to drink. Yet, Silver and Vulduin gave him a firm nod before continuing their grim discussion, but Vulduin grew impatient. "I'm not here to talk, Genesis. You better have a damn good reason for asking me to meet you here after what happened to Alfheim—"

Silver jolted from his seat. "Then pray follow me so I can show you—you'll appreciate this. Sir, please pardon us, for we will return momentarily."

General Araneus was slow to react, but he raised another drink as a toast to meeting the Shadow Emperor for the first time; Silver beckoned Vulduin upstairs behind the adjacent kitchen and approached the first door to one of the rentable rooms. Silver stood by the threshold, grinning ear to ear, though Vulduin growled from his cheerful demeanor when the world was burning. "Genesis, what is this about?"

Silver fixed his glasses. "Before I open this door, I ask that you please turn around."

Vulduin wasn't enthusiastic about his proposition. "Why should I?"

"You will thank me for this later. I promise you," Silver placed his right hand over his heart and raised his left, "Now, please, face that way." Vulduin slowly and reluctantly did, and when Silver was sure that he wasn't peeking, he opened the door. "All right, now you may turn around." Vulduin bit his bottom lip as he wheeled around, but what Silver surprised him with left him dumb.

"Hello, Vulduin." Waiting in the small and quaint room was the Empress herself, Aryl Aurora, his wife—

The two hadn't seen in other in the flesh since his arrest. Unsure of what to do or say, the paralyzed Vulduin reached up, patted his hair down, and held his mask to his chest.

Stricken from the throne and crown, Aryl hid within her cloak, but she removed the cowl, her unmatched beauty blazing like Divine's light in Vulduin's view. Unable to contain himself, he embraced her tightly, bringing her into a long, passionate kiss. When they finally broke apart, he kept his arms wrapped around her. "It's been far too long," Vulduin whispered, "I will never leave your side again."

CHAPTER 27: BLOOD ON THE ICE

The crimson sky turned to charcoal, and the rain hammered down as Silver stood outside Moonridge's tavern and looked over the horizon, his concentration and gaze fixated on Snowhaven's direction. Aracania paid no attention, relaxing after a delicious meal while laying ensconced within her coils, wings wholly unfurled against the green turf. Her deep breaths were like a forge's bellows, her rhythmic beating drums soothing, contrasting Alfheim's requiem.

Once he sobered, General Araneus soon joined him. "Since the Council planned their betrayal, I don't think there's any hope for Liongod and the others. The Lich may very well have the dragon eggs as we speak."

Silver bit his cheeks and searched through his jacket pockets, pulling out the letters he had received from Selena while she was in Rhumbek and Nuvak. Araneus peered over his shoulder and pulled out a sealed letter delivered from Snowhaven Vidar claimed was from her, waiting for reinforcements in the capital to establish their covert; upon comparing the handwriting, the general swore and crumpled the forged message before tossing it away.

He rubbed his temples when Aracania opened one leering eye, her tail flickering. "Only the Divines know the truth."

Silver's face drained of what little color he had, wishing he could teleport directly to Snowhaven. He was so close to finishing the Aether line project; Silver cringed at his lost research, for that was the second time the Lich destroyed his work. "I'm going after Liongod and the others," he said.

"Then allow Aracania and I to join you," Araneus pleaded, and the chittering Aracania clicked her claws against the rocks, agreeing with his declaration.

Silver refused their assistance, not wishing harm to befall them. "I'm sorry, sir, but your duty is here to protect the imperial family."

"No, not after what happened. I failed my men; how am I equipped to protect Their Imperial Majesties, let alone the Crown Princess?" Araneus hissed through his teeth when he met Silver's somber gaze. "Oh, blast it— Admiral, I may have sentenced her to death."

Silver snarled at him, not believing a word of it. "How could you have known?"

Araneus marched to the sleepy Aracania and leaned against her bulging stomach. "I failed to bring the Council to justice, and now the Empire has fallen. Pray forgive me for sending Liongod into the depths of Oblivion, Admiral—I had no idea. May the Divines help us."

Looking towards the darkness brewing in the far east across the ocean, Silver said, "Sir, you haven't failed, and the war isn't over yet," and turned sharply on his heels, heading back inside the tavern.

He trekked back to the room where he left Vulduin and Aryl alone; the two were in an intense discussion with Armageddon's map unrolled between them as Silver barged inside, the door swinging open. "I have something to say," he announced, expecting an objection to his plans, but Vulduin was surprisingly quiet. "I'm leaving to find Selena and Thor. I can't stay here any longer and expect them to return. You've held me back long enough, and I've had it: you will not stop me from going after them."

Vulduin and Aryl remained calm. "Then we won't," said the Shadow Emperor.

Silver didn't expect this response. "Pardon me?"

"My wife and I were planning on how we would rescue our daughter, and then you just waltzed in here to declare your intentions. I couldn't have planned that better myself."

Silver cleared his throat and straightened his shoulders. "Very good."

When that was settled, Vulduin turned to Aryl. "In the meantime, General Araneus and Aracania will safely escort you to Dark Blood Hold—I suspect Lord Vincent Godfrey will be expecting us soon." Glaring at Silver, he added, "You will rendezvous with us there once you rescue Selena and the others."

Aryl's eyes glossed over like a frozen pond. "You're not coming with us, then."

"Not yet. I have some unfinished business to address, but I promise we will meet again soon. I'll ensure General Araneus has a map to their hiding place." Vulduin kissed her forehead before marching downstairs to deliver the news.

Aryl, however, suspected this was their last union, and she asked Silver, "Do you know where he's headed?"

"I wish I knew, Your Imperial Majesty, but sometimes he doesn't tell me anything."

"I'm not the Empress anymore, so there's no more need for formalities." She dolefully looked down at the map. "If we win this war, Vulduin and I don't want the throne."

"I'm afraid I don't understand—"

"The rule of succession will apply, and the immediate heir will rise to power." Aryl's sapphire eyes gleamed when she made herself clear.

"That will be up to the Crown Princess; Selena has no interest in the throne," Silver said.

Yet, the former Empress turned away and sighed, ignoring his warning over her headstrong daughter; Silver, however, feared how Selena would take the news. Aryl watched the door before saying, "Vulduin isn't coming back, is he?"

"I-I have no idea."

After saying their farewells, Silver excused himself from Aryl's presence. He made his way out of the inn and rushed to find Araneus preparing Aracania for travel and Vulduin strutting away with haste and purpose. "Where do you think you're going?" Silver called out.

Vulduin's voice was quiet and hoarse, like he was about to cry or scream. "Just for a walk."

"Will you return?"

Vulduin stopped and abruptly turned around to face him, the two standing in uncomfortable silence. "If I take my walk and don't return, it means I haven't finished my walk."

Silver's face became inflamed when he understood Vulduin's meaning. "Your wife suspected this. I don't know what she will say if you leave again." Vulduin ignored him and continued his march. "I think you're making a huge mistake." Vulduin assumed his red dire wolf form and dashed towards Alfheim at dragon speed, making it clear he wouldn't reply.

Silver sighed as he watched the Red Wolf vanish over the hills and said: "May the Divines watch over you, my friend." He fixed his jacket and transformed into his white wingless dragon facade, beginning his long flight to Snowhaven.

The smell of sulfur and rotting flesh laded the air, stinging Vulduin's nostrils. He resumed his elf guise as he walked through what remained of Alfheim. The sky was painted blood red by the fires raging in the background, debris and dead bodies littering the once beautiful streets. Only Rune Citadel and the Council's headquarters remained unscathed among the smoldering wreckage. He looked up to see the dragon creatures circling overhead; Vulduin clenched his fists, preparing himself for a fight, but the masked behemoths ignored him entirely, flying over and perching on the remains of the Pyre.

His skin prickled when he heard Vidar's voice, making him want to vomit. The treacherous, pompous half-elf emerged from the smoke and dust, his eerie ice eyes piercing the veil. "There you are. I was wondering when you would show yourself again."

"Where is the Lich?" Vulduin asked coolly.

Vidar casually strutted forward with the rest of the Council following close; he hissed through his teeth. "I'm afraid you just missed him, Vulduin. He had important matters to deal with in *Snowhaven*."

"I want my daughter back. Where is she?"

Vidar taunted, "Does it matter? She's still very much alive for now."

Vulduin gritted his teeth and, without thinking, flickered his wrists, and thousands of steel chains shot out from his frock jacket sleeves, focusing the bladed tips on aiming straight for Vidar's heart. Instead of dodging, Vidar and the rest of the Council remained composed as the tangled mess of metal was upon them; Vulduin's shackles struck an invisible barrier protecting the betrayers.

"We were expecting you," Vidar sneered, and Vulduin swore; only the Lich knew the proper wards that could block his attacks. He retracted his chains, and Vidar continued goading him. "What's the matter? The Lich has shared some of his magic secrets with us for being so loyal."

Vulduin backed away and spat. "Damn you all to Oblivion."

"You've been running from us for over two hundred years, and now, there's nowhere else for you to turn. Surrender, and we'll let you live for now, or you can fight and die here. It's your choice, but make it quick. I'm rather busy at the moment." Vidar yawned.

Vulduin lowered his hands and hung his head in defeat. "If I go quietly, will you leave my family alone?"

"We just want you," Vidar pointed at him.

Vulduin nodded and held out his hands in surrender, and Vidar ordered his two associates standing closest to arrest him. The Shadow Emperor neither hesitated nor flinched when the Council cuffed his wrists and ankles nor fought back when a masked dragon swooped down and scooped him with its sword-like talons to be carried away to Mortemholdt, the dreaded prison isle floating over Lake Peril. Vulduin didn't falter.

*****

As much as Selena was happy to be rescued, she had to use Azrael as support upon returning to the old cell, leaning on him as she worked on standing for the first time since Medusa dragged her away. "You can do it.

Don't worry about me—put all your weight into my shoulder if you must."

Concentrating on her efforts, Selena ignored her body's unwillingness to cooperate; she fought until her muscles ached, but she was glad to be standing again. "Thank you."

"You can thank me once we get out. And here." Azrael summoned a pool of water within the palm of his hand and offered her a drink. "It's not much, but you'll need it. I placed a spell in it to help you get some of your strength back—like Silver's elixir."

Selena nodded and sipped from his hand without hesitation, instantly rejuvenated; it was like the sun's power coursing through her veins, and she was refreshed, her cheeks full of color. The fire within her blazing emerald eyes that Medusa couldn't extinguish intensified, and Selena was ready to fight back with a vengeance of a thousand dragons.

Happy to see that she reclaimed her lost vigor, Azrael urged her to follow, making their way back to Rahim's cell with haste and stealth. Rahim's eyes lit up like the stars when he saw her and rushed over, hugging her tightly.

Azrael, however, broke up their reunion. "We'll have time for that later." He placed his hands on the wall where he initially broke through Medusa's curse. He closed his eyes and muttered another enchantment in the demonic language; silence, and he confirmed, "We're directly below the crystal gardens where Thor and Doragon are imprisoned."

Selena's heart fluttered like a bird taking flight, and she and Azrael agreed to create an underground tunnel that would break through their wards. However, Azrael seemed a little hesitant about how they could dispel the enchanted crystals, but Selena remained determined. "We have to try," she resolved, "I'll destroy this castle if I have to."

Azrael clicked his teeth. "Pray don't alert Medusa, but once we free them, we must leave as soon as possible."

Rahim shuddered when Azrael and Selena got into casting positions. "Medusa and her army will chase after us once we've made enough ruckus."

"Yes, but with any luck, we'll be long gone by the time they're about to give chase," Azrael reassured, though his tone exhibited some reluctance, "We'll find a place to hide for a while before meeting up with Phantom Dust and the others."

Rahim stood back as Selena and Azrael began casting earth magic; she felt the energy rise within her body as she imagined the world moving. An explosion erupted from their hands, creating a large hole in the wall of their prison cube. Azrael climbed in first and summoned a small flickering flame burning from his palm once Selena and Rahim joined him.

Selena took over the creation of the tunnel with added stairs, clearing the way with magic, the pathway spiraling upwards to the gardens. Every few meters, she deepened the passageway as Azrael and Rahim followed until she made her last cast, and the trio arrived in the crystal gardens without the threat of Medusa's curse.

As much as Selena dreaded staying in Snowhaven any longer than necessary, she still admired the fairytale prison of rock and rainbow, but no sight was as beautiful as seeing her dearest companion again. Her eyes glimmered upon confirming that Thor and Doragon were safe and unharmed—with their belongings and harnesses —near the heated pools; though Medusa was a sadist, she kept her word that no harm would come to the dragons.

They whipped around, and their ecstatic roars made Niflheim weep from their reunion when Selena and Azrael dashed over and joined their companions in jubilation.

Happy tears trickled down their cheeks, and Selena buried her face into Thor's snout when she felt his mental touch. *I've missed you so much, my dearest one.*

Thor snorted and closed his eyes after herding her close to his breast, commemorating their silent communion. Doragon wrapped both Rahim and Azrael within his protective arms, and they grew ensconced within his coiled tail, licking and sniffing them until they pried themselves away.

The trio quickly harnessed both dragons and packed up their boxed belongings and weapons that Medusa and Holland had graciously and suspiciously returned to the stone gardens. When Selena gave Azrael a worried glance, he quickly shrugged it off, urging how fast their window for escaping was diminishing.

Thor snarled when Selena ensured all was ready. **I would forego all of this packing. Doragon and I ought to carry you three out while we still have the chance.**

We can't leave our belongings behind. However, Selena ruefully looked around, guilty of leaving the dragon eggs behind in Medusa's clutches, but Thor reassured her that they would rescue them once they reconvene with their allies.

I will not lose you again, my dearest.

Doragon roared and unfurled his massive gold and silver wings once Azrael was strapped and buckled. Though Rahim was ready after tightening his carabiners, Thor was hesitant in relinquishing his hold on Selena. Instead, Thor trapped her in his claws, holding her close to his chest.

He and Doragon reared up on their haunches and hovered from the light flutter of their wings. Selena could feel Thor calling forth the essence of stone and living nature as the ground trembled and massive boulders rained from the sky from his and Doragon's magic. Although they were protected from the attack, the castle's crystal gardens didn't stand a chance from the flaming meteor shower destroying all within the dragons' proximity. The colorful gemstones shattered like glass, and the gold-streaked mother-of-pearl walls crumbled from their wrath.

When the dragons exhausted their energy, and the onslaught stopped, their gilt-painted prison lay in ruins. Content that Snowhaven no longer confined them, Thor and Doragon began their flight until Selena saw a black hole materializing beneath them. Her heart sank when shadow hands pluming with dark Aether thrashed forth, reaching for their hind legs.

The trio looked back and saw the former Justiciar William Holland below, hands extended and fingers curled, watching his spell wrapping around the dragons, forcing them to make their descent. As he sneered, his justiciar disguise vanished in a column of smoke, leaving him donning his more comfortable Obsidian Order attire, the dark blue robes nearly hiding him in the shadows.

As Thor and Doragon were forced to land among the destroyed stone gardens, cursing under his breath, Azrael unbuckled himself and dismounted. He knelt before the stone, hands at his sides, and slowly brought them up as he stepped forward, creating a thick ice wall formed around him to act as a barrier from oncoming ranged attacks.

Selena unsheathed Dragonheart, the rose-tinted ivory blade gleaming against the snow and ice, ready for battle, and slipped through Thor's claws, with Rahim joining her once he found his revolver. The two stood with Azrael, ready for Medusa's army of the undead and the Obsidian Order now marching forward from the icy fortress.

Thor and Doragon roared in warning, wrapping their shielding wings around the trio; Thor roared and knocked away the approaching battalion with a swing of his thick steel-rod-like tail. He then opened his mouth and unleashed a powerful fire breath at another group deciding to take on his might, but they remained unaffected by his breath attacks and continued rushing in. Doragon charged with his horns and whipped his tail, countering two large groups circling close. Yet, another formation appeared behind the dragons, but Doragon wheeled around, unleashing a massive torrent conjoined with Thor's to force them back. Their combined power was enough to incinerate the soldiers, reducing them to ash piles.

As the alarms blazed around the citadel, alerting Medusa of their escape, fireballs rained upon them from the catapults lining the castle's high walls. From behind both Thor and Doragon came more of the soldiers marching through the halls, surrounding the dragons. Thor and Doragon roared as their hides became encased in flames, damaging the undead whenever they drew close.

Selena looked over at the water and intensely concentrated. Deep down, she knew that the powers of ice and water moved through her, and she needed to embrace a steely resolve within herself: Selena must be versatile and adaptable, able to turn her opponents' energy against them. Breathing deep, she held out an open hand and dragged her fingers like plucking stars from the sky. The pool's water bubbled, and streams shot up, dancing in the air. The tendrils followed her swift movements, expanding and snapping at the soldiers like a whip from every angle. Her water turned to ice at the tips, and they ripped through their enemies' armor and flesh; to her disappointment, their wounds healed as fast as she attacked them. "Regeneration?" Selena asked, horrified and confused.

Azrael created an ice tornado circling him as he launched into the air, and his ice vortex carried him across the destroyed gardens. While suspended within his crystallized maelstrom, he encased himself inside a frosted sphere, and giant ice spikes grew on its surface and exploded. Selena acted fast, summoning giant ice walls, blocking the jagged missiles from hitting her and her allies, but the soldiers besieging Azrael were impaled from his attack and collapsed into the snow. Once he finished his cataclysm, Azrael landed, and spears from the ice jutted from the ground with a flicker of his hand and launched at the next incoming wave.

Meanwhile, the determined Rahim worked on shooting down the blockading attackers marching forth; his time practicing with Selena and Azrael allowed him to enjoy the fruits of his labor. His quick precision took down six soldiers in a blink of an eye before reloading, which he accomplished in seconds, and resumed with his back to Selena's. However, when one flung throwing knives at him, Selena summoned a cold stone slab as a shield, catching the projectiles. Grinning, she kicked her earth wall down, and as it crumbled, the pieces flew at the soldiers, and the erupting wave carried them away.

Thor turned around and unleashed a light beam from his mouth, pulsating with energy. He aimed his attack at the demonic forces, sweeping his magical torrent across the ground. As soon as the light touched the soldiers, they immediately disintegrated into ash.

However, despite their valiant efforts, more of Medusa's troops swarmed around them, replenishing lost numbers in seconds. There was no end to the onslaught.

"What are we going to do?" Selena asked Rahim and Azrael in dismay as the trio backed closer to their weary dragons.

The soldiers suddenly stopped attacking and held their position as if they were waiting, giving the group a moment to rest, but the five cringed when a shrill voice shattered the air, making their skin crawl. "I've expected this treachery, but I thought you would have done this weeks ago." Whispering and hissing snakes tickled their ears as Medusa parted her way through the never-ending army and ran her fingers through her platinum blonde hair. "I'm disappointed in you, Azrael. Have you truly grown this weak to where you couldn't get through a simple curse?"

"Oh, to Oblivion with you."

She ignored him. Instead, she walked over to Selena, swaying her hips with every step. "I thought I could break you after you've been so helpful to my experiments—so unfortunate."

Selena gritted her teeth. "A dragon never yields."

"You're foolishly headstrong as you are brilliant." Medusa laughed as her purple eyes scanned the sea of undead soldiers until Ashur and the already harnessed Jade sauntered down the battered corridor, the Pearlscale's claws clicking against the onyx floors, and she beckoned them over. "I believe it's time you two make haste, as the Day of Eternal Darkness is nigh, and everything must be perfect. My little pet and my children should already be in Alfheim. You and Jade must prepare the dragon eggs at once while I'll take care of Azrael."

Rahim began to sob, ignoring Selena's and Azrael's hisses and snarls. "Niamh."

Ashur and Jade bowed and sneered. "As you wish, my Dark Lady." The Imperial Pearlscale sneered at them as he scooped Ashur within his talons, helping him mount the already prepared saddle. To Selena's alarm, she saw the chest with the Mythic Flight eggs belted behind Ashur's seat; her throat swelled, and her heart squeezed as the group dismally watched the venomous pair sweep off the ground like the gentle breeze under Jade's wings, making the long journey to Alfheim.

Medusa ignored their disgruntled sentiments, relishing her victory in the Empire's downfall. "Now the Dark Master needs you, Azrael."

His eyes widened, but Selena asked when Azrael withheld his suspicions about his role in the Lich's gambit. "Why do you need him?"

Medusa shrugged her shoulders, but the faint sheen in her eyes was as sharp as a two-edged sword. "I'm surprised you haven't figured out what the Dark Master intends with the dragon eggs." Selena scowled, but Medusa continued. "Since losing Ragnarok, our master had to find a different way to destroy your world and rebuild from the ashes. The powerful dragon eggs you graciously hand-delivered will allow us to open the portal to Oblivion, unleashing havoc and destruction upon this realm, thus amplified by the upcoming eclipse. Since he is a Divine, Azrael was the final key to unlock the gate."

Doragon roared and wrapped his arms around the growling Azrael, his golden eyes turning to slits, readying himself to strike Medusa down. Thor joined his side, hissing and arching his back with wings extended. **My dear, say the word, and we will strike her down now.**

Medusa jeered at the hostile Doragon and Azrael. "The Dark Master has turned your army against you, Death, and has amassed over one billion waiting to storm through." She stepped back and gestured to the surrounding army waiting on her command. "Remember the Orcs and trolls you fought in the Battle of Alfheim? The Dark Master himself has blessed them—their reward for their loyalty."

Selena gripped Dragonheart and stepped from Thor's shield. "You'll have to kill me first before I let that happen." She ignored Azrael's and Doragon's worried gazes.

Medusa's lips curled into a vicious sneer, and the sound of hissing snakes that always followed her returned. "Noble to the end, but no matter. We still have much to accomplish."

Medusa's minions resumed their endless battle, quickly overwhelming the group before they could retaliate. Fighting through wave upon wave separated Selena from the group as she danced through the infinite sea of soldiers, looping off heads with Dragonheart from every swing. Azrael followed Rahim, Thor, and Doragon as they worked their way through, determined not to be separated.

The two dragons spread their wings in preparation to snatch the three away, but Medusa anticipated their actions. Like Holland's spell, she manifested another black hole and called forth the spirits of darkness—the same demons Selena fought from the ancient dwarven ruin. They latched themselves to the two stampeding dragons, holding them in place. Azrael and Rahim backtracked and aided their escape by fighting off the demons. Thor's and Doragon's combined weights were of no consequence, for the spirits of darkness fought with the strength of ten dragons of Ulrich's might, keeping them grounded. When Azrael and Rahim realized it was no use, they defended Thor and Doragon from being overwhelmed when they couldn't fly, but the dragons relied on their breath abilities to protect Azrael and Rahim.

Selena, however, focused her anger on bringing Medusa down, determined to kill the snake. Amidst the pell-mell conflict, Medusa's cold voice whispered in Selena's ears: "You and your friends will die here."

When Selena turned around, she was soon face-to-face with the venomous snake; she raised her hands, and Selena levitated before being thrown across the stone gardens by an invisible force. However, Selena forced herself to land on her feet, sliding across the ice. Her look of trepidation was tempered as she glanced over her shoulder to see Medusa rearing up for a sneak attack.

Selena spun in time and summoned stone blocks to protect her from Medusa's sudden fire blasts, but the force of the impact pushed her near the edge of the deep, heated pool, and she nearly toppled into the water. She regained her balance and blocked more oncoming attacks as Medusa cast a barrage of elemental magic: fire, lightning, ice, water, earth, and poison, all used with such mastery. She dodged and held her hands up in defense, but Medusa's final blast stunned her before dropping Dragonheart and falling backwards into the pool, slowly sinking.

Hysterical, Thor cried out: **My dear, no!**

Selena began losing consciousness from Medusa's relentless attacks as she continued her slow descent, but an expression of determination appeared on her face. She spun around, created a mighty water whirlpool, and used her magic to launch herself straight for the surface of her monstrous tornado, breaking through the pool's embrace. She propelled into the air at incredible speed and towered over everyone high above the ice.

Medusa looked up at the swirling maelstrom of ice and water with dismay. Selena landed between her and the soldiers, swiftly moving her hands, and the water formed a protective circle. As it expanded outward in a shockwave, Medusa disappeared.

"Liongod, get out of there," Azrael cried out to her. He and Rahim ran after her, but they were quickly overwhelmed by the never-ending army. Azrael's eyes widened, and Doragon roared, fighting from their demonic hold with increased ferocity when their worst fears were realized.

Medusa reappeared right behind Selena with her sword at the ready, the blade a deep red color, and sliced off her left hand in one cut. Selena released her magic, the water barrier splashing and soaking into the snow and stone. First, an uncomfortable sensation stinging in her left arm, then it was on fire. Blood poured forth from her severed limb like water as the snow and ice were dyed crimson. Selena grabbed her arm, screaming in pain and horror, nearly losing consciousness from the agony.

Ignoring Thor and Doragon still fighting through the spirits of darkness, Medusa paced around her and taunted. "Do you love how sharp my sword is? It's like yours: dragon bone and steel, enchanted with the demon's fire from Oblivion. It's said to be especially painful against a Divine."

Thor and Doragon finally broke from the demons' hold through sheer will, and the two, with Azrael and Rahim's help, stampeded through the sea of undead soldiers, with Azrael praying under his breath.

They were all too late.

Selena heard a faint hiss tickling in her ear. The blood drained from her limbs, and built-up pressure swelled within her chest, her heart beating wildly fast, and her body went numb. Before Selena realized what had happened, her chest and back tore open by a blood-shaped spear, splattering her blood on the ice.

"Just as I said before," Medusa whispered, "you and your friends will die here."

Before slipping into the void, Selena heard Thor's voice screaming within her fading consciousness.

CHAPTER 28: THE LONG NIGHT

The tearful Rahim rushed through as Selena's lifeless, bloody body fell; Azrael created a wave of ice and stone, pushing Medusa and the still marching army back, propelling him to catch her and carrying them and Rahim towards Doragon. The three looked at each other with shimmering eyes, but Thor's terrifying roar shook the very foundation of Snowhaven, the castle of ice and stone trembling from his Divine wrath.

He forced his way through the line of soldiers still waiting to attack them, but most fled after seeing the rampaging dragon destroying all in his path. His massive paws crushed through the broken gems and stone from the once magnificent gardens as Thor charged directly after Medusa, but she raised her hand, and a blue barrier encased her in an arcane shield, protecting her from melee attacks. He crashed into it, but Thor was relentless, bashing his horns and claws against the wall of energy, not willing to stop until he could destroy the snake himself.

Rahim looked up from Doragon's protective hold and yelled, "Thor, stop," but the distraught dragon was caught in a blind rage.

Medusa smiled and flickered her wrists, her blue barrier exploding in all directions, sending Thor backwards, and she mocked, "You're weak. I just killed your rider. What are you waiting for, dragon? Finish me."

Thor recovered when her magic dissipated and hung his head, his deep breathing resonating with the growing waves rocking around the icy fortress; Medusa laughed when she invoked his fury.

"Oh no," Azrael whispered and tightened his grip around Selena's body. "We must get back. Doragon, please cover us."

Doragon snaked his head around the trio, wrapping them within his shielding wings and ensconcing them in his coiled tail. Meanwhile, Thor's crimson scales were imbued with a sinister aura, plumes of dark Aether energy wafting from his length. As his breaths grew deeper and heavier, lightning and fire struck the ground in front of him. With a swish of his tail, he summoned screaming winds and dust clouds circling him, tearing apart the castle from his wrathful firestorm. The brewing cataclysm threatened to render his allies helpless within Doragon's shelter.

Doragon roared, and Azrael, knowing that Thor would soon destroy the Water Kingdom capital, created a red barrier of arcane energy, protecting them from Thor's ensuing wrath. The ground quaked, and the howling typhoon destroyed the castle towers above them, carrying and throwing the debris of ice and stone into the violent waves rocking their fragile island.

Rahim banged his fists against Azrael's shield, ignoring the squall smashing against their bubble. "Thor's losing it. No…no!" He slammed his fists against the ice before drawing Selena closer. She was dead; Rahim didn't want to believe it. He couldn't— "This is your fault."

Before Azrael could ask what he meant, Rahim decked him hard in the jaw. "This is your fault!" he shouted, and Azrael stumbled back. "Selena is dead because of you. You planned this, didn't you? You knew she would die. Why didn't you help her or warn us?"

Azrael rubbed his cheek and hissed through his teeth; Doragon roared upon witnessing Thor's grief and torment. "We tried to stop it, but we're not to tell—"

Rahim silenced him. "I don't give a damn about your Divine forsaken code. Why did you let her die? Every time you looked at her, didn't you see how much time she had left? Didn't you? Blast it, answer me." Rahim's voice sounded fragile, as if it and his heart would break at any moment. He was about to strike Azrael again, but Doragon snarled at him to stop, his tail thumping against the barrier.

Medusa's goading and taunting interrupted their brawl, and she continued screaming and laughing when Thor's fury showed no bounds. "Show me what the Dark Master has granted you, dragon."

Rahim's fists trembled, but Azrael scowled when Doragon reminded him of their oath. **You're the promise everyone has to keep, and Death fulfills his oaths.**

Azrael bit his lip when remembering he and Doragon were oathbound to Her Imperial Majesty. They warned her and Phantom Dust that a possible danger loomed over their daughter without directly confirming her upcoming death day; the Empress made them swear to protect her, no matter what that meant, regardless of their code. With a determined gaze, Azrael reached for Selena's body; Rahim fought him, but Azrael pushed him away. "What are you doing?"

"I'm keeping my damn oath," Azrael said, "Doragon and I might not return, but no matter what happens, get yourselves out." Before Rahim could question what he meant, Azrael touched the ground with one hand. After muttering a prayer, he created a black hole underneath him, Doragon, and Selena. Shadow hands crawled out and latched onto Azrael and Doragon, pulling them and Selena's lifeless body into the abyss. Rahim screamed and moved away as they submerged into darkness, and the hole vanished.

The three were transported into an empty realm devoid of time and space, between the dead and the living. Azrael stood while carrying Selena's battered corpse in absolute emptiness. No longer a dragon, Doragon had transformed into a spirit particle floating above Azrael's head.

Azrael muttered a few words in the demon language, and a humongous, arched onyx door appeared behind a white veil; etched upon the gate was a giant skull in front of a reaper scythe. Engraved above was a banner bearing the words in the demonic language 'Soul Gate,' the archway decorated with carved shadow hands from Azrael's magic.

Azrael placed Selena's body down and approached the door; breathing deep, unsure of the consequences, he placed his hand on the stone gate. Doragon zipped overhead, his Divine light glowing against the shining obsidian vault; the door vibrated from their touch and creaked open. Selena's white soul curled on the floor within the dark abyss as if she were sleeping, waiting for Azrael to guide her to the next world beyond the living.

Doragon's spirit particle drifted forward and floated inside the gate. **Are you ready?**

Azrael was anxious; he didn't know what would happen if he ever brought anyone back. He fought through his fears and worries and nodded. He picked up her soul, as gentle as holding up an infant. As the gate closed and with Doragon following, Azrael walked back and set Selena's essence within her battered shell. As spirit and flesh melded as one entity, Divine's light imbued her body, bright like the sun, and the glow vanished.

To Azrael's relief, her wounds were healed upon reuniting her soul and body, but she still lacked her left hand, and her back refused to mend. Medusa used powerful dark magic to strike her down; Azrael hissed when realizing her Aether was twisted and that he couldn't help her be rid of the scars on her chest and back, the marks' dark energies wafting like plumes of smoke. Yet, she stirred in her spot before drawing her first breath; Selena was alive but unconscious.

However, Azrael's skin prickled when he and Doragon heard a terrifying laugh shattering the timeless and spaceless realm. "I knew you would fall for my trap."

The Lich took long strides as he emerged from behind the Soul Gate, his skeletal hands burning with an eerie green fire blazing against his voluminous layered black cloak. Horrific red pupiled-lights peered through the empty eye sockets of his grisly nose-less skull covered by a white mask. Yet, Azrael flinched when noticing the lower half of his facial covering chipped away; his pale, undead skin frayed away from his lips, revealing a wicked grin.

"Curse you, Venexus," the quivering Azrael muttered a few unpleasant words as Doragon's spirit particle darted over and hid inside his shirt. The feared necromancer waved his flesh-less hand and summoned a shadow hand that reached out and latched onto Azrael's leg, pulling him back.

"Don't blame me for your ignorance. You fell for my gambit by fulfilling your oath." The Lich's red pupils blazed in satisfaction. "You knew that we would meet again where it all began one day. I have all the dragon eggs, and now I need you." The undead necromancer created black pools around him, the acid giving birth to the tiny creatures walking forth. "I am the death of all things, older than existence itself, and now, your power belongs to me."

Azrael slashed his hand at the shadows latching onto him and recited his spell before the acid demons approached. The Lich may take him, but he needed to ensure Selena's safe return. *It's all up to you and Thor.*

"You will now serve me, Death. The Day of Eternal Darkness draws nigh, and there is no hope for your world anymore: it will perish in dark fire." The Lich's demons overpowered Azrael as the Divine's magic pulled Selena's body into the void.

Rahim recoiled when Selena reappeared next to him within Azrael's protective barrier. His eyes widened but searched for Azrael and Doragon, wondering what had happened. Yet, he tapped her shoulders, but Selena didn't stir; he set his ear against her chest and felt relaxed when he heard her heartbeat.

However, Thor was oblivious to Selena's return; he roared and let forth a dark purple and black Aether beam writhing in lightning towards the treacherous snake Medusa, who continued chanting, "Yes, that's it. Show me more."

Rahim reached over and banged his fists against the dome, pleading, "Thor, stop."

The heartbroken Thor couldn't hear Rahim; lightning struck in circular motions encircling him between beating his wings, and the dark storm turned violent. Not heeding the threat that could wipe them out, what remained of Medusa's demonic army besieged him with weapons drawn. Thor stood upon his haunches, wings unfurled as if preparing himself for a mighty roar. However, Rahim watched in fear and horror as the purple aura around Thor grew from collecting the energy of the elements; he created a black ring of darkness orbiting him, and with one final cry, he released it.

The ring grew to titanic proportions as it stretched outward in a shockwave, shattering the barrier protecting Rahim and the unconscious Selena and disintegrating Medusa and her army into dust, killing his enemies instantly in one wave. His unleashed magic continued expanding in every direction for leagues, leveling the three icy islands and demolishing all of Snowhaven's structures until only rubble of stone and ice remained.

Their isle rocked and trembled from the growing violent ocean waves, but Rahim rushed over, pleading, "Thor, stop this." Thor snaked his head over to look at him, his eyes clouded in a purple veil. He shook his head, and the swirling summoned storm grew heavy, lightning striking the ice, cracks spiderwebbing across the surface. The waters from the Turquoise Ocean turned into terrifying waves that could overturn a ship. "This isn't you; you're not thinking clearly, but please—Azrael and Doragon saved her."

Ignoring his fear that Thor would strike him down, Rahim ran over to embrace his neck, but Thor growled through clamped fangs and backed away. His body and wings trembled, and his scales reclaimed their crimson luster against the blizzard, and the purple glow disappeared from his eyes. Thor peered over Rahim's shoulder at his fallen companion, but he sensed her faint consciousness swirling in dreamland.

However, Thor's vehement storm grew and circled above their heads as the torrential rain and snow hammered down. The winds turned fierce as a lightning bolt struck between them and cracked the ice in two. Selena was separated from the two, swiftly carried away by the ocean's dark waters.

Gritting his teeth, Rahim grabbed Dragonheart as Thor quickly snatched him, holding him within his clawed cage, and flew into the storm to chase Selena. She was drifting on a piece of ice as the rough waves moved her further out, but it looked like she would fall off at any moment.

Rahim peered through Thor's claws and pointed at her, though he knew Thor could see far better than he could; Thor roared and followed Selena's scent, but just as they reached her, a vast wave knocked the ice over, and she tumbled into the depths below. Rahim held his breath as Thor dove through the icy waters and swam down against the current.

Selena's body was constantly being forced down by the rocking waves. Thor stretched out his free foreclaw and grabbed her before spreading his wings and swimming back to the surface. Yet, just as they poked their heads from the depths, another giant wave crashed down on top of them, forcing them to stay underwater. Thor arched his neck to look at his companion and saw the grave expression on Rahim's face.

This was the end.

As the two began losing consciousness, Thor cupped his wings together, and a small blue light appeared in the middle of his chest as he channeled the energy of the water around them. He unfurled his wings, and the light grew, creating an enormous air bubble. Thor turned in the water and forced his way to the surface, breaking through the ocean's icy embrace, his water spout erupting like a violent volcano. His mighty wingbeats put more distance between them and the slowly calming water, escaping the devastation he caused.

Thor swiveled his head and saw what remained of Snowhaven: only a sheet of ice covered in debris. The rain and snow lessened, and Thor's storm finally dissipated, leaving behind his summoned black and metal-hued clouds roaring like an angry dragon.

Thor ruefully set Selena and Rahim within his harness, the two collapsing beside their drenched bags and boxes. Ensuring Selena would be comfortable if she ever awoke, the grim Rahim dropped Dragonheart and wrapped her comatose body in a blanket of furs; wincing from the sight of her severed arm, he exercised extreme caution when covering the stump with a spare shirt. Hopeless by the long night, he asked, "What are we going to do now?"

Rahim then looked outward as Thor somberly flew into the dark and stormy horizon.

SOAR THROUGH
THE ARMAGEDDON TRILOGY

By C.D. MULLER

Don't miss out on these exciting adventures!

About the Author

C.D. Muller (also under the pen name Crystal Summers for romance) was born on December 9th, 1990. Of her love of *Harry Potter*, she discovered the magic of writing when she was fourteen.

She graduated from Patagonia Union High School in 2009 and attended college to study Computer Science and Programming. She participated in community events, such as writing plays for her local theaters and hosting author presentations for elementary classes.

Her husband's death heavily affected Muller's writing and art. She almost gave up on both but used her talents to help her cope with depression and anxiety. She currently lives in Tucson, AZ, with her new husband, newborn son, and three cats. For more information, go to https://crystaldsummers.com for updates and her social media.

www.ingramcontent.com/pod-product-compliance
Lightning Source LLC
Chambersburg PA
CBHW020332010826
48970CB00010B/110